The characters and events portrayed in this book are fictitious. Any similarity to real persons, living or dead, is coincidental and not intended by the author.

Dedication

This novel is dedicated to the many dedicated scientific researchers who devote their lives to advancing our knowledge and understanding of the worlds around us.

* * *

Acknowledgements

I would like to acknowledge fellow author, Delaine Coppock, whose encouragement kept this novel moving forward. Also, my good friend, Paul, who provided support and invaluable scientific and technical advice. To be clear, Paul bears no resemblance to any character portrayed in Coercion, and any and all errors and inaccuracies in the fictionalized technical and scientific data and descriptions are solely mine.

* * *

PROLOGUE

The white haired woman sat on the veranda of the elegant villa, nestled amongst the vineyards and wineries of the Massif de la Clape, in southern France. Her plush chair was positioned under the cover of the red-tiled half-roof, a few metres back from the ornate white stone balustrade. Deep blue cushions and a plush red blanket cocooned her aging body. The air around her was kept comfortably warm by heaters attached to the massive wood beams overhead.

Her large sunglasses softened the watery sun's glare, as she gazed across terraces of vines and fruit trees that stepped down, south towards the distant, sparkling blue of the Mediterranean Sea. The evening sun was starting to cast its light on the vibrant colours of the winter flowers and foliage in the ornate urns that were strategically located on the marble tiled floor around her.

The woman's right hand protruded from below the red blanket, and tapped slowly on the handcrafted table of yellow Lebanon cedar beside her. The arrival of an expensively dressed man, in his forties, broke the woman's silent contemplation, although the she made no acknowledgement of his presence. He moved a chair to a position that faced towards her, mindful not to impede her view.

"I am glad that you are finally here, Anthony. I have been waiting for your progress report. I'm sure that you understand the importance of this project." She said, turning her sharp gaze in his direction.

"The news from Beirut is excellent, Mother. The building is nearing completion, and is quite breathtaking. It will be a medical icon to father's memory for many decades to come. We are confident that it will be finished, equipped, and ready for the opening ceremony on May fifth, next year, as planned. Also, the latest information indicates that the research results that we have identified appear to meet our requirements, and will provide a medical centrepiece." Anthony shifted uncomfortably in his chair. "However, so far, our agent has been unable to conclude an agreement with the two researchers." Seeing his mother's face darken, he quickly added. "It will happen: it may just take a little more time."

"You don't have 'a little more time'. I gave you and your brother, Michael, a schedule, and I expect you to meet it. Failure is not an option, Anthony."

"We understand, but their research is already being discussed in medical circles, where there is excitement about the possibilities that it could present. To avoid any future difficulties, we must persuade them to sell it to us willingly."

"Then that is what you must do. Your father and I did not give up when we were faced with minor challenges and obstacles. We found ways to overcome them, and built the business empire that provided the lavish lifestyle that you have all enjoyed." She paused. "We must know everything about these two researchers, and do whatever it takes to persuade them to sell their research to us."

"I have had them thoroughly investigated." Anthony explained quickly. "They are brothers, Paul and Matt Berg, and both live relatively modestly. They do not have significant financial issues, and showed no real interest in our monetary offers. Our agent will meet with Matt Berg at his presentation in Turku, and will exert whatever inducements she can on him there. However, he has excluded making an exclusive sale, and stated that, if further research confirmed their findings, they would consider making their research available to everyone at a nominal cost."

"That is absolutely unacceptable. You must not permit that to happen." The old woman barked angrily, slapping her hand down on a blue cushion. "The advances made by those two researchers could revolutionize the medical treatment of viruses around the world. When we obtain exclusive ownership of their research, and develop it at our new Beirut hospital, we will be establishing the foundation for Lebanon to become the leading technical nation in the entire region. As oil diminishes in importance, scientific knowledge and technology will become the economic drivers and motivators of social change. Our family will accomplish all of that, and your father's name will forever be identified as its founder."

"There are many steps, from research to medical acceptance." Her son ventured. "We cannot be sure that the advances the Bergs appear to have made will prove out after further rigorous investigation."

"The fact that there is more research to be performed means that the full potential has yet to be determined. I have no doubt that it will become a major medical breakthrough, and it will save millions of lives worldwide. Your father and I had a sixth sense about these things. That was how we became so successful."

"They are showing no inclination to sell their research to us, or, in fact, to anyone else. How do you want us to proceed? "

"If they do not respond to our financial offers, then you must apply pressure. Where are their family or business weak points? Everyone has them."

"There is nothing obvious, with either of the Berg brothers. Neither of them have any known illegal activities, addictions or obsessions that we could use. They both live quite ordinary, uneventful lives. Their parents are both dead, and they have no close relatives. Dr. Matt Berg, the brother in London, lives alone. He has had affairs with various women, but has no committed partner. He is dedicated to his successful small high tech business."

"Can his customers be encouraged to cancel their business with his company?"

"We did look into that. However, his business includes some technical contracts for the British police and security agencies. I decided that approach is best left alone."

The woman absorbed the information with an irritated grunt. "What about the other brother? In Vancouver, isn't he? Are they close?"

"All reports are that the brothers are very tight, despite living far apart. Paul Berg, the brother in Vancouver is a widower, university professor, and researcher. His wife died three years ago, from cancer. Since then, he has buried himself in his research work. He has no significant outside interests." He hesitated. "Apart from his brother, his only other close relative is his thirteen year old daughter, Nicky. He is devoted to her, as is her uncle, Matt. She is a typical young Canadian teenager, a good student, not involved with drugs or alcohol, and has no particular boyfriend. Her current obsession is football. She is a member of the local team that won the Provincial championship."

"Ah." The old woman folded her hands together, and sat back with a satisfied smile. Anthony waited uneasily for her to continue. "The girl is their weakness, and that is how we will persuade the Bergs to agree to our terms. She plays football, does she? Good. That is when she is isolated and vulnerable."

"From what we know about Paul and Matt Berg, we will have to hold the girl, to coerce them to give us their research." Anthony mused. "That would have a shattering effect on the Berg brothers, but mere threats are unlikely to work."

"Thousands of us experienced heart-wrenching losses and deprivation during the futile wars in our beloved Lebanon. Your brother was killed. A short disruption in the comfortable lives of these few people is insignificant, particularly considering the magnitude of the medical and economic benefits that will be realized. Paul and Matt Berg might have noticed some interesting results from their research, but they don't have the range of abilities and resources that will be required to develop those results to their full potential. Our new state of the art hospital in Beirut, backed by our vast financial resources, will ensure that a dedicated, top research team will develop this seed of a medical advance as quickly and as efficiently as possible. We will bring our results to the world in a fraction of the time that would be taken by any of the pharmaceutical giants. We must do it. It is our family duty."

"I understand." Anthony acknowledged. "I will speak to Michael. We will do whatever is necessary to obtain this research."

"Absolutely. Now, Go: find out everything about this Berg girl, her football team, and her family. Bring me that information before the end of the week, and I will tell you how to proceed."

CHAPTER 1

Doctor Patricia Chen's two-week tour of pediatric facilities in China had started with visits to clinics in Hangzhou and Shanghai, and concluded in Beijing. It had been a demanding schedule. The final day had been a series of consultations at Beijing's Good Health Children's Clinic.

She had made a last walk through the Children's ward with her friend, Doctor Yang Chow. In the bed beside the door to the surgery, she had noticed an anxious looking little four year-old girl. Yang had quietly explained that the girl was being prepped for major surgery to resolve an irregular heartbeat that threatened her survival. The tiny waif was understandably scared. Tricia had sat, holding her hand and talking to her, for over an hour. The little girl had relaxed, as she chatted with the young, foreign doctor with the pixie haircut, and the reassuring smile. When it was time for the anesthetic, she had whispered "Night, night doctor", as she sank into sedated oblivion.

Tricia had glanced at her watch, as she settled into the car that the Clinic had provided to take her to the airport, and sighed at the thought of the Beijing traffic. There was no way that she would be there in time to catch her flight home. However, the Clinic driver had hurtled around narrow, shuddering cobbled back alleys, between rows of crowded, red-roofed, squat dwellings, dodging pedestrians, cyclists and an assortment of carts, in a close-your-eyes-and-hang-on ride. Ironically, when

Tricia had arrived at the Air Canada gate, in time for her flight, she was informed that a weather system had delayed the departure to Vancouver, for two hours.

The two-hour delay had turned into three, before they were in the air. It was well into the flight before the cabin crew had completed the usual routine of drinks, dinner, and Duty Free, and Tricia was able to put her glasses away, pulled the mask over her eyes, and snuggle under the blanket, for a possible few hours rest.

The cabin daytime lights came on, when they were an hour out from Vancouver. She retrieved her glasses and mobile, and checked for messages. She smiled at the text from Nicky that first welcomed her back, and then fretted that her Dad might not like the present she had bought him for his fortieth birthday. Tricia made a mental note to assure Nicky that he would love the antique, working model steam engine that she had discovered at the downtown 'flea market'. The thirteen year old could be counted on to be on 'texts alert', and would let her Dad know about the flight's late arrival. Paul Berg had probably forgotten that she was returning today, but thankfully, Nicky was good at keeping her Dad on track with the daily routines. Nicky and Paul were as close to family that Tricia had. It was good to be home.

The last thirty minutes of a flight always seemed to drag. Finally in the terminal, she made her way through the passageways, and shuffled along in the human crocodile through Customs and Immigration. She checked for the number of her flight's designated carousel, and trudged through the mass of travel-weary humanity to get a buggy for her luggage. With the various flight delays, the vast International Arrivals area pulsated with a bewildered, eclectic mix of flight worn travelers of every age and description. Tricia carefully circumvented a herd of tanned, returning sun-seekers trying to maintain a last breath of noisy jollity, in their shorts and hats that seemed appropriate when they had boarded their flight.

At barely five foot two inches tall, Tricia avoided the crowd surging around the point where the luggage first emerged from the bowels of the airport. For her physical comfort, she had established a routine of standing at the less crowded, far end of the carousel. It always took a while for the luggage to arrive from the plane, and she didn't mind the extra few seconds for her bag to reach her, if she could wait and retrieve it without being jostled by a crush of hot, tired bodies all around her

Her suitcase was bright red, and, she always felt a sense of relief, when it appeared, waving the blue ribbon that she had tied to the handle. She lifted it on to her baggage cart, being careful not to knock the duty-free bottle of Lagavulin single malt Scotch she had bought on the plane for Paul. Her Customs clearance, with its indecipherable red numbers, letters and squiggles, in hand, she headed for the line-up at the exit.

"Hey, Tricia! What's a beautiful woman like you doing in a place like this?"

Tricia looked around in surprise, searching for the familiar face that matched the cheery voice. Striding towards her was the ever-cheerful figure of Matt Berg, Paul's younger brother. She smiled and waved. Tricia liked Matt. He and Paul had always been close, and were quite similar in appearance, with only a four-year difference in their ages. They both had a mop of sandy hair and slim builds, with smiles that spread to light up their faces. Matt was slightly taller at six feet, and where Paul tended to be studious and conservative, Matt was the epitome of an effervescent researcher and entrepreneur. He was always bursting with enthusiasm for his latest scheme, and invariably fun to be around.

Tricia pulled her raincoat over her navy blue pantsuit, as she waited for Matt to catch up.

"Hey yourself, Matt. So glad you could make it. Paul wasn't sure if you would be able to come. He was afraid that you might be too caught up somewhere or other, Finland, wasn't it? "

Matt gave her a hug. "Of course I came. It's his fortieth birthday; I am not going to miss that. Yes, Finland. The meeting was in Turku. I just arrived from Helsinki, where have you come from?"

"Beijing. We were over three hours late because of weather. Helsinki? Is that to do with the project that Paul mentioned the two of you have been working on?"

"That's it. The meeting went really well. Wait 'till we tell you what we're in to."

Tricia laughed. "I'm sure it will be another exciting adventure that you will come out of with even more money. I've got my car here, so we can go and surprise Paul and Nicky together. I'll say 'Hello', but I won't stay: I'm a bit too tired." She glanced at him. "You should put a coat on. It will be cold and wet outside."

"Yes, right. Where did I put it? I'm sure it's in the front of my bag here somewhere. Have you heard anything from Nicky? I messaged her that I had arrived. How is she doing? She was really into soccer in a big way, last time I talked to her."

"Nicky's doing fine. Soccer is still her major obsession. She made the West Coast Warriors under sixteen team this year, and is absolutely thrilled."

"That's fantastic. Good for Nicky! Paul must be proud of her."

"Yes, he is. He never says much, but you know Paul. He even took a break from his work to come to most of her games with us."

"You take Nicky to her games?"

"Yes. Along with her friend Kim. Well, she is still only thirteen."

"Of course." He frowned. "That's right, she has her fourteenth birthday coming up in a few weeks. March twenty-seventh, isn't it? I mustn't forget it. How did she get to fourteen so quickly?"

Tricia sighed. "I don't know, Matt. I still remember Nicky as a toddler. The years just seem to fly by. Where is your Customs clearance?"

"Oh yes. I've got the damn thing in one of my pockets. Ah, here it is. Let's go."

As they shuffled their way along in the lineup, Tricia asked, "How's Lara? I thought you two were pretty serious. Paul thought she might be coming with you?"

Matt took a deep breath. "What can I say? Lara is a terrific person, smart, athletic, always fun to be around, and ready for any adventure: everyone loves her: she even laughs at my jokes." He sighed. "It's just that I have to be certain, before I make a serious commitment. So we are having a rest, at least for a while. Who knows?"

Tricia shook her head. "Oh Matt."

"I know; I sound like a foolish old romantic, but I'm convinced that my soul mate is out there somewhere. We just have to keep searching until we find each other." He gave a weak laugh. "In the meantime, there was a stunning Finnish cabin attendant on the flight here from Helsinki. Unfortunately, she was quite adept at politely rebuffing all of my attempts at conversation."

"Matt, you're impossible." Tricia groaned.

"Where is your car?" Matt asked, as they maneuvered their way through the crush of people greeting the arriving passengers, and out of the airport.

"My beloved Volvo is at Park-and-Fly." She pointed to where a group of tired passengers were shuffling around. "The stop is just over there. We're in luck, there's the shuttle coming now. We won't have to hang around waiting."

"We put our bags inside, on this thing, if I recall. So why don't you take the carry-ons, and that Duty Free bag that you've got, and I'll look after both of our suitcases?"

"Thanks, Matt. The drivers are quite helpful. If you get the cases to him one at a time, he'll help get them inside."

*****

Professor Paul Berg stood looking out of the front bay window, sipping a glass of Malbec red wine. His parents had built the two-storey wood frame house. It was nearly twice his age, but he and Nicky loved its every creaking board. Situated on a quiet residential street amongst cedar and fir trees, the inhabitants were near, but apart from, the bustle of the adjacent university campus. Outside, the lights along the driveway made the wet snow twinkle on its way down, providing a reminder that winter was not over, even on Canada's mild west coast.

Paul looked over, as Nicky wandered in. "I didn't realize it was so late. You surprised me when you turned the driveway lights on, and opened the gates." He said, adding after a few moments. "You said that Uncle Matt and Tricia had both messaged you to say that they had landed. Have you heard anything from either of them since then?"

The thirteen-year-old's fingers flashed across her iPhone. "Tricia messaged saying that she was in the Customs line.

That was just after uncle Matt's text, saying that he had landed. Nothing since then from either of them. Do you think Tricia will drop by on the way home, Dad? I hope she does. She says that she usually manages to sleep on the long flights."

Tricia had been a tremendous friend since Nancy had died, and she and Nicky had grown quite close. Paul could not have asked for a better role model in his daughter's life.

"She always works on the day she leaves, and with the flight being three hours late, she is probably going to be pretty tired, even if she did manage to catch some sleep." Paul pointed out gently. "I wonder what's keeping Uncle Matt? I would have thought that he would be here by now. Perhaps there was a line-up for a taxi."

Nicky flipped her blond ponytail self-consciously, as she fiddled with her phone, to avoid looking at her father. "You've known Tricia a long time, haven't you, Dad?"

"Yes. Since she and Mum were at Medical school together. They were close friends."

"She's nice, isn't she? She's really, really smart, and cute, too."

"Yes, I suppose she is. I have never thought about it. Matt likes her, too. We all get along pretty well."

"You two aren't, like, a couple, though?"

Paul gave his daughter a quizzical look. "No, it's not like that. We're just friends. We sometimes go together to a concert or play, if it's something we're both interested in, or where it's some social thing, where it's more comfortable for her to bring a partner." He stared out of the window. "I'm not much for social events. It's mainly Tricia who is involved in those sorts of things."

"She doesn't have a partner, that's why she asks you to go with her? She's not gay, though, is she? Not that it matters."

"As far as I know the answer is 'No' to both of those questions, but those are very personal issues. You and Tricia are quite close. If she ever decides she wants to talk to you about it, that is her choice, but you mustn't start prying into her personal life. What has brought this on?"

Nicky glanced towards the clock. "Oh, nothing. I was just wondering. It's been two weeks, and I kind of missed her."

Jake, the Golden Retriever, stuck his head up, from where he had been sleeping on the rug in front of the gas fireplace in the Family Room. He lumbered to his feet, and wandered past them to the front door, wagging his tail, and whining happily.

Paul looked out of the window. "Here's Tricia now. Jake must have heard her car. It looks like uncle Matt is with her."

"Come on in. Come on in." Paul said as he ushered them towards the Living Room. "When we heard your flight had been delayed, Tricia, we thought you might be too tired to drop by. How was your trip? I see you picked up a stray at the airport."

"It was Matt who noticed me in the baggage claim. It was a bit of a long day, followed by a late flight, and I was having difficulty noticing anything."

"I can imagine. Come on in and sit down, both of you."

"Thanks, Paul, but I'm really too tired to stay. I'm going to head home now. I will come by tomorrow, so I can catch up with all of you then. You and Nicky can have Matt to yourselves this evening."

"Of course. You must be exhausted." Paul said.

"I know how you must feel. I don't have much left, myself, and I have had a much easier day than you." Matt added.

CHAPTER 2

The following afternoon, the film of wet snow had turned to puddles, when Tricia arrived at the house. She let herself in, with the key to the front door that Paul had given her when Nancy's illness started to take its toll. As usual, Jake had recognized her car as soon as she turned onto the street, and was in the entrance hall to greet her. Paul called for her to come and join them in the Living Room. From her instant take, it appeared that Matt and Paul had been having a serious discussion. Matt was sitting at the end of the burgundy sofa, closest to the matching armchair, where Paul was sitting, looking decidedly tense.

"Hi both of you." She glanced from one to the other. "I'm not interrupting anything, am I?" She asked, as she sank into the other plush armchair, across from Matt, with a satisfied sigh.

"No, no, Tricia. We've been hoping that you would be able to make it. I'll make a pot of that green tea that you brought us from Hangzhou. You and Matt can swap jet-lag stories."

"Sorry I had to drop you off and run, last night, Matt, but I was totally beat. I went home, and climbed straight into bed. I did manage a couple of hours at the hospital this morning, before the jetlag hit me again, and I had to head home. I always find it takes a day or two to get adjusted to the time change, coming back this way. It's confusing to leave Beijing late Friday evening, and arrive in Vancouver earlier the same day. I still feel like a wet noodle. How are you doing?"

"Not too bad, thankfully. I find it's easier heading west from Europe, than heading east, like you did. That's a brute. I didn't last long after you dropped me off, either. I managed a couple of Scotches, while Paul and I chatted, before the old eyelids started to feel like they had lead weights on them, and I crawled upstairs. I slept like a log, until four o'clock this morning, at which point, of course, I was wide awake."

"Well, what was it, about three in the morning Finland time when we got here last night?"

"Yes, and about one o'clock in the afternoon, Finland time when I woke up. Unfortunately it was only four in the morning, Vancouver time. Sleep was out of the question, so I dug out some work, and kept myself occupied until I smelt the welcoming aroma of coffee coming from downstairs. I wandered down to that great kitchen that you and Nancy designed."

"That was one of the last things that we did, before the cancer took hold. It's a great memory." She said wistfully. "We had a lot of fun. Paul kept fretting, and had to be banished until it was finished. The French limestone flooring took forever to arrive." She smiled at the memory. "It's still difficult for me to realize that Nancy has gone. Sometimes, when I hear a noise in the kitchen, I look up, expecting her to come around the corner laughing about some crazy thing that has happened."

"You two were friends for a long time."

"Since High School. Nineteen years." Tricia took a deep breath. "I suppose Nicky was getting breakfast ready in the kitchen?"

"Yes. She not only had coffee brewing, but was also preparing the biggest breakfast you could imagine; some sort of non-meat bacon, eggs, potatoes, toast, and I forget what else. When Paul joined us, I asked if he was expecting company, since there was enough food for six people."

"I know how that goes." Tricia interjected cheerfully. "And he explained that it would only be enough for six, as long as Nicky wasn't one of the six. I've seen how much Nicky can eat, and she still stays incredibly slim and fit. So where is she?"

"She and her friend Kim have been upstairs in her room since they got home from soccer practice."

"Nicky's not in any trouble, is she?"

"No, no. There's something that Nicky and Kim want your advice on, well your support, really."

"Is it a girl thing? Should I go up and talk to them in private?"

"No. It's nothing like that." Matt explained. "I'll leave it there. Paul and the girls agreed to wait until you were here, to provide some of your sage wisdom."

"This all sounds very mysterious. I can't imagine what sage wisdom I could have to offer. My brain feels like mush."

As he brought the tea through, Paul called up the stairs to Nicky, that Tricia had arrived, which prompted the girls to come racing down, still in their sweats, from soccer practice. They both started to talk at once.

Tricia put down her cup. "One at a time, please." She pleaded. "Nicky, what on earth is all the excitement about?"

"You won't believe this, Tricia, I know I didn't." Paul groaned.

"You'll never guess what." Nicky burst out. "It's totally unreal. The Warriors have been invited to an under-sixteen soccer tournament in Beijing, China."

"It's an international tournament, and Nicky and I are both on the team." Kim chimed in.

Nicky could barely contain herself. "The whole team is soo stoked. Dad has the letter from the coach with all the details.

You know, I really, really want to go. Tell Dad that we have to go, otherwise we'll be letting the team down. Right Kim?"

"Totally."

Paul held up his hands. "Whoa. Let's try and take things one step at a time. Tricia has not even had a chance to drink her tea."

"Sorry Tricia. We just couldn't wait."

"Paul doesn't seem quite as excited." Matt chuckled. "It sounds like a great opportunity, to me, but we all agreed to wait for your opinion, Tricia, since you have lots of experience in China, and you know Beijing really well."

"Wow, nothing like hitting me with the heavy stuff on the first day back. When is this tournament?" Tricia gasped.

"It's at Easter: Spring Break. They come together this year."

"The tournament starts on March twenty-fifth, and lasts for one week." Kim added.

"There are teams from Singapore, Thailand, Hong Kong, Korea, Japan and all over. And from China, of course."

"Hold on, let's take a breath here. March twenty-fifth is only five weeks away, and with the time difference, I can tell you that you would want to arrive at least several days ahead. You would need up-to-date passports and visas. When did you hear about this?" Tricia asked.

"The first I heard about it was this afternoon. I don't see that there is any way that we can get everything done in time." Paul said, shaking his head. "The coach sent a letter home with the girls. Apparently, a team had to drop out, and one of the tournament organizers had heard of the Warriors, and suggested them as a last minute addition. One thing I don't understand, is why the organizers in China selected the

Westside Warriors for this international tournament?"

"Perhaps because we won the Provincial under fifteen tournament last year, Dad."

"And it's still the middle of winter in the rest of Canada," Matt pointed out. "So there are no teams currently playing in the other Canadian provinces."

"What about your passport, Nicky?" Tricia asked.

"We renewed it last year, just in case Dad could take me with him to see uncle Matt. Please, Dad. You have to say that I can go."

Paul waved the letter that Nicky had brought home from the team coach. "Well, according to this letter, it's not going to cost much. It says that the tournament is going to provide the housing and all the meals in Beijing, and a corporate sponsor has offered ten thousand dollars, to help cover all of the airfares. Do you know how many will be going, in total, Nicky?"

"Coach told us this afternoon that there will be sixteen players; the team eleven, plus five substitutes, and then there will be the coach, the team manager, and two of the girls' mums who are teachers. That will make twenty, all counted."

"That's a generous sponsor." Matt said.

"Coach told us that Air Canada had offered a really good team price for the twenty seats."

"What did your Mum and Dad say, Kim?" Paul asked.

"They want to talk to you and Tricia, since, you know, Tricia, like, knows so much about China."

"Well, what do you think, Tricia? You do know China really well."

"It sounds like a great opportunity. The girls will see Beijing, meet girls their own age from several countries, and play some challenging soccer games. I can message my friend Yang Chow, at the Beijing Clinic and ask her what she knows about this tournament, if that will make you more comfortable, Paul? She told me that she was involved in girls' soccer, to help get the teenage girls doing some sports."

"I would appreciate that. Well, it seems like you all agree." Paul smiled ruefully. "Let me think abut it overnight, Nicky, okay?"

Nicky rolled her eyes towards the ceiling, with a groan.

"Okay. But you will have to decide soon. Coach said we'd have to commit right away, so that everyone has time to get up to date passports for the visas, and make all the reservations for the flights and the residence where we'll be staying, and stuff. Tricia, you have been to China so often. I really want to go. Tell Dad he has to agree."

"Tomorrow." Paul said firmly.

Nicky gave a frustrated grunt. She turned, and with a classic teen, long-suffering sigh, she and Kim headed back up the stairs.

Tricia settled back in her chair. "Well, I wasn't expecting that when I walked in."

Paul shook his head. "You can just imagine how I felt, when Nicky suddenly dropped it on me. Do you think that the girls will be able to get everything arranged in time?"

"I would think so, as long as they all make sure that they have valid passports. I expect the tournament organizers will contact the Chinese Consulate here, in Vancouver, to arrange for the visas to be expedited for everyone in the group. That tends to be the way they do things in China." Tricia explained.

"I'm still nervous about Nicky going. She's still only thirteen. Is Beijing safe?

"Beijing is safer than many big cities, yes, but it is quite different from Vancouver. Nicky is still going to have to be careful, and stay with the other girls, and be careful what she eats. There are four adults going with them, who will doubtless be watching them carefully. If Yang Chow knows that Nicky and Kim will be there, they can always contact her if they need anything."

"I would really appreciate that. It would make me feel better to know that Nicky had someone in Beijing to contact, and I'm sure Kim's parents will feel the same way. But still, haven't things been a bit tense between China and Canada for the past few years."

"They have been, yes. Recently, China has been trying to improve its international image. I suspect that this girls' international soccer tournament is one of the attempts to show that China is an advanced, friendly country. That is a powerful motivation for them to make sure that this tournament is safe, and a public relations success."

"Well, you had a good idea, Paul, why don't you think about it overnight?" Matt suggested.

"Okay. But I'm sure I'll have more questions and concerns, Tricia."

"Of course, ask me anytime." Tricia decided it was time to move on. "On a completely different topic, what is this project that you two have been working on? You mentioned something about it at the airport, Matt, and promised to give me the full details."

"Okay." He nodded at Paul. "Why don't you go first?"

"Well, as you know, my work is in the area of nuclear medicine, treatments and imaging. For some time now, my research has been focused on the development of new applications of PET and SPECT. That is...."

"Yes, I am familiar with those: Positron Emission Tomography and Single Photon Emission Computed Tomography. They both provide great images for us doctors to work with."

"Of course you are Tricia. Well, as you know, the SARS and MERS outbreaks were two from the family of corona viruses. Then along came the devastating covid-19 pandemic, which was also a corona virus. Matt suggested that it would be useful if we could somehow tag the corona virus with an isotope, and monitor its activity, with imaging. That could potentially provide invaluable information on the efficacy of vaccines."

"It certainly would, if you could produce time phased images that showed the existence and demise, or not, of the virus for vaccines, and infections." Tricia agreed.

"Yes, well, about six months ago, I finally managed to tag Vanadium-48 to a common corona virus. The tomography to produce useful images has been a bit of a challenge. However, I'll let Matt take it from here."

"Okay, well while Paul was doing that, my team was working on isolating protein strings that might trigger a routine immune response against the most common corona virus, HCoV229E."

"I know that one." Tricia smiled. "I've had hundreds of young patients with it. It's the common cold."

"Absolutely." Matt continued. "The virus is readily available for research, relatively benign, and readily produces an immune response. We wanted to see if we could find a protein string that induced an immune response, and provided some basic images for us to work from. We seemed to be getting somewhere with a couple of them, so Paul came over to our lab in England, to run some tests."

"Right. I remember that. Nicky stayed with me, while you were away, Paul."

"Well, we rented some time on a local PET machine, in the middle of the night, the only time it was available. For night after night, we watched the images, to see if Paul's Vanadium-48 provided the images of the reaction that we wanted. The first few results were not very encouraging, but then one protein string appeared to show some very interesting results."

Tricia nodded. "That sounds quite promising"

"However, we were running out of the common cold virus to test, so I contacted a colleague at a medical research lab in Wiltshire, and she sent us a batch of corona viruses. She included a note saying that she was not sure what we wanted, so there were several groups of different corona viruses in the batch. We decided to attach Paul's Vanadium tag to all of them, and ran them, as a control group, through the protocol."

"Yes, I see. The images showing the non-effect of your protein string on that range of corona viruses would help verify the imaging you had produced with the common cold virus."

"Exactly. However, that's not what we saw."

Paul jumped in. "No. The images appeared to show a specific protein string that Matt was using produced a response that killed all of the viruses."

"What? I don't understand."

"Neither did we, Tricia. We got Matt's colleague to send us samples of all of the corona viruses that she had available, and the result was the same every time."

"Are you telling me that your protein string produced a

response that attacked every corona virus? That would be a stunning medical breakthrough." Tricia gasped. "It would mean that one vaccination would provide protection for every corona virus, from the common cold to covid-19, and including SARS and MERS."

"Hold on, there, Tricia. As you know, there are hundreds of corona viruses circulating around the world, mainly in animals, and we can't claim to have found the answer for all of them, or, in fact, any of them, really. We have only tested a few, but the results certainly look interesting, for the few that we used."

"What can I say? This is absolutely astounding."

"We mustn't get too excited, at this point." Matt added, "We have only got some very preliminary data. All we can say is that our research program showed unexpected results with the several corona viruses that we used. Our research was not even targeted at this result. It will take millions of dollars and several years, for us to run through a controlled research protocol that will confirm, or not, our current results. At this stage we are trying to generate interest in appropriate funding groups."

"From a personal perspective." Paul explained. "If this did work out, it would be a once in a lifetime achievement for Matt and me: a stroke of incredible good fortune, and something very precious to us. We don't want to just hand all of our research to someone else to, sort of, carry across the finish line."

"Just with what I understand that you have accomplished so far, I'm very impressed." Tricia acknowledged.

"There is one more thing." Paul said tentatively, glancing at his brother. "There is a slight theoretical possibility, and I must emphasize '*slight*', that there might be other, similar protein string combinations that would act with other viruses in the same way."

"That would mean that protein strings could be developed to trigger immune response against every virus?" Tricia gasped.

"No, well, yes in theory. I suppose that could be a remote possibility, but that is getting way ahead of the small step that we might have made." Matt hastened to explain.

Tricia was thoughtful. "I suppose there is no possibility of your invention being modified as a bioweapon? You know, if some group isolated a virus that was virulent and deadly, they could use it against an enemy, or threaten to use it, knowing that they were protected by applications of one of your protein strings?"

"No. No." Paul and Matt chorused together. "We have made sure that it can only be used for positive applications that are strictly benign." Matt explained.

"Yes, of course, you have already thought of that." She shrugged. "I have spent too much time near some rather autocratic regimes. It was just a thought that if it were possible for someone like, say, Kim Jong-un, to get hold of it, he could use a deadly corona virus as a powerful threat. At home or abroad." She added as an afterthought.

"We've thought about that, and we think we've got it covered." Matt said. "Paul and I are the only people who know the detailed design parameters, and we only have the records of half each."

"Thankfully, Matt was meticulous in recording the derivation of the protein string, even though we thought that we would only be using it as the zero impact control, for comparison." Paul interjected.

"Even so," Matt explained. "It was a pretty random

development, and it would probably take me a couple of months to reproduce the protein string precisely."

"Have you applied for any patents?" Tricia asked.

"Yes, we have filed several different patent applications, for those things that are eligible for patenting, with each one in a different international jurisdiction. There is no link between them, and they are all so different that only Paul and I know the whole set of patents that go together."

"In addition, we have each retained key details that are known only to the two of us. The programmed chips with all of our research information self wipe, if there is any attempt to copy them. We have independent back-ups, of course. That's pretty standard industry practice, these days. This way we have made sure that we will maintain total control over the development and application." Paul added.

"Sounds like you have thought of everything. What about meetings, like the one you were just at in Turku, Matt. Didn't you have to reveal a lot of details there?"

"Ah, the secret in those situations is to talk about what our research results show, without revealing any of the key details about how we did the research."

"All I can say is 'Wow'. It sounds like you two could make a lot of money from this?"

"Well, that's not really likely." Matt explained. "Besides, if this does actually work, we want it to be available worldwide, at a reasonable price. We don't want it to become a money tree for some huge company. That's why Paul and I are going to continue with the research, to produce some accepted, peer reviewed results."

Paul added. "A major reason for us to patent anything, at this point, is to preempt having any parts of our work locked out by researchers at major companies, who might be working in the same area. If it works, this could be a breakthrough in virus management that should be available globally, and particularly for the poorer countries."

"Hmm. You said you got a lot of interest, in Turku, Matt?" Tricia asked. "Anything firm?"

"Well, nothing firm, but, there was certainly a lot of interest, particularly from a company in Switzerland, and from a fascinating little man from Israel. He seemed to appear whenever the Swiss representative wanted to discuss the project with me. I think he was nervous about her company getting an exclusive licence. Of course, we have no intention of giving anyone an exclusive licence, at this point."

"She? Would it be accurate to assume that this Swiss representative was an attractive young woman, Matt?" Tricia asked drily.

"Well, yes, I suppose, she was." Matt said, a shade too indifferently. "We went out to dinner once, but it was all business. I have her card. Claire LeBlanc, with Medical Holdings, in Geneva. She said that they will contact us with a firm proposal shortly."

Tricia sighed. "I am overwhelmed. I have to have time to digest all of this. My brain is still a bit foggy."

Matt gave a wave of his hand. "We have been talking about us all this time, and not even asked you how you are doing, Tricia?"

"Apart from the jetlag, I'm fine." She laughed. "I got word from Yang this morning that the little girl who was going in for heart surgery, when I left the Beijing clinic, is doing well. The prognosis looks very positive. That made my day."

"It is always good news to hear that a young patient is on the road to recovery. Well done." Paul smiled.

"I didn't actually have anything to do with the medical side, really. I was just sitting with her while she waited to go into surgery. The dear little tyke was, understandably, a bit scared."

"Tricia, I've no doubt that it meant a great deal to her to have you there." Matt assured her.

CHAPTER 3

By mid-March, Nicky and Kim were moving into frenzy mode, as they got closer to their departure to China. Even Jake seemed to sense the excitement and ran around like a youngster. Finally the big day arrived. Despite Paul's' admonishments about getting as much sleep as possible before the long flight, Nicky was up by six thirty in the morning, dancing around in a cloud of excitement.

Paul had asked Tricia to come with him to see her off, adding that he would appreciate if she made sure that Nicky had packed everything that she would need. Tricia had suggested that Nicky take a supply of pain killers and personal hygiene products, including toilet paper, whether she thought that she would need them, or not. She found that those had been packed, but sighed when she made a check of her carry-on small backpack, and found several containers of make-up. She quickly moved them into a plasticized pouch in Nicky's checked bag, with a note, pointing out that they were too large, and Airport Security would have confiscated them.

The flight left at one o'clock that afternoon, and the coach and team manager had insisted that all of the girls should be at the airport between ten thirty and eleven. At ten o'clock, Paul, Tricia and a very excited Nicky bundled everything into the car, and headed for the airport.

They heard the team before they saw the group of excited, athletic teenagers chattering volubly, while being herded by four remarkably calm women. The coach had played on the Canadian team a few years earlier, and was well versed in the rigours and issues of international travel. Some apprehensive looking parents were standing slightly to the side, chatting amongst themselves. Every so often, one of the girls would dash over with a frantic last minute concern, and her parents would reassure her, and send her back.

As they came into sight Nicky burst out with horror. "Oh no. I'm the last to arrive. I knew it. Everyone has been waiting for me."

"Nicky, we are just fine. Your Air Canada flight doesn't leave for more than two hours." Paul said patiently. "That will give you plenty of time to report to the Air Canada counter for luggage drop, and then to go on and clear Security."

Tricia introduced a travel practicality. "Have you got some Canadian money in case you want to buy anything in Duty Free? All you might want is a magazine or something to read."

"Uncle Matt e-transferred me two hundred dollars. I've got fifty of it in my purse."

Tricia put her arm around the girl. "That was very generous and thoughtful of him. Don't spend it all at the airport."

"I won't. He sent me a message this morning, you know, wishing me luck, and all that. He used to play soccer, didn't he, Dad?"

"Yes, he was really good. He was on the university team, here, in Canada, and again when he went to graduate school in London. He doesn't play any more, hasn't for quite a few years, but I believe he has season tickets to watch Chelsea."

"You mean, like, live at the stadium? Every home game?"

"I think so. He and a friend have been going together for a few years, now."

"Wow. Do you think he would take me, some time?"

"You would have to ask him, yourself. And, of course, there is the small point that you would have to be in London, to watch Chelsea play."

"If I can bring up more immediate matters," Tricia interjected. "Do you have some Chinese Yuan for when you get to Beijing, Nicky? You shouldn't need it for anything, but it is always better to have some in case of an emergency."

"I've done what you said, Tricia. Most of my money is tucked away in my suitcase, but I have put six hundred Yuan in a separate compartment in my purse. That's about a hundred dollars, isn't it?"

"Yes. That should be lots. Do be careful with your purse. Always have it in front of you, with the zip closed, and the strap over your head and across your body. Airports are renowned hunting grounds for pickpockets and sneak thieves. Remember to take special care with your passport. Whatever you, do don't lose it. You've got my friend Dr. Chow's phone numbers and addresses in Beijing, just in case you need a local contact?"

"Yes, absolutely. Kim's parents were really pleased that Kim had someone to contact there, in an emergency. We both have Dr. Chow's contacts, including her email, in our suitcases, and saved on our iPhones. We plan to get a local SIM card for Beijing as soon as we get there. All the girls are going to do that. I'll be okay." She glanced at her father's tense features. "Don't worry, Dad. I am going to be with the team all the time, and Ms. Young and Ms. Raybourn and the two mums will be watching over us like mother hens."

Paul looked around. "Okay, I think it's time we said goodbye, and you joined your teammates. I'm sure that between you, Tricia, and Ms. Young you have covered just about every eventuality. Take care of yourself, Nicky, and have a great time. Tricia and I are really going to miss you. "

Tricia managed a tight smile. Yes, she would miss Nicky.

"Give me a hug Nicky. We will be thinking of you. My last piece of advice is to be careful what you eat and drink. Food in China is not the same as Chinese food in Vancouver, and sometimes it can upset your stomach. Have a wonderful time. The house will seem empty without you. Don't go chasing any boys. Love you."

Nicky hugged them both, then with her purse slung across her body, and her small backpack over her shoulder, she grabbed the handle of her luggage, and hurried over to join the rest of the team. Paul and Tricia stood watching her disappear into the crowd of girls at the Air Canada international counter.

Paul gave Tricia a rueful smile. "Well, I hope you'll drop by whenever you can. It's just me and Jake rattling around the house for the next week or so. I'm really going to miss her." He glanced wistfully over at his daughter. "I suppose this is the start of Nicky spreading her wings, and preparing to leave the nest in a few years."

"Oh Paul. I'm going to miss her, too, but she'll be back in ten days. It will be a few years before she thinks about leaving home." Tricia glanced around her. "I've been through this airport a hundred times, and never thought anything of it. But this is different, watching Nicky head off. She looks so grown up, compared with the ten-year-old of just a couple of years ago."

He had to swallow the lump in his throat before he continued in a slightly husky voice. "If you want, we can have some lunch, and then head up to the Observation Deck to watch her plane to take-off. It doesn't leave for a couple of hours."

"That's a good idea. We can get some really good Japanese food at a restaurant by International Security. Let's see, what Gate are they leaving from? There it is on the monitor. Gate D67. I think we can see it from the Observation Deck. The gates all have big numbers on them. I have often sat in the lounge, and watched my plane at the gate."

Paul and Tricia made their way past the throngs of passengers, clustered around the various airline counters in the busy departure hall. They stopped, for a last look back to where Nicky was talking excitedly with her friends. She must have sensed their watching, because she turned, and gave them a little wave. They silently wished her a good trip, and a safe return, as Ms. Young started herding the group towards the Security checkpoint, on their way to China, so far away. Tricia slipped her hand into Paul's, both gaining comfort from contact. In the silence of that moment, the relationship between the three of them subtly changed.

Paul kept busy for the rest of the afternoon wrapping up some work on the production system of a particularly promising medical isotope. Tricia went to the hospital, and stayed occupied catching up with some of her young patients. That evening they decided to go out for dinner to a little French restaurant that was in the neighbourhood. Afterwards, when they were each at home, they both went on to the Air Canada web site to check on the progress of Nicky's flight. It was on time and expected to land in Beijing in about four hours.

CHAPTER 4

Tricia's car was parked in the driveway, when Paul arrived back at the house from his early morning run. He had invited her to join him for breakfast, and was looking forward to the fresh warm croissants that she always stopped to pick up from the local bakery. It had been three days since they had watched Nicky's plane take off from the airport, and they were both missing her. Nicky was always such a presence.

As he came in through the side door, Tricia shouted to him. "Paul! Paul! It's Nicky! Come here. Quickly." The panic in her voice was unmistakable.

His wet running shoes slid on the limestone floor, knocking over the stool beside Tricia. He grabbed the kitchen counter, to stay upright.

"What's happened?" He gasped, when he saw Tricia' stricken face.

Tricia pointed at the screen. "I just got this email from Yang Chow. There is a similar email from the Warriors team's coach and manager, Ms. Young and Ms. Raybourn. They sent them to you, and Kim's parents, with a copy to me."

He stared at the words, struggling to absorb Yang Chow's message. He felt an icy hand squeezing his pounding heart, as his legs started to collapse beneath him. The message tried to be reassuring: that was impossible.

Nicky was missing.

Yang Chow explained that, according to Kim, the incident occurred on the street close to the residence where all of the visiting girls in the soccer tournament were staying. The team had had the afternoon off from training, and Nicky and Kim, along with several other Warriors, were just looking around at the shops, when a Chinese boy came over to Nicky and Kim and said he would like to practice his English. Suddenly, a car pulled up beside them, and a man jumped out. He and the boy started to push Nicky into the car. Nicky and Kim fought with them for a few seconds, before the man knocked Kim down, and the car roared away. Kim was at the Beijing clinic, under Dr. Chow's care: apart from some strains, minor cuts and some bruising, she was badly shaken but otherwise unharmed.

Someone had called the police, and they had been to the clinic to talk to Kim. Yang Chow assured them that everything was being done to find Nicky.

Paul stared at the screen, in disbelief, struggling to speak.

"This is insane. I can't believe it." He finally croaked out. Tricia righted the kitchen stool, and he collapsed onto it. "I don't understand. What has happened to Nicky? Where is she?" He made a supreme effort to calm down. "I can't think straight. What do we do? I'll call the police. No. That's not right. No point in contacting the Canadian police. What do we do?"

Tricia looked across at him, and immediately grabbed both of his forearms. "Paul, you're shaking! Look at me. My eyes. Look at me. Concentrate. Take a deep breath, and let it out slowly. Again. You must not let yourself go into shock. Try and calm down. Do you understand? Can you hear me? Breathe with me."

"Yes, yes. Okay." He looked at her, and followed her breathing, slowly, steadily, for several minutes. "Sorry. Hell of a shock. I'll be okay. Give me a minute."

"Keep looking at me. I made some green tea. Try drinking some: it should help. I've got some mild sedatives at home; I'll bring them back with me. Right now, Nicky needs us: we have to stay calm. Can you do that?"

"Yes. I think so." He took another slow breath, and gritted his teeth. "No, dammit, I can and I will." He held up his hands. "Look. I've stopped shaking. Well, nearly."

"We have to go to Beijing immediately. I'll come with you, okay?"

"What? Yes, of course. Absolutely. I'm really going to need your help. You can speak the language, and know China, and all that. Are you sure that you can just leave?"

Tricia flicked that issue aside with her hand. "There is a lot to do, and we will have to move fast. You have an valid passport?"

"Yes, Nicky and I renewed them last year."

Jake came in to the room and barked, confused with what was upsetting Paul.

"What about Jake?"

"Jake? Yes. Of course. Right. I can handle that. He can go to Nancy's parents. They love him; he reminds them of Nancy, and he's happy with them. I'll call them right now."

After a brief conversation, he gave Tricia a tense nod. "They are in shock. Doris burst into tears, and couldn't speak. She handed the phone to Gordon. He will come right over and get Jake. They live in Kerrisdale, just ten minutes away." Paul swallowed, and fought back tears, as he tried to continue. "Gordon and Doris said that if it's a matter of a ransom, they would give us everything they have. They absolutely adore

Nicky. Nancy was their only child, and they say that Nicky is so like her."

Tricia took a moment to blink back her own tears. "That is beyond generous of them." She took a breath, and forced herself to concentrate. "Your passport? Do you know where it is? You need to go and get it. The airline will need it. "

"My passport. Right. Yes. I'll go get it. "

"You go. I'll arrange things with my work." Tricia sent a brief message to her office, and started working furiously to search available flights to Beijing.

Paul returned, waving his passport. "Got it."

"I can't see how we can leave before tomorrow, at the earliest. The flights all leave around lunchtime, and you have to get a visa. That will take all day today, even if I use all of my goodwill with the local Chinese Consul."

Paul waved his passport frantically. "No. No. Wait. Think, Paul, think. I have a visa for China. I got one when Nicky got hers."

"What?" Tricia stared at him. "Really? You have a Chinese visa in your passport? Are you sure? Let me see."

"Yes. Well, Nicky was so excited about getting hers; I thought I might just as well get one, too. You know, she's going to have her birthday in Beijing, and I thought I, well, might, decide to go over and watch Nicky play, and see her on her birthday." He concluded lamely.

Tricia scanned the passport page with the visa for China. "Okay. Yes. You do have a Chinese visa." Tricia agreed, with surprise. "It's valid for three months. That changes everything." She pushed his passport into her purse. "I'll take your passport: the airline will need the details. There is space on the Air Canada flight at twelve forty-five, direct to Beijing.

I'm going back to my place to get my bag, and I'll book the tickets, and check us in online from there." She looked over at Paul. "We have to be at the airport by eleven, at the very latest. I'll leave my car here, and arrange for a taxi to pick us up here at ten fifteen. That's over an hour and a half from now. It's plenty of time, as long as we hurry." She gave him a reassuring smile. "We can make it."

"What do I need to take? What about money?"

"I have some leftover Chinese currency from my previous trip. Bring whatever cash you have, plus your credit and debit cards. You will need to have some Chinese Yuan when we arrive, just in case we get separated for any reason: you can get them from the banks and currency exchanges at the airport. I'll book us rooms at the Hyatt on East Chang An avenue; they know me, I've often stayed there." She checked her watch. "It only takes me thirty minutes to pack. I'll get everything done, and be back before the taxi gets here at ten fifteen. Make sure you're packed and ready to go with all the basics. The Chinese can be quite formal, so include a good suit, shirts, ties, and a couple of jackets. The weather will probably be a lot like Vancouver, so pack a raincoat and sweaters. Are you sure you can do that?"

"Yes. I'm okay, now. I'll be ready. After I forgot some essentials a couple of times, I made myself a list of everything I need to take, when I go to conferences."

"Have your wallet, cash, bank cards and phone with you as carry-on. If we forget anything else, we can buy it in Beijing. You must contact Matt, too. Just forward him the emails, and tell him we are leaving immediately for Beijing, and will contact him again when we know more."

Paul stared at a new message that had appeared on his laptop, and froze. "What the Hell is this?"

Tricia took one look at his ashen face, and leapt over to look at

the message. It read:
'This message has been sent to both Paul and Matt Berg.
Nicky is unharmed, and quite safe. We are businessmen, and want to make a transaction.
Nicky will be returned to you, in return for all of the details of the protein string and all of your research for the corona virus.
No doubt the documentation details that we require have been stored electronically, probably on the cloud. Please make sure that you can access them.
Professor Paul, you will proceed to Beijing, as everyone will expect.
Reply to this email with the name of the hotel where you are staying, and when you will arrive. Wait for further instructions.
Make sure that you bring everything that we have asked for.
Matt Berg will remain in London, and wait for further instructions.
Do not involve any third parties.'

"Dear God, what next?" Tricia gasped. "Matt will wonder what the Hell is going on when he gets that." She moved away from the keyboard. "Here. You must send him the emails from Yang Chow and the team manager right away."

Paul gritted his teeth, as he fought to concentrate. He straightened up. "There, I've forwarded the emails to Matt. I've tried to add a brief note saying that we are on our way to Beijing. It may have been a bit garbled. I said I'll call him as soon as possible."

"Will you be able to access everything they want, when we reach Beijing?"

"Yes, yes, as long as there is a good wifi connection. It's mostly on the cloud, as they expected."

Tricia grabbed her purse and headed for the door. "I've got to go. We have just lost a few precious minutes." She paused, and waved a hand at the screen. "Send a reply to those bastards, telling them that we will be staying at the Beijing Hyatt on East

Chang An. I've written it down, there, beside the computer. Okay? Make sure that you have everything packed and ready. As long as you are ready when I get back, there'll be enough time for the taxi to get us to the airport for the Air Canada flight."

Tricia threw a worried glance back at Paul, as she reached the door. He had replied to the email with the hotel details, and was staring at the computer screen.

"We've got to do this, Paul: for Nicky. We must not let her down."

The adrenalin was beginning to kick in. The initial shock had been overtaken by a look of fierce determination on his face. "We damn well will not let Nicky down."

As she left, he raced upstairs, pulled his suitcase out of the closet, and tossed it on the bed. He stood still, with his eyes closed. For a moment he was back in the hospital on the day Nancy had died. She was lying exhausted in the hospital bed, when she had summoned her remaining strength, opened her eyes, looked at him and said 'I'll be leaving soon Darling, but I'll always be nearby to help you and Nicky.' They were her last words.

Paul choked back the tears. "We need you now, Nancy. We really need your help now."

He opened his eyes with a new surge of energy, and started determinedly checking off the items on his list. He remembered Tricia's advice about what he should take, and was pushing in some items, when doorbell rang downstairs. It was Gordon to pick up Jake. His face was white, and he was fighting back the tears, as he gave Paul a hug.

"We are so sorry, Paul. What the Hell has happened? Is there anything that we can do? When do you leave for China?"

"Right now, Gordon. Just as soon as Tricia gets back. She's coming with me."

"That's good. She'll help with the language, and all that. I won't hold you up. Please keep us informed whenever you can. We have a key, and will check on the place while you're away."

Jake had picked up on Paul and Gordon's stress, but he knew the routine. Within minutes, he was sitting in the back of the car, his sad face staring out the rear window, as they pulled out of the driveway.

Paul finished packing his suitcase in record time. He stood stock still, his brain screaming in overdrive, as he mentally double-checked everything off his list. Done. He was still wearing his running clothes. He grabbed underwear, a newish pair of jeans, a grey knit shirt, and a cotton jacket with zip pockets for the things he would need on the flight, and checked his watch. He could just manage a fast shower.

He dropped his suitcase in the hallway by the door, beside his computer bag with his laptop and iPad. He checked his watch: six minutes past ten. He heard a car pull into his driveway.

"Good going, Tricia. You're back in record time. We're coming, Nicky." Paul muttered.

He shrugged into the jacket, and stuffed his phone and wallet in the inside, zipped pockets, congratulating himself for remembering a small stash of cash that he and Nicky kept for emergencies. He was ready to go.

Flinging open the door Paul found himself confronted by a large, powerful looking man standing beside a slim, athletic looking woman. The woman handed him her business card.

"Professor Berg? My name is Sara Little, and this is my colleague Kevin Blakey. We are with the Canadian Security and Intelligence Service. We would like to talk to you. May we come in?"

Paul stared at the business card, and then back at his visitors. "CSIS? What on earth does CSIS want with me? No, look, it's a really bad time. I am leaving for Beijing, right now. No, you can't come in. Go away."

"I am afraid that we must insist. We are aware of your situation, and it is important that we speak to you before you leave. It won't take long. If you refuse to speak to us here, we can, and will, arrest you. That would be inconvenient for everyone. I suggest that you cooperate, and we will be gone in a matter of minutes."

Paul was furious, but saw no option. He stood back, as the two CSIS agents pushed their way into the entrance hall.

"Professor Berg, the Canadian security services have a mandate and a duty to collect and analyze information for the protection our country, and its people, from potential foreign malfeasances." Sarah Little's voice was threatening by its quiet restraint.

She raised a hand to stop Paul before he could interject. "No. Do not interrupt. We have recently obtained information that there has been an interest in obtaining some unique medical research that you and your brother have developed. Our analysis has concluded that your research has the potential to be used by certain foreign interests for hostile acts, that could represent a threat Canada."

Paul stared from one to the other of his visitors in stunned disbelief, while his mind struggled to comprehend what he had just heard. Sarah Little was about to continue, but Berg waved his hand to stop her.

"Hold on. Give me a couple of seconds here. My daughter has been abducted in Beijing, as you appear to know. I am going through living Hell, and you have pushed your way in here with some story that Matt and I are involved in some research that has, what, possible military applications?"

Paul was angry, and getting more worked up by the minute. "This is fucking ridiculous. I have never engaged in any research program that involves any possible military application. In fact, our research protocol specifically states that we never will have anything to do with military research. It has nothing to do with CSIS, so you can just leave. Go on. Fuck off out of here."

Blakey took over. His tone was threatening. "You and your brother have identified a protein string and imaging system. The potential hostile applications of those are disturbing, particularly if it gets into the hands of an unstable, unfriendly group or government."

"What are you talking about? *If* our research works out, Matt and I *may have* identified a possible protein string that *appeared* to eradicate some viruses in the corona family. The actual rather pedestrian development was an imaging agent to test and confirm the efficacy of virus eradication. There is no hostile application to our system."

"Your daughter, Nicky, has been abducted in Beijing. By now, we expect that the kidnappers will have contacted you. They want your research, don't they?"

Paul was silent as he struggled with the kidnappers instructions not to involve any third party. His voice shook. "All Nicky wanted to do was play in a soccer tournament." He stared at each of them. He had to say something that would satisfy them, and get them to leave: he and Tricia must catch their flight. "Yes, they have messaged Matt and me. They have assured us that she is quite safe. Matt has been told to stay in London, and I have been told to go to Beijing. They have told us that Nicky will be returned to us, unharmed." He turned his gaze on Sarah Little. "We've booked in at a Hyatt hotel, on

Chang Street, I think it is, in Beijing. Leave us alone, and we will get Nicky back safely. We don't need CSIS playing James Bond, and screwing everything up."

The stone-faced CSIS agents were familiar with this reaction.

"Have they said what they want?"

"Forget that nonsense about our research. It will be money." Paul lied smoothly. "What else would it be?"

"Are you wealthy. Professor Berg? Is that why someone would grab Nicky?"

"I am financially comfortable. My brother, Matt, has made quite a bit from his business. He is devoted to Nicky, and told me that they can have it all. He thinks that between us we can raise about three million dollars, on short notice: maybe more, in a couple of weeks. From what I understand, that would be a lot of money in China." The lies flowed easily.

"We believe that they want your protein string research."

"The system is not even close to being proven, yet. If they wanted it, they could simply buy it." Paul carefully slid around the question.

"Where is Dr. Matt Berg?"

"As far as I know, he is in London, arranging for the money. For Heaven's sake, there is nothing for you to do. We will go to Beijing, and bring Nicky back safe."

Sarah Little shook her head. "No. You must leave this to us; we know what we are doing. We have dealt with this type of situation many times. It can be a dangerous game if you try to play it alone. Everyone wants your daughter to be returned to you safely. You have no idea of the sort of people that you are dealing with. Contact the Canadian Embassy as soon as you reach Beijing. There will be a team there to help you."

The two CSIS agents abruptly turned and left, leaving Paul staring after them. His mind churned through what had just happened. As he started to close the door, Tricia pulled into the driveway.

She glanced back at the official looking, black car that was pulling away. "Who was that?"

"Believe it or not, that was CSIS. I feel like I'm in an alternate reality. I'll fill you in on the way to the airport."

"The taxi was pulling up, as I drove in. Come on, let's go." She glanced at her watch. "Ten twenty. We'll make it in time."

As they pulled away from the driveway, Kevin Blakey spoke quietly to Little. "Can you believe him? Is he really that naive?"

"Maybe. I'm not sure." Sara Little pondered. "He is an academic, a scientist, living in his own world. I hope he isn't going to start trying to resolve this himself."

"Of course he is."

"Yes. Of course he is."

CHAPTER 5

On the drive to the airport, Paul explained the conversation he had had with the two CSIS visitors earlier. Tricia was astounded. However, she quickly brushed that aside as an irritating distraction, and emphasized to Paul that they had to concentrate on their primary task, which was to reach Beijing, and get Nicky back as quickly as possible.

"You've booked us in Business Class. I'm not sure I'm quite dressed for that. You look really smart." Paul noted, as he pocketed his passport, and scanned his itinerary and Boarding Pass that Tricia had sent to his iPhone.

Tricia glanced down at her Arctic Green cotton pants, Italian Terra Cotta cotton shirt, and Irish Green linen jacket. "This is my standard flight outfit. It's a matter of being comfortable, and having sufficient pockets. Business Class will save us some valuable time at the baggage drop and Security, plus, with the lie flat seats, we might manage to get some rest on the long flight. We're going to need it."

"I understand. Good plan. Just not what a university prof is used to, that's all."

Tricia gave him a long-suffering glance. "This is beyond important, Paul, and I can certainly afford it."

"Of course. Thanks. You've been an absolute rock, Tricia. How have you managed to stay so clear headed with all this blowing up around us?"

"I'm a pediatrician, Paul. I have to deal with children, often quite little children with heart wrenchingly tragic medical issues. I have had to learn to stay calm and keep focused, no matter what type of desperate situation I was facing. Right now, we have to focus on getting Nicky back."

Their Business Class reservations helped move them smoothly through the Air Canada baggage drop, and the express Security line, but they still consumed many precious minutes. At Tricia's insistence, Paul made time to withdraw some Canadian dollars at a bank machine, and exchange them for Chinese Yuan. They arrived at their Gate to be greeted by the announcement that the first stage of loading would begin shortly.

Paul glanced around, and spotted a public phone on the wall. "I'm going to call Matt. If I use the public phone, there is little likelihood of anyone listening in. Okay, after the CSIS visit, I'm paranoid." He agreed, in response to her questioning look. "I won't be more than a couple of minutes, and it will take at least twenty minutes to board everyone."

Tricia nodded. "Good idea. Matt must be wondering what on earth is happening." She gave a quick glance around. "I'm going to board right away. Just make sure that you and Matt don't keep talking: you must not miss the flight."

"No chance." Paul was puzzled. "What's wrong? You have that look, like something is bothering you?"

"It's probably nothing. I'll explain when we are on board. It's a wide body: our two seats are at the front, side by side, in the centre. We should be able to talk reasonably privately. Go and phone Matt." Tricia gave his hand a squeeze. "I'll see you on the plane. And don't forget your carry-on."

Paul managed a weak smile for the first time that day.

When Paul finally appeared, the cabin attendant was in the process of asking Tricia, for the second time, if she knew where he was. He responded to her greeting, as he shoved his carry-on in the overhead bin, and slumped down in the pod. Tricia had lowered the screen between them, to make conversation more private.

"Here's a sedative. There's a bottle of water beside you. How was Matt?"

"Worried sick. I've never heard him so upset. Like us, he just can't believe it. We all love Nicky so much. Neither of us can understand what's happening. How could a couple of boring scientists, like Matt and me, have done anything that would end up with Nicky getting abducted, for God's sake? I don't understand, and neither does Matt. We feel so helpless. This has to end: they can have whatever they want: we just have to get Nicky home safely." He shook his head. "That reminds me. What was it that was bothering you, earlier?"

"At the airport, there was a young woman, who seemed to be paying you rather a lot of attention." Tricia explained quietly. "She was hanging around on this side of Security, trying to look as though she was waiting for someone. I was behind you coming through, and I noticed her pick up her bag, as soon as she saw you were through. She dropped behind us, when she realized we were together."

Paul frowned. "There was a smart looking young woman in a red jacket, who came by when I was on the phone. I thought that she was just wandering around while she waited to board."

Tricia gave her head a slight nod. "That sounds like the one. Her clothes looked fairly high-end European. Attitude was relaxed, and self-assured. Best guess, I would say CSIS; at least, I hope she is, because I certainly don't want to find out that there is anyone else following you."

Paul looked grim. "There are always the kidnappers?" He rubbed his forehead with his knuckle in frustration. "I have never felt so bloody helpless, Tricia. I can't stand it. Where the Hell is Nicky? That poor kid. She must be absolutely terrified. I can't bear to think about it."

Tricia tried to give a reassuring smile. "Hang in there, Paul. We are going through Hell, right now, but we will get through it, and have Nicky back home in no time. I'm sure of it."

Paul reached over, and squeezed Tricia's hand. "You really are terrific. I don't know what I would have done without you. I thought I was going to collapse, at one point, but you stayed so calm and clear headed, you convinced me that we would work our way through this."

Tricia gave him a reassuring smile. "Here we go." She said, as they pulled back from the terminal.

"We're on our way, at last. How long is the flight?"

"About thirteen hours. Once we're in the air, and they have brought the meals around, we have to try and rest as much as we can, or we'll be no use to Nicky. The sedative should help. Try and remember that relaxation technique I showed you a while back."

Further conversation was drowned out, as the plane gathered speed, and roared into the air, leaving Canada behind.

As a physician, Tricia had trained herself to treasure sleep as an essential commodity that should be consumed whenever it became appropriately available. Her svelte frame was significantly smaller than average, and she was able to curl up reasonably comfortably, as she tried to coax her mind to relax and rest. However, she still found sleep to be elusive. Her mind would not stop churning through the bizarre series of events that had afflicted them over the past few hours. She was unable to make sense out of what had happened, and indeed, was still happening. How on earth could a couple as innocuous as Paul and Matt have ended up in this situation?

CHAPTER 6

Matt Berg stared at the phone, transfixed. This just could not be happening; first the insane email, then the emails from the manager and coach of the Warriors that Paul had forwarded. His initial reaction to the first email had been instant denial. It had to be a bluff; some crook who knew that Nicky was in China, and thought that they could scam some money out of him and Paul, before they could discover that Nicky was actually quite safe, totally immersed in the soccer tournament, and exploring Beijing with her friends. Paul's phone call from the airport made the reality undeniable.

Nicky had been snatched off a Beijing street.

Even over the phone connection, Matt had heard the fear and stress in his brother's voice. Any lingering doubts had vanished with Paul's account of his encounter with the two people from CSIS, who had arrived uninvited at his home. What had Matt completely confused was that the kidnappers had made it quite clear that what they wanted was all of the information and data related to his and Paul's research, including every piece of documentation that they had assembled. Obviously, they would give it to them. Paul had confirmed that all of his documentation was stored electronically on the cloud, so that they could both have access. They would give the kidnappers the access codes, so that they could whisk it off to another protected account, but how could they assure them that neither he nor Paul had already duplicated all of the files?

Gradually, Matt's brain began to unfreeze. Anger started to take precedence, and provided a powerful motivating force. He had work to do. Top priority was to do everything possible to get Nicky back safe and sound. In case the kidnappers decided they wanted some money, as well, he would immediately start liquefying whatever assets he could. His heart had warmed when Paul had told him that Nancy's parents had said he could have whatever they could raise. He knew that they were not wealthy, but they dearly loved Nicky, their only granddaughter, and the only living memory of their daughter.

As his mind moved into top speed, he spun through the places where the kidnappers could possibly have heard about their research. He locked on to his presentation in Turku, Finland, a few weeks earlier. There was quite a crowd there, about forty people, but he had made it clear that their research was still in its early stages, and would be made fully available for the benefit of everyone: so why this horrific kidnapping? He had to develop a plan: first, he would tell his lawyers to liquefy his assets, then, while they looked after that, he would troll through all of the attendees in Turku, to see if he could identify anyone who could possibly be involved in this.

He needed someone who had access to that sort of information. Vance Chestermann came to mind. He was an older technical specialist, of some sort, in the government, who had come to him for help in modifying some advanced audio/video monitoring equipment that had an intermittent bug in the design. After he had signed the Official Secrets Act, Matt had managed to isolate the weakness in the equipment's circuitry, and had corrected it. Vance had never said exactly what he did, but when Matt phoned his office one time, to his surprise, the call went to the Secret Intelligence Service switchboard in Vauxhall, London. He would call Vance for help.

Within the hour, Vance Chestermann was at the door of Matt's flat, along with a serious looking woman about Matt's age. Vance introduced her as Sandra Fellows.

"Vance and I are analysts in different areas at SIS." She explained. "We are aware of the research that you and your brother have developed, Doctor Berg."

"Call me Matt, please."

"Right, Matt. I think the first step is for you to tell us everything that you know about the abduction of your niece, Nicky Berg, in Beijing."

Matt went through everything he knew, which, he pointed out, was not very much. They were particularly interested in the emails from the alleged abductors, as well as Matt's recollection of Paul's phone call from Vancouver airport.

"That's about it." Matt declared. "My brother, Paul, and I are totally over our heads. We don't understand what is happening at all. We were planning to license the system to whoever wanted it. It doesn't make any sense for someone to kidnap Nicky to force us to give it to them. That's insane."

"Actually, Matt, we were alerted to your research some time ago. When we started hearing it mentioned in some unusual quarters, our technical people went over it." Sandra Fellows showed him a page on her tablet. "This is a brief summary of their concerns, following your presentation in Turku."

"There was someone there from SIS?" Matt asked in surprise, as he took the tablet.

They ignored his question, as they waited patiently for him to read the information. As he read, Matt looked more and more stunned.

"I don't know what to say. I can't believe it. What this person is saying seems possible. They make it look like it could become some sort of biological weapon, in the wrong hands." He paused, thinking back. "Wait a minute. Tricia suggested something like that, when we were describing it to her. Is this what this whole ghastly business is all about? Some crazed despot has kidnapped Nicky, to force us to give them our research?"

"We don't believe that it has necessarily only caught the attention of some crazy despot. You will have noted that the report suggested that that is just one possibility. Your research would be worth a great deal of money, if it proves out as a major medical advance." Vance said quietly. He produced a photograph. "Do you remember this person in Turku?"

Matt stared. "Of course. Yes. That's Claire LeBlanc. She gave me her card. She works for Medical Holdings, in Geneva."

"This woman goes by a number of names, but she does not work for any 'Medical Holdings', in Geneva, or anywhere else. She is a freelance collector and supplier of confidential information, at a price. And her price is quite high. You probably got to know her quite well, I suspect?"

"Well, sort of, I suppose." Matt flustered. "We went out for dinner just the once. She was great company."

"Yes, I imagine she was." Fellows said dryly.

"Dammit," Matt growled angrily. "If she or her client, whoever that may be, wants our damned research, they can have it. Just as soon as we get Nicky back, unharmed."

"Well. There is a bit of a problem with that, I'm afraid, Matt." Vance observed quietly. "Currently, you and Paul are the only two people who have all of the knowledge and documentation. There is one way that Claire LeBlanc's client, or indeed some crazy despot, as you put it, could make sure that they obtain permanent, sole possession of your research."

"What would that be?" Matt puzzled.

Vance let out a slow breath. "The removal of yourself and your brother, and his daughter, once they have the research."

Matt went ashen white. "You can't be serious? Are you telling me that Paul and I could be killed by some, some assassin, once we have done what they ask, and handed over all of our research, and Nicky...?" His voice trailed off.

"That makes it sound a trifle over dramatic, but it captures the concept, I'm afraid." Sandra Fellows confirmed.

Matt slumped back in his chair. "Good God. This simply can't be real. Surely there is something that you can do about this mess?" He looked from one to the other of his visitors.

"This is quite a tricky situation. The ultimate solution is to openly disseminate the details of your research worldwide. Once your work on the protein string is widely available, it becomes a universally known medical advance, its value financially, and as a weapon, is greatly reduced, and all potential threats are essentially removed. As an aside, I suspect that we know the genial little chap from Israel who you met in Turku; he is actually from Mossad. He probably recognized your Claire LeBlanc, and was doing his best to keep you away from her."

"This just goes from bad to worse." Matt shook his head. "Okay, so I'll contact Paul, and we will throw everything we have into the public domain. The only thing that matters is that we rescue Nicky, before any of this spins further out of control.""

"That is probably not the right answer, at the moment, I'm afraid, Matt." Vance explained reluctantly. "That would put

Nicky in a very bad position: she would have no value to the abductors."

"I don't think I want to hear this." Matt groaned. "So what do you suggest?"

"We are working closely with Interpol. What we have agreed is that they will look after your brother, Paul, on the Beijing side of things, and we will work with you on this end."

"What exactly does that mean? Which brings up another thing that has been puzzling me: Why did Nicky's abductors specifically instruct me to stay in London?"

"I suspect we have the answer to that," Sandra Fellows explained. "There was a procedure that was used by a group some years ago to avoid the inherent difficulties that arise with illicit purchases or exchanges. They divided the exchange into two parts, frequently in two different countries. In the case of a purchase, the product changed hands in one country, and when that was satisfactorily completed, a message was sent to the party in the other country, and the payment was made. Everyone stayed in place until the payment was confirmed. The divided jurisdictions make legal action difficult in both countries."

"How do you see that working with Nicky's kidnappers?"

"Your brother will stay in Beijing, and provide all of the software and documentation that the kidnappers have demanded. When they have checked it over, and are satisfied, they will release Nicky to you. You will message your brother confirming that she is safe, and the transaction will be complete."

Matt took a deep breath. "That sounds like we take all the risk."

"It is classic 'coercion'. They have Nicky, so you have no option." Chestermann pointed out.

"So are you telling me that Nicky has been flown to London?"

"I doubt it will be London, or even the U.K. I expect that you will receive a message shortly telling you to travel to somewhere in Europe. That way they keep you off balance, and don't allow us the opportunity to set up anything very elaborate."

"So, when I receive this message, I just jump on a plane, or ferry, or something and head off to wherever they tell me? Is that it? You will leave me swinging in the breeze in some foreign location where I have no idea what is happening?" Matt demanded angrily.

Sandra Fellows shook her head. "Not at all. A small team is on standby to go to the location where you are directed to go. They will provide all the covert assistance to you that they can, to help locate where Nicky Berg is being held. Our mandate is to get her back to you safe and sound."

"Okay. So what do I do now?"

"You pack a bag, and wait. We have to go and organize a couple of things. Immediately you hear anything, call me using this phone. We have to assume that they will be monitoring your existing communications." Vance handed him a card, along with a mobile. "Hang in there, Matt. We're with you all the way."

****

Once they were in the car, heading back to headquarters, Vance turned to Sandra Fellows. "What do you think? This looks to me like the first phase of a carefully planned operation, possibly with an intermediary broker to confuse the reality."

"Yes, the picture is starting to emerge in that direction. From what we have seen to this point, the outlook is very disquieting."

Vance let out a slow breath. "These situations rarely turn out well. The prospects do not look good for any of the Berg family."

"No indeed. In this sort of case, the endplay frequently results in the elimination of all of the outsiders involved; that would be Paul and Matt Berg, the girl, Nicky, and presumably the Chen woman who is with Paul Berg."

Vance Chestermann gave a grunt. "That's the way I see this unfolding, too. Working with Interpol this early improves the situation." He sighed. "Unfortunately, once the other party has complete control of the research, whatever happens after that we will have to wait to find out."

CHAPTER 7

Five thousand miles away, the old woman sat in quiet contemplation on the veranda of the villa in southern France. Tall red pots, bursting with spring flowers, were located at intervals along the ornate white stone balustrade that ran along in front of her. She had often found that her mind seemed to be stimulated by the soft fragrance from the mimosa blossoms that drifted and eddied through the warm Spring air.

Her private thoughts were broken by a cautious knock, followed by the arrival of a woman of indeterminate middle age. From the general appearance of the newcomer, it was apparent that she was a relative, likely the woman's daughter, the significant difference being that the younger woman's hair was still black.

"We have heard from Jasar, Mother. He is proving to be a good choice for coordinating communications"

Her mother glanced up as she pulled up a chair beside her.

"I am sure that the message that your son sends will bring warmth to his aging grandmother."

"He reports that the strategy that you conceived is working perfectly. Michael and Anthony, have already initiated the initial steps, and it will only be a matter of a few short days, and the project will be completed."

"Good." The old woman gave slight tilt of her head, signifying that she had expected nothing less. "This project is the most important thing left for me to complete, in my old age." The old woman stated. Her daughter cleared her throat nervously.

"Why are you making that noise, daughter? If you have something to say, then say it." Her voice, though soft, crackled with the power of command.

"It is Sehrish, mother."

"Ah, yes, Sehrish is a capable young woman." The woman smiled to herself, silently nodding her head. "She is very intelligent. She reminds me of myself at her age. I hope that it was not a mistake to permit her to attend university in Paris. She sometimes seems to have become infected with the current opinions of young French people. Our culture goes back five thousand years, to the Phoenicians. How can you compare that with some silly ideas that were only thought up a few days ago? I don't suppose she has had any thought of marriage?" She asked wryly. "She seems to get along well with that fellow Marc."

"She maintains that she will select the man she marries, if she ever decides to take that step, and she is emphatic that Marc is not that person."

The old woman grunted. "How can she possibly think that she possesses the experience to know who would prove to be a good partner in life?" She shook her head in exasperation. "What, then, is this latest concern with Sehrish?"

"She has said that she wishes to return to Africa. She says that is where she belongs. I suspect that there is a young man there that she wants to see. She has frequently mentioned someone called Antoine." The younger woman explained nervously.

"She has a job to do for this family." The old woman snapped.

"I understand, mother. I know that she will not let you down."

"Sehrish's opinions can be quite irritating. She has no idea what we have been through to create this life for her. Your father and I were young and just starting out. He was becoming recognized as a professor at the university, and I was beginning to establish my medical practice. Beirut was a beautiful modern city. Then all the trouble started. The Muslims and the Christians got in to a civil war, so the Syrians decided to join in, and started shelling our lovely city. Our home was destroyed, and your father and I lost everything, our lovely home, and nearly all of our treasured family heirlooms, mementoes, and possessions. We had to scramble through the wreckage, gathering what few valuables we could find. Your father had his ancestors' love of the sea, and the one thing that had survived was his boat. We left our homeland, and sailed all the way here, just as our ancestors had done, millennia before us."

The old woman paused, and gazed at the distant Mediterranean.

"I remember, mother. I had my twelfth birthday on that boat." Her daughter said softly.

The old woman continued, oblivious to her daughter's comment. "We had to start again, from nothing. Your father took whatever work he could find. Behind us, the entire region was becoming consumed with one war after another; Israel attacked Beirut; Iraq attacked Kuwait; the United States attacked Iraq; and on and on it went. By chance, your father met a colleague from Iraq, who had come to France, hoping to buy weapons. We looked around at the devastation of our lives and our homeland, and realized that the so-called Western countries had been profiting from the wars, with all of the weaponry that they sold to anyone who could pay their price. From his earlier work with the Lebanese military, your father still had some connections with armaments manufacturers, and the skill to design improvised explosives. He was able to supply the weapons that his colleague wanted. Others came to us, since we supplied products for which there was a great demand that was not met by the traditional suppliers, who were largely Western governments, including the one here in France"

The daughter remained silent. She had heard it all before, and knew that it was better to simply let her mother continue, until she ran out of steam. The old woman waved her hand around. "We created all of this from nothing. You and your children have lived in a lavish lifestyle because of what we have achieved. We had to do some harsh things, when that was necessary."

"We all understand, mother. Unfortunately, Sehrish has developed her own beliefs and attitudes, from her work in Africa. I am concerned that she will not participate, once she realizes that the girl is being held against her will."

"I have anticipated of that." She paused. "I will tell her that the girl requires total relaxation, while she is waiting for critical surgery. There is no need for Sehrish to be aware of the real reason we are keeping the young woman under sedation. Her task will simply be to use her medical training to maintain the girl in good health."

The daughter ventured to try and move things along. "I am sure that Sehrish will follow your instructions, exactly as you require. She is just a young woman. I will speak with her."

"Do that. Your father exploited a unique opportunity that he had detected in the vast world of information communications. All of our difficult business activities were conducted far from here. We have an inviolate rule that this house, this family, must never be linked to any business activities that could bring us into disrepute. Make sure that

Sehrish does not hear of the activities of Michael, in Beijing. She is quite close with her brother, Jasar: I don't want them talking. Thankfully, he is away at the moment. I will send Sehrish to Bergerac tomorrow, before he returns."

"It is important that you take care of these things, Mother. Thank you." She hesitated. "We have so many conventional assets, hotels, residential buildings, and a wide range of commercial businesses, I thought that we had left the old business approaches behind?"

"So we had. So we had. Your father invested wisely, sometimes he had to be ruthless, so that today, our family possesses diverse interests that can never all be destroyed, as our lives were in Beirut." Her voice rose as she continued. "You and your brothers don't seem to understand the significance of this last project. It will establish your father's name on a research hospital in Lebanon that will stand as an icon in the world to the medical and scientific talents of the Lebanese people." Her voice had grown loud with passion, until she was almost shouting. "The Bergs' research that we will acquire will serve as a catalyst that will advance the national economy to unprecedented levels, and generate a surge in national pride that will last for generations to come. It is the most important enterprise this family has ever undertaken. It may require some temporary harsh actions involving a few insignificant individuals, but it will succeed."

The old woman paused, panting for a few minutes, while she got her breath back, before she pulled herself to her feet. When she stood, her age betrayed her. She was stooped, and looked quite small and frail, as she steadied herself with her cane that had been hanging in the arm of the chair.

"There is a chill in the evening air. I will go inside. Tell Sehrish to join me for breakfast tomorrow morning. I will speak with her myself. When I was her age, I was already married, and was an established physician. She is a clever young woman, and well educated. It is important that she start to establish herself in our family."

"I will instruct Sehrish to join you for breakfast." The younger woman said to the slowly retreating back of her mother.

***

"Good morning, Grandmother. Thank you for inviting me to join you for breakfast."

"Come in, Sehrish, come in. Here, sit down. It is always a pleasure for an old woman like me, to have a young person join me for breakfast. It brightens the start to my day. The coffee and milk are both hot, and Marie has just brought the croissants, pastries and bread, right out of the oven. The fruit is not the best, but that is all that is available at this time of year."

"Thank you, Grandmother. It looks quite splendid." The girl murmured politely, as she took her seat at the small table, opposite the old woman.

"So what have you been up to? I understand that you found university in Paris to be quite stimulating?"

"Oh, yes! It was wonderful. The theatres; the music; the whole city absolutely reverberates with life, all day and all night." The young woman exclaimed, her eyes alight at the memory.

"You are now a qualified physician, just as I was, at your age. I am very proud of you. I still remember the feeling when I received my Doctor of Medicine. Now that you are back from your time in Africa with Medecins sans Frontieres, you must be keen to start the next chapter in your life?"

"Oh, yes. It was a tremendous experience, working in Africa for two years, and I do miss it. We felt that we were really accomplishing something important. I would like to gain some experience with the modern practices in France, so that I can take that knowledge back to Africa."

"I have arranged something that will help you there." The old woman held up her hand, as her granddaughter started to interrupt. "I am very proud of what you have accomplished, Sehrish, and have been pleased to provide you with a generous income for the past years. Now, I want you to do something for me."

"Yes, of course, Grandmother." A shadow flitted across the young woman's features. "What is it you want me to do?" She asked nervously.

The old woman frowned. "A young English girl will be in our care, for a short while, and I want you to look after her. She has a serious heart defect that requires surgery. Unfortunately, her mother got involved with an extreme religious sect, in England somewhere that refuses all surgery, and believes that prayer will save the girl. Her father is not so inclined. He managed to rescue her, and, through a mutual friend, asked for our help. It is essential that the girl be kept heavily sedated, in preparation for her surgery: any excitement could cause her heart to fail, as, I am sure, you will readily understand. The young girl will arrive in France later today, and stay in the Dordogne region. We have rented a small cottage near Cadouin, and I want you to go and take care of her. As soon as the surgeon in Bordeaux indicates that he is ready to perform the surgery, we will transport her there."

"I am not familiar with the medical protocols here in France. The procedures in Africa are quite different. I would really rather not be involved in such an important medical situation, Grandmother." The young woman fought to conceal her concern. "Why are we involved? Surely there is an experienced French doctor who can attend to her?"

"The mother has been searching for her daughter, to take her back to the religious cult, where they say she will be cured by prayer. The girl's uncle, her mother's brother, arrived in France in a few days ago, to look for her. Apparently he has received some information that she will be here, somewhere in the Dordogne region. He will expect her to be under the care of an established French doctor, and that is where he will start to look. You are recently returned to France, and therefore you are essentially an invisible doctor here, at present. That makes you a perfect choice to look after the girl."

"What about the medical equipment and drugs that this poor girl requires? How can I obtain those essential items?"

"They will all be available at the cottage. You want to experience medical practices, here, in France, and so you shall. You will go to the Dordogne, and assist a doctor, who I know, at the hospital in Bergerac." The old woman's voice brooked no dispute. "All you will have to do is check on the girl every day, and keep her sedated. You can monitor her health on-line, remotely, throughout the day. There will be comprehensive instructions for her care waiting for you there. I anticipate that the surgeon will be ready to proceed within a few days, a week at most. Your uncle Anthony will be there to make all of the arrangements, at the appropriate time. You must have no contact with him, at all. If you see him, you must act as though you do not know him. He will be watching for the girl's uncle. You must maintain your role as a young doctor, new to the region."

Tears started to form in the young woman's eyes. "I really appreciate how good you have been to me, Grandmother, and how you have supported me all these years. What you are asking of me is a family obligation." She took a deep breath. "Of course I must do it."

"I'm pleased that you understand, Sehrish." The old woman said softly.

"Who will be looking after the girl, and how will I explain my presence?"

"That has all been taken care of. An elderly woman is being well paid to look after her. She has been told that the girl is preparing for major heart operation, and needs to be sedated under your care, for a few days, until the surgeon is ready. She has also been told that the girl's uncle is looking for her, to take her back to the religious cult, and she must not reveal her presence, and must report anyone asking about her."

"Will there be any risk that I might be followed, Grandmother, when I go to check in on her each day?"

"Your uncle Anthony will be watching for anything like that. Just follow the normal precautions for any young woman, and make sure that there is no one paying too much attention to you. If you have any concerns, contact me immediately, and just say that you are concerned that you are being stalked. I will take whatever action is required."

"When must I leave?"

"Today, as soon as you are ready. I will send you an email in a few minutes, with the name and location of the doctor you will be assisting, and the address of the small, furnished gite in the city that has been arranged for you. Tomorrow, you will receive a message asking you, as a doctor, to provide confidential care for the young girl, and the address where she is staying. The woman at the cottage will be expecting you, a dedicated physician, who is there to help a young girl in a very difficult situation."

Sehrish took a last drink of her coffee, and stood up. "Thank you for inviting me to have breakfast with you Grandmother." She smiled. "Now, I must go and pack. I will perform my duties exactly as you ask. I will not let you down."

"I have every faith in you, Sehrish. Just be careful how you drive that little gold sports car of yours. You could not afford to replace it on the salary of a young physician."

The young woman understood the quiet warning. "I will be careful, Grandmother." The convertible Lexus had been an extravagant gift, when she had returned from Africa, and she loved driving it. She would do what her grandmother asked.

CHAPTER 8

Indeed, there was a young woman who was assigned to travel to Beijing with Paul. She moved along smoothly behind him and his companion, as they made their way through the International Departures area.

Interpol agent Michelle Denis had arrived in Vancouver two days earlier, and had been preparing to fly home to Lyon later that day. Fortunately, she was staying at the airport hotel, and was already packed, when her boss contacted her just before ten thirty to ask if she would take an immediate assignment to monitor a Canadian travelling from Vancouver to Beijing. She had accepted readily, since these international missions added to her accumulated leave days, and she would need a lot of time off shortly.

Michelle had quickly checked out of the hotel, hurried down for the Air Canada flight that had been booked for her. She had found a seat near the Security checkpoint, and sat with the photo on her phone, watching for her subject, a university professor, named Paul Berg. She would be on the same flight as him, and had been told to be alert for any other interested parties. In the unlikely event that she did observe any interest, to transmit photos or videos, back to Headquarters immediately. A team was being briefed, and would ready to take over from her in Beijing.

They had been flying for a little over five hours when agent Denis ventured forward to check on her subject. She pushed the curtain aside and surveyed the front cabin. There was no real reason for it, but she believed in paying attention to small details.

She could see Paul Berg's head, and there, coming out of the washroom, was the Chinese woman who appeared to be travelling with him. She had the seat beside him. Her instructions had not mentioned a travelling companion. On their arrival in Beijing, she would notify Head Office, and send them a photograph for identification.

A soft, firm voice interrupted her thoughts. "Excuse me, do you have a seat in this cabin?" Michelle had not heard the attendant come up behind her.

She turned around, and managed a disarming smile. "Not this time. I was just checking out Business Class for my next trip. I'll head back to my seat."

CHAPTER 9

CSIS Regional Director, Claude Noble delivered a curt directive to Sarah Little and Kevin Blakey to meet him in his office in half an hour. They knew what the topic was going to be.

Noble waved them into the chairs in front of his desk.

"What the Hell is going on with the abduction of the daughter of the UBC scientist?" He glanced down at the note on his desk. "Professor Paul Berg. I thought we were on top of this. At the last briefing you told me that the situation was under control. Now it looks like the whole thing could go pear shaped. And in China for God's sake."

His laser gaze hit first Little, and then Blakey. Sarah Little spoke first.

"You are familiar with the background, sir. An alert came from our Chinese office, several weeks ago, that a unusual invitation had been extended for a Canadian girls soccer team to take part in a tournament, in Beijing. It had not been initiated through the normal diplomatic channels."

Blakey leant forward slightly in his chair to take over the narrative. "Our concern elevated when we identified one of the girls on the team as the daughter of Professor Paul Berg, who was already on our watch list, along with his brother, Matt Berg, as a result of intercepted chatter concerning their recent research. We contacted the SIS in London, who were already alert to the situation, and we agreed to monitor communications involving both Berg brothers."

"The situation moved to amber yesterday," Little continued, "when the police in Beijing reported to our Embassy that a girl on the visiting Canadian soccer team, tentatively identified as Nicky Berg, had been abducted off a street in Beijing. This morning we learnt that another girl on the Canadian team, Kim Song, who was reported to have suffered minor injuries during the abduction, was in the Peking Union Medical College Hospital, under the care of Doctor Yang Chow. Our Embassy has confirmed this information independently. "

"What do we know about this Doctor Yang Chow, and the girl Kim Song? Do they have any connection with Paul or Matt Berg?"

Little answered. "Doctor Yang Chow and a Canadian doctor, Patricia Chen are old friends. Patricia Chen is also a close friend of Paul Berg and his daughter Nicky, the girl who was abducted. We have crosschecked the background of the relationship between Paul Berg and Patricia Chen. Chen trained together with, and was a close friend of, Paul Berg's wife, Nancy Thorpe, who died three years ago from cervical cancer. Patricia Chen has become close with both Nicky and Paul Berg. Kim Song is a school friend of Nicky Berg, and is also on the same soccer team. They all live in close proximity in Vancouver."

Blakey picked up the narrative. "As expected, on learning of his daughter's abduction Berg made immediate plans to fly to Beijing, and Chen went with him. She is a regular visitor to medical clinics in China, and has a long term multiple entry visa. They left on the direct flight this afternoon from Vancouver to Beijing, with Air Canada. We were concerned with the emerging developments, and visited Paul Berg around noon, to advise him of our concerns."

Little interjected. "He did not take our involvement well, although he did seem to comprehend the CSIS concerns."

Noble sat back in his chair. "Several questions come to mind immediately. First, was young Nicky Berg the victim of a plot to abduct her, in order to get Paul Berg to Beijing, where she would then be used to pressure him? Second, is she still alive, and if so, where is she? Third, what are the authourities in Beijing doing to find Nicky Berg? Finally, if this is a planned abduction to coerce the Berg's to give up their research results, do we know the likely players who could be behind it? Where are we with the answers?"

"Yes, sir those are the answers that we have been looking for since we started to get the information from Beijing." Little said. "First, if the purpose of abducting Nicky Berg was to get her father to travel to Beijing, it has succeeded. He is already on his way there. We are convinced that Berg and his brother will hand over all of the software and documentation relating to their research without a second thought, in order to obtain the safe return of young Nicky.
"The answer to your second question is that we don't know if Nicky Berg is still alive, or, if she is, where she is currently being held. The reason for this answers your third question, in that the Chinese authourities have been reticent in providing us with information on their actions in the case.
Finally, we have discussed the possible instigator of this abduction with our counterparts in MI6, in London, and Interpol. They suggested that the abduction could be being handled by a third party, on behalf of what they term the 'End User'. However, at this point, that is just speculation."

The Regional Director closed his eyes in exasperation. "Oh shit. I don't like this. We cannot permit some group of nutcases to obtain the potential bioweapon capabilities of the Bergs' research." He looked grim. "Right, well you two had better get going. The late Air China flight to Beijing leaves in about four hours, if I recall correctly. That gives you enough time to grab a bag and get to the airport. Ajit will make the reservations for you as usual."

CHAPTER 10

It was just after four o'clock in the afternoon, local time the following day, when the Air Canada flight docked at the terminal of the Beijing Capital Airport. Paul and Tricia were some of the first ones to disembark. She had flown into Beijing many times since the new terminal had first been opened for the 2008 Olympics, and knew it quite well. During the lengthy walk to the immigration counters, Tricia noticed that Paul was slowing down, and gazing at the vast structure of the glass and steel roof that soared around them. After the shocks of the past day, the human sea of bodies and the unfamiliar environment was obviously disorienting him.

She grabbed his hand. "Here, Paul, this way. This airport is so confusing. Thankfully, I've been here so many times, I have finally learnt my way through. It's not much further."

Despite being among the first passengers from their flight to arrive at the row of Immigration Desks, they still had to line-up at the end of a snake of passengers from previous flights. It seemed to take an eternity. Once they were through immigration, Tricia led the way down an escalator to the airport train that would take them to the baggage area, and the main terminal.

As they came through the sliding glass doors into the Main Terminal building, Paul stopped in his tracks. The journey to the baggage area had been suffocating, but when they entered the main area, the cacophony of human activity hit him like a solid wall of sound. He stood transfixed at the mass of people everywhere he looked. Tricia tugged his arm, and pointed to a middle aged man dressed in the ubiquitous dark grey suit, patiently standing at the barrier holding up a sign with 'Professor Berg and Doctor Chen' displayed on it. Tricia silently gave her friend, Yang Chow, her sincere thanks for insisting on sending a driver from the clinic to meet them.

The driver exchanged Mandarin greetings with Tricia, as he politely took the luggage cart away from a bemused Paul, and marched off through the moving mass of humanity, leaving them struggling to stay in his wake. The little parade pushed and jostled its way across the terminal to the elevator, then down to where a shiny black Audi was waiting for them.

As they pulled away, and left the airport behind, Tricia pointed out the haze that hovered in the sky to the South, above the massive metropolis of Beijing.

Paul settled back into the car, with a sigh. "So that's Beijing. Where are we going now? We should go straight to the clinic, and talk to Kim."

Tricia shook her head. "I think we should first go to the hotel. Your message to the person who contacted you and Matt was that we were coming here, and would be staying at the Hyatt hotel on East Chang An Street. I'm sure they will be watching for us to arrive, so we should check in, so that they know that we are here. The hotel is not far from the clinic."

"Good point." He stared at his watch. "What time is it? My watch says something after two o'clock in the morning. My eyes are having a bit of difficulty focusing."

"It's ten after six in the afternoon. Beijing is sixteen hours ahead of Vancouver. How are you feeling?"

"Not great. My mind is a soggy mush, and my body feels about the same."

"I take it you didn't get any sleep on the flight?"

"Not very much. I just can't stop thinking about Nicky. How can this possibly be happening? It's like we've passed into the twilight zone. I can't believe it. I just can't believe it."

She looked at his hands. "You're starting to shake, Paul. Take some deep breaths. We must try and stay calm."

It was rush hour in Beijing, and, once they had exited the main road from the airport, it seemed to be a battle to drive every few blocks along the choked arteries. It was after seven o'clock, before the driver finally negotiated his way off the city's main roads, through some narrow side streets of central Beijing, and onto East Chang An avenue. They slid past the neon lit fronts of restaurants, shops and small hotels, and pulled up the ramp to the front of the Hyatt hotel. The impressive curved glass entrance was a wall of light, and a sharp contrast to the low rise, shabby looking buildings they had just passed through.

As soon as the car stopped it was met by a cordon of enthusiastic uniformed hotel staff. The driver was not about to renege on his responsibilities, and jumped out of the car to supervise the porter with his passengers' luggage.

With that organized, Tricia explained to the driver that they would just check in with their luggage, and if he could wait for about half an hour, they would like to go to the clinic. That settled, Tricia led a bemused Paul through the luxurious lobby across to the check-in desk. As soon as she gave their names, the manager appeared, and greeted Tricia effusively, alternating between expressions of remorse for what had happened to Nicky, and welcoming her as a treasured guest. The story of the abduction of the Canadian teenager had been a lead on the news. He had upgraded them to two adjoining rooms on the Club Floor. Formalities completed, Tricia and Paul took the elevator to their rooms, where their luggage was already waiting for them. They didn't bother to unpack. After an attempt at a brief freshening up, they headed back down for the drive to the clinic.

"I'm actually starting to feel almost human again. How long will it take to get to the clinic?" Paul said.

"Not long." Tricia reassured him. "Usually about ten minutes. Remember that Kim has had a really bad experience, so don't push her too hard."

"I know. Look, why don't you take the lead? You're used to dealing with kids, and you're a woman, which might make it a bit easier for Kim to relate."

When the car pulled into the clinic driveway, Tricia felt a wave of reassurance to see the familiar physicians' entrance where she had visited so many times in the past. She had great respect for the calibre of medical care that was provided at the clinic, and was thankful that Yang Chow had immediately whisked Kim in here. Unlike hospitals in some parts of the country, this one was equipped with the most advanced medical technologies in China.

The state-run clinic had a Foreigners' Wing where most of the doctors had received foreign training and spoke fluent English. This wing with its fifty beds had been set-aside for foreigners, with private rooms at a modest cost. Tricia knew that Yang would have found Kim a room there. She hurried across to the reception desk, and waited agonizing minutes for them to locate Doctor Chow. She arrived within minutes, and was effusive in expressing her embarrassment that such a terrible incident would happen in Beijing. Tricia politely thanked her and asked about Kim, explaining that they wanted to talk to her as soon as possible. Yang reassured her that Kim was recovering from her ordeal remarkably well, but, despite her excellent progress, it would be prudent to keep her for one more night. Tomorrow she would be able to return to Canada with the rest of her soccer team. The coach and manager had heard from the parents, who were unanimous that they should forego the remainder of the tournament, and get the girls home as quickly as possible.

Yang Chow led Tricia and Paul through the maze of corridors and up a flight of stairs to a small private room where a pale-faced Kim was lying in a bed, hooked up to a battery of digital displays showing an array of her physical functions. She had a red, swollen nose, and the start of what looked like two black eyes.

Jane Raybourn the manager of the Westside Warriors team was sitting in the room beside Kim. She stood up with a relieved look when she saw Paul and Tricia with Doctor Chow.

"Professor Berg, I can't tell you how devastated we all are about what has happened to Nicky. I am sure that it is all a terrible mistake, and she will be back with you in no time. I dropped by to see how Kim was doing. We have been so careful with where the girls go during their free time. We absolutely insisted that they always stay in groups. Nicky and Kim were with several of the girls at the time. All the girls are in an awful way about this. They can't wait to get on the plane back to Vancouver."

"Thanks, Ms. Raybourn. Dr. Chow tells me that you have been calling in regularly to check on Kim. Her parents really appreciate that. I know Dr. Chow will have given her the very best care possible." Paul managed to sound in control.

"Yes, Doctor Chow has been terrific. I will leave now, and head back to the team. Bye Kim. I'll let the others know that you are doing really well." She stopped at the door. "I nearly forgot, we packed all of Nicky's things in her suitcase, and I left it with Dr. Chow, for you."

Kim gave the team manager a little wave. "Thanks, Ms. Raybourn. Hi Doctor Chen; Professor Berg. How did you get here so quick? Have you heard anything about Nicky? We're all worried sick about her. Is she missing? I don't understand what happened."

Paul made his best effort at a smile. "We're not sure where Nicky is, Kim. We're here to find her. How are you doing?""

"Like Ms. Raybourn said, Dr. Chow has been absolutely terrific. When Mum and Dad heard what had happened, they were messaging me, like, every fifteen minutes. Finally, I managed to phone them a little while ago. They were worried sick. They wanted to come here immediately, but it was going to take forever for them to get their visas for China. I'm really feeling lots better so I just want to join the team for the flight back home tomorrow. It totally sucks that all of this has happened. It, like, totally wrecked everything."

Tricia scanned the digital instruments. "Hey, Kim, according to all these readouts, you're doing great, considering. Luckily, we both had valid Chinese visas, and got the first flight, as soon as we heard what had happened."

Yang Chow gave a quick check of the current numbers on the digital displays, then turned to Tricia looking a little puzzled.

"It is strange, Tricia. Kim's symptoms were just a bit odd. I have some blood and urine tests in at the lab, and expected the results back later today. From Kim's reaction, I would say that she ingested some form of chemical. Perhaps someone was a bit careless or over zealous with cleaning the utensils or dishes that Kim used. That can happen. We should know more later. You told me earlier that you and Nicky didn't buy anything to eat in the streets at all, that is right, isn't it Kim?"

"Yes, Doctor. My parents drilled it into me before we left that I should stick to the food that was provided, and not be tempted by anything being sold in the street, or even in a store. The thing is, it all happened so quickly. I'm a bit fuzzy about exactly what happened before the girls loaded me into a taxi and brought me here." She looked away.

Tricia had been dealing with children of all ages for a number of years, and recognized the sign. She glanced over at Yang and Paul. "Can you just give me a minute, Yang? Paul?"

Once they had left, she turned back to the patient. "Okay, Kim. Come on, what happened? This is serious. I need the full story."

"I understand, Doctor Chen, totally." A pink flush started to creep into her face. "It's just, sort of, uber embarrassing." She took a deep breath, and looked out of the window. "We got off the underground train with Sharon's mum, and five other girls, and we were all just checking out the neighbourhood, before we went back to the residence. Nicky and I were sort of hanging outside some sort of food place that sold pastries and drinks and stuff." She paused, then continued, speaking quickly. "Well, this cute Chinese guy, I think he was a bit older than us, anyway, he came over and just started talking to us in English. He asked our names, where we were from, and what we were doing in Beijing, and all that sort of stuff. Then he asked if we wanted a drink. Nicky said that we were afraid of getting sick. He assured us that the bottled coke was fine, and he would get us some. We were, like, cooked from walking around Beijing all afternoon. The place looked pretty clean, so we said okay. It sounds so majorly dumb, now, but honestly Doctor Chen, he seemed really nice, and we were only, like, steps from the others.

"So anyway, he got a couple of bottles of coke, and I remember he poured it from the bottles into three paper cups. He asked if he could talk to us, and practise his English, and suggested we wander over to a little park place, just, like, twenty metres away.

"We headed over, talking, then some woman bumped into me and spilled most of my drink, right over the front of my shirt.

It was soo embarrassing. I was totally soaked all down my front. Then it starts to go all confused. A big, black car, you know, sort of like an SUV in Canada, but not as big, well it suddenly screeched to a stop beside us, and this man jumped out, I think he was in the front passenger seat, and threw open the rear door. The boy yelled something, and he and the man grabbed Nicky and started pushing her into the car. Nicky yelled, at least, I think she did. There was a lot of yelling, and I tried to fight them off. The man turned and punched me in the face and I fell down. I remember hearing lots of yelling, and people shouting, then Sharon's mum told a couple of the other girls to jump into a taxi with me and brought me here. That's all I can really remember." She started to cry. "It was awful. We were so stupid."

"You did great, Kim. You must have been putting up quite a fight for the man to have to hit you?"

She gave a self-conscious grin. "Well, I think I made him a bit mad. There was another person in the back seat, pulling Nicky in. When the man pushed me away, and started shouting at them to hurry up, or something, the boy was, like, bending over, pushing Nicky into the car. I was so mad, and I kicked him as hard as I could, you know, where it really hurts. He sort of squealed and fell into the car. That's when the man turned and hit me." She looked away, self-consciously. "Soccer balls aren't the only ones that I can kick."

Tricia stared up at the ceiling, struggling to avoid crying. "How was Nicky? She must have been terrified?"

Kim frowned. "Actually, I seem to sort of remember that Nicky seemed quite confused, but my memory is a bit fuzzy. It was all happening so quickly."

She called to Yang Chow and Paul to come back in, and went over and gave Kim a long hug. "Oh Kim. You have to be over-the-top careful, when you are in a foreign country. Thank God you're safe. We're really proud that you fought back like that. The others were terrific, too. It sounds like their yelling made them panic and get out of there as fast as possible."

Doctor Chow gave a tense look from across the room. "Yes, it was very good that everyone started shouting and making a lot of noise. I understand that several of the people in the shops heard them and came running to help as well. Unfortunately, these days in Beijing, it can sometimes be unwise for young girls to talk people who they don't know."

Kim grimaced. "Believe it. I really know that now. He just seemed so normal and nice."

Tricia turned to Yang. "You said you were waiting for some lab results?"

"Yes. They should be back soon. I am sure there won't be anything unusual. Kim can join the others, and fly home tomorrow. What about you and Paul?"

"We are staying at the Hyatt hotel on East Chang An Avenue. I've stayed there before, and the manager knows me."

Yang nodded wisely. "That can be quite beneficial in China."

Paul stifled a yawn. "I hate to say it, but the jetlag is getting to me, again. I think I should head back to the hotel."

"Yes, me too, Paul. Thanks for everything, Yang. And you look after yourself, Kim. We will see you in Vancouver."

CHAPTER 11

Michelle Denis also had a room reserved for her at the Hyatt on East Chang An Avenue, to be where Paul Berg was staying. Postponing unpacking, she set up an Internet connection at the desk in the room, and sat there for a couple of minutes organizing the wording of the message. It was only a confidential mission, so it did not require complex codes or special communication systems, but messages still had to be couched quite carefully. Michelle always worked under the assumption that her messages were likely to be intercepted by some third party, particularly in China, so she sent a message to the server in Singapore that would quickly and untraceably reroute it to Headquarters.

"Hi Danielle: Arrived in Beijing finally. Missed Paul when we were boarding at the airport, but he was on the plane, and has checked into the Hyatt hotel, so I will catch up with him later. Otherwise everything went okay. His friend seemed quite pleasant; sorry I have forgotten her name. You might know her from the attached photo. Call me later and we can exchange all the latest gossip. Michelle"

The greeting 'Danielle' meant that there was a 'D' grade, low level concern. The subject, Paul Berg was currently out of contact, and had been travelling with an unknown person. The final sentence requested identification of the unknown female, and requested a secure phone conversation later, to provide a detailed update, and receive further instructions.

There was little more that she could do at that point, so Michelle unpacked the essentials, and, after a quick shower, headed out to get something to eat. Airline meal times followed a curious schedule on the long flights to Asia, and she wanted to get her body on local time as quickly as possible.

It was three hours later when the insistent buzzing from her mobile phone told her that Head Office was returning her call.

Michelle had identified herself, and was instructed to attach her scrambling device. Once she had confirmed she had done that, the Head of Operations was connected to the call.

"We have received your text, Michelle, and have identified Paul Berg's companion as Doctor Patricia Chen. She is a Canadian pediatrician at the Vancouver Children's hospital, but makes regular visits to pediatric clinics in various parts of China. She is thirty-five years old, unmarried, and lives alone in the townhouse that she owns in Vancouver. She is a close friend of Paul Berg, although they are not considered a couple. Her parents emigrated from Guangzhou, China, to Canada thirty-six years ago. She was a close friend of Paul Berg's wife at High School, and when they were at medical school together. Berg's wife died of cervical cancer three years ago. I'm sending a more complete bio to you."

"Thank you, ma'am. That gives me a good understanding of who Doctor Chen is, and her relationship with Paul Berg. They certainly appear to be comfortable together."

"Do you believe that either of them noticed you following them from Vancouver?"

"That is possible, although I think it is unlikely. They might have noticed that I followed them through Security, but after that, I was just one of a couple of hundred other passengers, milling about at the boarding gate in Vancouver. On the flight to Beijing itself, Berg and Chen were in Business Class, and I was back in economy, so they did not notice me there. I slipped up front to check on them once, but I was only there for a minute or so, and they had their backs to me. Unless they were expecting someone to be watching them, there was no reason for them to have been looking for me."

"Did you notice anyone else who appeared to be watching Berg?"

"As always, the waiting area had the usual mix of bored passengers, with some idly watching their fellow travelers, but no-one appeared to be showing any undue interested in either of them."

"Where are Berg and Chen at the moment?"

"They are staying here, at the Beijing Grand Hyatt, in line with our information. At the moment, they are at the Peking Union Medical College Hospital, visiting Kim Song, Nicky Berg's friend who was hurt when Nicky was grabbed. Our contact here was able to provide some basics. Can you give me any more information? Are the local authourities looking for Nicky Berg here in Beijing, ma'am?"

"I can give you what information I have from the team that is there, to take over from you. It is looking like a deceptive approach that was used a couple of times in the past, although the last time we saw it operated was over a decade ago. At that time, there was a successful group that had a system of coercion that involved kidnapping someone important to the individual who had something that they wanted. The clever part is that they arranged for the trade of information in one country, having moved the kidnap victim to another, unrelated country, thus avoiding being seen to be overtly breaking any of the laws in either location. The 'trade' could be dismissed as simply a legitimate exchange. The owner being in no position to complain, while the victim was still being held. In those past instances, the kidnapped victim was always sedated, and didn't know where they were, or what was happening, when they were found. The kidnappers had long since departed before the local authourities realized the person was the victim of a kidnapping in another country."

Michelle started to understand. "Do we know the identity of the kidnappers, who want this research, ma'am?"

"No, we have not made an identification to this point. However, we have to assume that they could be a rather nasty bunch."

"If Paul Berg is in Beijing to hand over his research, where is Nicky Berg, if, as past experience suggests, she will be in some other country?"

"A short while ago, Matt Berg was instructed to go to Bergerac, in France. That may not be the final destination, but we have some indications that Nicky Berg has been taken to Europe, our information suggests France, probably as a medical patient on a private medevac flight."

"Ah, that is why we are involved?"

"Correct. We have been in contact with CSIS in Canada, and MI6 in the U.K., and the French Police Nationale. We all agree that we have to find Nicky Berg, and stop the kidnappers from obtaining the medical research from the Berg brothers. If we let this approach succeed, we could have all sorts of copycats."

"Where are the Chinese in all this?"

"Not sure. They might just be treating it as a simple criminal abduction of a teenage girl. We don't know exactly what their next move will be."

"What are my instructions?"

"For the present, stay close to Paul Berg, and keep me informed on everything that happens. Don't initiate contact with your

Chinese counterparts, at least, not at this point. We have a team in place to take over from you, but I want them to operate on their own for the time being. Our course of action is expected to evolve over the next forty-eight hours."

The Head of Operations closed the briefing. "That's about it, for the moment, thank you Michelle. Keep us informed, and contact me immediately if there are any developments with Berg or Chen."

CHAPTER 12

Paul had to wait until they were alone in the taxi heading back to the hotel, before he felt comfortable asking Tricia if she was able to learn anything useful from Kim.

She hesitated. "Well, sort of. Kim was able to give a pretty good description of what happened, despite being punched in the face, and knocked down by some thug."

Paul shook his head in disbelief. "Good grief. Poor Kim. This whole situation just gets more and more incredible. What in God's name is going on? What was she able to tell you?"

"She and Nicky, and a few other girls from the team were with Sharon's mum, returning from a visit to downtown Beijing. They had just left the subway, and were ahead of the others, walking back to their team residence, when they stopped to look in a store window, while they waited for the others to catch up. A Chinese boy came over, and started talking to them. He asked if he could practise his English, and suggested he buy them a Coke, or something. They were unsure, but he persuaded them, and suggested they take the drinks to the corner, where there was a bench in a small park. The others were still behind them, checking out some things in a shop. Nicky and Kim had only gone a couple of steps, when a car came to a sudden stop beside them; a man jumped out, and someone in the car helped the boy bundled Nicky into the car. They fought back, and that is when Kim kicked the boy in his groin, provoking the man to punch her."

"Why didn't anyone stop them? Weren't there any adults around? What about the other girls? Why didn't they stop it?"

Tricia frowned. "It was all over so fast. The thing is, Paul, from what she described, it sounded like it was planned."

"Oh God, no."

"Well, hold on a minute, Paul. That would confirm the message they sent to you and Matt. Whoever is behind this doesn't intend to harm Nicky, they are just using her as leverage to force you and Matt to give them all the details of your medical research."

"That's just bloody nonsense. Our initial findings are not worth kidnapping Nicky, to coerce us into giving it to them."

"Apparently, they think it is."

Paul rubbed his forehead. "So what do we do now? Any suggestions? I think I'm going mad. I've got to do something."

"There really isn't anything we can do, at this point, except try and get some sleep, and wait for whoever 'they' are, to contact us."

"There is no way I will be able to sleep, not knowing where Nicky is, or what has happened to her."

"We both need sleep. You were exhausted, at the clinic. We've been up for an incredibly stressful twenty-four hours. There is nothing we can do tonight, and we owe it to Nicky to be as alert as we can possibly be tomorrow morning. I have sleeping tablets that I brought with me. They're at the hotel. I'll give you one."

"Okay," Paul agreed, grudgingly. "Here we are now. Let's hope we hear from these bastards first thing tomorrow morning."

One of the advantages of staying at the Grand Hyatt hotel in

Beijing was that there were no surprises that otherwise might await the weary Western traveler in a traditional Chinese hotel. The two connected rooms that the Manager had arranged for Tricia were large and luxurious. Paul glanced around his room, with its invitingly large bed, appreciative that the manager had given them an upgrade. Tricia knocked on the connecting door, as he was sorting out the few essentials that he needed from his suitcase.

"Yeah. Come on in. We should leave the connecting doors unlocked, in case anything happens in the night."

"A good idea. Here's the sleeping tablet." She handed him a tablet. "Take this with a glass of water, from the bottle over there. Never drink water from the tap. Have you heard anything from Matt?"

"He sent a brief message a few hours ago. I only just got it. Apparently MI6 arrived at his door, and were amped up about what they saw as the dangerous, potential application of our research. He's clearly a bit shaken up. The MI6 people told him to expect another message from the kidnappers that will tell him to go to another destination. They think it will likely be somewhere in Europe. Apparently, they based this on some past experiences. He will get back to me again later."

CHAPTER 13

Paul did not have to wait long for the contact from Nicky's kidnappers. The next morning, he was drying off, after a shower, when the phone rang in his room. He leapt across, and barked his name into the instrument.

The voice was cold and mechanical. "Write this down." Paul scrambled for the pen and paper on the desk. "The Fangshan restaurant at noon today for lunch. It's in the Beihai Park, behind the Forbidden City. Just you and Doctor Chen. No security. We will be watching you. Bring some samples of the documentation that we require. Have you got that?"

"Yes, yes, I think so. The Fang Shang restaurant in the Bay High Park behind the Forbidden City, at twelve noon, today. Will Nicky be there? Where is she? Hello? Hello?" He was talking to a dead line.

Tricia burst into the room. "Was that them? What did they say?"

Paul was distraught. "All they said was that you and I are to go to some restaurant in a park behind the Forbidden City, for lunch at noon today. No 'security' was what he said. I presume that means 'no police'. And I am to bring some of the documentation." His gaze wandered blankly around the room. "He hung up when I started to ask about Nicky. This is fucking madness, Tricia. What are we supposed to do?"

"The restaurant, Paul. Did he say the name of the restaurant?"

"What? Yes. I wrote it down." He stared at the hotel note pad. "He said the Fang Shang restaurant, in the Bay High Park."

"Okay, that's the famous Fangshan restaurant, in Beihai Park. I know it. Did you say that we are supposed to have lunch?"

"Yes. How insane is that? As if I will be able to eat anything."

"Okay, I think what they are doing is making sure that we come alone. It would be difficult for a police surveillance team to remain inconspicuous while we have lunch. I expect that we will receive instructions to leave at some random point during the meal. Any watchers would be forced to reveal themselves, or risk losing contact."

"So what do we do?"

"We go and have some breakfast." She shook her head, as Paul started to protest. "Paul, we have to look after our bodies, and keep our minds sharp, and that means eating properly, and getting whatever rest we can. Nicky is counting on us."

"Okay. You're right. I know. Starving myself is not going to help anything."

"On a practical issue, can you gather the documentation they want, by noon today?"

"Yes, that won't be a problem. I have to decide what to show them. I'm not giving them too much until I am sure that Nicky is safe, and we have a fixed time when we will get her back."

"If you get some clothes on, we can go and get some breakfast, while you work that out." She said, casting a wary eye at the towel that was getting gradually lower around his waist.

By eleven o'clock, Paul had assembled a selection of documents that he hoped would satisfy the kidnappers. He was pacing the floor, desperate to get going.

"It's not very far to Beihai Park and the Fangshan restaurant. If we take a taxi now, we'll be there far too early." Tricia explained, when he told her he wanted to leave. "I've been thinking about that though. It's quite a pleasant day. If you are willing to walk through the Beijing streets for about thirty minutes, I have an idea. We'll leave through the Oriental Plaza shopping mall that is connected to the hotel, and walk north down the Wangfujing pedestrian shopping street."

"I'm not in the mood to go shopping, Tricia." Paul said tersely.

"I understand that, Paul. My point is that, if anyone is following us, with two of us, stopping and starting, and looking around, we should have a good chance to spot them. When we reach Wusi Street, we turn left, and that will take us to the Beihai Park entrance."

He gave Tricia's shoulder a pat. "Sorry. I was being stupid. That's a really good idea. This whole business is really getting to me. Nicky is the most important person in the world to me. I have to find her. I can't stop thinking about her, every minute. Where is she? Is she all right?"

Tricia put her hand on his arm. "I know, Paul. Nicky is a really important part of my life, too. I can only guess at the strain that you must be under. As soon as you are dressed, we can get going."

It was an unusually warm March day in Beijing, with a slight wind that had blown away the polluting smog, and left clear skies and bright sunshine. Tricia had suggested that they dress to blend in as just another tourist couple. She wore a salmon coloured sweater over a blue shirt with pale blue pants, and had suggested tan cotton cargo pants and a crisp off-white denim shirt for Paul.

They strolled along the sidewalks at a leisurely pace, avoiding the endless streams of pedestrians that seemed to flow in waves in both directions. Trying not to make it too obvious, she would stop and gaze in a shop window, allowing Paul to walk a short distance, before turning around, ostensibly to wait for her, while he scanned the street behind them. A bit further on, they reversed the procedure, with Tricia going ahead, and turning to check the faces behind them.

Tricia could see that Paul was visibly stressed by the cacophony of sounds that reverberated around them, and seemed to be deteriorating the further they went. She was relieved to see the massive gated entrance to Beihai Park, after they had been walking for twenty minutes.

She paid the nominal entrance fee, and led the way along the pathways, lawns and gardens. To try and help him relax, she tried talking to Paul about things that they passed, pointing out some that dated back over one thousand years. It had little effect. Paul was completely strung out, staring around every corner, and at every person they passed: her efforts to get him to relax were not successful.

The colourful, carved accents of the magnificent old building that housed the Fangshan restaurant were lost on Paul. He was too engrossed in looking for their contact to appreciate the ancient ambience of the locale.

They were early, but at the reception desk, the young woman attired in traditional Chinese costume located their reservation, and said that there was a table ready for them.

"I don't think that you are going to be able to identify your contact, by peering around at all of the other diners, Paul." Tricia suggested quietly. "I suggest that you, at least, look at the menu, or, perhaps, use it as a screen, if you must."

"I know, I know. The tension is killing me. I find it so damned difficult. I just want to give them what they want, and have Nicky back with us."

"What would you like to eat?"

"What? I have absolutely no clue. Can you order something for both of us? I'm not in the least hungry."

"Okay. We're a bit early, so if I order several courses, we can eat really slowly, and make it last for at least an hour. Here's the waiter coming over. I'll ask for a pot of green tea, and say we are having difficulty deciding. We'll be able to drag that out for a while. When I do order, I'm going to order the Fangshan Special Lunch for two. There will be endless dishes, which will take a while to come. I'm not hungry, either, but we should eat something to keep our strength up, for Nicky's sake."

They dawdled over the green tea, before Tricia gave their lunch order. As the endless succession of dishes arrived, Paul did his best to try some of them.

He glanced around. "This really is utter madness to sit here eating lunch. I have to do something."

Tricia reached across the table for his hand. "I understand. But we have been told to be here, and wait, and that is what we must do. I'm sure that we are being watched, to make sure that we are actually alone. And, of course, I suspect that there is the psychological play of getting us really wound up with tension, before the meeting.

The last of the lunch courses had been taken away, and still had not received any contact. Tricia finally signaled to the waiter for the bill. She suggested that they walk around the Park. Perhaps the contact would be made outside. As they walked through the door, Paul froze.

"It's Nicky! There she is." He gasped.

"Nicky? Where?" Tricia looked around frantically.

"Over there. She's with that woman. Come on. They just

disappeared around the corner."

"Are you sure that was Nicky?"

"Yes. She was wearing her jeans, and her Manchester United shirt. She had her Canada cap on. It was Nicky. I recognized her immediately. She was with a woman. They went round that corner."

He grabbed Tricia's hand, as they started to run. They rounded the corner, and stopped, looking around, desperately.

"There they are, Paul. They're leaving the bridge over there. It goes onto Jade Flower Island. Come on. Quick."

They raced across the elegant, white stone bridge, incurring the open disgust of those they passed, who were intent on absorbing the quiet, peaceful ambience of the park. At the far end of the bridge, the path split three ways in front of the ornately carved red gateway to the Yong'an Monastery. Which way did she go? Their vision was blocked by the profusion of budding willow trees, and the buildings around the hill that rose in front of them. The paths to the left and right circled the island along the lakeside; straight ahead, was the Monastery, and beyond, the path climbed up to the massive White Pagoda that towered above them.

"Which way, Tricia?"

"I don't know. If they are leaving the park, they will have headed around to the right. There's the East Gate exit that way."

"We'll go that way, then. Keep looking around."

He started to run. Tricia pulled him back. "We can't run, Paul. This park is a place of peaceful contemplation for the local population. If we cause a disturbance, the park officers will tell us to leave, and escort us out. Just walk at a steady pace. It's not far. Don't forget, they will have to walk as well."

The next few minutes seemed to take forever, as they wound their way around the edge of the lake, and were at the short bridge across to the East Gate exit. There was no sign of Nicky and the woman. Tricia approached an old couple sitting on a bench, absorbing the view of the iconic White Pagoda on the hilltop above them. She asked politely if they had seen a woman and girl cross the bridge. After some discussion, the old woman agreed that they had seen such a pair, but they had not crossed the bridge. They had carried on around the path.

Tricia thanked the couple profusely, and explained to Paul what they had said.

"Where does it go if they stayed on this path, then? Is there another exit?"

"There is the ferry to the north shore, and from there they could exit the park through the North Gate. Come on. It's just around the curve. We just might catch them at the ferry dock."

They left the path, and cut across the corner, in time to see that the ferry was getting ready to leave.

"Enough of the niceties, I have to run." Paul growled.

They careened down the slope to the dock, only to watch the water churn behind the ferry, as it pulled away. The woman and Nicky were sitting at the rear of the boat, with their backs facing the land. Paul called out to Nicky in one last desperate attempt to get her attention. The only sign that she heard was that the woman leaned over and said something to her. The girl took off her sunglasses, blond wig and cap, and turned around to look at them with a blank face that was devoid of any emotion. It was not Nicky. She was Chinese.

Paul staggered across to a bench, and slumped down, with his head down on his knees. "I don't understand. What was that all about? What was the point of it? They dressed a girl up to look like Nicky, and had us chasing her around the island. For what?"

Tricia sat down beside him, and put her arm around his shoulders. "I don't know, Paul. Perhaps it was to confirm to you that they really did have Nicky. That they knew Nicky well enough to be able to dress up a girl that looked just like her."

"Is it over then? Do we just head back to the hotel?" He rose unsteadily to his feet, and stood there, staring around, when his phone started ring in his pocket.

"Hello?"

"That was foolish of you to bring the authourities, Professor Berg. We told you not to. Now we will have to arrange for another meeting tomorrow. A day has been wasted. A day when your daughter could have been back with you. I will call again later, with specific instructions. This time, make sure that you follow them exactly."

He rang off, leaving Paul staring at the phone.

"Was that the kidnappers? What did they say?"

"Yes. They said that I didn't follow their instructions. They claimed that we had brought the authourities with us. I presume he meant the police. I have no idea what he meant. There are no police around here, are there?"

Tricia instinctively glanced around. "I didn't see any. Come on, let's head back. The quickest way is up the hill to the White Pagoda, up there, and then down to the bridge. Can you manage it?"

"What? Yes. I'm fine, just a bit shaken. I'm a physicist. My brain is not built for this high stress James Bond stuff."

They ambled their way up the hill to the base of the White Pagoda, then down to the intricately carved and coloured gateway of the Yong'an Monastery, where they paused for a moment.

"With or without its religious connection, it really is a magnificent piece of art, isn't it, Professor?"

Paul spun around, and to his intense annoyance, he found himself facing Sara Little from CSIS.

"Ms. Little, isn't it? What are you doing here? Are you alone or is the intrepid Mr. Blakey with you to complete your happy little CSIS team?"

"Kevin Blakey is with me. He is sitting on the seat, just over there. We would like to have a brief confidential chat with you."

"I take it, you've met Ms. Little before, Paul?"

"Oh, yes, Tricia. She and Blakey, over there, were the ones I mentioned, who came to the house. They are the brains trust from CSIS, which probably explains why our afternoon has been such a disaster." Paul was in no mood to be sociable. He made a show of looking around. "Where is the young woman you have had watching us?"

Little gave him a blank look. "I have no idea who you are talking about."

"Oh sure. Standard CSIS denial, I suppose." Paul was exasperated. "You and Blakey are the ones who have approached us, and wrecked our arrangements, so you can talk, we will listen, but only for as long as we feel necessary. If there are any questions to be asked, we will be the ones to ask them. Those are the ground rules. This is China, not Canada, and if you harass us here, we will have you arrested."

Throughout the exchange, Blakey had preferred to sit checking out the surroundings, and listening. The only person near them was a slightly built middle-aged Chinese man who was standing down by the water's edge, with his back to them, idly tossing bread to the ducks in the lake.

"Tricia, this is agent Blakey of the CSIS." Paul said dryly, as Blakey joined them. "I told you about their visit to the house. Now, apparently, they have come to work their Intelligence magic here. Agent Little seems to think that they have something that they urgently need to tell us. So speak geniuses."

Blakey was about four inches taller than Paul, and stood a couple of feet in front of him staring down right into his face. When he spoke, his voice was a low growl and there was no doubt of the threat it held.

"Professor Berg. We flew all last night to get here to help you out, so just drop the smartass comments. CSIS did not get you into this mess – it is clearly the result of something that you and your brother have done, and I suspect that, by now, you know that. We are just here to clean up your mess."

Paul had dealt with many confrontational situations during his career, and did not flinch. He glowered at the taller man. "Well, Mr. Blakey, let me clarify this for you once and for all. We have done absolutely nothing to get us involved with what you so absurdly think of as your world of international Intelligence. I am a university physics professor, and Doctor Chen, here, is an internationally recognized pediatrician. We are in Beijing, after the abduction of my thirteen-year-old daughter. We are totally innocent parties in this insane business, so don't start trying to play the tough guy secret agent with me."

As the two men glared at each other, the testosterone driven tension rose visibly, prompting both women to jump forward at the same time to get between them. Sara Little spoke first.

"Back off Kevin. That isn't helping."

The escalating tension evaporated with the injection of a new voice from behind the tense tableau.

"Not only that, Mr. Blakey, but if you break any of our laws, or cause any trouble, while you are on Chinese soil, I will arrest you, and you will be jailed, and deported." He paused, significantly. "Eventually."

The four of them turned in surprise to find that the middle-aged Chinese man who had been tossing bread to the ducks had moved silently up to stand a few feet away, where he had been listening intently to their exchange.

Sara Little stared at the new arrival. "I don't know who you are, but we have Diplomatic status at the Canadian Embassy. Because of the seriousness of this situation, involving the kidnapping of a young Canadian girl, the Ambassador has held discussions with your Minister of State Security. Your Minister is understandably concerned, and has provided us with written permission to work with the girl's family. The Canadian Embassy is in Chaoyang, and I presume you know how to contact your Minister, should you wish to confirm this." She said coldly.

"I am pleased to hear that. You will have therefore been made familiar with the laws of our country, and you will understand that I have the authourity to have you deported, if and when I determine that it is in China's best interest."

Tricia quickly stepped in to calm the situation, and with a courteous bow towards him, she made the customary Mandarin greeting, followed by request to permit her to introduce him to the group.

He made a stiff bow, to acknowledge this polite request to identify himself, and said in English. "I am with a Bureau of the Chinese Ministry of State Security, the MSS. My name? Well you can call me Mr. Renshu." He did not look at the two

CSIS agents as he spoke to Paul and Tricia, clearly identifying them as whom he wished to address.

Tricia smiled politely, then continuing in English, with a glance at Paul said. "Renshu in Mandarin roughly translated means 'benevolent forbearance'. Most appropriate I am sure. Thank you Mr. Renshu. Is there any small way in which we can assist you?"

"You speak excellent Mandarin, Doctor Chen, although with the slightest touch of an accent from your Canadian background, no doubt. You are well known to us, of course, since you have made many trips to China over the years to help treat the children in our hospitals and clinics. Your work is greatly appreciated."

Tricia accepted the Chinese compliment with a gracious bow.

Renshu continued. "You ask how you can assist us. We are aware of your own background, and that of the esteemed Professor Paul Berg, as well as the reason for this most recent hurried visit to Beijing. Your first visit, I believe Professor? It was brought to our attention after the local police visited the Peking Union Medical College Hospital. As I believe Dr. Chow explained to you, they are obligated under Chinese law to report unfortunate incidents such as the one that has involved your daughter, Professor. You appear to have found yourselves in a rather unpleasant situation. We are still gathering information to determine what lies behind it."

He turned to Little and Blakey. "Thank you for clarifying your status in our country. It would be useful if CSIS would provide us with all of their knowledge of the situation. I should point out that China is currently being very accommodating concerning your presence in our country. That is not necessarily a permanent situation."

Paul decided it was time for him to make a contribution to the conversation.

"Mr. Renshu, for our part, Doctor Patricia Chen and I are quite willing to provide you with all of the information that we possess. Our sole wish is to resolve the extremely unpleasant situation to which you refer. We have no idea how, or why we have found ourselves in this position, and we want the nightmare to end. At this moment, my daughter, Nicky, is missing, and we have no idea where she is, or who has kidnapped her. My sole wish is to have Nicky returned unharmed. We would be extremely grateful for any assistance that you could provide. "

Renshu nodded thoughtfully. "Ah, yes. I understand the terrible predicament that faces you, Professor Berg. However, I do not believe that there is any longer any reason for you to stay in the Beihai Park, and I suggest that you and Doctor Chen return to the Hyatt hotel, and perhaps get some rest. You have only arrived in Beijing recently, and I have always found jetlag to be quite debilitating. "

He moved deftly forward, steering Paul and Tricia towards the path to the bridge, and away from the CSIS agents. Turning to Tricia, he spoke softly in Mandarin. "Here is my card. It has my cell phone number on it. I would like you and Professor Berg to meet me for a meal tonight at eight o'clock at the Restaurant of Pleasant Memories. It serves food from my hometown of Hangzhou, which, as I am sure you are aware, is an ancient resort town on West Lake, South of Shanghai. It is a pleasant experience for me to dine at a restaurant that serves my region's traditional food, and one that I hope you will also enjoy."

Tricia accepted his card gracefully with both hands, bowing in accordance with Chinese custom, and responded in Mandarin. "It will indeed be a pleasure for us to join you, Mr. Renshu. I am happy to say that I am acquainted with the famous and beautiful town of Hangzhou. Professor Berg and I will be honoured to meet you at eight o'clock tonight at the Restaurant of Pleasant Memories that you suggest."

She understood that the invitation, followed by the business card, was an indication from Mr. Renshu that he considered that this meeting with Paul and Tricia had to come to an end. Politely taking one step back, Tricia turned and was about to translate his invitation to dinner to Paul, then stopped herself. The invitation and her acceptance had been made in Mandarin; obviously, Mr. Renshu had deliberately excluded the two CSIS agents. She would translate the invitation to Paul once they were alone.

Paul realized that something had been exchanged between Tricia and Mr. Renshu, but he had no idea what. What was clear was that she understood both the language and the appropriate Chinese social etiquette, so he determined to simply follow her lead. He watched to see what she did, then copied her, making his polite goodbyes to Mr. Renshu, with an attempt at a slight bow as they shook hands. It was with some relief that Tricia took his arm, and led him to the Yong'an bridge.

CHAPTER 14

"Surely, you don't really think our phones and internet could be bugged? Or worse, our rooms? To think that someone could be listening in to everything we say and do." Paul asked in disgust, as their taxi struggled through the afternoon traffic, back to their hotel.

"This is China." Tricia explained somberly. She raised her eyebrows, gave a slight nod towards their taxi driver, and lowered her voice to a whisper. "Since we are here because Nicky was abducted off a Beijing street, we have to expect that they will monitor everything we do. I don't see how else Mr. Renshu, could he have known that we would be at that park."

Paul glanced towards the driver and grimaced. "Oh. Right." He muttered. "I understand. It's awful, but if it's reality, I must factor it in. What about Blakey and Little? How did they manage to appear at the park?"

"What did you tell them, when they came to your door in Vancouver?"

"I told them we were about to leave for Beijing, although they weren't surprised."

"Did you tell them where we would be staying?"

"Yes, actually, now you mention it, I remember saying that you were booking us into the Hyatt."

"They probably had someone follow us from the hotel. We

must have missed them in the crowd. There was that woman who was on the flight from Vancouver with us. Despite Little's denials, she had to be with CSIS. Who else could she be working for? She would have contacted Blakey and Little."

Paul sighed. "My God, this gets crazier every minute." He leant his head close to Tricia. "I need to talk to Matt, but I don't want to have everybody listening in. Any ideas?" He whispered.

She rattled off some instructions to the driver. He grunted, swung the taxi across the road, and pulled to a stop in front of a large Western style hotel.

"Come on, we'll get out here." Once their taxi had left, she led Paul down a side street, and around the corner to a small Chinese hotel. "Wait out here on the street for me."

"What is this all about?" Paul demanded, when she reappeared.

"I went inside and ordered a taxi. It will be here in a few minutes. As far as this hotel is concerned, I am just a Chinese woman, calling for a taxi. If Renshu has us under surveillance, it will be a bit more difficult for him to track us. I'm sure he will be talking to that other taxi driver, and he will only be able to say that he dropped us at The Beijing Grand Hotel. The hotel won't have any record of us, and neither will its taxis."

"Good move, Tricia. Thank goodness your mind is working well. All I can think about is how to get Nicky back, as quickly and safely as possible. Whoever these people are, they can have whatever they want, as far as I'm concerned." Paul said grimly. "Okay, now what?"

"I need some information, before our taxi arrives. You know all about how mobile phones work. Paul. What it would take to block someone from monitoring the call? Also, what about Matt? If CSIS bugged your phone in Canada, and the MSS has been listening in to our conversations here in China, it's a pretty good guess that MI6 will have Matt's mobile phone bugged, too. This medical breakthrough of yours certainly seems to have got a lot of the intelligence agencies buzzing."

"Yes. Right. Let me think. I was watching a movie with Nicky a couple of weeks ago, and there was a group of characters running around with untraceable 'burner' phones." Paul continued thoughtfully. "They seemed to be able to buy these at certain stores. If Matt and I each had one of those, that could work, but I have no idea where to get such a thing, or if they are even legal."

Tricia smiled. "Actually, I think I know just the place. Here's the taxi."

"Where are we going?"

"To a market I know. It's not far: it's for locals, not the tourists." She pointed out of the window a few minutes later. "Here we are. Come on, out we get."

Paul stood on the sidewalk staring around at the ancient buildings that surrounded them. Tricia grabbed Paul's hand and led him through an archway into a bustling market full of locals, who were noisily negotiating their purchases with stall owners. Several people greeted Tricia, as they passed.

"The people here seem to know you."

"Yang Chow has a free clinic here on Saturday and Sunday mornings. I have helped her out a few times."

"What is this place?"

"It's just an ordinary Chinese market, where we can buy cheap, throwaway mobile phones, loaded for international calling. What they called 'burner' phones in that movie you watched." Tricia gave a tight smile. "Everything we do will be quite private: the people here will tell me if we are being followed."

"Great. But what about Matt? He will need one, too, or MI6 people listening in at his end will hear everything we say." His bow furrowed with concentration. "Wait a minute. Our research lab has its own server. If I called that server, I could program my office phone to forward Matt's call to my burner phone. I would just have to send him a message telling him to call my office number in say an hour and a half on a burner phone. Matt will know what that is."

Tricia exhaled. "That's great. There's a sort of internet café at this market, well it's pretty crude, actually, but you get the idea. You could send him a message from there."

Yes, yes. That could work. But when Matt calls, he and I would have to be somewhere where we could not be overheard."

"Like where?"

"Like alone in the middle of a large field with short grass. If there is anyone anywhere around, they should be naked, to make sure that they are not concealing a directional listening device. Some background noise would help to drown the conversation, too. Any ideas?" He asked sarcastically.

She stopped suddenly. "You said naked? Right?"

"Well, yes, but that was just sort of an example. I didn't actually mean 'naked'."

"I have a great idea. Come on, we have some purchases to make, and you have to contact Matt. We need a couple of burner phones loaded for international calling, and swimsuits, plus a waterproof pouch."

Paul stared at her. "A swimsuit? I don't believe it. Okay. Please explain, because I have no idea what is happening anymore."

"You want to call Matt, and you don't want everybody listening in, isn't that what you said? So we'll buy a throwaway phone from this market, but then we need to find somewhere where you can't be overheard."

"Right."

"Well, the hotel has a swimming pool in the basement, with a small waterfall thing
that cascades in beside a hot tub." Tricia explained, as she hurried him through the market.

Paul gave Tricia a grin of approval. "Very clever. The sound of the water will cover my voice, and anyone hanging around, and trying to listen in, will be really obvious. Not naked, but close. The cheap throwaway phone will provide privacy for my talk to Matt. Are you sure that there is a wifi signal at this pool, in the hotel basement?"

"Of course. This is Beijing. No self-respecting hotel in Beijing would have a dead area where there was no wifi. There is also a whole area of exercise room and juice bar in the area beside the pool, so there has to be wifi for those people."

"A couple more questions." Paul said thoughtfully. "Won't there be a lot of people hanging around the hot tub? Second question, how do I get the phone into the pool itself? Aren't I going to look a bit odd going for a swim with a phone?"

"Well, I'm hoping that there will not be many people in the pool; I've been there a few times, and it's always been quite quiet. You can put the phone in a watertight plastic bag that I'll buy at the market, and put it in the pocket of your shorts, or hang it around your neck. I have no doubt that you will not be the first person to be talking on their phone in the pool. Plus, of course, lots of phones are completely waterproof."

When they emerged from the elevator at the basement fitness

centre, Paul looked around in surprise. Directly in front of them were the entrances to two sets of sumptuous paneled change rooms, with white uniformed attendants seated behind their desks to check men into the one on the right, and women to the left. Looking down a short passageway Paul could see a glimpse of the freeform swimming pool, and facing it, various active machines in a glassed fronted exercise room.

"It looks like some strange tropical lagoon, but it should provide the privacy and exactly the ambient background noise we need to have a private conversation with Matt."

Tricia nodded. "So go get your shorts on and I'll see you back here in a couple of minutes. Don't forget the phone. Matt is going to call in," she checked her watch, "seventeen minutes."

Paul managed to understand the attendant enough to grasp the system for the locker and key. In a matter of minutes, he had changed into the navy blue swimming shorts, purchased at the market, and was back beside the pool. Tricia was already waiting for him there, wearing a pale green swimsuit with a white stripe, running from right shoulder to left hip. She presented a striking figure that had been noticed by some of the men in the exercise room, but all Paul's focus was on the pool area, and their immediate very pressing issues.

He glanced at the clock on the wall beside them. "Matt will call in about ten minutes. Where do we go?" He asked, looking around.

In front of them was a large freeform swimming pool with a small 'island' in the middle. The walls surrounding the whole area were built up with imitation rock that sloped up from the pool deck. There were imitation ferns, tropical plants and palm trees everywhere, and at each end, a hot tub was tucked into the surrounding imitation rocks. Overhead, the ceiling had been painted a deep tropical blue, with soft star-like lighting to enhance the whole ambiance.

"That hot tub by the little waterfall over there looks quiet, and should work." Tricia noted, pointing to their right.

"Absolutely. This is perfect. There are only a few people in the pool, and it will be difficult for anyone to overhear us without being really obvious. It looks like we will be able to see the whole facility from there."

The pool was a very comfortable temperature, as they swam up to the hot tub beside the waterfall. They sat under the waterfall, letting it cascade over them. Tricia spoke first.

"Okay. We will be quite private here, and free from watching eyes or listening ears. Matt should call any minute. Let's hope that your call forward through your office server and phone works."

"It will."

Paul carefully placed the phone on its plastic bag, on the dry surround of the hot tub.

"This is an absolute blasted nightmare," he gritted through clenched teeth. "Nicky has been grabbed, and here we are wandering around Beijing, with absolutely no idea what we are doing. We need to change the paradigm."

Tricia nodded. "Yes, they have been leading us around by the nose. At this point, we'll give them anything, and everything to get Nicky back, with no guarantee of anything on their part. They have us trapped in the ultimate coercion. There's your phone. That will be Matt."

Their conversation went on for some time, until Paul finally turned off the phone, with a long, slow exhale. "Well, you heard my side of the conversation, and can probably pretty well fill in what Matt had to say. Matt is convinced that we stay the course, and follow their directions. The two people, from MI6, told him that this particular routine had been used by a group some years ago, and always ended quickly, and with the hostage returned. He received a message to go to a town in France, some place called Bergerac, and that is where he is now, awaiting further instructions: just as we are. He made the point that if you are willing to stay, you will be a great help to me, particularly after he heard about our meeting with Renshu. He doesn't see that you are in any danger, as long as you don't get involved with the exchange."

"Not an issue. I'm staying."

"Have you seen that woman that flew with us from Vancouver? The one we think is with CSIS?"

"I think I caught sight of her in the hotel lobby this morning."

"Okay. We'll watch for her in the hotel lobby again, and if we see her I will simply walk up to her, and say that if she is from CSIS, we want to talk to her boss. If she is nothing to do with CSIS, she will just think I'm a bit weird. If we don't see her by tomorrow morning, we should head over to the Canadian Embassy, and insist that we speak to someone in CSIS. We can quote the names of Little and Blakey. That should trigger something."

Tricia ducked under the pool water, pushing her hair back as she surfaced. "When we see her, we should both approach her. It will be less intimidating."

"Good point. Let's get out of here. There's a clock over there: it's getting late, and we still have to get to up to our rooms and change, if we are going to be on time to join Renshu at the restaurant."

CHAPTER 15

As things unfolded, Paul and Tricia did not have to wait very long before they encountered Michelle Denis. They were crossing the hotel lobby, on their way to get a taxi to take them to the restaurant, when they saw her coming through the hotel doors in front of them. Agent Denis gave no reaction at seeing them, and continued on her way across the expansive lobby. She automatically tensed up when it was apparent that they intended to accost her.

Tricia spoke first.

"Good evening. I am afraid we don't know your name, but we saw you on the flight to Beijing. You seemed to be watching Paul. We presume that you are with CSIS, and we need to speak to the person in charge. You see, whatever, and whoever is behind everything that has been going on, it has to be cleared up and stopped. So please have the most senior person at CSIS contact us. We are in rooms 825 and 827 in this hotel, but you probably know that already."

Paul added. "This is very important, so please have them contact us as soon as possible. Thank you. Good evening."

Michelle Denis said nothing, restricting her response to a slow puzzled stare, before stepping around them, and carrying on walking across the lobby, to the elevator.

She was an experienced agent, but she had not anticipated Paul Berg and his friend being aware of her role, and confronting her. Their conclusion that she was a CSIS agent had really surprised her. She headed up to her room to make immediate contact with Headquarters to report. The assignment had gone far beyond the original direction of observing a Canadian university researcher and doctor en route from Vancouver to Beijing.

Across the lobby, on the other side of the bar, the Caucasian man and Asian companion, who had been in the lobby, ostensibly taking photographs of each other that morning, were now sitting enjoying a glass of wine. They watched the interaction between the Paul and Tricia and Michelle Denis with interest. Once the three participants had left the lobby they nonchalantly finished up, and made their own unhurried departure.

Secure in her room, Michelle connected on to the Internet and crafted an email, for automatic forwarding to Headquarters.

Hi Anna: Paul was here in the hotel lobby when I got back this afternoon. He and his companion came over to say 'Hi' as soon as they saw me. They have assumed that I am with our Canadian colleagues, and said they would like to talk to the travel organizer, right away. They emphasized that they want to close the transaction, without delay. Michelle

The communications staff in Headquarters received the message. The 'A' name signified it was top priority. It was forwarded on to the Head of Political Liaison, who then forwarded a copy to the Senior Intelligence Director, marked as 'Urgent'. Within an hour there had been a brief conversation between the two, and an immediate meeting had been scheduled for all involved staff.

The situation was deemed to have reached the 'Serious' level.

CHAPTER 16

The hotel doorman hailed a taxi, but Tricia waited until they had started down the hotel ramp before she told the driver to take them to the Restaurant of Pleasant Memories.

As they settled back in the taxi, Paul closed his eyes, and let out a long breath.

Tricia was the first to speak. "Well, I think that went as well as could be expected. She didn't say anything, but I think she understood the message. Now we see what happens."

"At least we have finally put one ball in play ourselves. Now, with regard to this meeting, I still don't understand why we are going through all of this, instead of having a normal meeting, at his office, or even at our hotel: they have private meeting rooms there." He grumbled, as they wound their way through a succession of narrow streets.

Tricia had impressed on Paul that an invitation to dinner from a government official with Renshu's obvious level of authourity, was more of an order than a request. She explained that it indicated that he wanted to have an informal discussion with them. Moreover, since the Chinese considered dinner to be formal occasions, she stressed that it was important that they dress appropriately, to signify respect for their host. Paul conceded when Tricia appeared wearing a very striking red silk dress with an exotic black motif that she had bought at the market. He settled on his tan suit and pale blue shirt, even reluctantly agreeing to wear the pink and blue pastel silk tie that she had also purchased at the market.

"It's just the way they do things here, Paul. A restaurant is sort of neutral ground. If we met at his office, he would be obliged to inform the Canadian Embassy, and they would insist on supplying a translator and a legal representative. Also, Mr. Renshu can charge the meal to his expense account, if he is meeting with someone related to a case that he is investigating. If he follows Chinese custom, he will probably not want to discuss anything to do with Nicky's abduction during the meal. That will come once the meal is finished. It can be very frustrating, but we must be patient: try and stay calm, and follow my lead. Mr. Renshu is an important official, and expects appropriate respect, even from foreigners."

"I don't know if I can sit making small talk, while I try and eat a meal that I really don't want. The only reason I want to meet with Renshu is to find out what the Chinese police know, and are doing, about Nicky's abduction."

"No. This is really important, Paul. However this evening unfolds, you must remember that Renshu is the only contact that we have here in Beijing who can help us find Nicky. No matter how much you are boiling over with frustration, you must control yourself, and follow my lead. Courtesy and respect are very important in China."

"You're absolutely right." He sighed. "Of course I'll do it. I'll do anything if it will help find Nicky, and get her safely back to us."

He looked down, as his eyes started to fill. "Since Nancy died, three years ago, I have been terrified of anything happening to Nicky. I love her so much. If you hadn't been here to help me through this, I don't know what I would have done. For the past few days you have been crucial in keeping me focused."

She slipped her hand into his, and gave reassuring squeeze. "The pain this awful business is putting you through must be unbearable. I love her, too, Paul. You know I will always be here for you both. We'll get Nicky back. I know we will. We just have to stay calm, and keep pushing forward."

Paul managed a weak smile. "We make a pretty good team, don't we? You, me and Nicky. She's a smart girl. A few weeks ago, she pointed out some things. She was absolutely right. You are really special. We would be totally lost without you."

Tricia was relieved from voicing a response, as the taxi turned down a side street, and slowed to a stop in front of an undistinguished looking restaurant in an a drab old building.

Paul stared out of the window, frowning at the garish, red neon signage. "Is this it?"

Tricia exhaled quietly. "Yes this is it. Don't be misled by the exterior. I looked it up: it has an excellent reputation for its food." She managed.

The manager was expecting them, and led them to a small semi-private room at the back of the restaurant, where Mr. Renshu was already established. He met them with the customary greetings and obligatory Chinese polite enquiries concerning their enthusiasm for dinner. Tricia gave the appropriate responses in Mandarin. Paul simply smiled and nodded.

It was clear that Mr. Renshu was a frequent and honoured customer of the restaurant, and was treated with deference and respect by all of the staff. Busboys scurried around making sure that the table was set, exactly to his liking, and that his guests were comfortably seated. Once Paul and Tricia were settled, small plates of appetizers appeared instantly, along with a pot of green tea that was poured into delicate teacups for each of them. Paul looked apprehensively at the small white china spoon with an intricate design in red and gold, nestling delicately in a matching small bowl. There were two sets of elegant chopsticks lying beside the bowl, and he decided that his only option was to try and follow Tricia's lead.

Mr Renshu led the conversation with polite enquiries about Paul's work, and his life in Vancouver, as the meal progressed with one colourful exotic dish after another. Paul managed to respond to Renshu's questions with brief answers, and was relieved when Tricia would expand on them for him. With Tricia's skillful guidance, they managed to keep the atmosphere formal and cordial.

As soon as they had finished with a dish, the servers whisked it away, and replaced it with something new. Paul had no idea what he was eating, and simply copied Tricia, both in using the chopsticks and bowl, and in deciding which foods to try. Several times Tricia nudged Paul with her knee, and gave a quick shake of her head to indicate that he should avoid a particular dish.

After about an hour, when Paul thought there could not possibly be anything else, a huge bowl of soup arrived. Renshu, who had enjoyed describing each of the dishes from his hometown, explained that in keeping with the custom of the Zheijang Province, this was the final dish.

"I hope that you enjoyed the meal." He said, when the soup was cleared away. "I have traveled outside of China a small amount, and I do appreciate that the foods of foreign countries can be difficult to accept. We tend to acquire our tastes for food from childhood, and your Canadian food is quite different from the way that we prepare our dishes here in China. Indeed, even within China, there are many regions where the food preparation is quite distinct, and I find some regional foods such as the spicy dishes from Szechuan are not to my personal liking."

Paul followed Tricia's lead, and managed some effusive praise for the meal, which Renshu accepted appreciatively. He looked reflectively from one to the other of them.

"If you are relaxed and your appetites satisfied, I think that perhaps we should discuss some issues of a more serious nature. If I may summarize?" He softly cleared his throat. "Regrettably, the interesting medical research by yourself and your brother, professor Berg, appears to have resulted in the commission of a serious crime, namely, your daughter, young Nichole, has been abducted off the streets of Beijing, and her friend assaulted.

"The Peking Union Medical College Hospital is highly respected, and its staff is fully aware of their legal responsibility to report any patients who appear to have been victims of criminal actions. It is of particular concern when the apparent victims are young Canadian girls who were guests here, in a football tournament. We take such criminal acts very seriously. The Beijing police are diligently searching for the perpetrators of this criminal act, and I have no doubt that they will be apprehended shortly. At this time, I would like to have an open and forthright exchange of information with you, so that we may all arrive at an understanding of your situation."

Tricia understood the reality and significance of such muted pressure in China, and gave a small bow of acceptance and understanding. Her interactions with her Chinese friends and colleagues had provided her with some insight into the pressure that could be brought into play by the all-powerful Chinese government. Paul looked unsure, prompting Tricia to make a gentle gesture with her hand, inviting Paul to respond.

"Oh, yes, of course." He glanced across at Tricia, who gave a nod of encouragement. "Doctor Chen and I completely concur, Mr. Renshu. We just want Nicky back, and this whole thing cleared up so that we can go back to our normal lives in Canada. It is a situation that we are completely unable to understand, but we are most willing to tell you whatever we can. Where would you like us to start?"

"Please start from the beginning. That would be from the point at which unusual things started happening."

For the next forty-five minutes, Paul and Tricia went over everything that had happened to them, starting with the invitation to the international football tournament, and culminating with their arrival in Beijing, after receiving the shattering messages that Nicky had been abducted.

Renshu listened attentively, stopping them occasionally, to have them clarify some point. Once or twice, Tricia switched to Mandarin to help with an explanation. When they reached the end of their account, Renshu sat back, and sipped his green tea thoughtfully.

"A most interesting story, Professor Berg. I think I am at liberty to tell you that it initially baffled us as much as it did you."

"I would like to ask you a question, if I may?"

"Please do, Professor."

"What was the point of that performance at the Fangshan restaurant, and in Beihai Park, this afternoon, with the girl who was dressed up to look like Nicky?"

Renshu nodded thoughtfully. "Yes, I understand that you would find that quite confusing. I believe that the kidnappers had several motives for that 'performance', as you call it. Firstly, requiring you to eat at the restaurant was simply to see if you would follow apparently meaningless instructions. That is a fairly standard tactic. Secondly, the girl dressed as your daughter, Nicky, was to confirm that you were actually dealing with the kidnappers. Also, it confirmed for the criminals involved here in Beijing that you really were Paul Berg, since a substitute would have been unlikely to recognize the specific football shirt as the one that your daughter frequently wore. Finally, that trip across the island to the ferry was probably an attempt to flush out any police presence that you might have arranged. That was why we stayed out of sight. Unfortunately, it appears that your two Canadians did not."

Paul shook his head. "I see. Right. I am so completely naïve at all this, most of the time I have no idea what is going on, or why." His voice broke. "I just want Nicky back, safe."

Tricia decided to intervene, and raised her hands slightly, palms uppermost, in a polite questioning gesture, recognized by Mr. Renshu. "So we have told you our side of the story. Is there anything that you can tell us from your side, Mr. Renshu?" She gave a slight bow towards their host. "I am sure that the MSS, the First Bureau of the Chinese Ministry of State Security would not have become involved unless they had a very compelling reason."

Mr. Renshu sipped his tea unhurriedly, before responding.

"Of course you appreciate that there are some factors that I am not at liberty to divulge. However, I can tell you that your brother and yourself, Professor Berg, seem to have garnered some intriguing international attention, some of it, unfortunately, quite negative. I am sure that it has been pointed out to you already, Professor Berg, that to be the sole possessor of the antidote to a family of unpleasant viruses, many of which have yet to make their unwanted appearance, could represent a very powerful biological weapon against any foe."

Paul interjected. "MI5 or 6, or whoever, made that point, to my brother in London, a few days ago, although not quite as forcefully. CSIS came to give me a similar message, as I was about to leave Vancouver. However, I must emphasize that we have not achieved anything like those dramatic results. We have only observed some surprising very initial outcomes."

Tricia was so animated that she started in Mandarin, before quickly changing to English, for Paul.

"Mr. Renshu, Paul and I want absolutely nothing to do with any of this intrigue that has entangled us. Paul and Matt's research findings are an unwanted distraction. They are more than willing to make them public, if it will end this situation. We have only one focus. We are beyond distraught that Nicky has been abducted, and we will do everything within our power to expedite her recovery and safe return. That is our sole concern. That is the only thing that is important to us. Is there anything that you can do to help us end this nightmare, Mr. Renshu?"

They waited anxiously for a response, but Renshu appeared caught up in his thoughts, as he stared silently out towards the vehicle lights that were flittering by the window, on the road outside,. For a moment they wondered if he had heard Tricia's question. Finally he turned back to them.

"My team is doing everything we can to bring the situation to a rapid, and acceptable, conclusion. However, information that we have received from several sources indicates that there are foreign interests involved."

"Who are these foreign interests, Mr. Renshu?"

"They are shadows, Doctor Chen. It is not a China issue. I believe that you have been coerced into coming to China for the very reason that the shadows have no presence here. To search for them here is to search for shadows." He paused. "I have recently confirmed that young Nicky was taken from Beijing on a medical flight to another country within hours of her abduction." Seeing the looks of horror on their faces, he hurried on. “We have no indication that she has been harmed.” He picked his words carefully. “The whole objective of the abduction was to pressure you into giving them the information that they have demanded.”

“I don’t understand.” Paul burst out. “Where have they taken Nicky? How on earth could Nicky be put on a plane to another country? What do you mean, ‘on a medical flight’?”

“Perhaps I can help there, Paul.” Tricia interjected. “I have encountered a number of cases where patients have been medevaced back to their home country. It is done when the patient can be transported safely, and it is believed that treating the patient in the familiar medical and social environment of their home country will be beneficial.”

“I still don’t understand. Why would they take her to another country?” he demanded, his voice shaking with stress.

“It a matter of legal jurisdiction, Professor.” Renshu explained patiently. “China cannot charge the perpetrators with kidnapping, if there is no victim in the country. If she is found in another country, it will also be difficult to make the charge of kidnapping there, since there will be no evidence of kidnapping in that country. As I explained, the situation is complicated.”

“What country do you think she has been taken to?” Tricia asked, taking Paul’s hand as he started to look close to breaking down.”

“Renshu hesitated. “We cannot be sure, but we have reason to believe that her destination may have been France.”

“France?” Paul gasped. “But France is not Nicky’s home country. She’s never even set foot in France.” Paul protested. “How can she possibly have been taken to France? Surely there will be a lot of immigration issues when a thirteen-year-old girl shows up in France without any family member? Nicky would certainly have had something to say about it."

"It is a simple matter for people, such as these, to produce false documents, Professor." Renshu explained. "Arriving as a patient on a medevac flight from China, it is almost certain that young Nicky would have been a sedated, and not in a position to be questioned."

"Wait a minute. France?" Paul grasped his forehead with hand. "Isn't that where Matt has been told to go, Tricia?" Paul's voice sank to a whisper. "What on earth have we become involved in? I feel like we have drifted into some bizarre twilight zone."

"I am not familiar with the term 'twilight zone', but I think I understand your meaning. It must seem like you have been pushed into a strange world, Professor. I cannot be certain your daughter has been taken to France. The MSS has a great deal of ability to deal with individuals who might threaten the welfare of our visitors, but that ability is limited to activities and individuals inside our national boundaries."

"We can't emphasize enough how much we appreciate everything that you are doing, Mr. Renshu." Tricia said, demurely, sensing the escalating tensions in the room. "We have no idea who is behind this awful situation that has embroiled us, and it has been made even more difficult to be in a foreign country. Your support has been a lifeline, particularly when there is no identifiable benefit for China."

Renshu stared across the room, saying nothing for several minutes before he replied. "Perhaps I have not made my position quite clear. I intend to apprehend the perpetrators of this scheme. They have committed a serious crime in our country. They will never benefit from the research information that they desire to force you to give them, Professor. We shall confiscate it as part of the evidence associated with a serious crime that was committed in China,"

"What? No, wait just a minute." Paul stuttered in disbelief.

Renshu quickly cut him off, as he stood up. "I will be in touch. You have my card. Call me immediately, if, and indeed, when anything happens that I should know about. I have no doubt that young Nicky's abductors will be contacting you again shortly. I hope that you enjoyed the meal. Good evening." He shook each of their hands, with a polite bow.

Paul was too stunned to react; he simply stood up and robotically, shook hands with Mr. Renshu, staring after him, as he left the restaurant.

"Is that it? I thought we were in the middle of a discussion?" He spluttered. "He just announces that China is going to take all of our research data, as 'evidence', then gets up, and walks out."

"Relax, Paul. The discussion was over. In China, when a meal or meeting is over, the host gets up and leaves quite promptly. There is no parting small talk like we have in North America, or Europe. The first time it happened to me I thought I had offended them, until Yang explained to me that it is just a social custom. I will ask the restaurant to call us a taxi."

Paul paced back and forward, unable to conceal his irritation at the way the evening had played out. He waited silently until Tricia had finished asking the manager to call for a taxi. When she had finished, he could contain himself no longer.

"This whole situation with that Renshu fellow is fucking ridiculous. I suppose we pay for that fucking meal?" He hissed between clenched teeth.

Tricia took hold of his arm. "Whoa, calm down, Paul. The manager told me that Mr. Renshu is a regular and valued customer. The meal has been paid for. However, although tipping is frowned upon, I suggest that we leave one hundred

Yuan on the table."

Paul closed his eyes, and made a supreme effort to calm down. He tossed a couple of notes on the table, and threw up his hands. "I still don't get it."

Tricia put her hand on his shoulder. "Let me explain what I understand happened this evening. Mr. Renshu works for one of the Bureaus of the Chinese Ministry of State Security, the MSS. From the little that I know about them, they have the reputation of being quite secretive about which internal bureau is responsible for what. However, from what Mr. Renshu said, I gather that he is charged with the responsibility for internal security within Beijing and possibly other regions in China. Since Nicky, a young foreign visitor, was abducted from a Beijing street, with the intention of forcing you and Matt to supply medical research to a potentially hostile party, he is determined to root out and neutralize the source of the criminal activity."

Paul was exasperated. "And a dinner here, followed by a quick chat, has answered all his questions? That's nothing like what I have been led to believe about the Chinese police and security forces."

"This is China. Things work differently here. When you interview a prospective new member for your research team, how much time do you spend with them?"

"What? That's totally different." He shook his head in irritation. "I have already read their work, and talked to other researchers and faculty who know them. The interview is sort of a formality to confirm everything I already know." He stopped, and let his gaze slide up to the ceiling. "Oh. I see. You're saying that's what Renshu was doing. He just needed to get us talking to confirm the information that he had already gathered about us. Good God. Did we do okay? What's he going to do now?"

"Yes, I am pretty sure that we did just fine. I interpret his parting comments to mean that Mr. Renshu intends to resolve only the crimes that have been committed in Beijing. That, at least, is something. Let's get back to the hotel."

"Great idea. Those are the most welcome words I have heard this evening. One last question. You obviously understood this business of sending Nicky to France on a medevac flight. That absolutely stunned me. How on earth can that happen?"

"It actually happens quite often. If someone is injured, or taken seriously ill, on a visit to a foreign country, the insurance company, or the individual's family, if they can afford it, might decide that it is preferable to fly the patient back to their home country for treatment in what is essentially a flying ambulance. Western countries generally perceive medical care in China as to be at a lower standard than in Europe or North America, and prefer to fly the patient to their home country for treatment."

"And Renshu seems to think that Nicky was heavily sedated and flown to France." He swallowed. "Poor kid. When she wakes up, she'll have no idea where she is or how she got there."

"Yes. That's one reason that we have to make sure that Matt is there to meet her, when she wakes up." Tricia asserted firmly. "Here's the manager to tell us the taxi is here. Come on, Paul."

CHAPTER 17

The next set of instructions from the abductors arrived with breakfast the following morning. Paul and Tricia were having a light breakfast of coffee and pastries, in the hotel, when a waiter approached, and gave Paul an envelope.

"Where did this come from?" Paul barked at the shocked waiter.

"A gentleman asked me to give it to you, sir. He said that he had to leave, and asked me to give it to you." He stammered. "I saw him leave the hotel." He added, hoping that this might calm the agitated guest.

Tricia interrupted, to smooth the exchange. "Thank you for giving it to us. We would like to contact him with a reply. Did you recognize him? Have you seen him before?"

"No, I have never seen him before this morning. I do not think he is a guest in the hotel."

"Could you tell us what he looked like?"

"He was ordinary. His English had an accent, European perhaps. Not Chinese. Not old, and not young."

"Was he white skinned? Or black, perhaps brown?" She added, when the waiter looked confused.

"White. Yes."

Realizing there was no additional information to be gleaned, Tricia thanked the waiter, who turned and walked quickly away.

"What does the note say, Paul?"

"It's brief and to the point. We are to go to the Summer Palace at eleven o'clock this morning, and bring a sample of the information they require. We are to enter through the Southwest Gate, and make our way to the Buddhist Pagoda, on Longevity Hill, acting like tourists. They will be watching to make sure that we are alone. Do you know the Southwest Gate of this Summer Palace place?"

"Yes, yes. I've been there several times. We must contact Mr. Renshu immediately, and tell him."

"Is that wise? The note says that we are to be alone. They mean, 'No police.'"

"It is essential. Mr. Renshu is MSS. It would be foolhardy to try and keep this from him. Come on, let's get back to the room and sort this out."

Despite the uncertainties of the Beijing traffic, they managed to arrive at the Southwest Gate of the Summer Palace at a few minutes before eleven o'clock. For the past hundred years, since it had become a public park, the Summer Palace had been a treasured oasis for the residents of Beijing, and it was busy, as locals and tourists took advantage of the perfect Spring day to absorb the tranquility of the setting. Paul was too wound up to appreciate his surroundings.

They followed the kidnappers' instructions, joining the general flow of people walking beside the lake to the Grand Pavilion, an elegant and structure of red pillars with a double pagoda style roof, with intricate carvings in brilliant red, blues and greens that gave it a magical appearance. It was lost on Paul. He was constantly looking around for any sign of someone showing an interest in them.

Tricia held Paul's hand, in an attempt to blend in with the tourists around them, quietly urging him to stay calm, as they waited for the kidnapers to contact them. To make themselves obvious to any watchers, Tricia bought tickets for one of the dragon boats that shuttled visitors around the lake. On any other occasion, it would have been a pleasant boat ride. The sun was warm, as the boat skimmed through the deep blue water, past the panorama of ancient buildings that dotted the verdant shoreline.

Paul and Tricia were oblivious to the passing scenery, consumed by the eerie feeling that someone was watching their every move. If Renshu had his team in place, there would be at least two groups watching them.

They disembarked at the dock at the base of Longevity Hill, and entered the Jade Waves Palace, following the flow of visitors along the Long Corridor, between walls of endless exotic paintings that depicted birds, flowers, and landscapes as well as scenes from history and mythology. They emerged in front of a massive ornate gateway that that led through various buildings and courtyards up the two hundred foot high Longevity Hill, eventually to the Buddhist Pagoda that the kidnappers' note had identified.

Tricia could feel Paul struggling to stop his hands from shaking. They had still not been contacted, as they started up the steps, to the highest building in the Park, the Tower of Buddhist Incense, with its three-storey octagonal Pagoda. They were alone when they paused for breath at the first level of the Pagoda. Their nerves were stretched to breaking point. In an effort to provoke some contact from the kidnappers, they posed openly, pretending to be admiring the vista across the lake and around the entire park.

"Where the Hell are they?" Paul muttered, staring at everyone around them.

There was a family moving around on the level above them, and behind them a young couple, a Caucasian man and an Asian woman, had paused to take photographs. No one appeared to be trying to make contact. As they were standing beside the marble railings, what sounded like two large insects flew over Paul's head. He flapped his hand at them, glancing up to see if it was small birds or insects. The quiet was suddenly ruptured by the couple behind them yelling at them to get down. The woman raced across, and herded them around behind the back of the building.

The man barked at her. "Get them down from this place." He pointed. "Over there. Go down those stone stairs over there." He looked at Tricia. "Go with her, as fast as you can. Go."

Paul did not move. He stared around, totally confused. "What's wrong? What's happening?"

"Shut up and go."

Tricia responded to the man's command, and, grabbing Paul's hand, pulled him over to the short flight of steep stairs that the man had indicated. They scrambled down the steps to a white gravel path that led across to a wide stone stairway. Tricia headed across the gravel to the stairway that led down the northern side of the hill, pulling Paul with her.

As they paused at the top of the stairs, Paul glanced back. He could just see the man who had stayed behind: he was now crouching behind a pillar, his eyes moving constantly, scanning from side to side.

A cacophony of noise had erupted from the balcony above where they had been standing: raised Chinese voices were shouting, amid the sound of running feet. The Asian woman raced up beside them, and gave Paul a push.

"Keep going, fast. I stay with you." She growled.

"Who are you?" Tricia gasped in Mandarin.

"Friend. I look after you." She barked back, in accented English.

Paul stumbled a few steps, the woman catching him before he fell. "Thanks. I don't understand. What's all the noise about? All I heard were insects buzzing by. What's going on? "

"Not insects. Bullets."

"What the Hell are you talking about? Bullets? Who on earth would be shooting, and at what?"

"At you. When you move around the terrace, you become visible target from the hill across the lake. Someone was watching you, waiting for a clear shot."

"Oh, come on." He gasped for breath with the effort of talking, as they sped down the stairs. "It was probably just some stupid kid, or a careless hunter, or someone practicing with his rifle."

"The Chinese aren't allowed to have guns." Tricia grunted.

"Silenced rifle, two fast shots together, long distance: a professional shooter." The woman asserted. "They concerned when you go up Longevity Hill, amongst buildings. They took shot, in case you head down back here, out of sight. As we do now."

They paused to catch their breath at a turn that brought the hill opposite back into view between the trees. "

Do you think they're still out there?" Paul stared at the hill, and frowned. "If they were shooting at us, from over there, both shots went well above us. At that distance, given the temperature, and assuming a muzzle velocity of about eight hundred and fifty metres per second, with a bullet weight of around fifty grams." He turned, and stared back up at the balcony that had been above them. "If it was a professional shooter, he must have seriously miscalculated."

The woman let out an exasperated grunt, and gave Paul another shove to get him moving.

"Now is not the time for physics calculations, Paul." Tricia gasped. "I know where we are going. At the bottom of the hill, we will come to SuZhou Market Street: there are more than fifty tourist shops and boats: all sorts of other tourist stuff. It's not far from the North Gate, the main gate to the whole Palace. We should be safe there with lots of people around. We can get a taxi from there."

Paul got the message, and raced on down the steps with Tricia. "I feel like I am going to throw up." He gasped, between heaving breaths. "That woman says that she and the man back there were here to look after us. Do you believe her?"

"We have to. Just keep going, Paul."

"How do we know that it wasn't one of Renshu's people who took a shot at us?"

"Because this is China, and Renshu is Chinese National Security." She gasped. "If he wanted us to disappear, we would simply be taken off the street under some trumped up charge, and never be seen or heard from again. He wouldn't bother with a gun. Someone took a shot at you. This is beyond an upset student who got a bad grade. If there is someone shooting at people in Beijing, Mr. Renshu is going to be a whole level past angry, when he hears about it. Come on; let's get down to the safety of the crowds in Market Street. Our top priority is to get out of here."

Once they reached Suzhou Market Street, they were engulfed in a bustling, sauntering throng of tourists enjoying the warm afternoon. Tricia led the way, shouting and pushing her way along the rough walkway to the North Gate. Their path was choked with people, between the colourful stalls of Chinese souvenirs that were backed up against the high outside stone wall of the park on one side, and a Venice like canal on the other.

As they struggled to approach the massive, ornate and brightly coloured North gate, an older guard saw them, and yelled at a taxi that had just dropped off a young Chinese couple. Tricia grabbed Paul's hand, and pulled him through the throng.

"Could you hear what that guard was saying, Tricia?"

"There was too much noise. I couldn't catch it exactly, but he appeared to be ordering the driver to stay where he was."

Tricia shouted a brief exchange with the guard in Mandarin. He kept nodding and feverishly waving encouragement, as he shouted replies, clearly intent on getting them into the taxi as quickly as possible.

"He mentioned Mr. Renshu. This is China. We don't have a lot of options. It looks like an ordinary taxi. We might as well get in."

On cue, a younger guard rushed over and flung open the door of the taxi so that they could pile in. He closed it with a flourish, as the taxi took off with a squeal of tires.

"I'm completely lost." Paul groaned. "What was that last bit all about?"

"The guard said he had instructions from Mr. Renshu." Tricia explained. "He was told to get us out of there." Paul was sweating profusely. "Are you okay?"

"Are you really asking that? No, but I'll manage." He gritted out. "What happened to that woman who shepherded us down the stairs?"

Tricia shook her head. “I don’t know. She just sort of disappeared in the crowd, when the guards at the gate started calling to us.”

“Who was she? And who was that man with her, the one who stayed behind, up at the top. Were they Renshu’s people?”

“I don’t think so,” Tricia puzzled. “They never mentioned him.”

“Then, who were they?”

“I have no idea.”

CHAPTER 18

It was late Wednesday night in Beijing, just after seven thirty on Wednesday morning, on the West coast of Canada, when Sarah Little and Kevin Blakey connected with CSIS Regional Director Claude Noble, over a secure Embassy line.

Noble got straight to the point. "What are the latest happenings with Paul Berg over there?"

Little took the lead. "Well, we've had some developments, sir. Yesterday afternoon we encountered Doctor Chen and Professor Berg after they had lunched at a restaurant in a Beijing park behind the Forbidden City. They are now aware that we are here. Before we could get into any substantive discussions, however, we were interrupted by a Chinese man who called himself Mr. Renshu, and had identification stating that he was with a Bureau of the MSS, that's the Chinese Ministry of State Security."

"I know what the Chinese MSS is. What the Hell was he doing with Berg?"

"We never got the chance to find out, sir. He demanded that we provide him with a full briefing on everything CSIS knows about the situation, and told us if we refused he would have us arrested, jailed, and eventually deported for being illegally in China. Blakey and I could see no benefit from arguing the point."

“It sounds like Berg is the headline act in an international intelligence parade over there. Are you any closer to confirming the identity of who is behind all of this?”

Blakey stepped in. “No, sir, unfortunately not.”

“This could devolve into something quite unpleasant. You had better find out who the Hell it is, and fast. Anything else?”

“Actually there is, sir. Berg and Chen went to the Summer Palace this afternoon. While they were there, someone took a shot at Paul Berg. They were on the terrace of a Buddhist temple near the top of a hill. Our local agent was monitoring from nearby. She reported that two bullets narrowly missed Berg. Judging by the sound, it came from a silenced gun of some description.”

“Shit. But Berg wasn’t hit?’

“No Sir, although unfortunately a Chinese mother on the balcony above was hit. There was a Caucasian man and an Asian woman behind the Bergs going up the hill, and they took very professional defensive action. She instantly moved them out of the line of sight, while he stayed behind to cover them. The woman herded them down the back of the hill to a busy shopping strip by the main North Gate. From our agent’s report, they seemed to immediately recognize the whistles as coming from bullets, and worked as a team in their defensive maneuvers.”

“Who were they?”

“We don’t know. They just faded away, when the official security people arrived.”

“This is not good, and appears to be escalating. Have you heard any hints as to who the sniper was?” The Director growled.

“No, sir.”

"Is that all?"

Blakey and Little confirmed that it was.

"Let me know immediately if you need support over there. Keep me informed, by the hour if necessary, and for God's sake don't let this turn into an international incident. Canada's political relations with China are at a sensitive enough stage already. I have been informed that Interpol is aware of the situation. They have been notified that you are there, and their people may contact you."

CHAPTER 19

Michelle Denis was also quick to update her Head of Operations about the shooting.

"Thank you Michelle. This brazen shooting at the Summer Palace significantly changes the situation. I have told the team that I sent, to take over the surveillance of Berg and Chen in Beijing, immediately. I have another mission for you.
"MI6 has informed us that Matt Berg has been directed to go to the town of Bergerac in the Dordogne region of southwest France, and await further instructions. There is a strong probability that the Berg girl is being held somewhere near there, and Matt Berg has been relocated there, in preparation for her release.
"You are to leave immediately for Bergerac. The tickets, and all the details you need, are in a package that will be given to you at Beijing airport. A car will be waiting for you, when you land at Bordeaux.
"We are concerned that there may be no intention of permitting the girl, or either of the Berg brothers to survive. Your remit is to locate Matt Berg and Nicky Berg, and get them out alive."

"Will I have backup, ma'am?"

"I will move a team in place to provide support. This is a delicate mission, Michelle. I believe that our best chance of success lies with your moving around on your own, below the radar. You know the situation, and I have every faith in you."

“I appreciate that, ma’am.”

“Now that it appears Nicky Berg may be being held here in France, it is imperative that we find her, and bring her out alive. I appreciate your continued commitment to this situation, as it has evolved. Your original remit was for a simple watching brief over Paul Berg on the flight from Vancouver to Beijing. You were scheduled to have returned to Lyon days ago, for personal leave. Bergerac is quite close to Lyon, but I will understand, if you ask to be relieved.”

“Thank you ma’am. I would like to stay involved with this operation. As you said, I am familiar with the individuals involved, and they seem like decent, ordinary people who have become embroiled in a situation that is none of their making. Every indication is that it will be brought to a conclusion in the next day or two. As far as my personal situation is concerned, the current estimate from the surgeon is later next week. And, as you pointed out, Bergerac is quite close to Lyon.”

“Right. Go ahead, proceed to Bergerac, as arranged. Keep me informed of your progress. Let us hope for a successful conclusion within the next few days.”

CHAPTER 20

When they got back to the hotel, Mr. Renshu, was waiting for them, slowly pacing across the vast lobby with the deliberate step of imposed calm. Tricia could read his body language. Tense shoulders, short clipped stride, head scanning the lobby in quick jerky movements: he was angry. More appropriately, he was furious.

As soon as he saw them getting out of the taxi, Renshu strode over to meet them at the door. Typical of life in the People's Republic of China, despite his non-descript appearance, the hotel staff clearly understood exactly who and what Renshu was, and anxiously cleared the path for him.

Renshu extended his hand as he approached. "Ah, Professor Berg, and Doctor Chen, I am pleased to see you safely back here." He shook each of their hands. "I must apologize for the incident that occurred at the Summer Palace this afternoon. It is embarrassing for myself and my team."

"Yes, the bullets that happened to stray our way this afternoon were most unfortunate." Tricia, acknowledged, in an effort to help Mr. Renshu save face.

"There were several quite strong gusts of wind where we were, near the top of the hill, and I believe that affected the bullets' trajectory." Paul contributed, having picked up on Tricia's tone. "In such circumstances, it is always unclear whether we were the recipients of good or bad fortune. Good that no-one was hit, but bad that the bullets came near us in the first place."

Mr. Renshu's eyes betrayed a brief flash, while the rest of his face remained devoid of any emotion.

"Unfortunately, I must clarify one point. One of the bullets did hit someone. There was a young Chinese couple with their eight-year-old daughter up above where you were standing. They were admiring the view from an upper balcony of the Buddhist Pagoda. A bullet struck the young mother in the hip. She is in serious condition in the hospital. It is hoped that she will not be permanently paralyzed. It is a tragic reality that when guns are fired, innocent people frequently get injured."

"That's just awful." Tricia gasped. "Is she going to be alright? I should have stayed to help her."

Renshu looked grim. "We sincerely hope that she will fully recover. A Caucasian tourist who happened to be nearby gave her immediate basic medical care, until our highly skilled doctors arrived, but I regret to say that the injury is serious."

"That was fortunate that there was someone with some medical training who stepped in to help. Do you know who he was?"

"Unfortunately, he left, without giving his name."

As a courtesy, Tricia switched to Mandarin. "We are so sorry to hear that a young woman, a mother, was hurt this afternoon, Mr. Renshu. Please let us know if there is anything that we can do."

Mr. Renshu responded in English. "Perhaps we can find some quiet place to sit, where we can talk? Ah yes, the concierge has kindly kept a corner over there reserved for us."

Paul glanced around. "Is it wise for us to been seen openly meeting with you here?"

"Yes, Professor Berg, it is probably the best arrangement for yourselves at this time. If there are any interested parties watching us, I want them to understand, very clearly, that you are under our protection. Any attempts to embarrass or harm you in any way will be dealt with very severely."

Once they were all seated and out of range from any inquisitive listeners, Mr. Renshu picked up the conversation again.

"It is quite unacceptable for that sort of thing to happen here in Beijing. As Doctor Chen will understand, it is a great embarrassment and a serious loss of face for all of my team. I was concerned that someone might try and approach you, and confront you in some manner, so I instructed my staff to discretely watch you, and make sure that nothing happened to you. They tried to apprehend the culprit, but so far have been unsuccessful. Now we will move forward from here."

A dark flush started from Paul's collar and moved up through his face. "You had your people watching us, and you let someone take a shot that injured an innocent young mother? Is that the best you can do?"

Tricia grabbed his arm. "Calm down, Paul. It was impossible to predict that someone was going to take a shot at us from another hillside. Please carry on Mr. Renshu."

Renshu gave a slight gesture with his hand in appreciation of her face saving interjection. "Thank you, Doctor Chen. After our discussion last evening, two things were clear to me. The first is that you, Professor Berg, have become involved in some issue, or incident, I am not sure which is the correct English word, but it has evoked the interest of at least one foreign group. The second point that became clear to me was that you are most likely entirely ignorant of the issues that are swirling around you. Would you agree with my summary?"

Paul's facial colour had returned to a more normal hue, and he grunted and nodded his head in agreement. "Yes, that sums things up pretty well. I'm sorry I started to get a bit unhinged there, a moment ago. This is all really getting on top of me. We have no idea what is behind all this that is happening to us. It seems like the whole thing has taken on an insane life of its own."

He paused to flash Tricia a contrite glance. "And you too, Tricia, I apologize. I have no idea how Matt and I ended up involved in the middle of this, but it has to end."

Renshu gave a tight empathetic smile. "I understand your concerns, Professor, and I agree. You will not be, in the clear, is I believe the proper idiom, until the interested party is no longer interested."

"Will it all end once we have handed over all of the information they want? If that is the case, they can have it all, right now. From what you explained last night, I suppose I should say that you can have it. I don't care any more: it just has to end."

"This is a tricky situation, Professor. You have made the point, forcefully, on several occasions, that the safe return of your daughter is your primary concern." Renshu picked his words carefully. "I can confirm what I said before, it appears most likely that your daughter is no longer in China. My responsibility is limited to resolving the crimes that have been committed here. My interest in the material relating to the research conducted by you and your brother relates solely to its status as evidence of those crimes."

"What are you trying to say?" Tricia gasped. Paul went ashen white.

"The safety of your daughter rests in the hands of the authourities, wherever she is being held." He shrugged. "My jurisdiction is limited to the crimes that have been committed in China. Unfortunately, Professor, those crimes are centred around yourself, and your medical discovery. The latest being some madman firing shots in the Summer Palace, and injuring an innocent Chinese mother. We will not tolerate such behaviour, and will take whatever steps are necessary to put an end to it, and that includes arresting everyone that we determine to be involved. I hope that you understand your position, here, in China, Professor, and you Doctor Chen."

"I understand completely." Paul gritted through clenched teeth, as he stood up. "Thank you for making everything clear, Mr. Renshu. Come on, Tricia, there is nothing further to discuss here. I must speak to Matt."

Tricia caught up with him, and grabbed his arm. "Stop, Paul. You're understandably upset, but we have to keep clear heads. Come on, we'll walk to the Forbidden City and Tiananmen Square. There's a teahouse there that I know. It's about a ten minute walk along Chang 'an Avenue. There's small stream, in a sort of linear park that runs parallel to the Avenue. It's usually pretty quiet, and it will give you a chance to cool down."

She guided him out of the hotel, down to the park that was actually a stretch of grass that bordered both sides of a small stream. After continuing for a few strides, Paul started to slow down, until he came to a full stop.

"I'm sorry, Tricia: I'm behaving like an ass. I have to keep reminding myself that Nicky is the only important piece of this madness, but the constant stress is scrambling my brain. I don't know how much more of this I can handle. I feel like I'm losing my mind." He scrunched his eyes tightly closed. "I'm really afraid I might suddenly collapse."

Tricia faced him, and held his hands in hers. "I know, Paul. We've been hurled into a world that is completely foreign to us. We have to try and ignore all of the background noise, and concentrate our focus on those things that we can control. You can do it. We can do it. And we will."

"Right. Yes. Right. I need to talk to Matt. We don't exactly where he is, or what the Hell he has been doing. In fact, I'm so confused right now, I have no bloody idea what the time is in Europe, if that's where he is."

"Okay, right now, let's try and relax, and carry on walking along here for a while, Paul. How have you been sleeping?"

"I haven't. I was afraid to take the sleeping pills you gave me, in case I slept though an important call."

"Okay. Tonight you take a pill, and make sure you get some sleep. Okay?"

"Okay. You're the doctor." Paul mumbled sheepishly.

"If there are any calls, I'll hear them, and wake you up."

CHAPTER 21

Matt sat at the bistro table, in the Place Palissiere, oblivious to the profusion of colour from the spring flowers that surrounded the little square. His gaze settled on the statue of Cyrano de Bergerac, with his large nose angled skywards, and Matt thought how he, too, had become an actor, lost in a tangled plot, on an unknown stage.

His mind churned over and over the conversation ha had with Paul a couple of hours earlier. Matt had been incandescent. He and Paul had faithfully followed the abductors directions, quite prepared to do whatever they asked to ensure Nicky's safe return. Now, after Paul and Tricia had been sent on a couple of fools' errands around Beijing for two days, not only were they no closer to resolving the situation, and recovering Nicky, but someone had taken a shot at them. Vance Chestermann and Sandra Fellows had warned him in London that something like that could happen, but he had never given it serious consideration. To make things worse, that Chinese policeman, Renshu, or whatever his name was, had made it clear that his only interest was to arrest the perpetrators of the crimes committed on Chinese soil, and confiscate all of Paul's and Matt's material relating to their medical research, as 'evidence'. He had no concern for Nicky's plight. He considered her to be someone else's problem.

"China intends to come out of this whole debacle the big winners," he grunted to himself, "leaving us as the losers, and Nicky in a frightening situation. And here I am sitting in this French town apparently waiting obediently for my next instructions from the kidnappers."

They were being played like puppets. It was time to change the game.

He had not become the head of small, highly successful, team of scientific researchers, and serial entrepreneurs, in a market dominated by multi-billion pound companies, by letting his team get pushed around.

Matt mentally ticked off the points that he knew, or suspected, about Nicky's kidnapping.

First, it had been carefully planned, with the objective of obtaining his, and Paul's, research findings that had appeared to trigger a generic immune reaction to the covid viruses tested.

Second, his Intelligence contacts in London had indicated that the strategy that was being employed, namely to coerce compliance by temporarily kidnapping a person of value, had been employed before, albeit in the distant past.

Third, his Intelligence contacts believed that it was likely that Nicky has been moved to Europe, and since he had been told to come to Bergerac, Nicky was probably being held somewhere nearby.

Fourth, based on the previous experiences that he had been told about, there was reason to hope that Nicky would be released, presumably to himself, once the successful exchange had been confirmed in China.

Fifth, he had concluded several days ago that to keep Nicky safely

sedated meant that there had to be a physician involved. That would most likely be a physician who had been brought in for that specific responsibility. The city of Bergerac was the largest urban centre in the region, and had thus probably been selected as a good place for the physician to blend in invisibly.

Matt sat back, and stared across the square. There was still another basic problem that had been troubling him. What were the kidnapper's plans for Paul and himself? After all, once Nicky was safe, what would stop them from reworking all of their research? For the kidnappers to leave such a loose end could reduce the value of the research material they had obtained to zero.

What an unpleasant thought. When they had met in London, Matt had suspected that Vance Chestermann and Sandra Fellows had been holding something back. Now he was pretty sure he knew what that was: they didn't see how the kidnappers could allow Paul and himself to survive. The outlook for Nicky and Tricia was probably equally grim.

He had made some progress, over the past few days, but, after Paul's phone call, it was clear that time was getting short. Sandra Fellows had sent him a cryptic message yesterday morning, to look for a gold coloured Lexus sports car, being driven a young female doctor who had recently arrived in the area. He had located the car and its driver, and followed it yesterday afternoon. Now he had to determine whether yesterday's trip was to a daily destination, or just a one-time thing.

However, to start filling in the missing pieces, he would need some credible cover. If the kidnappers thought he had any idea where Nicky was being held, they would move her immediately, and he would have to start again. He had switched his rental car, that was a start, but not enough.

He reached robotically for the cup on the table in front of him, knocking it, and spilling most of the coffee into the plate, where an untouched pain au raisin and croissant now floated in lukewarm coffee. He stared down at the mess, grunted, and looked around for a waiter.

The nearest waiter was standing a few metres from his table, with an irritated young woman, who was complaining that she wanted a table outside. The waiter was trying to explain that there were no outdoor tables available at the moment, but if she should return in half an hour he would make sure to keep one for her. Matt recognized her. She had been checking in to the hotel when he had walked through the lobby earlier. He had a sudden thought.

“Mademoiselle, you are welcome to share my table.” Matt called across. “Perhaps the waiter can bring me a replacement along with your order?”

Perhaps this young woman could provide the cover he had been looking for, he thought, standing up, as she slipped smoothly into the chair opposite him.

“Thank you. I have just arrived here at the end of a lengthy, and rather tedious trip.” She sighed. “I am in desperate need of a strong coffee, and possibly some pastries, and couldn’t bear the thought of traipsing around Bergerac any longer.” She glanced at Matt’s plate as the waiter whisked it away. “Although, personally, I prefer the coffee and pastries to be quite separate. I suppose that is a matter of personal taste.”

Matt smiled, and raised his hands, palms up. “I confess, I can be a bit clumsy on occasion. I believe that I saw you earlier this morning in the lobby of the hotel?”

“Quite possibly, if you are staying at the Saint-Clare?”

“Indeed. I am.” Matt extended his hand across the table. “Matt Berg.”

“Pleased to meet you, Matt Berg. I’m Michelle Denis. So what brings you to Bergerac.”

“I’ve been sent here to meet someone, but they have yet to

show up. I have spent the past couple of days, doing very little, apart from sitting around, and spilling coffee over my pastries in all the local villages. How about you?" Matt tried to sound casual.

Michelle glanced around. "Ah, here are our coffees and replacements. Perhaps we should keep the pastries well away from your coffee?" She suggested with raised eyebrows, and a smile.

"I promise to be more careful, this time." Matt assured her.

They were silent while the waiter put their orders on the table.

"You were going to tell me what has brought you to Bergerac." Matt reminded her.

"Oh yes, well our Head Office is in Lyon, where I'm officially called an analyst, but my role is frequently to be a sort of a roving janitor, doing the final clean-up after the main business has been settled. My boss felt there were some loose ends to be tidied up here, so here I am. Despite Lyon being so close, what with one thing and another, I don't know the Dordogne area very well. I have only been here a few times, and that was years ago. Your French is very good, but I suspect it is not your first language. English, perhaps?"

"You flatter me. My French can be a little strained at times, but I do my best. I work out of London. I like to visit the Dordogne region, preferably out of the main tourist season, when I can enjoy exploring the numerous beautiful Bastide villages. Are you enjoying the region?"

"I haven't had the chance to see very much, yet." Michelle waived her hand around. "Bergerac is an attractive town, but I had hoped to fit in visits to some of those Beautiful Villages that you mentioned. Unfortunately, it looks like I will only be here for a few days, and my instructions to come here were so last minute, that I don't really know where to start."

"I would be pleased to take you to a couple of places, if you have the time." Matt offered. "I am at a bit of a loose end, until my contact makes an appearance, and it would certainly be a pleasure for me to have company for a change. It's a great time to look around the local villages. They tend to get a bit crowded when the tourists arrive here in herds during the summer."

Michelle frowned at him thoughtfully. "I'm not sure. We've only known each other for about thirty minutes." She put her head on one side. "You seem to be decent, and you did let me sit at your table." She flashed an easy grin. "Of course, I will require references."

Matt smiled. "That sounds like a 'maybe'. I'm free later this afternoon: we could drive to a couple of interesting places that I have been wanting to visit." He hesitated. If you would agree to join me for dinner in one of them, you would be doing me a tremendous favour. The restaurants around here are fabulous, but I hate eating alone, so I've been surviving on Croque Monsieur, and other take away food."

"Thank you for the offer. I would like to, but I'm still suffering from jetlag." She glanced at her watch. "Right now, I have to go back to the hotel, to check my messages from Head Office. Let me think about it. I'll leave a message for you at the front desk, after lunch, if I can make it."

"Great. Just leave a message for Matt Berg."

CHAPTER 22

Once again, as soon as she was back in her hotel room, Michelle wasted no time in updating the Head of Operations.

"This is a secure line, Michelle?"

"Yes, ma'am. I've connected the scrambler. I have made contact with Matt Berg, and he has offered to take me for a tour of some local villages this afternoon."

"That was quick work. I presume there is an objective to your driving around the Dordogne with him?"

"Yes, ma'am. The pick-up this morning was straightforward. I was just about to ask if I could join him, when he invited me. He was most persuasive about taking me for a drive this afternoon. Dr. Berg is a smart chap. I suspect that he may have already got an idea of where young Nicky Berg is being held, and wants to use me as cover, while he checks out some specific location. I'm interested to see how that coincides with our general idea of Nicky's location."

"Where are you going, and when do you leave?"

"I haven't agreed to go with him, yet. I didn't want to appear too keen. I am going to leave a note for him at the hotel's Front Desk. My expectation is that he has a destination in mind, and I want to know where that is."

"Be careful. The support team is in place, and ready to make a quick extraction, if and when we give them the word. This is a very delicate situation. We have to coordinate any actions between Beijing and Bergerac. Our primary objective is to get everyone out alive. Our secondary objective is to stop the Bergs' research falling into the wrong hands." She sighed. "Let us hope that it is possible to achieve both."

"Yes, ma'am. I understand."

"Let me know the minute you locate Nicky Berg."

"Absolutely, ma'am."

CHAPTER 23

"So where are you taking me, Matt Berg?" Michelle asked, as they turned east on the main road that followed the Dordogne River out of Bergerac.

"Well, you said that it was some time since you had been in the Dordogne, and wanted to see what it looked like now, so I thought we would just have a drive around. There is so much to see, historical sites and lots of popular tourist destinations, plus, of course, the beauty of the villages and countryside everywhere. That's the Dordogne River beside you. Bergerac was a major port at one time, with wine as its main export."

"I did recognize the river." She noted wryly. "I said I didn't know the region very well, not that I am totally ignorant. I spent a few weeks around here somewhere, a long time ago. You know how it is; you never want to have vacations close to home. How is it that a Canadian knows so much about the Dordogne region?"

"How did you guess that I'm Canadian?"

"You have traces of a French Canadian accent, at times." Michelle smoothly covered her slip.

"My parents loved the Dordogne, and brought us here in the summers, when I was a teenager. It was a bit of a shock, at first, being immersed in French, everyday and everywhere, but for a teenager, it was a good way to learn; hanging out and trying to talk with the French kids."

“You said ‘us’, do you have brothers and sisters?”

“A brother, Paul. He’s in China at the moment, sorting out some business.” Matt changed the subject. “I went for a drive this way yesterday: we’ll pass through several villages that seem quite depressed, I’m not sure why. Most of the villages around here appear to be thriving. See what you think. We’ll be at the first one in a couple of minutes.”

“I think I know the answer to that, Matt. There is some tragic history of this area, from the last war. When the Germans were racing north from Italy to face the invading Allies, the local Resistance groups tried to slow them down. Many people were killed in some of these villages. It can be difficult for people our age to understand, but sometimes, the villages seem to have had difficulty recovering from those horrors, even today.”

“That is very sad. I should have realized that there had to be some kind of history.”

“This is a BMW. A nice car for a rental.” Michelle moved to an easier topic, relaxing back in her seat.

“Yes. They gave me a Peugeot, originally, when I arrived at the airport a couple of days ago. I wanted something with a bit more zip, so I went there first thing this morning, and they had this one available. I had just got back when you saw me spill my coffee this morning.”

“You drove all the way to Bordeaux airport this morning to change your rental car?”

“No, no. I flew in to Bergerac airport, and rented the car there. British Airways has a direct flight from London City airport to Bergerac. So it was quick and easy to change the car there.”

“Is that what you English call ‘exchanging horses in the middle of the river’?”

He smiled. "You're close, but I think you're thinking of the saying 'changing horses in mid stream'. We say that when someone changes their plan when they are already half way through. "

Michelle shook her head. "I will never understand your strange sayings."

"Well, your English is excellent, far better than my French. I'll turn off just ahead. There is an old paper mill that's interesting. Apparently this was a popular place to make paper, it had something to do with the water. Many of the original buildings are just ruins, but there is a sort of museum there, and the water still flows through the original channels. It's worth a quick stop."

They spent a short while wandering around the old paper mill, before continuing on their way.

"That was interesting. So where to now, tour guide?"

"Next stop is Monpazier: one of the Listed Beautiful Bastide Villages that are so famous."

"This is exactly the type of village I have been hoping to see." Michelle exclaimed. "Somehow, these villages feel like the rural roots of France. If I recall my French history correctly, it was Edward the First of England who built a number of Bastide villages around here, in the thirteenth century. The Bastide style of construction was to lay out the streets in a grid pattern, inside the walls, so we shouldn't get lost." Michelle searched her memory. "Wasn't Edward also the Duke of Gascony?"

"Sorry, my English and French history are really weak." Matt admitted. "There's the stone wall and gateway, with the parking lot ahead on the left. I'll park, and we can walk in. I've always wanted to visit Monpazier again. The last time I was here has to be years ago. According to what I remember, there is a magnificent square with a surprisingly well preserved open market hall."

The sun broke through the clouds to greet them, as they wandered around the streets, absorbing the centuries of history that the ancient stone buildings encompassed. They stopped to read the wall plaques describing some particular historical event that had occurred there.

"I could immerse myself in this scene for hours." Michelle sighed, as she moved around with her mobile phone, to get the some photographs of the beautiful old buildings.

"How about we get a coffee, or a glass of wine, at that bistro over there beside the square?" Matt suggested.

"That sounds like a great idea. It's so idyllic, relaxing and people watching in an historic square, on a sunny spring afternoon, you may have difficulty moving me. "

They sat and watched the activity in the square, chatting easily about everything and nothing for a while, until Michelle noticed that Matt seemed to be anxious to move on.

"You keep checking your watch, do we need to get back?"

"No, not at all. It's just that I wanted to head over to a small village, with a magnificent fifteenth century cloister, called the Cloister of Cadouin." Matt explained. "It was originally part of a twelfth century Cistercian abbey, and is listed by UNESCO as a World Heritage Site. I don't want to rush you: we can certainly stay here for as long as you wish. Unfortunately, access to the Cloister closes at six, and the drive will take about thirty minutes." He looked at his watch. "That will give us a little over an hour to absorb the beauty of the architecture, and to experience the peace and tranquility that seems to emanate from the whole setting. There is also a restaurant across the square from the abbey, where I was hoping that you would join me for dinner."

Michelle smiled, as she stood up. "It sounds completely entrancing: a beautiful UNESCO World Heritage Site, followed by dinner in a real French village restaurant. Absolutely irresistible. Lead on."

Michelle contentedly enthused about the sunny pastoral scenes that they passed, taking photographs, as they that twisted and turned their way along the quiet country roads. She explained that this was the French country scene that she always pictured, animals happily grazing in lush green fields, guarded over by a traditional stone farmhouse that sat like a sentinel on a nearby rise.

Clearly, the Cloister of Cadouin was a popular tourist destination, since, as they started to get close, they were greeted by signs providing directions to the locations of parking lots for visitors. Michelle was surprised when Matt suddenly turned onto a side road, and slowed to a more sedate pace.

"We are coming into the outskirts of the village: there are only a few kilometres to go. This is sleepy rural France, so I have to slow down a bit. I enjoy exploring the back roads around the village, but I don't want to hit a loose farm animal, or even a farmer who is wandering across the road, not expecting to encounter a tourist careening along his quiet lane." Matt explained.

When he turned on to another road, following a signpost that indicated it led to the village centre, Michelle noticed his hands were tight on the steering wheel. He slowed right down to stare intently at a small cottage on the other side of the road. She quickly took several photographs of the cottage, noting its name, and its location relative to the village centre. Matt was too fixated on the cottage to even notice.

Michelle found the Cloister of Cadouin to be every bit as enchanting as Matt had described, and was sad when they were ushered out at six o'clock. It was too early for dinner, but a perfect spring evening to take a leisurely wander through stone archways, and along cobbled side streets. The evening sun was casting its golden glow over the village, as they paused to admire the beauty of the buildings that dated back to centuries long past. Every corner was like a step back in time. When the sun started to slide behind the surrounding hills, dozens of traditional style streetlights came alive, bestowing a magical ambiance on the whole village.

"It's starting to cool down." Matt noted. "Perhaps it's time for us to retire to the restaurant across from the Cloister. I have heard that it's very good. We can see what they have to offer this evening."

It turned out to be everything they had hoped for. They paused in the entrance, absorbing the familiar aromas and ambiance of a traditional country restaurant in rural France. All around, bustling waiters moved smoothly between kitchen and tables, carrying dishes that sent a proliferation of mouthwatering messages to the senses. A waiter came and guided them to a reserved table beside a window. Michelle gasped with delight that it was like looking out on a scene from history, with the antique style village lights creating interplay of light and shadows throughout the square that brought the beautiful edifice of the abbey to life.

Dinner in a rural French village was always a leisurely affair, and Matt noted that the restaurant must have a good reputation, since most of the other diners appeared to be local. Having studied the menu at length, they both picked out several dishes from the Daily Board. Matt suggested that as Michelle was French, she would doubtless know the wines better than he, and perhaps she would like to select the wine.

The wine and food were both excellent. As the meal progressed, Michelle found that she was having to drive the conversation. While Matt was polite and adept at responding to any topic that she initiated, he seemed distant and preoccupied. It became evident that his mind was occupied with quite another issue.

Their meal progressed uneventfully, until a yellow sports car slipped quietly across the square in front of them. Their main course had been placed before them, but Matt seemed so gripped by the sight of the car that for a moment, Michelle thought that he might jump up, and race outside after it. Once it had gone, he exhaled.

"I'm sorry. That was very rude of me." He tried a tight smile. "I thought it was someone I knew. I've been wanting to see them for some time."

She smiled back. "That was a very striking car, and the driver was an attractive young woman. I can understand why you would want to meet her."

"No. It's nothing like that. Absolutely not. Not at all, I can absolutely assure you of that. It's a business thing." He made a deft change of topic. "Thank you for agreeing to visit some of the local villages with me this afternoon, and join me for this dinner. It has been the most enjoyable afternoon and evening that I have had in a long time. I actually managed to forget work for a little while. Well, apart from a few minutes ago, and I humbly apologize for that, oncc again."

Michelle put her head on one side, with a grin. "Well that's a good attempt at a recovery, so I think I'll forgive you, this once. This really is a splendid meal, and the local wine is excellent."

They finished the remainder of the meal with casual exchanges, like any couple getting to know each other for the first time. Somehow, the rapport between them seemed to have undergone a change. Matt was more relaxed, as they segued into comfortable discussions about the Dordogne region. Michelle explained that she had studied some anthropology at university, and intrigued Matt with descriptions of the incredible vestiges of civilizations of the earliest humans who had settled in the hospitable, temperate Dordogne and Vezere river valleys, many thousands of years ago.

They had developed a comfortable rapport by the time they left the restaurant, and were driving back through the dark country lanes. When they came to the quaint village of Moliere, Michelle suggested that they see if there was somewhere to stop for a coffee. Matt readily agreed, and eased the car through the ancient archway into the village square that seemed to have an almost magical ambience in the still warm spring evening. Across the square they saw a bar, with groups of locals enjoying late night drinks on a small patio area that was outlined with a string of small lights. Matt parked the car, and they ambled across to join them.

It was approaching midnight, before they were entering Bergerac once again. Michelle was slightly surprised when Matt stopped at the front door of the hotel to drop her off. His explanation was that he had to park the car some distance away, adding that he hoped to see her again soon.

CHAPTER 24

The following morning, Michelle contacted the Head of Operations, to provide an update of her afternoon and evening with Matt Berg.

"I am assuming that this is a secure line, Michelle. Please give me a comprehensive report on your time with Dr. Matt Berg. I will be recording it. Did you manage to learn anything significant?"

"Yes, I believe that I did, ma'am. We left Bergerac in the early afternoon in his rented BMW."

"Is the make of the car relevant?"

"Actually, I think it is. When I commented on the car, he said that he had rented a Peugeot when he landed at Bergerac airport, a couple of days ago, and switched it that morning."

"Huh. Interesting. I think that you're suggesting that he didn't want to keep using the same car, in case it was recognized. Go on."

"That was my thought, ma'am. He gave a rather feeble explanation for the change. I deflected the conversation by deliberately mixing up one of the English sayings. I have found that frequently works quite well. We headed east, on the D660 beside the river, staying on that road when it turned sharply south towards the village of Couze et Saint Front. There are the remains of a paper mill and paper making plant just after the turning, and Berg pulled in there, ostensibly to show me the museum, and what is left of the plant. However, he seemed to be more interested in the traffic that had been behind us on the road, than in anything to do with paper making. We stayed for about ten minutes, before leaving again."

"And you believe that he stopped to see if you were being followed?"

"That was certainly my impression. I noticed that he kept checking the rear view mirror, as soon as we left Bergerac. The road is fairly open in stretches, allowing me to make use of the side mirror, but I did not identify any vehicle that was following us."

"What was your cover story during this trip?"

"I told Berg that I had only visited the Dordogne region once many years ago, and did not know it all that well. I said that I had heard a lot about the Listed Beautiful Villages, and was anxious to see some of them for myself. From the paper mill, we carried on the D660 to Monpazier. We wandered around for some time, finishing up at a table beside the ancient square."

"Did Berg appear to have any particular interest in Monpazier, or the area around there?"

"No ma'am, he did not. We walked around, without any particular focus, and he was quite willing to wander anywhere that I suggested. At my suggestion, we sat by the square and had a coffee. I took a seat with my back against a wall, and a good view of the entire square. There were not many people there, and they were coming and going. I did not detect that we were attracting any undue interest from anyone."

"Where did you go from there?"

"After we had been sitting for a while, Berg started to look at his watch, and seemed anxious to leave. He said he wanted to show me the Cloister of Cadouin, explaining that it closed at six. He said that it is a World Heritage Site, and well worth a visit. However, it seemed to me that he was operating to a timetable.

"We drove along the relatively quiet route D2 direct from Monpazier to the Cloister of Cadouin. It was an easy run, and I was surprised when he turned down a side road, as we approached the village. He slowed right down, with some excuse about animals on the road, or something, but I had the distinct impression that he was looking for something, and that he had carefully selected the route from Monpazier, and the time when we would arrive."

"You think that he was looking for something that would indicate where the girl, Nicky, was being held?"

"That is exactly what I thought. When we came to a small cottage, Berg stared at it. The cottage was on his side of the road, but I managed to photograph the front of the cottage, and the name that was displayed prominently at the roadside. There was a small, sleek car parked by the front door. It looked bright gold coloured. A similar vehicle that got Berg's attention, when we were at the restaurant: together that evening. From Berg's reaction, I believe he considers the cottage and that car to be significant."

"Good work getting the photos you sent me. I have people checking the GPS, and the cottage with the name, 'Santuaire Paisible'. Did Berg react to your taking those photos?"

"No, ma'am. He was so fixated on the cottage, that he gave no indication that he had even noticed."

"Well done, Michelle. I sent a team to check it out immediately. They have reported that it looks like a very high prospect, and will continue to monitor it using drones with infrared cameras. Anyone leaving the cottage will be brought in. Did he ever indicate what had interested him in the cottage?"

"No. I asked him later, and he just shrugged, and said he thought he had caught sight of a friend's car parked there. After seeing the Cloister, and walking around for a short while, we went to a restaurant across the square from the Abbey. He had already made a reservation there, for a table beside the window. It was just a typical country restaurant, with candles on the tables, and the evening's selection written on a board."

"I suppose it has occurred to you, Michelle, that Matt Berg might have developed a romantic interest in you?"

"I think that we can totally discard any possible thought in that direction, ma'am. He spent more time over dinner looking out of the restaurant window at the village square, than he did looking at me. Thankfully the meal was excellent, because the conversation was a little strained, at first." She quickly changed the topic, although not quite quickly enough for her supervisor not to notice the catch in her voice. "Which brings up the other interesting incident. We were about half way through our meal, when a sports car, similar to the one I photographed in the driveway of the cottage, drove slowly through the square outside. This time, I could see that it was definitely gold. Berg froze. It only lasted a few seconds, before he regained his composure, gave a self-conscious grin, and apologized, saying that he was sure that the young woman driving was a friend. Although the lighting in the square was patchy, I did get a slightly better look at the car this time. It was definitely a high-end sports car. I didn't recognize as a European model, so I did a search online through all the Japanese sports cars. It was a Lexus LC 500. I had no chance to get the licence number. One other point, it moved through the square very quietly, so I suspect that it was the hybrid version. There was a young woman driving it."

"That is interesting, Michelle. I will have the team be on the lookout for a gold coloured Lexus LC 500 sports car. Since it appears likely that Bergerac is a location of interest, I will initiate the search there. It's an unusual vehicle, and the city is not that big:. If it's there, we should find it quite quickly, along with the young woman driver."

"How do you want me to proceed from here, ma'am?"

"Keep close to Matt Berg. The information from China indicates that something is expected to break in Beijing within the next forty-eight hours. When that happens, everything is going to start moving very fast. From the latest intelligence that we arc getting, it is starting to look like the kidnappers' original plan is beginning to unravel."

"That is my impression, too, ma'am. I had the feeling in Beijing that it was taking much longer than expected to make the exchange. The shooting at the Summer Palace seemed to create a major change. Someone had crossed a line, and that brought Mr. Renshu and the Chinese authourities into it, in a big way. They were furious that an innocent Chinese citizen had been seriously injured."

"We must not allow the situation to get out of control like that, here in France. Locating and rescuing Nicky Berg is now our top priority. We will confirm shortly if she is being held at that cottage. It appears that Matt Berg may be in possession of some important information. It is time for you to tell him who you work for."

CHAPTER 25

Paul Berg endured a restless night in his hotel room. He had been unable to stop his mind churning over and over the same things all night; eventually he had given up any attempt at sleep. He pulled on a pair of shorts together with a favourite exercise shirt, and headed down to the exercise room as soon as it opened, at six o'clock, and worked out on the treadmill and with weights for over an hour, before heading back for a long shower. He had hoped that the exercise and the shower, would help his mind slow down, but it seemed to have little effect. He moved on to the lounge for breakfast, consuming a substantial serving of scrambled eggs and something that passed for bacon, along with several cups of coffee. Still, his mind kept churning, and he covered numerous paper napkins with copious cryptic notes.

He had made no progress since he and Tricia had arrived in Beijing, and was beyond frustrated.

There had been two abortive attempts to interact with the kidnappers, most recently, the one the previous day that had resulted in a completely innocent young mother being shot. When he had told Matt on the phone, the previous evening, Matt had recalled that his MI6 contacts had suggested to him that the two of them could become targets for groups that did not want their medical discovery falling into the wrong hands. Who the Hell the 'wrong hands' were, neither of them had been told.

Matt had been vague in relating his activities, since he had arrived in Bergerac. Paul knew his brother well enough that he was sure that he was holding something back. Matt had always been reluctant to claim progress, or forecast success at anything until it was absolutely assured. He was even still cautious about their medical breakthrough, pointing out that they had only tested the possible vaccine on a sample of viruses in laboratory equipment, never even performed a large-scale trial.

When he could not face any more coffee, Paul had headed back to his room. He was restless after all the caffeine.

Tricia knocked on the connecting door, and came in to join him. She looked completely relaxed in lime green Capri pants, and a short, white denim jacket over a light blue turtleneck top.

"I could hear you pacing around. How are you managing?"

"I don't know. I'm going out of my mind. We've been here two full days already, and we're no closer to finding Nicky." He shook his head in despair. "I don't know what to do. The frustration is killing me. I was in such a rage this morning; I just wanted to smash everything in sight. Pretty stupid, huh? Thankfully, I decided to go to the exercise room instead, and go through a major workout. It helped. I've calmed down a bit; well sort of."

"I can understand how you were feeling. The past couple of days have been unbelievably frustrating. At least the kidnappers have made contact, although, each time, it seems like they were just toying with us. My interpretation is that they have been watching us to see if we would cooperate with them. I'm expecting that you will be contacted again, probably this morning, with yet another arrangement for a meet. I suspect and hope that this third meeting will be the real thing."

Paul glanced around the room, and made a sour face. "Look, let's go somewhere, where we can talk; outside of this hotel."

"Right. Come on. I know a place quite close, where we can get a coffee and a decent breakfast."

"Okay, but I don't think I can look at another cup of coffee."

One of the exits from the hotel led directly into the Garden Court of the massive Oriental Plaza mall. Tricia led the way through the intimidating maze of high-end stores.

Paul stared around, "Good Lord, this mall is huge, and it's full of all the expensive stores that I can't afford to let Nicky even go in at home. Thank goodness there are signs in English pointing the way to the Hyatt hotel. If you weren't with me, it could still take me hours to find my way back."

Tricia rapidly had them settled in a small restaurant on the second level, with a pot of green tea in front of them, and some food on the way.

She was focused. "You seemed to want to say something back at the hotel?"

"Yes, well. I've been thinking about my talk with Matt last night. I know him really well."

"Of course."

They were silent while the waiter put plates of pastries, cheeses and cold meats on their table. Paul waited until he had left, before continuing.

"I know Matt can often sound optimistic, but he has a sort of cagey way of talking, when he has something on his mind, and isn't ready to talk about it yet. With our research with the protein strings, he said nothing to me until he had repeated a long string of tests on every variant of the virus that he could lay his hands on."

"So what do you think he is holding back, now, Paul?"

"I'm not sure. But I am sure that he is working on something. Everyone seems convinced that Nicky is being held in Europe, and, since the kidnappers have sent Matt to this Bergerac place, she is probably somewhere around there. Whatever it is, he doesn't want to say anything, yet."

"Why wouldn't he say anything? That's crazy, and Matt is a really smart chap. If he has any idea where she is, he should call the police, and tell them to go and get her."

"Maybe not. You're right he is really smart, and he tends to think in broader terms than me. That's what had me thinking. If he has come across some lead that is limited to just the general area where Nicky is being held, and the local police start running around the countryside creating all sorts of fuss, the kidnappers are bound to get wind of it." He grimaced. "It doesn't bear thinking about what might happen to Nicky, at that point." He shuddered. "Even if they just moved her to some other country, we would be worse off than we are now."

"I see what you mean." Tricia said thoughtfully. "The kidnappers still would not have the information that they want."

"This is a very clever scheme that they have come up with. Nicky will be freed at the same time that they have got everything that they have demanded. Both parties recognize that there must be no significant time separation between the two events that occur in two countries, thousands of miles apart. It is sort of a long distance stand-off. We won't release the full documentation unless and until we know that Nicky is safe: the kidnappers won't release Nicky until they have the full documentation."

"I follow what you are saying, but isn't that what the kidnappers have said they would do?" Tricia puzzled.

"That's what they've said, but I don't think Matt believes them. And after thinking about it, neither do I. Renshu and the CSIS people are convinced that the kidnappers are a real nasty bunch, and Matt hinted at that too, last night."

Tricia's face went white with anger. "What about Nicky? We have to do something to stop this." She gritted through clenched teeth.

"I believe that was the message that Matt was trying to get across to me last night. We need help, and there doesn't appear to be anyone around."

"Excuse me, sir and madam."

Paul and Tricia looked up in surprise. They had been talking so intently that they hadn't noticed the restaurant manager approach them.

He was bobbing his head nervously, so Tricia switched to mandarin. "Yes? Is there a problem?"

"Not at all. No. Not at all. Is this gentleman Professor Paul Berg?"

"Yes, he is."

"A gentleman left this at the desk, and asked that we give it to Professor Paul Berg. He indicated that this was the gentleman he was referring to."

The manager placed a plastic carrier bag, on the table. It was gold coloured, with '***dunhill***' emblazoned on it in dark brown lettering. It appeared to be a standard bag given to customers of that store. He started to move away quickly.

"Wait. Who left this for Professor Berg?" Tricia demanded, in mandarin.

"I don't know, madam. I have never seen the person before.

He was not from Beijing. He did not leave his name." He said, before he scurried across to the safety of his station.

Paul stared at the object sitting on the table in front of him. "What the blazes is this?"

"The manager said a man left it for you at the desk. He said he did not know the man, but he was not from Beijing. I take that to mean he was not Chinese. The manager seemed nervous."

"God, I hope there isn't a poisonous spider or snake, or some deadly chemical in there." Paul peered at the package apprehensively.

Tricia took a deep breath. "Well, there is only one way to find out." She gingerly pulled the bag towards her. "If there is anything bad, take me straight to Yang Chow at the Clinic. They have the facilities there to deal with most things, after all, they have to be prepared for whatever some inquisitive child has got themselves into."

They gave a simultaneous sigh of relief, when Tricia declared the bag was empty, apart from a single, folded sheet of paper, with "Paul Berg" printed on the outside. Paul took the paper and carefully opened it on the table. They both stared at the message.

"Put the agreed initial material that supports your research in this bag, and bring it to this store at nine thirty this morning."

"That's forty minutes from now." Tricia gasped. "You have everything they want ready to go, don't you?"

"Yes. Yes. It's back in the room. It's mostly files of paper: the results of the trials that Matt printed out. We're not giving them any electronic information until we are confident that Nicky is released, or just about to be." He looked into the ***dunhill*** bag. "This should easily be big enough for it. I've been carting it around for the past two days, trying to give it to them. Where the blazes is this '***dunhill***' store? Do you know?"

"Yes it's in this mall. Come on, we don't have much time. We have to get back to the room, collect the stuff, and get back here again. The ***dunhill*** store is not far from here."

They pushed the bill and a fistful of Chinese currency at the pay clerk, as they raced out of the restaurant, and ran, dodging and bobbing their way through the shoppers, back to the hotel.

There were two elevators that took guests up to the hotel's Club Floor, but the indicator showed that one was on its way up, and the other seemed to take an eternity to reach the ground floor, as it stopped at what seemed to be every floor on the way down. When it finally did arrive with a group of seven Americans, one overweight, middle -aged man put his arms out, blocking the others from leaving.

He demanded of Paul, "Is this the ground floor? We've stopped at just about every damn floor. Why can't the Chinese Commies provide proper controls in English in their elevators? They're just damned buttons. That's communism for you. Can't get anything right." He turned back to the others in the lift. "This looks like the lobby, finally. Come on folks."

Tricia looked at her watch as they ran down the seventeenth floor corridor, and reached their rooms.

"Twenty-two minutes to go. Lots of time left. Oh damit," she cried, staring at a notice hanging on her door. "Look at that. My room is undergoing 'essential plumbing repairs', and will be unavailable until nine thirty. 'The Management apologizes for the temporary inconvenience.' Damn and blast. I need to pee."

"No problem, Tricia. Come on. My room is free, and that's where all of the stuff is. We must keep moving."

Minutes later, they were back at the elevator with the **dunhill** bag containing Paul's papers. The doors opened, and they piled in. They only gave the other occupants a perfunctory glance. There were three other people in the elevator: a man in a Hyatt employee's jacket, was operating the lift, and a couple who looked to be in their thirties had their backs to them, and were fiddling with a red suitcase.

Paul and Tricia faced the doors, ready to make a fast exit. They both let out a relieved sigh as they started downward. The lift came to a sudden stop between the fourth and third floors.

"What the Hell is going on?" Paul groaned in disbelief. "What's happened?"

"Relax, professor. We don't have much time. Do exactly what we tell you."

Paul and Tricia spun around to face the couple behind them. "Who the Hell are you? What do you want?"

The Asian woman pointed at Tricia. "Take off your Capri pants, jacket and top, as quickly as you can, Doctor Chen."

"No, I will not. What sort of sick perverts are you?" Tricia demanded angrily, as Paul stepped between them.

"Stay away from us. What is it that you creeps want? Just leave us alone. Who are you?"

The woman had handed her floppy hat to the man, and was already starting to peel off her red, designer jeans, grey silk jacket, and pale blue cashmere jumper.

"They are Interpol, Professor." Explained a familiar voice from beside the control panel. "Please do as they say. It really is important, and there is not a lot of time."

"Mr. Renshu." Tricia gasped, spinning around. "What is going on?"

"Our apologies for the dramatics, but everything has started to unfold rather rapidly. Yes, we are Interpol agents, Professor Berg, Doctor Chen." The young man explained, quickly showing them his identification. "After someone took a shot at you, yesterday, we decided that it would be best if my partner and I took your places for the exchange." He gestured to the woman who was already standing in her bra and panties, holding her clothes. "Please switch clothes as quickly as possible, Doctor."

"What about me?"

"You're much easier, Professor. Put on my maroon jacket, and this New York ball cap, and pair of aviator sunglasses, and you're ready to go. I am already wearing blue jeans and a blue shirt, essentially identical to yours. The doctor was a bit too difficult to match, so the women are going to have to switch clothes. Fortunately, they are close to the same size."

"This is ridiculous." Paul snapped. "You two are hardly a perfect match for us. You won't fool anyone."

"People see what they expect to see, Professor." Renshu intoned. "They saw you earlier, in the shopping mall, in those clothes, and that is what they will see again. Look how easily you were led to believe that the girl who you saw in Beihai Park was your daughter, just because of the clothes she was wearing. Please do as they say, quickly."

"Oh, what the Hell." Tricia muttered, shrugging out of her jacket, pulling off her Capris and top, and handing them to the woman in exchange. "Okay, now what?" She demanded as she struggled to zip up the red jeans.

"You, Doctor Chen, are going to the airport for the Air France flight to Paris that leaves in a couple of hours." The woman said, as she pushed her head through Tricia's light blue turtleneck.

"No. That I will not do." Tricia said firmly. "Paul will have to stay here, because he has the information, and is the only one who knows all of the technical details. I am going to stay with him. He doesn't speak Mandarin, and doesn't now his way around Beijing."

"You must go, Doctor. After the shots at Paul, yesterday, it will be safer and better for you both, if you leave Beijing." The woman insisted. "From Paris you will fly to Bergerac and join Matt Berg there. You will wait with him for the girl, Nicky Berg, to be released. From Interpol's past experience, you will be told when and where that will take place. She will need to be met by someone she recognizes, and there should be a doctor to check her over. You will be invaluable, filling both of those roles."

"This is very important, Doctor Chen. I will make sure that Professor Berg is looked after here in Beijing. Please do as they say." Mr. Renshu intoned firmly.

Paul put his arm around Tricia's shoulders. "As you pointed out, I have to stay, but if it will help Nicky, you must go." Paul said softly. "I can manage here."

"Okay, but what about my passport, and all of my personal things that are in my hotel room? There is a plumber in there, I can't get in." She paused, as realization dawned. "Oh, right. I suppose that was you?"

"Yes. Everything is packed in your suitcase." The woman said, tapping the side of the red suitcase, and handing Tricia the handle. "Your passport and tickets are in the front pouch. Here, take this floppy hat, and put these sunglasses on."

"What about Nicky's suitcase with all her things? I picked it up from the clinic, where Susan Chow was holding it for me. It was in my room. Nicky will need it."

"Yes, we saw it. It's in the car." The woman said as she adjusted her hair, a wig that had been hidden by the hat. It was a match for Tricia's pixie cut.

"What car?"

"When we reach the ground, Professor, you and Doctor Chen must wait for a moment, to let the other two get clear." Mr. Renshu instructed. "Once they have gone, you leave, and turn right out of the lift, go through that exit to the small mall, and on through there to Wangfujing Street. There will be a black BMW car waiting to take you both to the airport.

"That's a pedestrian street." Tricia said.

"Not where car is waiting. It becomes a pedestrian street further along." The man explained. "Give me the **dunhill** bag. Thanks. We're ready to go."

"Wait. I insist on some evidence that," Paul stumbled over the words, as he choked back a sob, "that Nicky is still… is still"

"I understand. I will deal with that for you." The man cut in sympathetically. "We will obtain a current video of your daughter."

Paul wiped the back of his hand across his eyes. "Right. Okay. Yes, thank you. Now what do I do, after Tricia has gone through security at the airport?"

"The car will be waiting for you and bring you back. You will be staying in your room, as before, that way you can answer the phone. From here on, I will pose as you, and make all physical contacts with the other side. We look a bit alike, so that should not be a problem, but we cannot be seen together. Forty-eight hours and this will all be over."

"We must keep moving." The woman muttered. "The lift must not stay stationary any longer, or it will attract attention."

"Yes, yes. We're off again." Mr Renshu proclaimed, as the lift started to descend once again. "Here we are, now hurry everyone." He looked over at the lobby clock. "It's nine twenty already."

CHAPTER 26

Everything had gone smoothly for Paul and Tricia as they left the hotel. The car was waiting on Wangfujing Street, and the driver had its engine running when they reached it. Before he whisked them out of the city, and onto the expressway to the Beijing Capital airport, Tricia insisted on checking that they did indeed have everything. She found her ticket and passport were in her suitcase pocket, as promised, and Paul confirmed that Nicky's suitcase was in the boot, with her empty carry-on backpack pushed inside the large front pocket.

Tricia was familiar with the airport, and was able to find her way to the Air France counter, to drop her and Nicky's bags, without too much difficulty. From there, it was through the airport's labyrinth, to the security checkpoint for International Departures. Paul offered to take her carry-on as they stepped on to the escalator, and her hand slipped into his when he took the bag. It gave them both a sense of comfort, and they were still holding hands when they stood together at the row of five portals that led into the International Departures area. They were finding it difficult to say goodbye. Tricia studied her boarding pass, as though it contained some cryptic message, and Paul kept looking at the big Departure board, behind them. They were looking at anything but each other.

Paul broke the impasse. "Tricia, I'm." He coughed. "I'm going to really miss you. You have been an unbelievable strength and support through all of this. I simply could not have managed without you."

She blinked back tears, as she smiled up at him, and squeezed his hand. "You just take care of yourself, Paul. Things look like they are going to come to a head in the next day or so. Are you really going to hand over all of your work to these awful people?"

He pursed his lips. "We'll just have to see how all that plays out. Matt and I have talked, and agreed that we both have some thinking and some work to do. It looks like I'm going to be pretty well shut up in my room for the next little while, so I will have plenty of time. I wish that you were going to be next door." He let out a slow breath. "Two days max, they tell us, and it will all be over. We will all be together again; Nicky, you, me, and Matt. Tell Nicky how much I love her, and I will be back there just as soon as I can."

"I will."

Paul took a deep breath. "I know this is not the time or place, Tricia, but I have to tell you that life just isn't the same when you aren't around. You're really special. I know Nicky feels the same way: we both do. She tried to ask me why we weren't, you know, together. She could see it. You, me and Nicky. We sort of belong together." He pursed his lips, and sighed. "I have to just say it. I've been in love with you since I don't know when, but didn't know what to say. You have such an interesting life: I couldn't see why you would be interested in me, a stodgy university professor." He clenched his jaw. "Dammit, I'm making a complete mess of this. I hope I haven't embarrassed you. I shouldn't have just blurted it out like that, while we are standing here. I'm sure you aren't remotely interested in me, in that way."

Tricia blinked hard several times: she didn't want her tears to embarrass him. "For an intelligent man, you really can be a bit slow, sometimes, Paul Berg. I fell in love with you a long time ago. Nicky asked me about us, too. She knew. I thought you weren't interested. So did Nicky." She reached up and kissed him softly.

He looked around, and gave sheepish grin. "Not exactly a romantic setting, I'm afraid. I've been wanting to tell you, well, ask you, well, you know, say something. I could never find the right place and time. And now, I've made a complete mess of it."

"You were perfect. Sincerity is much more important than a contrived performance or setting. This is a moment I will always remember."

Paul held her tight and kissed her. "It is a moment that I will always remember, too." He pretended to be giving it serious consideration. "Although, I must say, the image of you standing in the lift in your underwear certainly takes a close second place."

She rolled her eyes, and flashed an impish grin. "Well I hope you enjoyed the view. It was totally unfair. That woman knew she was going to change clothes, and was wearing modest cotton undies, while I was flaunting my all, in wispy little pieces of silk and lace."

Paul held her close. His gentle kiss was charged with emotion. "Nicky was absolutely right. You are fantastic." He turned his head, reluctantly, to look up at the digital clock that hung above the Departure portals. "I hate to say it, but you must go, or you will miss your flight. Say 'Hi' to Matt, and hug Nicky for me."

"I will." She gave him one last kiss, and headed through to the Security Checkpoint.

"Nicky's suitcase is in checked baggage." Paul called after her. "Don't forget to pick it up at Bordeaux."

Tricia glanced back over her shoulder, with a tolerant smile. "I won't."

Paul stood watching Tricia head through Security, and across the hall. She turned, and gave one last, little wave, before she disappeared out of sight.

He stood, staring after her, trying to decide what to do next. He really did not want to go back to his hotel room, and sit there on his own, but he had no idea where else to go. Tricia had always been his guide around the city. A group of passengers bustled by him, chatting excitedly, prompting him to move away from the entrances. Across the way, the big board displayed all of the departing flights, so he went over to look for her flight. The Air France flight to Paris was scheduled to depart in fifty-two minutes. To the right of the board was a sign in English, with an arrow pointing up the nearby escalator to an observation area. He could watch Tricia's flight take off from there.

Paul found a seat at an empty table beside the vast glass wall that looked out on the aircraft apron. He could see planes from a variety of airlines and countries all lined up at their allotted gates. There was the massive Air France Airbus, three away, at the ramp with the large number twenty-one on the side. He looked over, and checked the monitor that displayed the various flights in order of their scheduled departure: a smaller version of the board that he had been looking at downstairs. Air France to Paris was scheduled to leave from Gate twenty-one, in seventeen minutes.

Paul stared at the line of round windows of the Air France plane, squinting, trying to see if he could recognize Tricia's head. It was hopeless. The windows were too small, and she was too far away. He did remember that she had been relieved to see that she had a Business Class ticket, so she would be at the front of the aircraft. He had forgotten to ask her what her seat number was. He felt close to her, just knowing that she was on that plane.

"Professor Berg, we thought you might be here."

Paul jerked around in surprise at the familiar voice, and groaned. It was Sarah Little and her sidekick, Kevin Blakey: his least favourite CSIS operatives.

"Agent Little, what are you two doing here? Leaving, I hope?"

Sarah Little ignored his jibe. "We're just here to watch the planes. Has Doctor Chen left?"

Paul turned back to the window, in time to see the Air France plane push back from the Gate, and turn, ready to make its way to the end of the runway. He watched silently, as the huge plane revved its engines, and laboriously lumbered around the corner of the Terminal building, and out of sight.

"If it is any of your business, Dr. Chen is on a plane that is just about to leave China, so you won't be able to harass her any more."

Sarah Little moved around behind Paul, and said softly. "You know, Professor Berg, you may find it difficult to believe, but we really are on your side." She stood up. "We'll leave you, but if you need us, perhaps I should say, *when* you need us, contact the Canadian Embassy." She took an embossed business card from her jacket pocket. "Here's the Embassy card, with the phone number, they will get hold of us."

The Air France plane eventually reappeared at the far end of the runway, and Paul watched, as it started its thunderous sprint that would release it to soar gracefully to the freedom of the skies.

CHAPTER 27

Paul was relieved to find that the car that had brought them to the airport was, indeed, still waiting for him. Rather than return to the hotel, he asked the driver to drop him at Tiananmen Square. That was the only place he could think of, in downtown Beijing that he knew.

He meandered along, mingling with the eclectic mix of visitors and locals around him. They all seemed to be enjoying the warm spring weather, as they wandered around the Square, taking in the sight of the Forbidden Palace across the road. There was an impressive display of vibrant flowers adorning the entrance to the nearby Great Hall of the People, the government building that watched over the happenings in the Square.

He noticed an intriguing looking round building that was reflecting the afternoon sun, and decided to wander along the busy Chang 'an Avenue to have a look at it. A sign in English announced that it was the National Centre for the Performing Arts. Up close, it was even more dramatic, not really half a sphere, more like half an egg in shape, that gave the impression that it was floating in an artificial lake. The floating half egg was made out of some sort of metal with a great expanse of glass at the end. It was the most strikingly dramatic building Paul had ever seen, and he wondered if Tricia had ever been to a concert, or anything, there.

There was a park-like expanse of green space that surrounded the lake, where people were walking, or quietly sitting, absorbing the peaceful ambience in the heart of the throbbing cacophony of the crowded city. Partly obscured by some foliage, Paul noticed a rhythmic motion, away to his right. Moving closer, he saw that it was a loose group of men and women quietly immersed in their regular Tai Chi routines.

The bizarre events of the morning had left him totally drained, and Paul looked around to see if there was somewhere where he could sit down. He spotted an empty bench along a pathway between the flowerbeds, and sank down, with a heartfelt sigh. He was totally alone in Beijing. Tricia was on a flight to Paris and beyond. He had no idea where Nicky was.

He understood how the situation was what it was: he had to stay in Beijing for the handover, and to provide any technical information that might be required. It didn't help. He was, alone in the massive city of Beijing, not knowing his way about the place, and totally unable to understand the language. His only refuge was the Hyatt hotel, where there were people who spoke English, so at least he would be able to communicate, and find something to eat.

It had all happened so fast.

He took a deep breath, and looked around at the Chinese men, women and children who were taking a moment in these peaceful surroundings to regenerate their batteries, and move forward in their daily struggles. The clock was ticking, and this was no time to feel sorry for himself. He had some heavy thinking to do, plus some complex technical challenges to work on, before he gave the documentation to the kidnappers. Wherever they were, Tricia, Nicky and Matt were counting on him.

"Do you speak English?"

"Pardon? I'm sorry, what did you say?" He looked around, and saw that there were two young women standing beside him. Classic tourists: worn jeans; baggy tops, with inane messages on them; sunglasses, and high priced cross-trainers. They reminded him of his graduate students.

The girl with the long blond ponytail smiled. "I just asked if you spoke English, and obviously, you do. We've read that there is a great little teahouse along here somewhere that is the real traditional Chinese. We thought you might know where it is."

Paul managed a polite smile. "I've only been here a couple of days, and don't know my way around Beijing at all. However, I have been to a traditional teahouse along past Tiananmen Square, and I think that may be the one that you are looking for. Just stay on this side of the road, and go past the entrance to the Forbidden City across the road, and Tiananmen Square on your right, and you will come to a strip of restaurants and businesses. You can't miss it."

"Thanks. Sorry if we disturbed you." The dark haired girl gestured across at the egg-shaped National Centre for the Performing Arts building. "It's an incredibly peaceful setting, set in the middle of this small shallow lake, with a park all around. Have you been inside?"

"No, as I said, I only been here a couple of days, and I've been a bit busy." He looked around. "How do you get in? I hope you don't have to wade through the lake."

"No." They laughed. "There's an impressive entrance just over there, and you walk down steps and through a passage under the water. You pop up inside the building. The interior is absolutely stunningly beautiful."

"You really should take a tour, it's amazing." The blond girl urged. "I'm Stefanie, by the way."

"And I'm Julie," the other girl added.

"Pleased to meet you. I'm Paul. Your English is excellent, but I suspect that there is a hint of a German accent?"

"Quite right." They exclaimed in unison. "We are from Karlsruhe, in southern Germany." Julie explained.

"I know it well." Paul said. "There's a research lab there that I have visited a number of times. How long are you staying in Beijing?"

"Just a few days, then we are off to Shanghai, or somewhere, we're not really sure yet. How about you?"

"I hope to be finished up in a day or so, and then I'll head back." He looked at his watch, and stood up. "Time I was going, I'm afraid."

"It was nice to have met you. You said the Chinese teahouse was this way?" Stefanie asked, pointing toward Tiananmen Square.

"Yes. I'm going that way, I can walk with you, and point it out, if you like?"

"That would be great."

They started down the road, with the girls chatting away happily about the visit to China, the first time they had ever visited anywhere in Asia. They explained that they both worked for Lufthansa, and so their tickets did not cost too much, and they got a great rate at their hotel.

Paul felt obliged to contribute to the conversation. "I'm staying at the Hyatt hotel, that is down the road a bit further."

"That's where we're staying." Julie exclaimed. "Lufthansa gets a special rate there, so it works out to be a pretty good deal, with the two of us sharing."

"It seems like a pretty good hotel, and it's central. My, er, partner has been here quite a few times. She knows the city quite well, so she booked the hotel and arranged everything. I don't know Beijing, at all. I just tagged along. If I wander too far away from this main road, Chang 'an Avenue, I'm lost." He groaned

"That's great, though." Stefanie enthused. "Your partner can show you around. This city is so huge and crowded, it is a bit overwhelming."

"Unfortunately, she had to leave early this afternoon, and head back. I still have a couple of things to do. It should be wrapped up, within the next forty-eight hours, then I'm heading out."

"What do you do?" Julie asked.

"I'm a physicist. I teach physics at the university, and do some research. Actually, I suppose I do more research than teaching."

"That's really interesting. I hope you're not a spy, or anything, you know, selling physics secrets to the Chinese?" She laughed.

"Good Heavens no. Why on earth would you think that?"

"Well, at home, we hear so much in the news about China stealing Western technology secrets, and everyone else spying on China with spy satellites, and things." The girls mocked serious expressions. "We don't want to get arrested for being seen with a foreign spy."

"No. I am just a boring university professor. No excitement here, I'm afraid." He managed a weak smile.

"That's a shame." Stefanie sighed. "From all of the stuff the media has reported, we thought there would be secret agents around every corner in Beijing."

"You can't believe everything that's reported in the media." Paul suggested.

"But, if you do happen to see Daniel Craig anywhere," Julie added, with a giggle. "I'm definitely interested."

They had reached the small commercial development, and Paul pointed out the row of businesses set back from the road.

"Here you are. That's the teahouse that I was talking about."

The two girls thanked him, shook his hand, in polite German fashion, and headed towards the teahouse. He decided to cross the road at the next set of traffic lights and walk beside the stream, along the linear park that led back to the hotel.

Back in his hotel room, a few hours later, Paul was working furiously when the phone rang. He made a quick check of the time, and knew that it was too early to be Tricia calling from Paris, during her stopover. He reluctantly answered it.

"Paul Berg."

"Ah, good, Professor Berg, glad that you are there." Paul recognized the voice of the Interpol man from the lift. "Everything went well. We've passed that test. They want to complete the rest of the transaction tomorrow night. The location will be the National Centre for the Performing Arts, where you were this afternoon, except it will be inside tomorrow evening. We insisted that the exchange take place there, because there will be a lot of people attending the various performances. We will be told the precise time later. Remember that the exchange of information must be completely satisfactory for the release of your daughter. Make sure that you are punctual, and ready with the material they have demanded."

"What about Nicky? How is she? I have to see a video, before I supply anything else."

"Agreed. That is essential. They have promised to send a video to your email tomorrow morning that will provide all the verification that you require."

"Videos can easily be doctored."

"Yes, I understand. That is why I insisted that you must be in phone contact with your brother for the transaction to proceed. He must confirm that he can see Nicky, and has spoken to her, and that she is well."

"That sounds acceptable, but I won't make my final decision until after I have seen the video." Paul reluctantly agreed.

"I understand. I'll contact you tomorrow with final details. Before you go, who were those two girls you were talking to this afternoon?"

"What?" Paul was shocked. "Are you having me watched?"

"It is for your own safety, Professor Berg. Someone has already tried to shoot you. There are people here who definitely don't have your best interests in mind. Who were those girls, and what were you talking to them about?"

"For Heaven's sake. They were simply two German tourists from Karlsruhe. They work for Lufthansa, and are visiting Beijing for a few days, before heading on, to Shanghai, I think they said. They asked me if I knew a traditional Chinese teahouse they had heard about that was close to Tiananmen Square. The only one I know is the one I went to with Tricia, and I told them where it was. We were both walking in the same direction, so we went together. That's all."

"Except, they didn't go into the teahouse, at all. As soon as you had left, they turned around and got in a taxi to go who knows where?"

"Well, perhaps they decided that they didn't like the look of the teahouse, or perhaps it was closed. Did your spies check for that?

"That's not the point. The point is that two women, who you have never met before, struck up a conversation with you. For your own safety, you must not do that."

"They were simply two young German tourists, that's all." Paul was getting exasperated. "They chattered away about the National Centre for the Performing Arts, and a couple of other innocuous things. They aren't spies, and they aren't out to kill me, or kidnap me. I appreciate that Interpol has a difficult job to do, but you have to accept that there really are ordinary people, living ordinary lives, doing ordinary everyday things. Now, I have some work to do to make sure that I have everything ready for tomorrow evening. Goodbye."

He settled at his computer again. He had a lot of work to do. He had ordered food, and a pot of coffee to keep him going. He had a long night ahead of him. It was probably going to take him all night, and most of tomorrow morning. It was the most challenging and important night's work he had ever faced.

He must succeed.

From nowhere, his mind conjured up the memory of Nancy's final words, as she lay in the hospital bed, with minutes of her life remaining. When she had opened her eyes for the last time, they were surprisingly bright. She had smiled at him and said, "I have to leave now, Paul, but when you need me, I will always be there to help you look after Nicky."

He closed his eyes, and whispered, "Nicky really needs you, Nancy. If you look after Nicky, and keep her safe, I will deal with the rest of this nonsense."

CHAPTER 28

In the elegant villa nestled amongst the vineyards and wineries of the Massif de la Clape, in southern France, the white haired woman was seated in her familiar red-cushioned cedar chair on the palatial veranda. It had been overcast, before the clouds had cleared, leaving a cool, clear evening. The old woman was wrapped in a brightly coloured wool shawl, with the red blanket across her legs: she did not permit the vagaries of weather to interfere with her Spring ritual of evening coffee on the veranda, where she could gaze at the view that reflected all she and her husband had achieved.

As was her custom, she did not acknowledge the arrival of her daughter, only gracing her with a glance, as she repositioned the vacant chair, and settled it into her angle of vision.

"What is the latest information, daughter?"

"Michael has informed Jasar that the project is nearing completion, Mother. All of the material will be delivered within the next twenty-four hours, on schedule with your plan. That will complete the Beijing project."

"Has Michael experienced any interference with the process, thus far?"

"He assured me that the expected interest from the Chinese authourities has been appropriately contained, and will present no obstacles."

"I presume that he has followed my instructions, and he has not compromised our position, at all?"

"Absolutely not, mother. He assured me that neither Paul Berg, nor the woman with him, is aware of his role. The only remaining step will be the exchange, and the release of the young Berg girl in France."

"What is the latest information from Sehrish in that regard?"

"Sehrish has performed exactly in accordance with your instructions, mother, and has provided daily reports on the condition of the girl. She has assured me that the girl has been heavily sedated, but remains in good physical condition. Anthony has been monitoring Sehrish's activity, and has not detected her activities attracting any undue attention. Once I receive confirmation that our client has received the material, and is satisfied, I will order Sehrish to remove the girl from the gite, and take her to Bordeaux, where she will be released."

"Sehrish is driving that garish gold coloured sports car?"

"Yes, mother."

"I hope that your information is correct, and that it has not attracted any unwanted attention."

"Anthony has discretely followed Sehrish, and confirmed that there has been no vehicle that has taken the same route as her on more than one occasion."

"So she was followed on at least one occasion?"

"There are not a great many roads in the area, mother, and naturally there will be other cars going along the same general route. She changed her route each time, and Anthony never saw the same vehicle following her on the different routes."

"Hmph. Keep me informed as the project is concluded, and bring Michael back from China the moment he is no longer required to be there. I will be glad when this is over."

"Of course, mother."

Once she had left the room, and was out of her mother's hearing, the woman muttered to herself. "Once this is over, I'm going to make sure that Sehrish is able to make her own choices, and lead her own life."

Behind her, the old woman heard her daughter muttering, and gave a grim smile. "I am still the head of this family." She asserted quietly to herself. "And they are all still my responsibility."

CHAPTER 29

Charles de Gaulle airport was an impressive complex of escalators enclosed in glass tubes in a confusing, futuristic pattern, criss-crossing through an open atrium. Tricia had managed to get a few hours sleep on the long flight, but the combination of jet lag and stress had started to take its toll. After she had battled her way through Customs, and the crowded main terminal, Tricia found that she had to race for what seemed miles, to get to the departure gate in time for her domestic flight to Bordeaux.

The flight arrived in Bordeaux just after ten thirty in the evening. Since the drive to Bergerac would take nearly two hours, Tricia opted to stay the night at a nearby hotel that the accommodating woman at the airport Tourism Desk found for her.

The next morning, Tricia was up early, but it was still approaching seven o'clock, by the time she had completed the car rental formalities, and loaded up the car with her and Nicky's suitcases. Finally, she was on her way to Bergerac, and feeling pretty good. The early morning traffic was heavy around the Bordeaux ring road, but once she had negotiated her way on to the Autoroute, the traffic largely disappeared, and it was an easy drive for the rest of the way.

Paul had kept his promise, and booked her a room at the hotel in Bergerac, where Matt was staying, but it would not be available for a few hours. She tried Matt's room, but there was no answer. It was nine thirty in the morning, Bergerac time, which would make it three thirty in the afternoon, in Beijing.

Tricia needed coffee. And something to eat. But mostly, she needed coffee. Strong coffee.

She wandered out of the hotel, and stood on the street, looking around for some sign of one of the famous French cafes, or bistros. It was a pleasant, sunny, spring morning, and coffee at a seat outside would help to blow the fog from her brain. She heard someone coming out of the hotel behind her, and turned to ask them if they knew where she could get a coffee and something to eat.

Tricia stared in disbelief. "I don't believe it. You're that CSIS woman who followed us to Beijing. What on earth are you doing here?" She gasped, and then added in a voice that tolerated no dispute. "We have to talk."

Michelle Denis stopped in surprise. "Yes, I think we do. The question is, what are you doing here?" She looked around. "Where is Paul Berg? Is he here? When did you arrive in Bergerac?"

"Paul is in Beijing. I arrived in Paris last night, and got here less than an hour ago. It has been a demanding twenty four hours, and I need coffee and food. Do you know a café somewhere, where we can have a quiet talk?"

"Yes, come on. I know a place. We can talk when we get there. It's only a short walk, if that's okay?"

"I can walk, thank you. Apart from being hungry, I feel great." Tricia gritted.

Michelle led the way to the bistro in the Place Palissiere, where there were several vacant tables: they quickly agreed on the one on its own, in one corner.

Tricia spoke first. "It seems like I've been travelling for days. I need a coffee, and some pastries, or something. My French is non-existent, unfortunately."

"I was born here. French is my first language. I can order for both of us, if you agree? How would you like your coffee, a small cup of strong black, or Americano, which is a large cup but weaker, with a little milk, or café crème, which means they will bring a jug of hot milk with your strong coffee in a large cup?" Michelle tried to sound cordial.

"Thanks. That would be great. I'll start with a small cup of strong black coffee, and some croissants, or whatever they have: any pastries will do. I would like a coffee cream, or whatever you called it, to follow the small, strong coffee."

Once the waiter had taken their order, Michelle was the first to speak. "I don't understand, Dr. Chen. How did you get here, and why did you leave Beijing?"

Tricia put up her hand to stop her. "Stop. No. You go first. You obviously know who I am, but I don't know your name, or what you were doing following Paul and me to Beijing, and now showing up here. Who are you?"

Michelle nodded. "Bien. Okay. I will break the glass."

"I think you mean 'break the ice'."

"Ah, yes. Thank you." She smiled. "I still have difficulty with the English sayings. My name is Michelle Denis, and I am a senior agent with Interpol."

"You're not with CSIS? From Canada?" Tricia asked, surprised.

"No. I'm not sure what gave you and Professor Berg that idea. I was assigned to monitor Professor Berg on the flight from Vancouver to Beijing, following the abduction of his daughter, Nicky. Interpol believes that Nicky Berg was abducted to coerce Paul and Matt Berg to hand over all of their medical research, regarding a medical protein string. There is also information that young Nicky Berg has been moved from one national legal jurisdiction to another, namely from Beijing to France. The fact that there are several countries involved has brought the various crimes under the umbrella of Interpol, in collaboration with the national police forces, of course."

"Interpol? Could I see your identification?" Tricia's tone made it clear that it was not a request.

"But certainly." Michelle pulled her Interpol identification pouch out of her pocket, and pushed it across the table, with a perplexed frown. She was even more puzzled as Tricia scrutinized the identification intently, and then tested the card, apparently to make sure that it was the genuine article.

"It seems genuine." Tricia shook her head. "I don't understand. Don't you people in Interpol communicate with one another?"

"What are you talking about? What other people?"

"That couple in Beijing who have taken over from Paul. The man and woman who are going to impersonate Paul and me. They didn't give their names."

The flicker of surprise that crossed Michelle's features was quickly hidden by a coffee cup.

"Of course. That couple. We had a busy time, yesterday evening, and I have not been brought fully up to date with the Beijing operation, yet. Why don't you tell me exactly what happened?" She gave a friendly, collaborative smile. "That way, I will be better prepared, when I speak to my boss later today. Where did you meet the team, on the first occasion?"

Tricia took a deep breath. "We only met them once, and it was a bit bizarre. We were having breakfast in the shopping mall that adjoins the Hyatt hotel, when Paul had got a message to bring the proof of principal material to one of the stores, in the next forty minutes. There was enough time, but we had to hurry to our rooms to collect the material. When we got to our rooms, my room had a notice saying that it was out of service, with a plumbing problem. Paul gathered up the material, and we raced back and got in the lift. As you can appreciate, we were totally preoccupied, and didn't pay any attention to the three people already in the lift I don't know exactly, but I think it was around the fourth floor that the man with his back to us, who was operating the lift, suddenly stopped it between floors. That's when we discovered that the other occupants were Mr. Renshu, the Beijing police or Intelligence officer, or whatever he is, and a couple about our age, an Asian woman and a Caucasian man. They identified themselves as Interpol agents, and knew all about Nicky and the exchange. They said that because of the shooting in the park on the previous day, they were going to take over the actual physical exchange, pretending that they were Paul and me. They looked a bit like us, and as they pointed out, the other side had never actually met either of us.

"They said that Paul had to stay, to gather up all of the required material, and provide any technical answers that might be required. They told me to change clothes with the woman. She had packed all my clothes and things from my room into my suitcase. She was the 'plumber' that had kept me out of my room while she did it."

"Wait. You and the woman changed clothes in the lift?"

"Yes."

"Mon Dieu. You're right. That was bizarre. Why not use Paul's hotel room?" Michelle muttered. "Okay. Go on."

"Paul and the man were both wearing blue jeans and a blue shirt, so they already looked alike from a distance. The man did give Paul his maroon jacket, and a blue baseball cap. They told us that there was a car waiting to take us to the airport, and my passport and tickets to Bordeaux were in the pocket of the suitcase. Nicky's suitcase was also already in the car. I was to come to Bergerac, and be here for the release of Nicky, which would be in the next forty-eight hours. It would help if Nicky saw a friendly face, when she is released, plus I am a pediatrician. So here I am. What's your story?"

"Thanks. That is certainly an interesting account." Michelle said pensively. "That will really help when I speak to my boss." She looked at her watch, and pulled a face. "Which I should have done fifteen minutes ago." She jumped up. "Sorry, I have to dash. Meet me outside the hotel at noon, and I should be able to put everything into perspective, for you. This promises to be a busy day."

"Where's Matt Berg, do you know?" Tricia called after the retreating figure.

"I haven't seen him today." Michelle called back, as she moved swiftly across the square, past the statue of Cyrano de Bergerac, and up the wide stone steps. Once out of sight of Tricia, she broke into a run.

CHAPTER 30

Michelle hurried back to her hotel room to relate Tricia's strange story to the Head of Operations. This was a crucial day in the entire operation, and if Tricia's story were correct, it would have major ramifications on how the remainder of the day would be played out.

The first question from the Head of Operations was the one that Michelle expected.

"It is a bit of a coincidence that this Chen woman should show up, there, today. Do you believe her?"

"Yes, ma'am, I do. She did not give any of the usual signals that she was making any of it up. I checked, and she did arrive in Bordeaux last night on the Air France flights from Beijing via Paris, and stayed at an airport hotel overnight. She rented a car this morning, at the airport, and the hotel here, in Bergerac, confirmed that she walked in to the lobby at around nine this morning. What is the word from Beijing? Do the reports from our team corroborate her story from that end?"

"Well, we obviously didn't have anyone in the hotel lift to corroborate that curious part of the story. My take is that that was a control technique to persuade Berg and her to comply with their plan. The reports from Beijing do bear out most of the other parts. At any time, did you have eyes on a couple that resembled the man and woman that Chen described?

"No, ma'am, I did not. They sound like professionals, so

they would have made sure that they were absorbed into the background, until it came time to make their move."

"Yes, indeed." The Head of Operations said thoughtfully. "The way this whole business is evolving certainly suggests that it was following a plan, but that the kidnappers are now having to improvise. The crucial first step was to arrange to have Nicky Berg's soccer team invited to the tournament in Beijing. Everything flowed from there: the kidnapping that forced Paul Berg to fly to Beijing: the fast move of Nicky Berg to France, another legal jurisdiction: the strange events in Beihai Park that confirmed the group was actually holding Nicky, and provided a warning to Berg that he was being watched. Then there was the shooting at the Summer Palace, and that was when they seemed to lose their plan. On the following day Renshu was involved, when they made the bizarre move in the lift to convince Berg and Chen to have two apparent 'Interpol agents' take their places, and handle all of the Bergs' material, allegedly, on their behalf."

"Yes ma'am. I agree. Whatever happens, I am not even sure what criminal charges can be presented here in France. The kidnapping did not take place here, and anyone involved here can claim that they have simply been looking after a sick young girl. That is if she is found alive. If she is not, then there is no record of why she is even in France, and no apparent motive for anyone to have killed her. I had the impression that thought has been bothering Matt Berg."

"Where is Matt Berg?"

"I don't know where he is at the moment, ma'am. I haven't seen him since he dropped me off outside the hotel, thirty-six hours ago. However, I expect him to resurface at any time."

"Is he going to be a problem? If you think he is, then he must be removed from the active arena."

"I understand, ma'am. If there is any sign of a problem, he will be restrained, and promptly removed."

"Back to the Chen woman, can we use her to replace the opposition player, who we have identified there in Bergerac? She *is* a physician."

Michelle thought for a few moments. "That is a good idea, ma'am. She would have to understand the situation and agree. From my brief exposure to Chen in Beijing, and here, I think she would be able to pull it off. And she is motivated. That would strengthen that part of the plan. The key opposition player was secured late yesterday evening, and is being contained. She admitted everything immediately, tearfully claiming that she was pressured by her family to be involved. She claims that she had no idea that the Berg girl had been kidnapped. She insists that she was told that the girl was being prepared for a major surgery, and that she was in hiding because her religious family opposed it. There is clearly a risk involved in having her go back to the gite this afternoon. Introducing Chen as her replacement would reduce that risk."

"Chen has done a lot of traveling in the past twenty-four hours, a key factor is whether she physically and mentally fit enough to carry it out."

"I confirmed that she had stayed in a Bordeaux airport hotel last night. She seemed in good physical shape, ma'am, and was definitely mentally alert, when we met this morning."

"You're meeting with her again at noon. Lay out the operation that we have planned for later today. Make sure that she understands the seriousness of the situation. Explain the role that she would have, and, if she is willing to take it on, determine if you are completely confident that she will be able to do it. If you don't think that she will be able to handle the pressures and risks, then stop at that point. Do not press her.

However, in that case, she will have to be securely sidelined until the operation has been completed. If you judge that she is willing and able, she will need a compressed briefing. She should meet the opposition player that she will replace." She paused. "Are you comfortable making this last minute adjustment?"

"Yes, ma'am, perfectly comfortable."

"Good. Make sure that Chen and the Berg girl have vests. The support team will be in place this afternoon."

"Has there been any sign of a local presence, ma'am?"

"We have not detected any indication of local watchers, which is a bit disconcerting, given the circumstances. However, we can't be sure, since the precise location was not confirmed until yesterday, so we must be prepared. I am having second thoughts about the identity of the initiator of this whole action, but whoever it is, they may not want to leave any loose ends." She paused. "I will be happier when I know where Matt Berg is. We don't want him running around on some solo action."

"Yes, ma'am. I understand. I will make sure that Matt Berg does not disrupt the operation."

"Good. It is crucial that we coordinate the timing of actions between Bergerac and Beijing. A private plane will be waiting for you, at Bergerac airport, from eighteen hundred hours this evening: you will escort Nicky and Matt Berg to Paris, and on from there. The ongoing arrangements are in place. A courier will be waiting for you with the usual package, when you reach Paris."

"Will Dr. Chen be travelling with us, now that she has shown up here, ma'am?"

"Yes, Chen must go with you. I will have her added to the

passenger lists. I would like you to stay with the others in Paris, Michelle, provided that does not create an issue for you?"

"How long will I stay with them, and what will my role be?"

"You will escort them on the flight, provide the local team with a full briefing, and return to Lyon on the next flight. I have arranged for a doctor to provide assistance to Nicky Berg, and a small team to take over liaison, and security. They will really have mostly social responsibilities. I do not expect any problems, but they will be prepared to deal with it, as required."

"Thank you, ma'am. That should present no conflict with my personal commitments. When can I expect Paul Berg to arrive?"

"According to the operational schedule, he will arrive in Paris on the Air France flight early tomorrow morning."

"Very good, ma'am. I should go and meet with Dr. Chen, and explain the situation. I am reasonably confident that she will want to take the role. She is an impressive woman."

"Yes. Good luck, Michelle. Check in again, when you all get on the flight to Paris."

CHAPTER 31

Tricia was pacing back and forth, impatiently, on the pavement outside the hotel, when Michelle arrived. She strode across to meet her.

"Good. You're here. I want to know exactly what is going on. First and foremost, do you know where Nicky Berg is? Is she safe, and unharmed?" She demanded.

"Come on, let's walk to that café again, where we were this morning. It's not far, the tables are spaced far enough apart to have a private conversation, and we really should both have something to eat. It's going to be a long day."

When they reached the café, Michelle pointed to an unoccupied table that was on its own, beside a flowerbed. Once they were settled, Michelle started to explain. "Yes, we know where Nicky Berg is being held, and we have been assured that she is reasonably well, safe and unharmed."

"What? You know where she is, and you have not rescued her? Why on earth not?" Tricia gasped.

"Please, Dr. Chen, Patricia, let me finish. There is a lot to go through, and very little time. We identified where Nicky was being held the night before last, and confirmed yesterday that she is currently there. I have to say that Matt Berg was very helpful in locating her.

"This afternoon, we are mounting an operation, both here and in Beijing, to conclude this entire business. Because of the way that both Nicky's abduction, and the demands for Paul's and Matt's material have been planned, there has to be coordinated, precise timing in our actions in both places. It is believed that the objective of everything that has happened is to obtain sole possession of the results from Paul and Matt Berg's medical research.

"We have located a young doctor who was sent to Bergerac to look after Nicky: she has assured us that Nicky is sedated, but in good health."

"Who the Hell is this young doctor? I hope that you have her locked up."

"We have had her confined since yesterday evening. She claims that she had no knowledge of, and absolutely no part in Nicky's abduction, and that, when she arrived in Bergerac, she received a message to look after the girl, who was waiting for a major operation. She showed us the message that she received, and has cooperated with us, but denies that she knows anything more about the situation involving the young girl. That is where you come in."

"Me?" Tricia puzzled. "What can I do?"

"The gite where Nicky has been held is owned by a couple who are currently living at their home in England. They simply rented it for a month, over the Internet, to what they believed to be a respectable Canadian family, and know nothing about the actual tenants, or Nicky. An old woman was hired from the local town to take meals to the gite each day. She has been told that Nicky is waiting for an operation, and needs rest for a week or so, to gain some strength. The only other people who are ever at the gite are an older woman who stays in the gite with Nicky, and has been told the same story as the woman who brings the food, and the young doctor who we have apprehended: she visited Nicky every afternoon, to check on her, and confirm her sedation."

"That hardly sounds like much of an obstacle. I still don't see why you haven't just initiated a police raid, and rescued Nicky." Tricia protested.

"Because Paul was told that Nicky would not survive any rescue attempt that was made before they receive all of Paul's and Matt's research material." Michelle explained patiently. "He was also assured that Nicky would be released once it has been confirmed that the material that he has handed over contains everything that they have demanded."

"I still don't get it. Paul and Matt are quite willing to hand over whatever the kidnappers want."

Michelle took a deep breath. "This is where it gets unpleasant. It is unlikely that the kidnappers will want Paul or Matt to reproduce their research work, once this is over."

It took Tricia a minute or two to grasp the implications of of what Michelle had said. "Oh my God." She gasped. "I know what you are trying to say. Paul and I went through this. You are afraid that the kidnappers have a 'scorched earth' plan. As soon as they have everything they want, they plan to kill Paul and Matt, and most likely Nicky as well."

"That is our current concern." Michelle agreed somberly.

"You seem to have a plan, what do you want me to do?"

"At nine o'clock this evening in Beijing, Paul will hand over all of the material they have demanded to the intermediary group. They will examine the material for one hour. If it is deemed complete, at around four o'clock this afternoon our time, here, they have instructed the young doctor to take Nicky from the gite, and drive her to Bordeaux."

"Bordeaux? I don't understand. I thought the whole point of Matt Berg being here in Bergerac was to hand Nicky over to him here?"

"The doctor has told us that, yesterday, she was instructed to reach Bordeaux between six and six thirty, a busy time, where Nicky will be left at a location to be specified later, in or near the city, with a note attached to her, saying who she is, and to contact the police."

Tricia's face went taut. "You don't believe that will actually happen, do you?"

"We simply don't know what to believe. We have to be prepared for the worst case scenario."

"What about me? Why am I here with Matt?" She stared at Michelle. "They want Matt and me together. Good Lord. What do you want me to do?" Tricia asked huskily.

"We want you to take the place of the young doctor. If there is anyone watching her, you have a similar build, and in her clothes, no one will notice the substitution. You will drive her car up to the gite at three fifteen, in exactly the same way that the regular doctor has been told to do, and stop right in front of the door. We have sketches and photos to show you exactly where to stop. It is four strides from the car to the door, so you will have the cottage in front of you, and the car behind you blocking the lines of sight."

"Wait a minute, I can't do that. I only arrived in France last night, and I don't know my way around this area at all. All I've done is drive here from Bordeaux airport, following the directions that a chap at the rental company put into the car's GPS for me. Thankfully, he also switched it to English."

"There will be a blue Citroen sedan guide car. You just have to follow it. If anything should go wrong, and you lose the guide car, the directions will also be given to you by your GPS, and you will have an ear bud, so that I will be in contact with you all the way. Once you reach the village, the gite itself is easily identified by the sign, 'Santuaire Paisible', at the entrance to the driveway."

"What about the woman who is staying at the gite? She will see immediately that I am not the young doctor."

"According to the doctor, once the old woman who brings the food has left, she has been instructed to clean the gite this morning, to remove all traces of their presence, and will leave early this afternoon. She will not be there when Nicky is removed. You will simply have to walk in to the cottage, collect Nicky Berg, take her out into the car, and drive away."

"How certain are you that Nicky will be the only person in the gite, when I get there?"

"As soon as the young doctor confirmed Nicky's location, we had a drone overhead, with an infrared camera to provide us with the number and location of people inside.

"I want to be as precise as possible. Once I am in the cottage, the jeet, or whatever you call it, then what? Do you know where Nicky is?"

"Yes. The doctor confirmed the images from the drone. She is straight down the short passage, in the back bedroom, on the right. She was seen moving yesterday evening, and the doctor told us that she is usually starting to come out of the sedation, when she gets there. Nicky will be quite groggy, but may recognize you. If she does, that will be a help."

"I could give her an injection of adrenaline, to provide a boost."

"Good idea. You're the doctor. Tell me exactly what you want, and we will get it for you."

"Okay. What else?"

"There will be a set of clean clothes for Nicky: underwear, jeans, casual shoes, socks, shirt, sweater and jacket, in a bag that I will give you. You will have an earpiece, and I will be in constant communication with you. You will be wearing a vest, and have one in your bag, for Nicky."

"Hold on. What do you mean, we'll be wearing vests? Are you telling me that we will be wearing a bulletproof vest? You think that we might be shot at?" Tricia's voice had gone noticeably higher.

"No, no. Not at all. It's just standard procedure whenever there is the possibility of hostile involvement. In this case, we have not detected their presence. If there is the slightest sign of any opposition activity, we have people positioned to immediately deal with it. We just want to be ultra cautious. At precisely three forty-five, you will leave the gite with Nicky, get her into the passenger seat, and drive directly to Bergerac airport. The blue Citroen sedan will be waiting outside the gite when you leave. Follow that car. It will guide you along the D27, through Moliere to Lalinde. When you get to Lalinde, the road goes around the downtown, past a small lake. Opposite the lake is a parking area, in front of a hotel. The blue sedan will pull in there, and you will follow it in, and switch to another car. They will lead you to the Bergerac airport, and Matt and I will meet you there. The sports car will be taken back to its usual parking space in the town."

"That sounds pretty straight forward. Apart from the car change in Lalinde, I am just going in to the empty gite, collecting Nicky, and following a lead car to the airport."

"Remember, precise timing is essential. We are coordinating with the time that Paul hands over the material in Beijing, which means that you must leave the gite at precisely three forty-five, unless you receive other instructions."

"Got it. Wait. Hold on. I don't understand. Paul isn't handing over the material, the Interpol agent from the hotel lift is taking his place for that. Paul is just there to provide technical assistance."

Michelle pursed her lips. "Unfortunately, the two people that you encountered in the lift are not associated with Interpol. It was another clever ploy. Paul believes that he is handing the material to this man who will then act in his stead, in delivering it to the next party. In fact, that *is* the delivery. This way, Paul believes that he is not directly in the loop, and he is likely to tell the false Interpol agent if there are any problems with the material that he is giving to them."

"But Paul will have spent some time face to face with the fake Interpol agent, and will be able to describe, and identify, him? Oh. That confirms your assessment." Tricia whispered.

"Yes, I'm afraid it does. That is why there is only a small window of time between when he hands over the material, and when the other side is still in the process of determining that they are satisfied with it. That is when Paul must be removed from the situation, and at the precise same time, you must remove Nicky from the gite. If Paul is removed too soon, they will have time to direct that action be taken against Nicky, similarly, if we went in with a raid, and Nicky is removed too soon, Paul would be placed in extreme danger."

"That is your plan? What if there is an unexpected delay, at either end, Beijing or here? Everything will turn into a total disaster?"

"That will not be allowed to happen. I will be in constant radio contact with you, and we will be in constant contact with the Beijing team that is looking after Paul. Yes, there really is an Interpol team close to Paul, just not the couple you encountered in the lift."

"Okay, so you have a plan that sounds pretty solid, but what is the fallback position?"

"What do you mean?"

"Well, Nicky and I are supposed to meet up with you and Matt at the airport, where you have a private plane to take us to Paris. Supposing something happens to one of us. You, know, a car breaks down, or there is an accident on the road, and we can't get through, what do we do?"

"Right. Good point." Michelle says thoughtfully. "If these plans have to change for any reason, I'll contact you with alternate arrangements."

"Okay. I suppose that sounds like a reasonable backup plan."

"However," Michelle said with a reassuring smile, "All you have to do is drive up to the gite, and go in and get young Nicky out, and into the car. It is just a normal, everyday pick up, and I have no doubt that everything is going to work exactly as planned, and we will all meet up at Bergerac airport, at five thirty this evening."

"Yes, of course. I am just being overly cautious. So what do we do now?"

"I will take you to meet the young doctor whose place you will be taking. Her name is Sehrish, she comes from a wealthy and respected family, and has recently returned from working in Africa with Medecins sans Frontieres. As one physician to another, you will explain that if she is prosecuted for her involvement in Nicky's kidnapping, she will go to jail for a long time, and never be allowed to practice medicine again. However, if she fully cooperates, and tells you everything that you need to know, and you are able to pick up Nicky successfully, she will be transported back to her prior location in Africa, and there will be no charges against her."

"What choice does she have, faced with that?" Tricia snorted.

"We hope she understands that." Michelle looked at her watch. "One irritating issue is that we don't know where Matt Berg is."

"I think I can help you there." Tricia remarked. "He is just coming down the steps behind you."

Michelle turned around, and waved Matt over, with a sigh of relief. "Matt, come and join us. Tricia arrived this morning. We've been looking for you."

"Hi Michelle. Hi Tricia. What are you doing here?" He looked around. "Is Paul here, as well?"

"Hi Matt. No, Paul is still in Beijing. It's a long story. Where have you been? You look like you haven't slept in days."

"Yes, well, it has been a while. Paul and I have come up with an idea about our research. I chartered a flight to Lyon, to discuss it with an old colleague of ours, at the Faculty of Medicine."

"Sorry, Matt, but we absolutely don't have time at the moment." Michelle interjected firmly. "We picked up the young doctor, last evening, after she had been to check on Nicky, at the gite. You were right: it was at the cottage called 'Santuaire Paisible', near the Cloister of Cadouin. She has been quite helpful. Tricia is going to interview her, right now, and then, at two thirty this afternoon, Tricia is driving to the gite in place of the doctor, and bringing Nicky out. They will drive to Bergerac airport, where you and I will join them. We will all leave, on a private plane, at five thirty tonight for Paris, and then on from there."

"Whoa. Looks like I'm back just in time. I have to go and grab my stuff."

"Good point, Matt. I will have to pack up my things, as well."

"You don't need to worry about that, Tricia. We'll look after that for you. Your luggage, and Nicky's, will be with me, waiting for you at the airport."

Matt gave Michelle a worried look. "What about Paul?"

"It's a really tight schedule. Paul must be brought out at exactly the same time as Nicky. Timing is crucial. Come on, Tricia, you've got to go and have a talk with young Doctor Sehrish."

"One thing, Michelle, when Tricia springs Nicky, I'm going to be right there with you, wherever you are." Matt stated. "We can go to the airport together, to meet Nicky and Tricia."

Michelle took Tricia to a small cottage, where a very distraught Sehrish was locked in, with female guards. Michelle explained that, under Interpol security protocols, she had recorded, but not been physically present at the earlier questioning conducted by Interpol interrogators. As soon as she saw Tricia, Sehrish blurted out an apology, insisting that she had no idea that she was involved in a kidnapping. She explained that a doctor had heard she was back in the country, and contacted her, asking her to look after a girl who was awaiting heart surgery. His letter had said that the girl's mother wanted to return her daughter to a religious cult, where she believed that prayer would cure her. Because Sehrish did not have an established practice, she could attend to the girl without attracting attention from the mother, or anyone helping her.

Tricia sat in the armchair opposite her, and talked to her quietly, gradually getting Sehrish to calm down. Her English was good, and she was visibly shaken, as Tricia explained the difficult situation that Sehrish was in, and how her best chance to avoid the loss of her medical licence, was if she cooperated totally. Sehrish promised that she would do anything they asked.
Michelle interjected that Tricia would need some of her clothes, and the use of her car. The young woman agreed instantly, telling Tricia to take anything she wanted. Sehrish's hands shook so badly, as she fumbled for her car's key fob that

she dropped it, in her haste to give it to Tricia.

Tricia made the young woman go carefully through every detail of the house, and the room where Nicky was being held. Sehrish reassured them that, as far as she knew, there was no one watching the gite, and it should be simple for Tricia to drive up, park the car, and go inside and collect Nicky. Yes, the young girl was in good physical condition, and would be only half awake, and a bit confused, just as if she was coming out of a long, deep sleep. Tricia asked the name of the drug that she had given to Nicky, and noted that with some adrenaline she should fully recover quite quickly, and there should be no lasting effects.

"What clothes do you usually wear, when you go to the gite?"

"It's only been four days. I've been wearing pretty much the same thing, each time. Dark blue wool pants, a white shirt, and a casual, maroon light jacket. That's sort of my unofficial medical outfit. All my stuff has been brought here: it's in the suitcases somewhere. There are several pairs of pants, and about five shirts." She gave Tricia a quick assessment. "We are close to the same size: you might have to roll up the pant legs a bit. I put my clothes to be washed in a white bag. The rest are clean. Take your pick."

Satisfied that she had all of the information that she needed, Tricia turned to leave. "I'm sorry that you got involved in this, Sehrish. It should all be over in a day or so, and, as long as everything is as you described, I will ask that you be sent back to Africa. I suggest that you stay there for a couple of years, and let this all blow over."

"Thank you. I can't wait to get away from all of this. I just want to be in Africa, and start being a doctor again, doing something useful. The people I worked with there are absolutely fantastic."

Tricia detected a flicker of warmth, when Sehrish spoke of her co-workers in Africa.

"Is there someone special in Africa, perhaps?" She asked softly.

Sehrish looked down shyly. "There is a French Canadian doctor; Antoine." She hesitated. "We became very close. I miss him terribly. He asked me to move to Quebec with him, but my family ordered me back to France."

"Is he in Quebec, now?"

"No. When I told him that I was leaving for France, he decided to stay on in Africa."

Tricia gave her a warm smile. "You love him, don't you? Go back to Africa, and if it is right, go with him. You have your whole life ahead of you, Sehrish. You were coerced into doing something you would never have agreed to. You are an intelligent young woman. From here on you must make your own decisions, and do what you want to do. It's your life."

"Thank you. You have been very understanding, particularly considering what I have done. Now, please, you must go and rescue that young girl. What we did to her and her family is unforgiveable."

"Her name is Nicky: she is very special to me. I will get her out." She turned, rattling the key fob as she and Michelle reached the door. "One last thing. I take it there is nothing unusual about your car? It looks like a pretty fancy sports job? Anything I should know?"

"No. It looks really sharp, but it operates just like any other four speed stick shift. Third gear can whine a bit at high revs, but the dealer told me that's normal for that ratio. Apart from that, there's nothing unusual."

As soon as she was outside the room, Tricia grabbed Michelle's arm. "There's a problem."

"What is it?"

"I can't drive her car. I've never driven a stick shift. I would be foolish for me to attempt it, now. Plus, if there is anyone watching, it will be obvious that it's not Sehrish driving."

"Oh, merde." Michelle groaned. "Okay. We need another car. An automatic. The only automatics I know of are rental cars. Every French woman can drive a stick shift."

"Well, I'm not a French woman." Tricia snapped. "I've got a rental, it's a BMW, with automatic. I could use that, but it won't be the fancy gold sports car, if anyone is watching."

"It will have to do. Where is it?" Michelle asked brusquely

"I parked it in one of the hotel's parking spaces, when I arrived this morning. The keys are on the desk, in my hotel room. I'll have to go back and get them."

"There isn't time. We have to go over the route to the gite where Nicky Berg is being held. I'll call Matt, and tell him to get the keys, and bring the car here for you."

"How will he get into my room?"

"One of our people is already in there, packing up your things. I'll call Matt."

Matt called back to confirm that he had the keys, and had located the car. He said that he was bringing it to them, and should be at their location in about ten minutes.

Michelle sighed. "Okay, that's solved." She checked her watch. "We don't have much time. We have to get you on your way. Let's get you into some of Sehrish's clothes. I also want to go over your route with you, so that you have an idea of where you are heading." Michelle tried for a reassuring smile. "You'll do fine. Just follow our blue Citroen sedan guide car. I'll inform them of your change of cars."

CHAPTER 32

Tricia followed the blue Citroen sedan in her BMW rental, out of Bergerac, and along the main road, beside the Dordogne River. The sky was grey overcast, with the promise of rain later in the evening. They trailed along in a line of steady traffic through the series of small villages, until they entered Lalinde, where they made their way slowly along the congested one-way road through the town.

She was right behind the blue guide car, when it had to stop for the traffic light, at the intersection for the bridge across to the south side of the river. She realized that must be where Michelle had explained that the road would go around Lalinde on the way back, and somewhere along there, they would change cars in the parking lot opposite a small lake. The lights changed, and she followed the Citroen as it made a right turn across the bridge over the Dordogne River.

The traffic thinned on the other side, and it was easy driving along the winding roads of the rural countryside, only slowing as they passed through the small villages scattered on the rolling hills of the area. She saw a sign to Moliere, and remembered that was the village that Michelle had said they would go through on the way back. The gite where Nicky was being held was not far now, and Tricia started to feel the tension building in her stomach. She took some deep breaths, and tried to relax. What was she expected to do if there was someone with Nicky in the gite? What sort of shape was Nicky in, after being sedated for days?

Matt had given Tricia a long hug before she left. When she had finally pulled away, her forehead was damp from his tears.

"Bring Nicky back to us, safe and sound, Tricia." He had whispered. "You can do it, if anyone can."

She clenched her jaw, and tightened her grip on the steering wheel. Matt was right. She could do it, and, by God, she would.

"You're getting close. Just stay calm. We are with you all the way. It's just a simple pick up. Nothing to it."

Tricia jerked in surprise at the sound of Michelle's voice in her ear, sending the car momentarily across the centerline of the road, before she quickly corrected. She felt for the earpiece in her right ear, out of sight under her pixie cut hair.

"You gave me quite a start, there, Michelle. Can you hear me okay? The blue guide car is right in front of me. I can see the sign for Cloister de Cadouin just ahead, and the first houses are coming into sight."

"I can hear you perfectly. How do you feel?"

"Nervous. Don't worry. I can do it. If there are any problems, I'll let you know. Where is your backup team?"

"We don't want to put on too much of a show, in case there is anyone watching, so they have stayed out of sight. Don't worry, the team is in place nearby, if it should be required."

"Do you think there will be any problems?"

"No, we don't think so, but it can never be totally ruled out. Remember to drive right up to the front door, that way, if there is anyone watching, you will look a lot like Sehrish."

"Apart from the strikingly different car."

"Well, yes, apart from that. They'll probably think that she has changed cars, as a security measure. Have the key ready."

"It's in my pocket. There's the gite. I can see the sign 'Santuaire Paisible' at the start of the driveway. Here we go. I'm a bit early."

Tricia slowed as she turned up the short driveway, and pulled around easily in the gravel courtyard, and up to the front door. She grabbed the bag that Michelle had given her, from the back seat, and made the three steps to the front door, forcibly ignoring her trembling knees. She rapped on the door, and waited. Relieved that there was no sound from inside. She managed to put the key into the lock with only a slight fumble. She pushed the door open, stepped inside, and closed it behind her.

The silence was eerie. She called out, 'Bonjour'. That was all the French she knew. No response. She looked around. It was a simple cottage: as the young doctor had described, there was an open door to the living room beside her, and two doors opposite, to the dining area and kitchen. She peered in the living room. Nothing. Everything was clean and tidy, as though no one had been there. Good. Exactly as Michelle had predicted.

Dining room? Tricia froze. There was a woman sitting at the table with her back to her. Tricia's legs felt like jelly.

"Bonjour." She managed to croak out again.

The woman did not move.

She tried again, louder. "Bonjour."

Nothing.

Tricia's mind was racing. Was the woman asleep? What was she supposed to do? Hit her over the head? Her hands were shaking, and she would probably miss her head entirely. She was a doctor: whacking people over the head when they were asleep was definitely not part of her medical training.

"Calm down, and think, Tricia." She commanded herself silently. "You took that Women's Self-defense course. You can handle an overweight middle-aged French woman. And you're wearing a bullet-proof vest. Confront her."

She walked around to face the woman, just as Michelle's voice burst into her ear. "What's happening, Tricia? Speak to me."

"You told me that the woman was going to leave the gite. She's still here." She hissed.

"Do you need assistance?"

"No. She's dead."

"Are you sure?"

"Of course I'm bloody sure. I'm a doctor." She snapped back quietly.

"Mon Dieu! You didn't kill her, did you?"

"No, of course I didn't bloody well kill her. She was dead when I got here. She's slumped at the table: it looks like a heart attack. There's a note in French in front of her. I can't read French."

"Can you send a picture of the note to me?"

"Okay. Here it comes."

"Where's Nicky? Has she seen the dead woman? If she hasn't, close the door, and don't say anything about it. I'll send a cleanup team."

"I haven't heard anything from Nicky. I'm just going to find her."

Tricia pulled the door to the dining area closed tight, and, heart pounding, she made her way down the passage to the bedrooms at the back. She glanced in the bathroom as she passed: toilet, washbasin, and shower, sparkling clean and empty. She pushed open the last door on the right.

There she was. Nicky was lying in the bed, squinting at her, looking totally bewildered.

"What's happening? Is she there?" Blasted into Tricia's ear.

"What? Yes." Tricia swallowed hard, and took a deep breath. "She's here: she's here. She's looking at me." She gasped.

"Good. Stay calm, Tricia. Nicky is counting on you."

"Yes. I've got it." Tricia gritted quietly. She smiled at the girl in the bed. "Hi Nicky. How are you doing?"

"Tricia? Tricia? Is that really you?" Nicky rasped.

"Yes, Sweetie, it's really me. How do you feel?"

Nicky closed her eyes tight, then opened them again, and blinked a couple of times. "Really, confused. Like really, totally confused. What's happening? Where am I? The doctor and the other woman wouldn't tell me. Where are they?"

"They've gone. I'm here to take you home." Tricia dropped the bag on the floor, and ran over to give Nicky a hug. She sat back, wiping away the tears that had filled her eyes. Her pediatrician experience took over. "Let me look at you. Your pupils are dilated. Let's see if you can follow my finger." She held her forefinger in front of Nicky's eyes, and moved it slowly from side to side. Her eyes followed a bit, stopped, then jerked back to the finger.

"Okay, not too bad. Can you sit up?"

"I don't know. I think so." Nicky pushed her legs out from under the bedcovers. "Can you give me a bit of a hand?" Tricia reached an arm around her shoulders: Nicky was several inches taller than her, but between them, Nicky managed to sit on the edge of the bed. "Pretty wobbly, but I'm up. Sort of."

"Well done, Nicky. You're doing great."

"Sorry, Tricia, I just can't help it." She tried to wipe away the tears that had started to stream down her face. "It's been really difficult. That doctor woman kept injecting me, just as I started to sort of wake up. I knew that it would make me go back to sleep. I hated it. I was so scared. Each time I thought that this time I would never wake up again. And now you're here. I just want to go home. I've missed Dad and you so much, and Jake." She added with a weak smile.

"That's okay, Nicky. I understand. What you have been through must have been absolutely awful. Why don't you just sit on the side of the bed for a moment? I've got an injection in my bag here that will wake you up and clear your head."

"What? No. No. No more injections, Tricia, please. Please don't." Nicky started to shake, and sob uncontrollably. "I don't want to go back to sleep again."

"I promise you, Nicky, this one will wake you up, and help clear your head. I don't want you to go to sleep again, either. I want you wide awake."

"Honestly, Tricia?"

"Honestly, Nicky. Please trust me. Ready? Here we go. It will just take a minute or two."

"How is she, Tricia?" Michelle asked quietly.

"Pretty good. Pretty good, aren't you Nicky?"

"Yes. I think so. Hey, my head is, sort of, starting to clear a bit. Whoa. That feels way better. Nowhere near perfect, but better." She managed a weak grin. "My legs still feel like wet noodles. Where are we, Tricia. What's happening? There were two women here. Are they still here?" She looked around nervously.

"No, no. They're gone."

"It's all a bit fuzzy, sort of like a bad dream." She sniffed, and wiped her eyes. "More like a nightmare. I thought they were speaking another language. Not Chinese, though. I sort of thought it was French." She stared down at the flannel nightie that she was wearing, and pulled a face. "Not too cute, huh? Where did this come from?"

Tricia reached into her bag. "Okay, Nicky, here are some clean clothes. I want you to get dressed. I've got a car outside, and when you're dressed, we are going to leave. Can you manage that?"

"I think so. How long have I been in bed? I can't think when I last washed or showered." A look of alarm flashed across her face. "I need the bathroom. Where is it? Can you help me? I need to go: like right now!"

They stumbled together down to the bathroom.

"What the heck? I'm wearing a fucking diaper. And what's this gross bag thing? Sorry, Tricia."

"That's okay. Here, let me help. Can you manage now?"

"Yeah. I think I'm okay from here. Thanks."

"I'll wait outside. Give me a call when you need help."

Outside in the passageway, Michelle asked. "How is she? How soon is she going to be able to leave?"

"She's a tough kid, Michelle. Her mind is recovering fast, and she has a strong body. I can't predict exactly, but I can promise that I will get her out of here on time, and we will meet you at the airport. Nothing is going to stop me getting Nicky out of this place." She growled, grimly.

They made their way back to the bedroom, where Tricia laid

out the clothes from the bag. Nicky looked at them critically. "The jeans are okay, and I like the Nike runners. The rest will work. At this point, as long as they fit, no prob." She sniffed, and wrinkled her nose. "Good grief, I stink. And my hair is disgusting." She pushed her fingers into her tangled blond mop. "No time for a shower I suppose? No, I thought not."

It was a struggle for Nicky to pull on the clothes, her arms and legs refusing to cooperate with the instructions sent by her brain. She was breathing hard when she sat back on the bed, to let Tricia help her with her shoes and socks.

"You're looking much better, already, Nicky. Here, let's pull your hair back into a ponytail. It will keep it out of the way for now. That's better. You need to put this on."

"What on earth is that?"

"It's a vest to protect you. Look, I'm wearing one. It's just routine protection. Nothing to be concerned about."

"It's a bullet proof vest, Tricia." She gasped. "They wear these in the movies. What's going on? Where are we?"

"It's a long story, Nicky. I'll explain as we go. We're in France, and...."

"France?" Nicky croaked. "What the heck are we doing in France. How did I get here?" She started to cry. "I'm so confused."

"It's okay. You've been through a lot. I don't have time to explain everything right now. Please, just trust me. We're in France, and we've got quite a long drive ahead of us, and I will explain as we go. Is that your purse over there?" She handed it to Nicky. "Here. Check to see if your passport and stuff is there."

"Yes, it looks like it's all here. My passport, and my iPhone." She held it up, with a croaky squeal. "Even my cash is here."

She added, rummaging through her purse. "Unfortunately, it's Canadian dollars and Chinese Yuan. You've probably still got a bunch of Chinese money, too. Not a lot of use, if we're in France."

"I gave all my Yuan to your Dad, when I left Beijing."

"Dad's still in Beijing? I don't understand." She groaned.

"It's a bit complicated. He had to stay behind for another day or two, but he's fine. He'll be joining us in here in France. If there is anything we need, I exchanged my Canadian dollars for Euros, and got quite a few more in Bergerac. I've also got my credit cards, if we need them, so money won't be a problem."

Nicky shook her head in disbelief. "Bergerac? Where the crap is Bergerac? France? I can't believe this. It's all just too weird. That explains why I kept hearing people talking in French. I thought I was dreaming. Where are we going, now?

"We're driving to Bergerac airport, and taking a flight from there. It's a nice drive through the countryside. The women you heard talking French, that would have been when the woman who was with you all the time was talking to the doctor?"

"That, too. But during the day, sometimes I was just awake enough when the woman would come in on her own. She would stand beside the bed and start talking to someone. I was, like, right out of it, and couldn't open my eyes. The other person, it sounded like a man, had a sort of electronic voice, you know, like it was coming over a speaker. It was the same after the doctor left."

Tricia froze. She looked around the room frantically. "Did you hear that, Michelle? Damn it. The place is wired."

"Mon Dieu, of course it is. We should have known. That's why we couldn't locate any watchers. They didn't need watchers, they are wired in. Get out of there now. Immediately. Once they realized that you were not Sehrish, they will have sent a back-up team. Go. As fast as you can. I have to call Beijing and let them know that we're blown. Go, now." She shouted.

"Nicky. Come on. We have to run as fast as we can."

"I don't understand. What's happening? I'm not sure about the running bit. Can I hang on to you?"

"Yes. I'll help you. Come on. I've got your purse. As fast as you can."

Tricia threw the straps of both purses around her neck, grabbed the bag in one hand, and held Nicky around her waist with the other. Nicky looped her arm around Tricia's shoulders, and with Tricia taking part of her weight, they managed a fast shuffle down the passage, and out of the front door. Tricia tossed the bag and their purses, on the back seat, as Nicky pulled and twisted her way into the passenger seat.

Tricia jumped into the driver's seat, and stared down the driveway. No sign of the blue guide car. They were leaving earlier than planned.

"Belt on, Nicky? Let's go." She floored the accelerator, and the BMW responded with a roar and a spray of gravel, as it leapt forward.

"Look out! There's a car racing down the road towards us." Nicky shrieked, pointing at the road to the gite.

"Hang on." Tricia growled through clenched teeth. They reached the gate seconds before the other car. Tricia flung the BMW around ninety degrees, and headed towards the oncoming car, in a screech of tires. They passed each other with only inches between them. She caught a glimpse of two Asian men staring at them.

"What's going on, Tricia? Who are those men?" Nicky moved

her head so that she could look behind them in the side mirror. "They're turning around and coming after us. Wait a minute. A farm tractor and trailer has pulled out of a driveway, and is going slowly along in front of them: it's in the centre: it's blocking the road. They can't get past."

"Thanks, Michelle." Tricia muttered quietly.

"Tricia, you've got to tell me what's going on." Nicky gasped. "This is getting really scary."

"Okay. Right. Do you remember being in Beijing, China, with your soccer team?"

"Yes, sort of. It's all a bit fuzzy." Nicky muttered.

"You were grabbed off the street in Beijing, and brought to France, to force your Dad and uncle Matt to give some people all their research work on a sort of medical breakthrough they had just made."

"Where's Dad and uncle Matt? Have they given them the stuff they want?"

"At this moment, your Dad is in Beijing handing over everything they asked for. Uncle Matt is here in France."

"Who were those Asian men in that car, and what did they want?"

"I'm not sure, Nicky. I think they wanted to stop me from getting you out."

Michelle's voice burst into Tricia's ear. "What's happening now? Are you clear? Where are you?"

"I don't know where we are, exactly, Michelle. We had to avoid a car with two Asian men that came racing toward the gite. A farm tractor and trailer conveniently came out of a driveway, and blocked the road. I take it that was you? Right now, we're just trying to get away from here as fast as we can." She glanced across at Nicky. "What's happening in Beijing?"

"Okay, yes, our team has taken care of that car, for the moment. I'm trying to get a read on the Beijing situation. It's a bit chaotic. They obviously had someone listening in to the gite. When they realized that you weren't Sehrish, everything went pear shaped. I'll tell you more, as soon as I get some reliable information. In the meantime, try and find out where you are."

"See if you can see a signpost, Nicky."

"Okay. Who's that you're talking to?"

"Michelle Denis. She's with Interpol. You've probably heard of them."

"Interpol? This is totally getting crazier by the sec. There's a signpost ahead. It says we are heading to a place called Le Budge, Le Boodge, I'm not sure how to pronounce it. It's spelt B U G U E."

Tricia slowed the car. "Thanks, Nicky, I see it. Okay, Michelle, the sign says we are heading for Le Booson de Cadouin, and then L e B U G U E. Can you find where we are?"

"Yeah. Le Bugue. Got it. Keep going."

"You'll tell me where to turn for Bergerac airport?"

"There's been a slight problem. The flight from Bergerac airport is cancelled I'm afraid. Matt and I are heading for Bordeaux. Interpol has a centre there."

"What? So we need to head for Bordeaux?

"Probably not a good idea at the moment. The men who came to the gite will have identified your car, and may be looking for you."

"So, where do we go?"

"Keep going for a while. When you come to a town where you feel it's safe to stop, look for a comfortable hotel, and get a room for the night. Matt and I will get a flight to Paris later tonight. I'll contact you with an update from Bordeaux, or, if that's not possible, from Paris as soon as we get there.

"What? I'm driving through the middle of fucking France, Michelle, with no idea where we are, I don't even speak the language, and you've got both of our suitcases, with all of our stuff. We're lucky our passports were in our purses. Now you tell me to keep going until we find somewhere safe to stop? Is that the best you can do? At this point, I have no idea how I would know if somewhere was safe."

"Yes, I'm afraid that's the best I've got, at the moment, Tricia. Everything has been happening at once. It's a very fluid situation. Try and stay calm, or it will upset Nicky, and she has been through enough, already. Just buy whatever you need. We'll sort everything out, but it will take time."

"Thanks a lot. Michelle." She took a deep breath. "You will have gathered that we are in a bit of a situation, Nicky. The great Interpol plan appears to have gone sideways."

"I might be able to help a bit. I've taken a couple of years of French at school. My pronunciation is not very good, but I think I can manage some of the everyday stuff." She gave a quick grin. "Unfortunately, we never did a section on useful French expressions, when you are driving around, lost in the middle of France, after escaping from kidnappers."

Tricia laughed, and gave Nicky a reassuring smile. "You're terrific, Nicky. Between the two of us, we'll manage just fine. I have enough cash, plus credit and debit cards, with your French, we will work out a solution for ourselves. And our plan will work."

"We'll be okay, Tricia, I know we will. We've got away from

that cottage place, and no one is coming after us, that I can see, and I'm feeling better every minute. That shot you gave me really made a difference. I'll see if I can get a GPS on my phone. The screen's a bit small." She pointed at the dash in front of them. "That screen's got to have maps and GPS. Let me see if I can get it going." She tapped the screen, and it came to life. "There we go. That good, it's in English, well sort of: the French words are a bit mangled. Anyway, I should be able to get it going for us."

"Good work, Nicky. Here's Le Bugue coming up."

"Where do you want to go?" Nicky wrinkled her nose, as she checked the road signs that were coming up, and the options on the screen. "It keeps showing Paris as a destination."

"That's it, Nicky. Put in Paris. We'll bloody well drive there." She tapped her earpiece. "Did you hear that, Michelle? We're driving to bloody Paris."

No response.

"Paris, wow. Okay." Nicky noted. "It shows that we go across some river, and come to one of those traffic circle thingies. There should be signs for a place called Brive la Gallard, or something like that. I'm not sure how to pronounce the last word. It's GAILLARDE. Here's the bridge over the river."

"And there's the traffic circle thingy." Tricia smiled. "Now where is the road off to this Brive la whatever?"

"There it is. We just passed it."

"Okay, no problem, I'll go around again." She said lightly. "Here we are. Now we're on the road to Brive la whatever. The sign said eighty kilometers. It should take less than an hour. Way to go Nicky. What do we do when we reach this Brive place, can you see?"

"It looks like we get on the A20, that also seems to be called the

E9 road, that sort of takes us all the way to Paris."

"Hey, we're on our way. We'll make it, Nicky."

Nicky reached over, and gave Tricia's arm a quick squeeze. "Thanks for coming to get me, Tricia. I can never thank you enough." She was quiet for a moment. "What's Dad doing, do you know?"

"Not really, Nicky. It's all a bit confused in Beijing, from what Michelle said. We planned to meet up in Paris. I'm sure we will see him when we get there."

Nicky sat back, quietly looking out of the window at the passing countryside, and towns. When she had been silent for over half an hour, Tricia decided it was time to ask.

"Are you feeling okay?"

"Mm, yes. Sure. A bit tired."

"You look kind of worried, Nicky. What's wrong? Are you worried about your Dad? I'm sure he will be just fine. There are Interpol agents looking after him in Beijing."

"No, it's not that. It's just. Well you're a doctor, aren't you Tricia?"

"Yes, of course. What is it? Are you sure you're feeling okay?"

"Yeah. I feel fine." She managed a weak grin. "Well, not totally great, but lots better." She turned her face away and looked out the window again. "It's just: you said that someone sort of grabbed me in Beijing, and flew me to France, somehow, and I was sort of asleep all the time?"

"That's about how it went. I think they flew you to France in a medevac, that's a medical flight."

Nicky took a deep breath, before the words came rushing out. "When I was like asleep, did they, you know, like, mess around with me at all?"

Tricia saw the red flush creeping up her neck. "I think you are wondering whether you have been sexually interfered with?" She asked quietly.

Nicky nodded her head. "Uh huh. Yeah." She whispered.

"I don't think so, Nicky. In fact, I am pretty sure that did not happen. You would know if someone had been messing about down there. They had a woman staying with you at the gite, and the doctor was a young woman who spent the past couple of years in Africa with Medecins sans Frontieres. She seemed quite ethical, when I talked to her. She says she thought she was looking after a young girl who needed an operation, but her family in England had religious beliefs that wouldn't allow it. I really don't think that she would have allowed anybody to do anything like that. I can give you a check-up, later, if you like, but I'm sure that you have nothing to worry about." Tricia glanced across at her young companion. "If you would prefer it, I can have a female colleague of mine examine you. She's very good, and really nice."

"Thanks. I'll let you know." Nicky settled back. "Hey, look. We're coming to a major intersection. The GPS says take the second exit onto the E70 or A89." She stared at the screen. "Oh, right. They are the same road. What did that sign mean, when it said there's a toll road ahead?"

"It means that we will have to pay to travel on this road. I don't know if my Canadian credit cards will work here. I'm glad I got some Euros, in Bergerac. There's cash in my purse, on the back seat. Can you reach it? There are some coins and notes in the change purse. That should do."

"Got it. There are some coins that I don't recognize, and some paper money in the back." She inspected them. "Yes, it says 'Euro' on them. Where do we pay?"

“I don’t know, Nicky. We’ll work it out. I’m sure the toll roads will be set up to make sure everyone pays. Where do we go next?”

“According to the GPS, we stay on this road, until we get to the A20 which is another main road that goes north most of the way to Paris.”

“There’s a sign: I think it says that the intersection for the A20 to Paris is coming up, just ahead.” Nicky pointed out, a short time later. “It says it’s four hundred and sixty four kilometres to Paris. Here we go, Tricia. We’re on the A20, on our way to Paris.”

Tricia tapped her earpiece. “Did you hear that, Michelle? We’re on the A20 heading for Paris.” She smiled at her young passenger. “Settle back, Nicky, it’s going to be a few hours of steady driving before we reach Paris.”

“No prob. I am getting a bit hungry, though.”

Tricia chuckled with relief. “That’s my Nicky. Let’s get along this A20 a little way, and then you can start looking for somewhere to stop and get something to eat. I’m feeling a bit hungry, too. It’s probably the combination of the tension, and not having eaten much since coffee and croissants about five hours ago. I hope you can manage to order us some food, because my French ends at ‘bonjour’.”

CHAPTER 33

Paul had worked all night, and was finishing up in the late morning, when his Interpol contact had messaged him to bring all of the material to the National Centre for the Performing Arts, at nine o'clock that same evening. Along with the message was a short video of Nicky beside a television screen that was showing the CNN early morning news for that day. She looked vacant, and confused with what was happening, but appeared to be in reasonable health. The video could have been faked, but, no matter what, Paul new that he was compelled to proceed with the transaction, since that was the price for gaining Nicky's freedom.

As the meeting time got close, Paul got all his research material together, and headed down to the Hyatt lobby. The Doorman said he would give the taxi driver instructions, in Mandarin, to take him to the Arts Centre: Paul could only hope that he would end up in the right place. It was shortly after eight thirty, when he arrived at the imposing steps to the entrance on West Chang An Avenue. He checked his watch, for the tenth time, and confirmed that he still had ample time to find his way through the most unusual entrance. It went down, and along a short tunnel under the artificial lake, then up an escalator into the spectacular, towering interior of the huge Arts Centre. The walls around him were all glass with metal framing that soared upwards in a graceful curve to form the start of the roof.

Paul stood on the gleaming grey stone floor, looking around

impatiently for his contact. At precisely nine o'clock, the Interpol man appeared from the far side of the massive lobby area. He took the briefcase that contained the material the kidnappers had demanded, and told Paul to wait in the modernistic café, that he pointed out, on the mezzanine above them.

By nine thirty, Paul was getting impatient. He was too stressed to admire and appreciate the impressive architecture of the building around him. His attention was fixed down below, on the atrium, where he had entered the building, nearly an hour ago. The coffee and cake that he had felt obliged to order sat on the table in front of him, untouched. Beside them was his mobile phone, ready for Matt's call.

He checked his watch for what now seemed like the hundredth time. It was thirty-five minutes since he had handed over the package to the man from Interpol. Paul still didn't know his name. He had noticed the woman, sitting across, in the corner of the café.

The random thought tumbled through his mind that she looked somehow different. Her hair was different, but there were other things, too. She didn't look anything like Tricia, now. The fact that she was quite slight was emphasized by the impressive size of the man sitting with her. He looked like a caricature of a Chinese thug. They never took their eyes off him. There was no attempt to disguise their function, although what they thought Paul might do, he had no idea. He was alone in Beijing, did not speak a word of the language, and did not know his way around. He just wanted to get this whole business over with, and get the call from Matt, telling him that Nicky was with him, safe and sound, so that he could leave Beijing and China, and they could all go home. Until then, he had to simply wait.

On the other side of the immense atrium, Paul could see the

man from Interpol sitting in the café below, casually watching two men, who were sitting at the table adjacent to him, going through the material from the briefcase. Presumably those other men were the technical experts.

There was a burst of noise, as a crowd of Asian concertgoers entered the café, talking excitedly. They moved around together, trying to decide whether to sit at the long, curved counter style table that ran around the perimeter of one side of the café, or to sit at individual tables. From his time working with Japanese researchers, Paul was sure that they were speaking Japanese.

"Hello, professor. My goodness, fancy running into you again. Beijing isn't such a huge city after all."

Paul looked up in surprise to see the two young German tourists that he had met, yesterday afternoon, in the grounds of the Arts Centre.

"Oh, hello. Stefanie and Julie, isn't it?" He stammered.

"Can we join you?' Julie asked, smiling, as the two of them sat down.

"Yes, well, actually, no. It's not at all convenient, at the moment. I'm waiting for someone." He blustered. This was a situation that Paul absolutely did not need at that moment. "Look, I don't want to be rude, but I am engaged in a really important meeting here. Right now, actually, so I must insist that you leave."

The girl, called Julie, leant forward on the table, still smiling, spoke in a quiet voice that conveyed an urgent command.

"Professor Berg. Pick up your phone, and anything else you have here, stand up, and leave with us immediately. You must leave right now."

"What are you talking about? Who are you? I simply

cannot leave now. My daughter. It's impossible. You don't understand. Who are you?"

"We are from Interpol." Stefanie hissed. "Nicky is safe. We don't have time to explain, now. We will explain as soon as we have got you safely out of here."

"Interpol? If this is some sort of joke it is in very bad taste, and you have made a major mistake. That chap in the café on the opposite side of the atrium, and the woman sitting over there, well you can't see her now, because that crowd is in the way, but they are from Interpol, and I am working with them. It is crucial that nothing goes wrong at this point. Just leave. Please go away, and leave me alone."

"These young women really are from Interpol, Professor Berg, the other couple are not. Don't make a fuss. Do what they say, and leave with them immediately."

Paul spun around to face the speaker who had whispered in his ear from behind his chair. "Agent Sarah Little? What the Hell are you doing here?"

"Trying to help these young women rescue you, Professor. Now go." She ordered.

"I can't. It's Nicky: my daughter. You must understand? You know all about it. I have to wait to hear from Matt that Nicky is free."

"Nicky's safe. She's with Tricia. Things have gone a bit sideways, but they're safe. Come on. Now. You're wasting time." Stefanie commanded in a voice that brooked no dispute.

Paul grabbed his phone, as he was lifted bodily out of his seat, and virtually carried out of the café, down the stairs, and across the atrium, between the two young German women. To anyone watching, he probably looked like he was a bit drunk, and had met up with two close friends. Together, they were heading out with their arms around each other, probably looking for another bar.

As they reached the top of the escalator leading down to the exit tunnel that went out to West Chang An Avenue, Paul saw a familiar figure standing guard.

"Mr. Renshu?" Paul gasped.

"Good evening, Professor. I am pleased to see that you are leaving." Renshu said politely. "Otherwise, I would have had to arrest you, along with the other criminals that we are about to detain. I wish you a pleasant flight. Goodnight."

Before Paul had time to respond, the two young women propelled him down the escalator, and along the tunnel. Julie was talking urgently on her phone as they went. His own phone started to ring.

"Matt? Is that you? Where's Nicky? Is she all right?"

"Paul, yes it's me. Nicky's safe. Tricia's got her. She's driving the two of them in a rental car."

"Is Nicky all right? Has she been hurt?"

"Tricia says that Nicky is fine: a bit groggy after being sedated, but otherwise, just fine. I'll explain everything when we see you. It's over, Paul. Thank God, it's over. Now you must do exactly what those people from Interpol tell you, and they will get you out of China as quickly as possible. See you soon." Matt paused for a second. "Tricia's a very special woman, you know, Paul."

"Yes, I know." He replied softly into a dead phone.

Paul's head was spinning. A matter of minutes ago he had been sitting alone in the Arts Centre café, now he found himself standing in the night air, at the curb of West Chang An Avenue. A taxi pulled to a halt in front of them. Stefanie had the door open before the vehicle had come to a stop. There was already someone sitting in the rear seat.

"Hop in, professor. You don't have a lot of time."

"Agent Blakey. I should have known that you would make an appearance."

"Just get in, professor."

Paul did not have a choice, as he received a firm push from behind that propelled head first into the taxi.

"Goodbye, professor." Julie called, slamming the door.

"Have a nice flight." Stefanie added, as the taxi cut back into the stream of traffic, provoking hoots from a driver, who had to brake to avoid a collision.

"Blakey, what the Hell is going on? Do you know?" Paul pleaded, as he sank back in the seat.

"I know some of it. The Interpol team in Bergerac found where your daughter, Nicky was being held, and Doctor Chen went to the gite, that's what a rental cottage is called in France, to get her. She took the place of the woman doctor who had been checking on her each afternoon."

"What on earth possessed Interpol and the French police to send Tricia in to rescue Nicky, instead of one of their expert teams?" Paul demanded in disbelief.

"Because it was essential that the people who had abducted Nicky believed that everything was still going according to their plan. It was also a tremendous help that Nicky knows Doctor Chen, and that she is a physician: a pediatrician which is even better. Timing was absolutely essential for Interpol to rescue your daughter, and get you out of China alive."

"Alive? What do you mean, 'get me out alive'?"

"There was good reason to believe that they intended to eliminate you, your brother Matt, Nicky, and probably Doctor Chen."

"Good lord. The scorched earth approach." Paul muttered.

"Exactly. No witnesses. Anyway, things went a bit pear shaped. The kidnappers had installed monitoring equipment in the gite, and realized that Doctor Chen was not their doctor. Chen and Nicky had to make a fast exit, Bergerac airport was out, for some reason, and everyone had to make some spontaneous decisions. When that happened, you were at risk, so we had to get you out. The two Interpol agents, Stefanie and Julie, did a great impromptu job."

"They were lucky that crowd arrived at the café just at the right moment. There were people watching me like hawks. I have no idea what they thought I was going to do."

"That wasn't luck, professor." Blakey stated drily. "Agent Little told the leader of a group of some fifty odd Japanese concert goers that the Centre had arranged for complimentary drinks and food for them in the café at nine thirty."

"Oh. Right. Smart move. What about Renshu? What was his role in all of this?"

"He's Chinese security, and he did his job. That was all. He plans to make a couple of arrests, and confiscate all of your material as evidence. Renshu and China have come out as the big winners."

"Well, perhaps not." Paul mused.

"What do you mean?"

"What? Oh, well, medical research only rarely translates into major medical advances. Most fail to pass the rigorous regime of clinical testing. Where are we going, by the way? Everyone kept wishing me a good flight."

"You are going to the airport." Blakey looked at his watch. "You'll be in plenty of time for the Air France flight to Paris, later tonight. That's where your brother, Tricia and Nicky will be waiting for you. Here, I've sent the address of the hotel where they will be staying overnight to your phone. It just came through. Apparently there has been some slight change of plans."

"Are we going to be safe, even in Paris?"

"Yes, you should all be fine in Paris."

"What about the person who took a shot at us in the park the other day? Who are they? They're still out there."

"No, not really."

"What do you mean? Someone shot at us. We heard it go by, and it hit the young mother on the deck above us"

"We have contacts in Beijing, and they assured us that there was no evidence of any shooting in the park. That is standard Chinese code used when the perpetrator has been caught, and has disappeared into the secretive Chinese penal system."

"Oh. Right. I still don't understand that bizarre scene in the elevator, when that couple took over, and posed as Tricia and myself?"

"Renshu was really angry that you two had been shot at, on the Pagoda of the Summer Palace." Blakey explained. "Our understanding is that he arranged for the two people to pretend to be Interpol agents, and persuade you to accept them as intermediaries for the handover of your material. He also arranged for Dr. Chen to leave China immediately, on a flight to France, for her safety."

"Oh. I see. I think." Paul was stunned. He tried to clear his head, and deal with the immediate issues. "We have to stop at the hotel. All my clothes and stuff is there. It's crucial that I have my laptop, and all my research material."

"It's all been packed up for you, Professor: there is someone waiting for you with it, at the airport. We switched your return ticket from Beijing to Paris instead of Vancouver, so you are in Business Class. It should be a very pleasant flight."

"Are you and Agent Little staying on in Beijing?"

"No. We're on a flight tomorrow afternoon." Blakey peered through the windshield, as the taxi slowed to a stop. "Here we are. This is the Departures entrance."

They hurried through the airport, searching for an Information Board that would direct them to the Air France Check-in area. After a couple of wrong turns they saw the Air France sign in the distance.

"There it is, professor, and here is our man with your boarding pass and luggage. Since you were unaware that you were catching this flight, we took the liberty of checking you in, on your behalf."

"Is that permitted?" Paul questioned.

Blakey gave a long-suffering sigh. "Here. Take your checked bag to the drop off counter, over there."

"Of course. Right. Thanks."

"Okay, Professor Berg. You're all checked in, and you've dropped off your bag, so it's clear sailing from here." Blakey said, when Paul returned. "We just have to follow the signs to the International Departure portals. You should have plenty of time to get through Security before the boarding call for your flight."

"I know where that is." Paul grunted. "I was here to see Tricia off, on the Air France flight to Paris."

"Oh, right. It's been quite a day. I had forgotten that you were here with Dr. Chen. Apparently she has been quite active, since she arrived in France. Going in on her own, and getting your daughter, Nicky, out of the gite where she was being held. The last I heard, something went sideways, and Dr. Chen was driving Nicky all the way to Paris, where they would join your brother Matt and an Interpol agent at that hotel address I gave you. That Doctor Patricia Chen is quite something."

"You're the second person to tell me that, this evening." Paul murmured.

Paul reached out and shook Agent Kevin Blakey's hand. "Thanks for all that you and Agent Little have done. I apologize for being a bit churlish, at times. It's been difficult. You know, Nicky being kidnapped, and my being in China, where I don't understand a word of the language. I can't believe that it's all over. It is all over, isn't it? Nicky is safe, isn't she? Renshu has all of the material that I handed over, and I was told that he was going to arrest the people involved. Matt and I had nothing to do with any of that, so we can't really be blamed."

"Yes, it's over. Your daughter is safe, and you are all in the clear. Interpol deserves most of the credit. We just helped where we could. Through you go. A few hours from now, you will be in the air, sitting in your Business Class seat, with a drink in your hand, well on your way to Paris, and your family."

CHAPTER 34

Tricia and Nicky were in a steady flow of vehicles on the A20 Autoroute, heading north towards Paris. The sun was starting to sink down towards the horizon away to the West, but the light was still good. The driving was easy, as they ate up the kilometres through the French countryside. Tricia kept a steady speed in the right lane, only moving across to pass the heavy lorries that were hauling their cargo through the length of France.

She glanced across at Nicky, who had been quiet for a while, looking out at the passing scenery.

"How are you doing? Okay?"

"Oh yeah. I'm just, sort of, trying to chill out. I still feel weird, sort of waking up and being in France, and all the other stuff." She waved her hand at the window, "That's, like, real French countryside out there, you know, French fields with French cows and French sheep and that stuff, all around. Now, tonight we're going to be in Paris. It's just totally so ridiculous. Paris is a really big city, isn't it? Have you ever been there, before?"

"Yes, it's a big city. I was there, once, a long time ago. I can hardly remember it. I went with your Mum, after the end of our first year at university. I remember getting sick from the water. You shouldn't drink the tap water in Paris: don't even use it to brush your teeth. It'll give you the runs for sure."

"Yuck, got it." She hesitated. "Do you think of Mum,

sometimes? You were really good friends, weren't you?"

Tricia was silent for a moment. "Yes, I think of your Mum quite often. She and I were really good friends for nearly twenty years: we met at High School, and were together all through Medical School, and afterwards at the hospital in Vancouver. I really miss her. You must too?"

"Yeah. I do. A lot." She bit her bottom lip. "I know this sounds really weird." She paused. "In that cottage, at night, I sort of half woke up, and Mum was there by my bed, and she was talking to me. She told me that I was going to be all right. She was just sort of quiet and calm." She gave a quick look at Tricia. "It was probably the drugs, and stuff, and I was just sort of dreaming." She twitched her mouth, self-consciously. "So that's why when I saw you, I wasn't sure at first if you were real. Sorry, Tricia, that must sound totally crazy."

"No, it doesn't, Nicky." Tricia murmured.

They were comfortably quiet for the next few kilometres.

"I can't wait to see the Eifel Tower." Nicky broke the silence with a change of subject. "There's a photo of it on the front of our French textbook at school. How long will we be in Paris?"

"I really don't know. The original plan was for us all to fly to Paris, and then to go on somewhere from there. I was never told the details. Agent Michelle Denis, from Interpol, thought she would have plenty of time on the flight to explain everything, but that never happened."

"Things didn't quite go as planned, did they?"

"No, they seldom do. But we're here now, and on our way to Paris, even if it is by a somewhat different route. Which brings up a more immediate issue, we should probably stop for gas, and we could both use a break and some food. Those signs we've passed a couple of times that say something like Air de something; they have a bunch of pictures on them. I think that means a rest stop, with a café and gas station."

"Yes. That's what it looks like. Here's another one coming up now. It says 'Aire de Limoges', and it seems to have lots of things, like gas and food, and stuff. It says '1500 m' underneath. I think that must mean it's fifteen hundred metres ahead. Yes, here's the slip lane, now."

"There are quite a few cars pulling off. I'll just follow them. If it's not what we think it is, or we don't like the look of it, we can just get back on the A20, and try the next one."

"It looks pretty good." Nicky said, as she peered around. "There are lots of people going in and out of what looks like some sort of shopping mall. Straight ahead, there's a couple of gas stations, or whatever they are called in France. I hope there are some places to get something to eat."

"I think I'll fill up with gas, first." She said as she guided them to a stop beside a set of gas pumps. "Here we are. This is a bit confusing. I don't want to put diesel in the car by mistake. You don't happen to know the French for petrol and diesel, do you?"

Nicky frowned in concentration. "I remember, we did this. Yes, in France, gas, or petrol, as they call gas in the UK is 'super', and diesel is called 'gazole'. I'll hop out with you, and see what it says on the pumps."

"That's good, look, it says inside the gas cap to use 'super'." Tricia stared at the pumps. "Oh lord. The pumps are all coloured with letters and numbers on them. What do you think, Nicky?"

"I'm not sure. Sorry, I'm not much help. I'm not old enough to drive, yet, so I'm not really into this stuff."

"Excuse me madam, do you require some assistance?" Tricia looked up to see a smartly dressed, middle-aged man, at the pump behind them, filling a sleek looking silver car.

"Well, yes, thank you, actually, I could use some help. Are you familiar with these French pumps?"

He smiled. "I think so, madam. I am French, and have lived here for all of my fifty-one years. Let me finish here; it will only take a small minute, and then, perhaps you will permit me to be your guide."

True to his word, he was finished quite quickly.

"The pumps were changed a few years ago, to make them all the same throughout the EU. The pumps for petrol, in France it is called 'super', they are usually green, and all have a circle with an 'E' and a number which indicates how much of the biofuel it contains. Diesel pumps are usually black, and all have a square, with letters, and some numbers. You see, here, on your petrol cap it says that this car uses petrol, or 'super' as we call it, and so it must be filled from the green pump. E85 is the most powerful, so, for this car, I would suggest that you choose that one, but any green pump will do, if you are unsure."

"How do I pay?" Tricia asked, staring at the pumps, credit card in her hand.

"Ah yes. You pay at the booth over there. Sometimes foreign credit cards do not work too well, so it will be much easier to pay with cash. Is this your first time in France?"

"Thank you so much for your help. Yes, it is my first time in France. In fact, I only landed yesterday evening, and I am really not at all familiar with French customs." She smiled. "But, fortunately, I do have cash to pay at the booth." Tricia looked around. "The sign on the autoroute said there was a rest stop here, with quite a list of facilities. Is that it over there?"

"Yes, indeed. If you turn right, after you leave this petrol station, you will enter the parking area for the rest stop." He said, pointing towards the red tile roof on a long, gray stone building, visible above the neatly trimmed bushes that topped a small grass bank.

"Is there somewhere there, where we can get something to eat here?" Nicky asked.

"But most certainly, mademoiselle. Inside, there are many different places providing food. You can get everything from sandwiches to full meals in quite agreeable restaurants. There are also many shops, plus toilettes, and all the usual amenities."

"Thank you so much. You have been most helpful."

He shook her hand with a smile. "It has been my pleasure."

The parking area was laid out in curved rows that sprayed out in a fan shape, with each row separated by a line of small trees that were starting to show signs of pink blossoms. There were large decorative bowls of spring flowers, daffodils and tulips of every colour, spaced regularly between every third tree, along each row.

"Whoa, this is really cool, with all the trees and flowers and things." Nicky approved as they started walking towards the building.

The pedestrian paths were all identified in red tiles, and came together at a circular plaza, in front of the main entrance, where a stone fountain gently tumbled water down an artistic assembly of rocks, into a large, round pool. The building itself was horseshoe shaped, with several sets of large entrance doors in the middle of the horseshoe, and the two curved wings flowing out and away, on either side.

Inside, the building was just as elegant. Tricia looked around.

There was a wide central aisle, with storefronts for businesses of every type on both sides. "Goodness, it looks like there are hundreds of shops and food outlets. Unfortunately, all the notices are in French. It could take us forever to find a washroom."

"There's an Information Booth over there." Nicky said, pointing ahead. "The sign says that they speak English, but I know 'toilettes' is French for toilets, so we should be able to manage, even if they don't."

The woman at the Information booth did, indeed, speak English. She gave them a map that showed them where the nearest washrooms were, and marked all the cafes and food outlets.

They made their way through the crowds of travelers and locals, who had come to the rest stop to shop and eat. Some of the French teens were checking out Nicky, as they passed, but she was too busy scrutinizing all the different clothes and techie stuff in the shop windows to notice. As they passed various cafes, Tricia tried to understand the various food options from the menus that were display on boards outside. Nicky was able to help with the basic food names, but their lack of familiarity with French food made it difficult to decipher exactly what many of the menu items were.

"How hungry are you, Nicky, or more importantly, what do you think you can manage? I don't know what you have been eating for the past few days, but I don't think we should go for anything too adventuresome, in case your stomach isn't quite ready for it."

Nicky sighed. "Yeah, I don't feel, like, you know, too food comfortable. I was sort of out of it, when they wanted me to eat. It was kind of difficult for me to eat, too, so they only gave me a little each day, and it was pretty basic, sort of mushy type food. Right now, I feel as if I'm starving, and could eat loads of anything, but I don't think I should eat too much, like, fried stuff and French food that I've never eaten before. I have a feeling that it might not sit too well, and we still have a long way to go."

Tricia gave a wry smile. "The woman at the Information booth said that these rest stops were about every twenty kilometres along the Autoroute, but we don't want to end up having to stop at every one, to use the washrooms."

"No. That is definitely big on my 'avoid' list. That would be gross." Nicky said with a shudder. She hesitated for a moment. "There was that Subway that we passed, back there? It's a bit lame to eat at Subway for my first ever meal in France, but I know what their sandwiches and salads are like, at home, and if they're pretty much the same here, I think I can manage that without any big problem. Actually, a large French Subway salad really sounds just about perfect. Is that okay, Tricia? It's got tables and everything, and it looks sort of French."

"That sounds like a perfect choice, Nicky. Done. Subway it is. What will be really good for me is that they have large, overhead pictures of everything on the menu, with the French name underneath. I'm pretty sure that I can manage, by pointing at what I want." Tricia laughed.

"That was so good." Nicky purred, as she put down her empty apple juice container, and sat back. "Perhaps we should get something to take with us?" She suggested, hopefully.

"Sure. Why not? We still have a long way to go." Tricia checked her watch. "It's closing in on six thirty: we should be on our way again. It's starting to get dark, and we still have several hours of driving. Here's some Euros, why don't you get some drinks and cookies, or something, while I text Michelle, and see if there is any news."

Nicky returned to the table with a bulging bag.

"That looks like it will keep us going for a while." Tricia observed. "Michelle texted back that they were at Bordeaux airport, and about to board their Paris flight. She's given me the name and address of a small Paris hotel, in the Sixteenth Arrondissement, where she has booked rooms for all of us. She said it has a good, quiet location, in a residential area."

"Sounds great." Nicky hesitated.

"What wrong, Nicky?" Tricia tried to keep her concern out of her voice.

"I don't want to sound like a wimp, but sleeping alone in a strange room, is a bit scary, after the past few days."

"Of course." Tricia smiled. "I'll text back to Michelle, and ask her to book us two rooms with a connecting door. I'm sure she can arrange it. Will that be okay?"

"Yeah, that would be great. Thanks."

"There. That's done." Tricia said with a reassuring smile. "Off we go, then. But first, a quick trip to the washroom."

"Good plan."

As they passed the Information Booth, on the way from the washroom to the exit, the woman they had spoken to earlier called out to them. "Excuse me, Madame."

"Pardon? Are you calling to me?" Tricia looked around in surprise.

"Yes, Madame. Your two friends were here asking after you. I'm sorry, I didn't quite know where you were, but I didn't think that you had left the Rest Stop, already. If you want to find them, they went that way." She explained, pointing away to the left.

"I didn't think anyone knew we were here." Tricia said in a

strained voice. "What did these people look like?"

"They were two Asian men. Quite smartly dressed in suits. Hardly any French men wear suits these days." She saw the tension in Tricia's face. "They were most polite. They described you and the young lady, so it seemed all right. I told them you had asked about the restaurants, I hope that was acceptable?"

"When did they leave here?" Tricia choked out.

"About ten minutes ago. Oh dear. Have I done anything wrong?" The woman looked from Tricia to Nicky anxiously.

"They are very dangerous men. If they come back, can you say that you haven't seen us? Please. It is very important."

"Mon Dieu. I'm so sorry. Yes, I'll try and put them off. They seemed so polite, and they seemed to know you. You go. I'll call Security."

"Tricia! Look. There they are, over there. They look like the men who were in the car that tried to chase us, as we left the cottage place. They're going from shop to shop. They're searching for us." Nicky said frantically. "They just went into that shop that sells leather purses and stuff."

"Come on, Nicky. This way. Quick. Run."

They ran down the opposite leg of the Rest Stop, dodging around the families who were wandering through, taking a break from driving.

"Where are we going to go?" Nicky sobbed. "I'm scared. Don't let them get me, Tricia. Please. Don't let them get me."

"I promise you, that will not happen." She gritted back. "We are a bit ahead of them. Look for a Security Guard. I saw several of them walking around earlier. Come on, we'll go into this shop, and ask them to call Security."

They dashed through the shop doorway beside them, looking around frantically for an attendant. There were only two in sight, and they were both dealing with customers. Tricia rushed up to one of them.

"Excuse me. It is an emergency. Please call Security, immediately."

The woman looked affronted. "Madame, Je m'occupe de ce client." She sniffed. "Je ne parle pas l'anglais."

"Emergency. Call Security. Now."

It was no use. The woman shrugged, and turned her back on them, muttering to the customer about the rude English.

"Come on, Nicky. We have to try somewhere else."

They raced across the aisle, into a shop that sold electronic equipment.

Tricia stood in the middle of the store, and shouted. "We need help."

A very precise man emerged from the rear of the shop. "Madame. Je suis le gerant. I speak little English. Please rest calm. What is the problem?"

Tricia thought quickly. "Security. Call Security. There are two men. Bad men. They attacked this young girl. It is very bad. Please call Security."

"Venez. Come. I call Security." He led them into the back room where an office desk and two chairs were surrounded with unopened boxes of electronic equipment of every type. There was little room for them to stand. He gestured towards the chairs, as he locked the door, and made a call on his phone. They were both too tense to sit down.

"What's he saying? Can you understand him?" Tricia

whispered.

"He called Security, I think. He said there were two, something or other, English women disturbing his shop. I think that's what he said, or, at least, something like that."

"That's good. I don't care what he said about us, as long as Security shows up."

They waited for an eternity of less than five minutes, until there was a knock on the door. The manager opened it, and let in a woman wearing a black jacket with Securite in yellow letters.

She had a brief exchange with the manager, as she took out her notebook. Looking down as she wrote, she sighed in accented English. "What is it, the problem?"

"There are two dangerous men who are looking for us. Asian men. We just want to get to our car and leave." Tricia explained.

The woman looked up, with a disdainful glance towards Tricia and Nicky. She froze, with her pen poised, and stared from one to the other.

"Moment, please." She turned away and spoke urgently into her shoulder radio. Turning back, with a tight smile, she said. "Please wait. Someone comes to assist you."

They stood, helpless, waiting, wondering what on earth was going on. There were two raps on the door, and the man who had helped them at the petrol pump walked in.

"Ah. We meet once again. Permit me to introduce myself. Chief Inspector Lacombe, of the Police Nationale, at your service." He flipped back his jacket to show a badge and gun clipped to his belt.

"I am pleased to see a policeman, but what do you want with

us? I don't understand. Was there some problem with my paying for the petrol? I paid in cash." Tricia pleaded.

He smiled, and gave a Gallic wave of his hand. "Rest assured, Madame, it has nothing to do with that." He pulled a mobile phone from his belt. "I need to know if you have ever seen these two men before."

Tricia stared at the video that he was showing her. "Yes. Perhaps. I think we saw them earlier today. They were chasing us in a car. It was terrifying. Who are they?"

"How about the young Mademoiselle? Have you ever seen these men before?"

Nicky's hand was shaking as she reached for the mobile. "Yes, I think so. As Tricia said, they tried to chase us when we were leaving that cottage place." She fought to hold back the tears. "It's sort of complicated." She mumbled.

"Of course: I understand. You have had some difficult days. Please do not be alarmed, either of you." He tried a reassuring smile. "These two men arrived a brief time ago, and have been showing photos of you, and asking people if they have seen you."

"What?" Tricia gasped. "Who are they? What do they want with us?"

"We intend to find that out, Madame."

"It's me they want, isn't it?" Nicky sobbed. "Because I got away from them."

Tricia put her arm around the shaking shoulders of the young girl. "They are not going to get near you again, Nicky. I will make sure of that."

"I can assure you, that is my intention, also, young Nicky."

"How did you know her name?" Tricia demanded.

"Because, Doctor Chen, a police alert was sent out by Interpol, with your names and descriptions, along with the details of the vehicle that you are driving."

"Michelle." Tricia breathed.

"Your vehicle was noted, as soon as you passed the toll booth. I was nearby, in Limoges, and caught up with you just before you turned off for this rest stop. While I was driving, I received some background on your situation. I have a granddaughter, and I was very annoyed to find out what had happened to you, young Nicky." He shook his head in disgust. "Here in France. It is intolerable."

"So what will you do about these two men?"

"I will arrest them and decide that their papers are not in order. We will hold them overnight to sort out the problem. That will give you plenty of time to reach Paris. If they are in France illegally, tomorrow they will be put on a plane back to wherever they are from."

"What if they jump in their car, before you can arrest them?" Nicky pleaded.

"We know which is their car, Mademoiselle." He smiled. "It is not able to travel anywhere." The Security woman by the door had a brief conversation into her phone, and nodded at the Inspector.

"The two men are currently being questioned in another part of the shopping centre. You are able to leave safely." He explained.

"Thank you. Thank you so much." Nicky and Tricia gasped together.

The police Inspector spoke rapidly to the store manager, and then turned to them. "You can leave by a rear door from this shop. Fortunately, the shops on this side have a door on to the car park. I will escort you back to your car. "

Minutes later, Tricia and Nicky were back in the car, speeding along Autoroute A20 towards Paris.

"I haven't stopped shaking." Nicky sobbed. "I thought I was going to throw up in the backroom of that store."

Tricia had been silently repeating her calming mantra that she used in stressful medical situations. She was relieved that her hand didn't shake, as she reached over and gave Nicky's arm a reassuring squeeze. She let out a long, slow breath. "Yes, indeed. It was pretty scary there, until Inspector Lacombe walked in. Thank goodness Michelle sent out an alert."

"Holy crap, Tricia, what would have happened if she hadn't?"

"We must try not to dwell on 'What ifs', Nicky." Tricia said, with as much reassurance that she could muster. "Let's just be thankful that she did, and it all worked out."

"If these people want the research stuff that Dad and Uncle Matt have got, why don't they just give it to them, then they would leave us alone, wouldn't they?"

"Your Dad and uncle immediately agreed to everything these people asked for, Nicky. Unfortunately, so far, they don't seem to want to accept 'Yes' as an answer. I'm sure it will all sort itself out shortly." She explained grimly.

"One thing I don't understand." Nicky puzzled. "How did those men find us? I understand how the police and Inspector Lacombe were alerted, when we went past that toll booth place, but those men couldn't have had that information."

"I don't know. Perhaps they happened to see us." That had been bothering her, too. Tricia decided she should change the subject. "How far did that sign we just passed say it was to Paris?"

"Three hundred and sixty one kilometres. The GPS says we should be there in under four hours. The road number seems to sort of change a couple of times, but this Autoroute is also called the E9, and we stay on that all the way into Paris."

"It's getting dark, and starting to rain, so it may take a bit longer, but, once we get there, and meet up with your Dad, uncle Matt and Michelle, it will all be finally and completely over, Nicky." She gave the young girl her best, reassuring smile. "Now we just have to try and relax for the next few hours. Paris, here we come."

Inspector Lacombe walked through the building, to the room where the two men were being detained. He stopped, and gave a curt nod to the police officer standing outside the door.

"The microphone is in place, and working, Kim?"

"Yes, sir. I could hear them quite clearly, most of the time. My Korean is a bit rusty, but I was able to understand nearly all of what they said. It has all been recorded, so my translation can be checked." Officer Kim explained.

"Who are they, do we know?"

"Yes, sir. According to their identification documents, they are registered as immigrants, and arrived in France together from South Korea four years ago. However, it appears that they were both born in North Korea, and managed to make their way to the South. They say that they are related, cousins possibly. Their documents show them as members of the Security staff at the hospital in Sarlat. The hospital confirmed that."

"What did they say? Give me a brief summary."

"It sounded like they do not have permanent resident status in France. They both kept repeating that they must find a way to stay in France, and discussed various things that they could do to make that happen. One of them even suggested injuring each other, so badly that they would be sent to hospital here."

"Why on earth would they want to do that?" Lacombe asked in surprise.

"Well, sir, for some reason, they seem to think that if they were so badly disabled while they were here that they were unable to work and lead a normal life, they would be allowed to stay in France. It seems that their status as residents of South Korea is unclear, which could mean that they would be deported back to North Korea. They are convinced that if they are sent back there they would face a very unpleasant death."

"I see." Lacombe was shocked. "Did they say anything else?"

"Yes, sir. I thought that one of them said something about Lebanon, and referred to someone, but I couldn't catch the name. He spoke quite softly, and the other one told him to shut up immediately, so I couldn't hear exactly what they were saying."

"It sounds like they suspected that we might be listening." He frowned. "Lebanon?" He shook his head. "I don't understand."

"If our techs can enhance the recording, I might be able to hear it a bit more clearly."

"Right. Good work. Get on that as soon as possible. Top priority." Lacombe was concerned. "I don't like the sound of this. I will alert Paris, and go there myself, at once."

CHAPTER 35

Tricia kept a steady pace on the Autoroute to Paris, with Nicky following their progress on the GPS, and noting where they were, each time they passed a sign. By the time they reach Chateauroux, the rain was coming down in a steady drizzle. Thankfully, they were just one of a stream of vehicle lights slicing through the darkness along the Autoroute, heading relentlessly towards the Capital. The hum of the tires, the rhythmic thwack of the wipers, and the lights of the oncoming vehicles blended into an hypnotic sensory ambience. Tricia shook her head, and asked Nicky if she could try and find a radio station to provide some background noise, to break the monotony.

"Sure, no prob. We should be able to pick up some local stations, that way, we can sort of follow our progress by the towns we go by." She worked the radio, until a signal came in reasonably strong.

They saw clusters of lights, as they passed through and around various towns and villages. A well-lit sign said it was two hundred kilometres to Paris. Nicky rummaged in the Subway bag to retrieve a bottle of apple juice. "Do want anything to eat or drink, Tricia?"

"I could use a drink. Could you take the top off, and hand it to me?"

"Yeah, sure." She handed her a bottle. "It feels like the shot you gave me is starting to wear off a bit."

Tricia glanced across. "That's okay. Just have a nap if you want. It's pretty easy driving at the moment, just steady line of traffic, and no intersections or anything."

Nicky sat up, and gave a shake. "No, I'm okay." She made a face. "Sleep is really not that attractive for me, yet." She stared down at the GPS. "It looks like we'll come to the A10 at some point, we get on that, and it will take us all the way to the outskirts of Paris."

Tricia noticed that Nicky was munching away. "What did you get to eat from Subway?"

"There are some chocolate chip cookies. They're really good. Sorry, I couldn't bring you any coffee. Perhaps we should have another stop. You could have a coffee, and I could use a washroom, before we reach Paris. We've made really good time so far."

"Coffee and a washroom visit sound like a good idea. Can you see if there is a Rest Stop coming up anywhere?"

Nicky busied herself with the GPS. "There's a rest stop called the Leo Resto – Aire de Val Neuvy." She spelt it out. "That looks about ten minutes ahead. We should see the first sign for it shortly."

"That sounds perfect, Nicky. It will give us the chance to fill up the car with gas, or should I say 'Super', and I can get a coffee, to put some life into me, before we venture into the challenges of the Paris streets."

"And I can hit the washroom," she laughed. "You said, at the Subway, back at the other rest stop, that Michelle had reserved rooms for us at a small hotel in that sixteenth area place: I forget what it's called. If she gave you the address, I can put it into the GPS, and that will direct us straight there from this," she stared at the screen, "Aire de Val Meuvy Rest Stop."

"That sounds great. Once we get to Paris, you will have to help me with directions. It's going to be a bit tricky, driving through the city, at night in the rain, even with the streetlights."

"Sure. I'll look for the names of the streets that we need to take."

Nicky was quiet for a while, prompting Tricia to glance across to make sure she was okay. "Everything all right, Nicky?"

"What? Oh sure. It's just that I can't believe that it's all over. It really will be, once we all meet up in Paris, won't it?"

"Yes, I'm sure it really is over. Inspector Lacombe has detained the two Asians. Your Dad has handed over the material that those people wanted, whoever they are, and now we are all going to meet up in Paris. Everyone has what they want. There's nothing left to do. It's all over."

"Why Paris? Why not Vancouver?"

"That was Michelle's idea. Uncle Matt, you and I are all in France, and we would have to go through Paris, or some other major city to fly back to Vancouver, so she thought that your Dad could fly here, and we could all be together quicker."

"Oh, yeah. I get it. Makes sense." She peered though the rain swept windshield, as they went past a sign. "Hey, that was a sign for the Aire de Val Meuvy Rest Stop. Five kilometres, and it had those little icon things for gas pumps and a coffee shop, plus some other stuff."

"That's good. I could use a break." She sighed. "And a coffee. I'll text Michelle that we're there."

They pulled into the Rest Stop, and were both pleased to be able to get out and stretch. Tricia now knew the routine for getting the right 'Super', and that she had to pay at the booth. In no time, they were sitting in a mall coffee shop, both enjoying a drink, and, in Nicky's case, along with an impressive looking sandwich.

"What is that you've got there, Nicky? It looks most interesting."

"It's called a Croque Madame. It's basically a grilled ham and cheese sandwich with some sort of sauce, and a poached egg on top. It's really good."

"Plus a salad and some fries."

"Oh, yeah. The salad came with it, but I asked for the fries." She grinned. "The French for fries is 'frites'. I can remember all the important French words."

Tricia pulled a piece of paper out of her pocket. "Here's the address of the hotel in Paris that Michelle gave me at the other Rest Stop. I scribbled it down as she was talking. I hope it's complete."

Nicky scrutinized it. "Looks okay. Hotel something Tour Eiffel, Rue Felicien David. I'll put it into the GPS in the car, and see what happens."

"Well, I suppose we should be moving along." Tricia said, as she finished her coffee, and stretched. "It's been a long day, but it can't be too much further now. Ready to go, Nicky?"

"Yeah, sure." She paused. "Tricia, that man, sitting on his own at the table by the door. He's been trying not to make it obvious, but he's been sort of looking at us, ever since he came in from the parking lot."

Tricia made a casual glance around, as though she was looking for the washroom. "You mean the youngish man in the open blue zip jacket, with the sort of pink shirt underneath?"

"Yeah, that's him. After what happened at the other Rest Stop, he makes me nervous. He's not after me, is he?" Nicky's voice quavered.

Tricia leant across the table to whisper. "I don't think so, Nicky, but after our previous experience, I'm not going to take any chances. That women's washroom that we used earlier, the door with 'Femmes' on it, is close to the exit into the mall. We'll make like we're going to the washroom, and deke out into the mall. With luck he won't notice us go."

"Okay." Nicky glanced around. "That group of English Seniors looks like they're all together, in one of those tour group things. They seem to all be getting ready to leave: we could try and mix in with them, as they head back into the mall."

"Good idea, Nicky. Let's go. We mustn't run. At least, not yet." She added.

They walked as casually as they could over to the washroom. Once inside, Tricia held Nicky out of sight behind her, giving her hand a squeeze, as she held the door open a crack, so that she could see back into the restaurant.

"What's happening Tricia?" Nicky breathed.

"The group of Seniors are taking forever." She moved to get a better look. "It looks like two of the men are arguing over how much tip they should leave. That man is staring at this door."

"Is he coming?"

"It looks like he is going to get up. I can't really see him very well. There's a woman with a tray standing in front of him, looking around for a table. Oh, someone walked by, and bumped the woman: she dumped her tray over him. He's really ticked."

"Can we just run for it?"

“Wait just a minute. The tour group of Seniors want nothing to do with it. That’s got them moving. Come on. Come on. Here they come. Ready?’

The talk outside the washroom door got louder, before the door flew open, and a short, stocky older woman, with fluffy white hair, and large blue framed glasses bustled in.

She stopped in surprise. “Oh. Excuse me. Is there a line-up?” She stared first at Tricia, and then at Nicky hiding behind her. “Wait a minute. What’s going on here? Is something wrong?”

“Yes, there is. We have to get away from a man out there.” Tricia explained quickly. “We need to get into the Mall, and out to our car without him seeing us. It’s complicated. He wants to grab Nicky.”

“Please don’t let him get me.” Nicky pleaded, fighting back tears.

“Who is he? He’s not police or her parent, or anything? Have she done anything wrong?” The woman frowned.

“Absolutely not. We don’t know who he is. The police know all about it. Nicky’s a witness to a crime. I’m a doctor, and they asked me to look after her, and bring her to Paris, where the police are expecting us. We’ll be safe once we get there. We only stopped here for a break. I don’t know how he found us. We just have to get on the road again.”

“Please help us.” Nicky gasped. “He’s going to hurt me if he gets me.”

The woman spun around, and spoke to the woman behind her. “Ethel, tell Henry and Bill to get a move on, and come here.”

The tall, slim woman, apparently named ‘Ethel’, backed out through the door, and signaled to two men who were shuffling along in the middle of the crowd of Seniors.

"What's wrong, Maud?"

"There's a man in the restaurant who is after this young girl. She's a witness for the police. This woman is a doctor who is taking her to Paris, where the police are expecting her. You two walk behind them, so that they can get out of here, without him seeing them leave. They just need to get to their car." Maud told them, crisply.

"Right ho." He squared his shoulders, and patted his substantial stomach. "Just walk in front of me and Henry. You're both such wee little things, you'll be completely hidden by our bulk. We'll have you out of here in a jiffy."

"You and Henry don't have to walk like your underwear is too tight, with your shoulders touching." Maud groaned. "Try to act natural."

Tricia grabbed Nicky's hand; they slipped past the woman, and walked ahead of the two men in the middle of the group heading out into the Mall.

Once they were safely in the shopping area, and out of sight of the restaurant, Tricia turned to the two men. "I think we're safe now. I'm sure he didn't see us leave. Thank you so much. Please thank the women for us, too."

"Yes, thanks. You've no idea." Nicky managed, a trembling hand wiping at her damp eyes.

Tricia put her am around the girl. "Come on, Nicky, there's the main exit to the parking lot, over there. Let's run for it!"

They raced out of the Mall, and across the parking lot to their car, making sure that they kept a row of vehicles between them and the window of the restaurant.

"We've done it, Nicky. Well done." Tricia sighed, as they pulled out of the Rest Stop parking lot. "I'll keep an eye on the rear view mirror, if that man was watching us, I'm pretty sure he didn't see us go."

"I can't stand much more of this." Nicky gasped. "Why won't they just leave us alone?"

"I don't know: it's awful. We're both so jumpy, he may not have been interested in us at all, but we have to be sure." She tried to be reassuring, forcing a smile for her young companion. "Don't worry. Next stop is the hotel in Paris. Well join the others, and all this stuff will be behind us."

Tricia accelerated the car along the Autoroute, flicking occasional glances at the rearview mirror.

"Can you GPS the route for us, from here to the hotel?"

"Yeah. No prob." Nicky busied herself putting the address of their destination into the GPS. "I'm okay now we're out of there." Her voice was still quavering. "Sorry I keep being such a wuss. Here we go. It looks like we stay on this main road, the A10, until we turn on to the Boulevard Peripherique. We go a little way on that, and then we sort of, like, slide off to go across a bridge called the Pont du Garigliano. The GPS will give us directions as we get there, so it looks pretty easy."

"I hope so. The traffic is starting to get heavier. I suppose we're joining the Paris throng. Does it say how long before we get to the address of the hotel?"

Nicky stared at the screen. "Yeah. There it is. It says it's seventy-two kilometres from here, and the GPS says it will take about an hour. It's getting closer every minute as we scoot along here. There are no major stoppages showing on the GPS. Looks like we'll get to the hotel between ten thirty and eleven, providing there aren't any traffic problems, or junk."

"Or if I take a wrong turn." Tricia added, trying to keep a lighthearted mood.

"You're doing great. That won't happen." Nicky assured her. "Can you see anyone following us?"

"I'm not sure. There have been some headlights that pulled onto the Autoroute behind us, and have stayed behind us for the past little while." She flicked her eyes to the rear view mirror. "No, that's okay. They've put their indicator on. They're turning off.""

Nicky let out a long breath. "Who's going to be at the hotel? Do you know? Is Dad going to be there?"

"I don't know, Nicky. Uncle Matt and Michelle should be there. Michelle said it was about an hour and a half flight to Paris from Bordeaux. Of course, then they have to get from the airport to the hotel, and I have no idea how far that is: I never left the airport the other day, when I arrived from China. Michelle did say that your Dad was flying out of Beijing late in the evening sometime, but it's a long flight. It took me nearly twelve hours, all together, but there was some sort of delay when we arrived in Paris, and our plane had to circle for a while. Then there is the whole time thing, with Beijing being six hours ahead of France, so I don't know what time it was in France when he left Beijing."

"My head is sort of fuggy. I can't seem to work out all that time difference and flight time stuff. He'll be here tomorrow for sure, though, won't he?"

"Assuming he gets a direct flight, yes, your Dad should arrive in Paris tomorrow. In the morning, I would think."

"Oh, okay." The GPS started giving out a message. "Here we go. Up ahead is where we jog around a bit, and start heading for that Boulevard Peri whatever, and the Gaggly bridge."

"Got it. There's the sign the GPS is talking about. It's a good thing they have the road well marked. With the rain making the roads wet, and the traffic starting to pick up, we will have to slow down. It will be much slower when we get onto the city streets, and I'll have to really concentrate."

They were quiet, as Tricia joined in with the steady flow of vehicles that were heading through the suburbs, into the centre of Paris. A valley of buildings loomed around them as dark shapes in the rainy night. Streetlights provided cones of yellow light, revealing shining water drenched roads, and, here and there, umbrella covered pedestrians hurrying through to wherever they needed to go. Occasional shop fronts were illuminated to show off their wares, apparently hoping to entice customers in, when they opened in the morning.

"There's the sign for the Boulevard Peripherique." Nicky called out, and they followed the car ahead of them as it swung gently through the curve, around to the left, and joined the Boulevard.

"The exit to the Gaggly whatever bridge is not far, according to what I can see on the map." She stared ahead through the windscreen. "That must be it. Just ahead. Where all those cars are exiting away to the right. Yes. There's the bridge."

"Got it. We must be nearly there." Tricia exhaled.

"Hey, Tricia! I can see the Eiffel Tower, just along the river. It's all lit up with little lights. That is so totally awesome. Did you see it?" Nicky enthused.

"I'm a little occupied at the moment, Nicky. Do I have to turn here on to the Avenue de Versailles, for the bridge?"

"Yeah. Here's the Avenue de Versailles coming up. We turn right, where those cars ahead are going. Then we go along there a bit, and turn left onto that bridge ahead, according to the GPS map."

"I just caught a glimpse of the Eiffel Tower. You're right: it really is something with all those lights. It stands out, even on a rainy night like this." Tricia said, as they exited the bridge, and headed down into some residential streets.

"Sorry I got a bit excited back there. My mind is such a mixed up mush. I feel great for a while, then it suddenly goes, and I feel sort of down and depressed, then, after a bit I'm all amped up again. It's like a cycle."

"It's understandable. Your mind and body will take a while to adjust after all the drugs, plus everything else that you've been through."

"Yeah. I suppose so." She gave a confused grin. "I'm still struggling to get my head around the idea that we're in France. It's sort of hard to explain, but since I woke up, and saw you, and all that has happened since, it has felt a bit like I'm kind of in another dimension."

"I feel a bit like that myself. Hey, we're nearly there. Thank goodness there doesn't seem to be much traffic, here. We can take our time." Tricia shrugged her aching shoulders with a sigh. She carefully negotiated their way through the cars and other vehicles that were parked on both sides of the wet roads. There were mostly houses lining the streets, although they did pass a corner store and occasional brightly lit wine shops that were still open, as well as two bakeries that would be coming to life in a few more hours. Nicky was intrigued by the small restaurants with their menu boards that were still displaying 'Le plat du jour', under their awnings.

"Here's another intersection, Nicky. Look out for the Rue Felicien David."

"There it is." She said, pointing to the street ahead on the right. "We've made it." She peered through the windshield. "I think I see the sign for our hotel: it's lit up just ahead. Isn't it called something with 'Eiffel Tower' in the name?"

"Yes, that's it." Tricia confirmed, as they drew closer. "Now I just need to find somewhere to park."

"There's a place. Can we fit in there?"

"Yup. We're in. Thanks for all of your help navigating, Nicky. You were great. Let's try and run inside, without getting too wet. We just have to get checked in, since we don't have any luggage to worry about. Michelle and Matt should be here already, and hopefully they will have our bags inside waiting for us. "

The first people they saw, as they pushed their way through the revolving glass front door, and entered the lobby were Michelle and Matt sitting on a plush, kidney-shaped couch, waiting for them. Their faces lit up, and they sprang forward, Michelle running across to hug Tricia, and Matt and Nicky flying into each other's arms. Everybody was talking at once.

"Tricia. Nicky. You finally made it. Fantastic. How are you both? You must be exhausted, driving all the way here from the Dordogne. Matt and I have been on the edge of our seats, waiting for you to walk though the door. I was receiving updates on your progress, every time you went through a tollbooth, but the last one was a while ago. You have been absolutely fantastic Tricia, driving all the way from Bergerac, really, in one go, particularly considering that you don't speak French, and have only been in France for twenty-four hours."

"It was certainly a long drive, but my navigator, here, was a huge help. Michelle, this is Nicky Berg, who you have heard so much about recently, and Nicky, this is Agent Michelle Denis of Interpol. Nicky has been terrific, she even helped with the French. I don't know what I would have done without her."

Nicky wouldn't let go of Matt, so she exchanged a little hand wave with Michelle.

“Honestly, how are you, Nicky?” Matt asked, holding her at arms length, so that he could look at her. “You’re looking pretty good.”

“It was awful, Uncle Matt. I’ve sort of totally lost about four days.” She tried to fight back the tears, as she hugged him. “I couldn’t believe it when Tricia appeared. At first, I thought I was seeing things. I could hardly walk. I won’t even mention the disgusting diaper. Uber yuck. Then we had to rush out, and the car with these two men came racing down the road to get us. It was totally hideous, and really scary.” She swallowed, as she paused for breath. “Tricia was great. She did this amazing skidding right turn, and we got away. We thought we were safe, and then, after a couple of hours driving, we stopped at this Rest Stop place, and these two men came, and were looking for us, but this nice cop, Inspector Lacombe, that was his name, wasn’t it Tricia? Well, he helped us and arrested the two men or something. Anyway, he got us to our car, and we just took off again. Then when we stopped again later, there was this man watching us in the restaurant. It was really scary. We had to hide in the middle of a group of really nice old English people to get out to our car.”

“It’s okay, Nicky. It’s all over. You’re safe now.” Matt hugged her tight, as he gave Tricia a puzzled look.

Michelle pulled Tricia aside, and whispered. “What’s this about men looking for you at the Rest Stops?”

“I’ll fill you in with all the details later. We actually have you to thanks. Inspector Lacombe heard your police alert to look out for us, and caught up with us at the Rest Stop near a place called Limoges, or something like that. He helped us out of a bit of a difficult situation.” She muttered quietly in reply.

“When’s Dad going to be here? Do you know?” Nicky asked, looking first at Matt and then Michelle.

"At this moment, your Dad is on the overnight flight from Beijing, and is due to land early tomorrow morning. Of course, he has to clear Customs, and all that, and get a taxi from the airport, so he should be here around breakfast time." Matt explained.

Nicky looked around at the others, sheepishly, her face wet with tears. "I know it's a bit weird, because I was sort of asleep for days, but I suddenly feel kind of, like, really, really tired." She managed a small smile. "Would it be okay if I just went to bed?" She gave Tricia a questioning look.

Tricia took only a second to understand her unstated plea. "Yes, of course. I'm with you, Nicky. It's been a really long drive, plus we had a couple of rather stressful rest stops. I'm beat. I don't think there is anything urgent that has to be done tonight, is there Michelle?"

"Not at all." Michelle recognized that a message had been sent and received, between the two. She would find out later from Tricia how serious the issue was. "How about we meet down here at eight o'clock in the morning? The hotel does quite a good breakfast."

"Great. Nicky and I will head on up to our rooms. Do you have our keys, or do we get them from the Front Desk?" She looked at Michelle and Matt questioningly.

"You will have to get them from the desk. They will want to see your passports, too. It's quite usual in France." Michelle explained. "I've filled in most of the guest registration details for you, already, there's just your passport numbers, and signatures. You've both got your passports handy?"

"Yes." They answered in unison, as they dug out their documents.

"That's good. Your luggage is already in your rooms. Two

rooms, side by side with a connecting door."

Michelle noticed a flicker of relief flash across Nicky's face, and understood the silent message that had been exchanged between her and Tricia.

CHAPTER 36

While Tricia and Nicky were enjoying their reunion with Matt and Michelle, Sarah Little and Kevin Blakey were connecting with CSIS Regional Director Claude Noble.

Noble was curt. "I read your message that things were winding up in Beijing. What are the details?"

"Well sir, it does look like it is over. There was a tightly organized operation, last night, planned and executed by the Interpol team." Sarah Little recounted. "At exactly the same time as Paul Berg was at the National Centre for the Performing Arts in Beijing, handing over all of the material that the kidnappers had demanded, Dr. Tricia Chen was at the gite in the Dordogne area of France removing young Nicky Berg. It had to be precisely timed, so that the kidnappers were not aware that Nicky Berg had been rescued, until Paul Berg had handed over the material, and he had been removed to safety."

"Explain." Noble barked. "What was the threat that Berg was facing?"

"There was a credible concern that the kidnappers intended to eliminate the Berg brothers, Nicky Berg, and Patricia Chen. That way, there wouldn't have been anyone left to reveal the details of how and why the Berg brothers had given them sole rights to their research." Blakey explained. "That was why everything had to be timed so that the Interpol actions didn't provoke any panic reactions by the kidnappers, in either Beijing or Bergerac. The plan was for Paul Berg to hand over the material, and as soon as it had been verified and accepted, I would be ready with a taxi to whisk him to the airport. From there, he would immediately be flown to Paris, to join his family. At the same time, Dr. Chen would take Nicky Berg from the gite to Bergerac airport, where they would join Matt Berg and an Interpol agent, and fly to Paris on a chartered flight, to meet up with Paul Berg."

"Why was Patricia Chen selected to go in alone to rescue Nicky Berg? That task is routinely assigned to an extraction team that has been trained for it?"

"The particular situation and circumstances under which Nicky Berg was being held were quite unusual. She was heavily sedated, and there was only one woman who was with her in the cottage each day. That attendant only left the cottage when a physician attended Nicky Berg for a brief time every evening. Interpol has identified that physician, and arrested her. She is a young dedicated physician who had spent the past two years working in Africa, and gave every indication of having strong ethics. Her story is that she received a request to look after a young girl who was waiting for a major operation, and had no idea that the girl had actually been kidnapped."

"She has cooperated with Interpol willingly, and provided detailed information about Nicky Berg's condition, and the schedule and layout of the cottage." Little explained. "She also told Interpol that when it was confirmed that Paul Berg had handed over the required material, there would be no one else in the cottage since the woman attendant would have already left. It was decided that Dr. Patricia Chen would go in on her own, in the place of the physician. The advantages of using Dr. Chen on her own were that if anyone were watching, she would appear to be the regular physician, and would not raise an immediate alarm, plus Chen is a pediatrician, and Nicky

Berg is very familiar with her."

"I take it that things did not go exactly as planned?" Noble said drily.

"No, unfortunately not, sir." Sarah Little agreed. "Apparently the gite that was being remotely monitored. Chen and her Interpol contact realized in time for Chen to get away with Nicky Berg, just as a hostile team was arriving. The meet at Bergerac airport was cancelled when something went sideways with the private jet that Interpol had chartered to take them to Paris. We're still trying to get the details."

"Okay, what is the situation, at this time? Give me all the details that you have. "

"Interpol got Paul Berg out of the Arts Centre, and I drove him to the airport, and put him on the plane to Paris. He should be landing there early tomorrow morning, Paris time." Blakey recounted. "The fellow from the Bureau of the Chinese Ministry of State Security, Renshu, stepped in, and arrested several of the people involved in the handover of the Bergs' research data."

Sarah Little took over. "According to the latest information that we have received from our Interpol contacts, Matt Berg and the Interpol agent drove to Bordeaux, and caught the flight to Paris. They arrived this evening, Paris time. As we explained, Dr. Patricia Chen and Nicky Berg had to scramble out of the gite, when they realized it was being monitored. Unfortunately, they were left high and dry, when their charter flight from Bergerac collapsed, so Chen decided she and Nicky would drive to Paris. It took them over six hours, but we have just heard that they have arrived at the hotel where Matt Berg and the Interpol agent were waiting."

"Okay. So it sounds like it has been pretty well wrapped up. Who has the material that Paul Berg handed over?"

"Renshu, and the Chinese."

"Damn. So, if I can summarize," Director Noble said. "Renshu and the Chinese have all of the material about the medical breakthrough that Paul and Matt Berg achieved: Nicky Berg is with Dr. Patricia Chen, Matt Berg, and an Interpol agent at a hotel in Paris, awaiting the arrival of Paul Berg, who is on a flight from Beijing. Finally, several of the individuals involved in the events in Beijing have been detained by the Chinese police."

"That about summarizes the current status, sir." Blakey and Little agreed.

"Do you see any existing threat that could possibly continue to endanger the Canadians, namely, the Bergs and Chen?"

"No, sir, we don't think so." Sarah Little said uncertainly.

"You're not sure. What is the outstanding threat?"

"Apparently Patricia Chen and Nicky were pursued by a pair of Asian men when they left the gite. Two men, possibly the same two, were searching for them at a Rest Stop on the way to Paris. A member of the Police Nationale had been alerted by Interpol, and intervened. They were arrested. That particular incident appears to have ended there. However, Dr. Chen reported that there might have been another attempt to abduct them at a later Rest Stop. They managed to evade the individual involved, and continued on to Paris."

"Question. How did the Asian men know that Chen and the Berg girl were at those particular rest stops?"

"That's not clear, sir. The Interpol agent told us that the French police are still interrogating the two men at the first one. As far as we can determine, the individuals behind this whole scheme are still out there in the wind. However, we have no solid intelligence that indicates that they still pose any level of threat to Chen and the Berg family."

"What about the man who posed as Paul Berg, and his female partner, the woman who had been posing as Dr. Chen? What has happened to them?"

"They seem to have disappeared, sir. The man is now believed to be a French freelance. Interpol is hopeful that they will be able to identify him. The current thinking is that the two of them were private operatives working for Renshu. He was very annoyed by the shooting at the pagoda, and hired them to keep Berg and Chen safely out of the danger zone. That explains why he was operating the lift for that strange scene where Chen swapped clothes with the woman. It also explains why Chen was sent to France."

"You have no idea who the woman is, or where she is?"

"We did some analysis of current active female operatives with our colleagues in other agencies, and there is a loose fit with an operative known as 'The Chameleon'." Blakey explained. "Few details are known about her, but she is thought to be a Eurasian, who hires out primarily to recover materials, or facilitate difficult exchanges. This has included recovering kidnap victims in the past. There are no known photographs of her, but, apparently, she is so adept at changing her appearance that she would not be recognizable from one time to the next."

"Could she present a threat to the Bergs or Chen? They have seen her, up close, and could potentially identify her."

"We are not sure that it was the Chameleon. Our best estimate has only a fifty percent probability. If it is the Chameleon, she has worked for friendly national security and intelligence agencies before. We do not believe that she represents a threat to the Bergs or Chen, and may even be working on their side. I understand that we have used her on a number of occasions, in the past."

"Okay. Keep looking into the possibility that there still could be operatives intent on removing the Bergs and Chen. Is there anything else? If not, that appears to wrap it up. I'll see you both back here tomorrow morning. I should advise you that I am hearing murmurings of political moves to rewrite this whole narrative. Apparently there are international sensitivities that could be disturbed if this episode became public. I will be able to bring you up to date tomorrow."

With that, the communication was terminated.

CHAPTER 37

Paul trudged his way wearily through the Paris airport. He looked around at all the escalators going in various directions, and found it totally confusing. The few hours' sleep that he had managed on the plane, was the only sleep he had had in over forty-eight hours. He recognized some other passengers from his flight, and followed them: thankfully, they went to the line-up for Customs and Immigration. He was driven by the knowledge that Nicky, Tricia and Matt were all here in Paris, waiting for him.

Whenever he thought of Nicky, Paul's head spun. He kept going over Matt's words in the call that came through as he was being rushed through the tunnel out of that Chinese arts centre place:
'Nicky's safe. Tricia's got her. She's driving the two of them in a rental car. Tricia says that Nicky is fine: a bit groggy after being sedated, but otherwise, just fine. I'll explain everything when we see you.'

What did 'fine' mean, after an experience like the one that Nicky had endured? Why did he mention that Tricia was driving them in a rental car? The plan was that they were all going to Bergerac airport, and flying to Paris from there. Blakey had said that something had gone wrong. What had happened? If they weren't going to the Bergerac airport, where was Tricia driving them? Had Tricia and Nicky managed to get a flight to Paris? If not, where were they? One thing gave Paul comfort: if things were getting difficult, there was no one that he would rather have looking after Nicky than Tricia. She was smart, and seemed to be panic proof.

He took a deep breath. Tricia had only been gone for two days, but he already missed her so much.

Paul shook his head slowly, and muttered to himself that he just had to be patient for a little longer. Matt would explain everything, when he got to the hotel.

The Customs agents seem to be going painfully slowly. He desperately wanted to get through Customs, out of the airport, and into a taxi heading for the hotel where Blakey had told him they would be staying.

Finally, it was his turn, and he was through. He followed the signs with the English word exit, and the French 'sortie', plus the picture of a taxi.

There was a wait in another line at the taxi rank, but eventually, it was his turn. The driver put his luggage in the back, he showed him the address of the hotel that Blakey had written down, and, finally, with a honking of horns, and a few French curses at the other drivers, they were off.

Paul walked into the hotel lobby, and saw Nicky standing by the ancient looking elevator, looking bemused.

"Nicky!"

She looked across, her jaw fell open, and her face lit up, as she rushed across and threw her arms around him. "Dad. Dad. You're here. You made it."

"Yes, of course I made it. I wasn't going to leave you a moment longer." He tried to swallow the frog in his throat, and sound casual.

"It was awful. I was sort of, like, kidnapped, then Tricia rescued me, and we drove all the way to Paris. It took positively hours, and she was totally fantastic." The words were tumbling out. "I missed you so much. They drugged me, or something, and I don't remember the past few days, until there was Tricia just sort of standing there. It was incredible. I thought she was a ghost, or something at first, then I realized she really was there. I had to get dressed, because I was wearing this awful nightie thing, and you won't believe it, but I was wearing a diaper, simply too totally gross. Then Tricia realized that they were listening to us, and knew she wasn't the other doctor, and we had to run for the car, except I couldn't run, and Tricia had to help me sort of shuffle out, as fast as we could, and there was this car coming racing towards us, and we just missed it and took off."

"Hey, there's no need to cry." Paul said, as she started to sob uncontrollably. "We're all here. It's all over, finally it's over, and we're all back together again." He was blinking back the tears, and hugging her like he was never going to let her go.

Nicky wiped her eyes. "I was so scared. I don't want to ever leave you again. There were these men and they were chasing us at that Rest Stop, and we didn't know who they were or anything, then this man who had shown Tricia how to fill the car with gas, 'Super' they call it, well anyway, he came in, and told us he was with the French police, and said they would be arrested, and led us out the back way, and we just took off. My knees were shaking so badly, I could hardly walk."

He kissed the top of her head. "I'm here now, and you're safe. Where are the others? You're not on your own here, are you? Tricia and Matt are here, somewhere, too, aren't they?"

"Yes, we're here, bro." Matt called out as he appeared around the corner. "Come on, we need a hug, too. It's been quite a wild time."

There was a cough. "Monsieur?" The taxi driver was standing behind Paul, with his bags.

Paul glanced around. "Oh yes, of course. I'm sorry. Matt, have you got some Euros? I owe this man for the taxi from the airport."

"No worries. I've got it." He paid the taxi driver, and joined his niece in hugging his brother.

Nicky broke free, finally, looking around. "Where's Tricia? She was right behind me when I came down."

"I saw her with Michelle, around the corner, over there, just now." Matt said, pointing across the lobby. "They were deep in discussion about something."

"Michelle? Who's Michelle?" Paul asked.

He was answered by Tricia appearing with Michelle Denis beside her. "Hi Paul. Thank goodness you're here. We've all been wondering what was happening with you." She was slightly flustered, uncertain about their new relationship. "Let me introduce Agent Michelle Denis of Interpol."

Michelle stepped forward with her hand extended. "Hi Paul. We were never properly introduced in Beijing."

Paul stared. "Michelle Denis? I thought you were with CSIS?" He shook his head. "You were in Beijing. How did you get to France? There is an awful lot that I need explained."

"I was sent on to Bergerac to work on facilitating Nicky's release. Thankfully, despite a few bumps, everything worked out. Matt was a tremendous help, and Tricia was absolutely amazing. She went in alone, and got Nicky out, and drove all the way to Paris."

"I told you, Dad. Tricia was awesome. She rescued me several times." Nicky exclaimed.

Paul looked at Tricia, unsure if he should rush across and kiss and hug her. He decided to leave her the option; he opened his arms wide, and gave his best welcoming smile. "Do I get a hug from Nicky's hero?" He asked softly.

Tricia strode across the lobby into his arms. She buried her face in his chest, and then looked up so that they could share a welcome kiss.

"How are you? I can never thank you enough for looking after Nicky. You were absolutely incredible. I've missed you so much." He whispered.

"Me too. You have no idea. It was quite a drive from the gite to Paris. Nicky and I felt like we were totally alone, racing right through the middle of France, a country neither of us knew. If we hadn't had a GPS, I don't know where we would have ended up. Nicky was absolutely tremendous. She was a great help with her knowledge of French. All we could both think about all the way was what was happening to you. We had no idea if you were still in Beijing, or if you had actually caught the flight to Paris, or where you were."

Paul hugged her, and kissed her again.

"Whoa." Nicky gasped in surprise. "There's obviously been things going on, while I've been out of it."

"How about we all move into the dining room, and get some coffee and breakfast?" Matt suggested. "Are you up for that Paul? If you check in at the front desk, and show them your passport, they will have your bags taken up to your room for you."

"That sounds like a good idea. I'll hang on to my laptop, though. I must contact Nicky's grandparents in Vancouver, and give them the good news that Nicky is with us, safe and sound. As soon as I've done that, coffee and a real French croissant? Lead me to it. They brought some breakfast around on the plane, but I couldn't face it."

He came back from registering at the desk. "I need to catch up on everything that has been happening. I've heard about Tricia rescuing Nicky from the gite where she was being held, and some French policeman helping them get away from two fellows who were looking for them at a rest stop. I still have no idea why the original plan collapsed, you know, about you all meeting up at the Bergerac airport and flying to Paris. How on earth did Tricia and Nicky end up driving all the way here, yesterday?"

Matt put his arm around his brother's shoulders, and led him towards the dining room door. "Come on. Let's all go in. You can send your message, while we sit down, relax, and share our stories about the past couple of days, over coffee and breakfast."

"I think perhaps, I'll leave you all to your breakfast." Michelle said apprehensively. "I am just an outsider."

"Absolutely not." Matt declared. "You must join us. You are a key member of the group. Michelle has been the brains behind everything, Paul. I don't want to even think what would have happened without her. She was our contact with Beijing, alerting us to your evolving situation, and keeping everyone calm when things started to get a bit hairy. Michelle, no argument, you are one of us. Come on."

"Okay. I will be enchanted to join you. Thank you." Michelle was quietly pleased that Matt had insisted that she join them for breakfast.

The group wandered back into the hotel lobby, after a prolonged breakfast that was filled with exchanges of accounts of the happenings of the past couple of days. Two elegantly dressed gentlemen approached them.

"Please excuse us, Mesdames and Messieurs. Allow me to

introduce ourselves: I am Jean-Claude Voisier, Senior Secretary in the Ministry for Europe and Foreign Affairs, and this is my colleague, Lucas Tremblay from the Canadian Embassy. We would like a brief word with everyone, perhaps, in the small room over there. Merci."

"This doesn't sound like it involves me." Michelle observed.

"Nor me. I'm with you, Michelle." Nicky added.

"Non, non. We would like everyone to attend, including you, Agent Denis, and you Mademoiselle Nicky." Lucas Tremblay explained firmly, as he and his colleague shepherded them past the lifts into the small meeting room that they had reserved.

Once they were all settled in the chairs around the meeting table, Jean-Claude Voisier cleared his throat, and began. "First, let me welcome you all to France, and at the same time apologize for the experiences that you have had to endure, most notably you, Mademoiselle Nicky. It is absolutely intolerable that something like that should happen in France."

"Before we begin explaining the reason for our meeting with you, it is necessary that we attend to some administrative details." He gave a Gallic shrug of resignation. "Because my Canadian colleague and I will be discussing issues involving," he pursed his lips and gave a quick sideways flick of his hand, "how shall I say, perhaps difficult relationships that our governments may have with another country, you are all required to sign the Official Secrets Acts for our two countries."

"Wait a moment. I have been through enough of this nonsense already, thank you very much." Paul fumed, as Tremblay handed out official looking documents to everyone. "I don't intend to sign the anything, and if you are going to talk about something that your governments want to keep secret, then I am absolutely not interested, and I am leaving."

Lucas Tremblay placed the final documents on the table in

front of Tricia, who was sitting beside him. "Unfortunately, you have no choice, Professor Berg. You are all Canadian citizens, and a failure to sign the Official Secrets Act, when, as in this case, you are in possession of information that could be damaging to Canada, your failure will be taken as an implicit violation of the Act, and you will face criminal charges in Canada."

"I am afraid it is considered to be a serious violation that will be respected in France, Professor." Jean-Claude Voisier added sympathetically. "You will be arrested, and put on a flight back to Canada, where you will have to face the charges that my colleague has identified." He punctuated this with another Gallic shrug.

"This is outrageous." Paul growled.

Tricia finished signing the two documents, and turned to him. "We might as well sign, Paul. Even if it is blatant government coercion, we have no rational choice."

He signed the two documents, and flung them across the table to Tremblay. "There. It's done: now get on with all this secret nonsense that you alluded to."

"We thank all of you for your cooperation." Monsieur Voisier walked slowly around the room, as he spoke. "My Canadian colleague and I are fully aware of the unfortunate occurrences that have befallen you over the past number of days. It all started with the brilliant medical advances made by you, Professor Paul Berg, and you, Doctor Matt Berg. Unfortunately, an unscrupulous group ignored the potential humanitarian benefit that was your goal, and plotted to obtain all of your research for themselves. They made some tentative exploratory forays to try and legitimately obtain all of the rights to your advances, but were not successful. Whereupon, they embarked on an unscrupulous plan to achieve their desired outcome. They arranged for young Nicky to be invited to visit Beijing as part of a soccer tournament, to create the opportunity they required.

"Using a local intermediary that they were able to coerce into their iniquitous plot, they had young Nicky Berg abducted from the street in Beijing, anaesthetized, and flown to France, where she was held." He nodded acknowledgement toward Nicky. "Paul Berg was then told to fly to Beijing, and bring all of the material relating to the advances that he and his brother had made. At approximately the same time, Dr. Matt Berg was told to travel to the town of Bergerac in France, ostensibly to receive Nicky when she was released.

"Thankfully, Interpol was alert to the plot, and Agent Michelle Denis was sent first to Beijing, and then to Bergerac to analyze the situation, and secure the safety of Paul, Matt and Nicky Berg, and, as it transpired, Doctor Patricia Chen, who had accompanied Paul Berg to Beijing. Interpol was concerned that the interested party might conclude that their long term interests would not coincide with all of yours."

Nicky's gasp resonated loudly in the otherwise totally silent room.

"I know that I am making a summary of the events, and you are all too well aware of the details." Voisier continued. "Moving to the end of the story, you are all safe here in Paris, but China has obtained all of the material that was to be given to the kidnappers. Not a desirable outcome, but the best that was available. Now we come to the crux of the matter.

"The governments of France and Canada, and many of our allies, have determined that the details of this abominable episode must not be made public. Firstly because it might well provoke what you call 'copy-cat' incidents, and secondly because we do not want it to be known that China has essentially stolen a very significant medical advance. Therefore, it has been decided that there will be an official account, to which you will all adhere. It is the following:

"Nicky Berg was taken severely ill while she was in Beijing with her soccer team. A passing motorist recognized that she was in distress, and stopped, bundled her into their car and took her to the Beijing Children's Clinic, where Doctor Yang Chow attended to her. Because of the language difficulty, there was an initial misunderstanding by the other members of the soccer team who were present. Her father, widower Professor Paul Berg, and his friend Doctor Patricia Chen rushed to Beijing. Thankfully, Nicky recovered after a few days, and they all went to rest and recover for ten days, on an island in the Caribbean.
"The French and Canadian governments have agreed on this plausible story since it will minimize any potential national embarrassments, and keep you away from unwanted media attention for ten days. By the time you return to Canada, the media will have other stories to pursue, and you will be able to continue your lives quietly, out of the media spotlight."

"That's utterly ridiculous." Paul burst out, incredulous. "That story will never hold together. What about Nicky's friend Kim, and the other girls? And Doctor Chow certainly will not endorse that complete fabrication."

"I am sure that they will all agree with this account of events, monsieur. Nicky's friends from the soccer team have already been told that she was taken ill, and rushed to the clinic by a passing motorist. They were confused, but everything happened so quickly, and since they did not speak Mandarin, and were unfamiliar with China and Beijing, they have gradually accepted that version of events. The situation with Nicky's friend Kim was the most challenging. However, her family is Korean by birth, and to avoid any possible difficulties with Canada, they have agreed."

"How do you explain all of us here in Paris?"

"Poof." Tremblay shrugged. "It is the obvious route to connect from Beijing to the French island. We have already supplied the Canadian media with that update of the incident involving Nicky, and it has been widely distributed. The Chinese authourities have welcomed, and supported this version of events, and told Doctor Chow that she must adhere to that story: it is China, she has no option." Lucas Tremblay added.

"What is this nonsense about us all going to some Caribbean island?" Paul demanded.

"The French government will cover all of your expenses, including your to flight to the island of Saint Martin that will leave tomorrow morning, and your living expenses on the French half of the island for ten days."

"What sort of place has been arranged for us to stay in? I hope it's not some dingy two star hotel." Paul groaned, still struggling to come to terms with the sudden arrangements that had been imposed on them.

"Appropriate accommodation has been arranged at a large villa, near a very pleasant beach. There is full maid service, plus a chef, so you will be well looked after. There is also an excellent doctor, Doctor Francoise Dubois, who specializes in pediatric trauma, and has agreed to see Nicky for an hour each day."

"Why do I need to see a doctor?" Nicky sounded close to tears.

"You've been through an awful lot, over the past few days, Nicky." Tricia gently explained. "It's a really good idea to see someone like Doctor Dubois, to help you process everything. If I had been through what you have, I would certainly want to see a specialist. I've met Francoise Dubois: she's a really nice person and an excellent doctor. You'll like her."

"She won't inject me with anything, will she? I don't want any more injections."

"No, she'll just take all the usual tests and measurements that doctors do, and talk to you. You don't have to do or talk about anything you don't want to. It will just sort of be an easy chat for an hour to help you get past any uncomfortable memories."

"You mean like being kidnapped, drugged, escaping, and then being chased across France by thugs, that sort of thing?" Nicky managed a wry smile.

"You know, I think a few days in the sun, on a beautiful French island in the Caribbean is just what I need. How about you, Matt?" Paul said, giving his brother a knowing look.

"Sounds absolutely perfect, to me." Matt had got his brother's message. "And I certainly hope that you will be coming with us, Michelle?"

"It sounds wonderful, just exactly what you all need. I am going to have to check my schedule."

"Bon. That is settled." Jean-Claude Voisier sounded slightly relieved. "A package with your tickets and all of the details will be delivered to the Front Desk later this morning. Your flight leaves tomorrow shortly after noon. It is quite a long flight, but Island time is six hours behind Paris, so you will arrive tomorrow in the late afternoon, island time. Saint Martin is an integral part of the French Republic, so the facilities and services are the same as those that are available in any area of France. Now you have the whole of today to explore and enjoy Paris."

"What about clothes? All I have is my stuff for the soccer tournament in Beijing. What is this Saint Martin place like, monsieur Voisier?"

"It is largely a holiday island at this time of year. Shorts and shirts are the main dress code during the day. Swimsuits are frowned upon in the main town of Marigot, where there are some excellent shops. The island also has some very fine restaurants, if you decide you would like to get dressed up and go out for dinner."

"One last thing." Lucas Tremblay gave a winning smile. "To celebrate the conclusion of this unpleasant experience, I would like you all to join me for an aperitif at Wilde's bar in L'Hotel this evening. It has a famous history as a popular spot for Oscar Wilde, and many other celebrities. Would six o'clock be suitable? It is close to the Rive Gauche, the Left Bank, with its many fine restaurants, where you can have a most enjoyable dinner."

Tricia, Matt and Paul were so overwhelmed by what they had just been told that they automatically murmured their agreement and thanks. Nicky looked concerned.

"Will I be allowed in this Wild bar place?" Nicky asked anxiously.

"But absolutely, mademoiselle. I would never have suggested anywhere that would not be appropriate for you." Tremblay reassured her. "You might find some of the letters on the walls quite interesting."

With a friendly au revoir, the two men departed, leaving the little group still trying to process the latest turn of events.

"I hadn't exactly planned on ten days on a Caribbean island." Matt mused.

"I think that Nicky and I are going to have to go on a shopping sortie this morning." Tricia noted with a laugh. "Is there anywhere near here where we can go, Michelle?"

"The Rue de Passy is a short walk away, and has quite a few shops that should provide an excellent selection." Michelle Denis explained. "I know the area quite well, and would be delighted to be your guide."

"And what do Matt and I do, while you women are filling your shopping bags?" Paul asked with a smile.

"You could both probably add a few things, as well." Tricia observed. "How smart is this Wild bar, Michelle, where Lucas Tremblay is meeting us this evening?"

Michelle gave a brief side tilt with her head and shrugged. "It's very traditional, and has kept a sort of late nineteenth century ambiance, in keeping with the Oscar Wilde era. At six o'clock, we will be early, when it's popular with the conservative, embassy types for pre-dinner drinks. Parisians are quite fashion conscious, so most of the women will be wearing fashionable outfits, and the men will have jackets, or suits. Later in the evening, when the main crowds arrives, there will be quite an eclectic cross-section of patrons and you would see quite a few flamboyant fashions."

"I can manage the jacket or suit part," Matt stated. "How about you, Paul?"

"Yes, Tricia insisted that I bring a suit, so that should work. I'm still not sure what you and I are going to do this morning."

"Why don't you two walk along the Seine to the Trocadero, opposite the Eiffel Tower?" Michelle suggested. "It's not far, and should be quite pleasant this morning. Matt speaks French quite well, so you can stop for a coffee and pastry at one of the bistros along the way. I suggest we meet back here again around twelve, and take taxis to Montmartre. It is very quaint, with some interesting restaurants hidden among the cobbled streets. There is one where I like to go, whenever I'm in Paris. We can have lunch there, and, after lunch, we can explore Montmartre."

"I think I remember my French teacher talking about Montmartre. What is it Michelle?" Nicky asked.

"Montmartre is like a small artists' village on a hill, in the eighteenth arrondissement of Paris, Nicky." Michelle explained. "Its quaint cobbled streets and alleyways twist and turn their way up the hill, occasionally emerging into unexpected squares, from where you can catch glimpses of Paris below you. Everywhere you go, there are dozens of colourful little shops, cafes and restaurants, packed in beside each other. At the top is a famous church, the gleaming white, beautiful Sacre-Coeur Basilica. It can be seen from all over Paris, and from the Sacre-Coeur, you can see all of Paris."

"I think you will love Montmartre, Nicky." Matt added.

"That's settled, then. Matt and I will meet you back here at around twelve, and we will all go to Montmartre for lunch." Paul concluded.

"I have one request." Michelle added. "I would like to go up to my room and freshen up a little. I suggest we meet down here, in the lobby in fifteen minutes?"

This was met with general agreement.

CHAPTER 38

Michelle had her own reason to return to her hotel room. She needed to supply the Head of Operations with an update of the current situation.

"Good morning, ma'am. I thought I should bring you up to date."

"Go ahead."

"I arrived at the hotel with Matt Berg early yesterday evening. Patricia Chen and Nicky arrived much later, around twenty-three hundred hours. They had a bit of a rushed departure from the gite where Nicky was being held, but our team was on hand and able to intercept their pursuers. Chen decided to drive right through to Paris. There was an incident at a Rest Stop near Limoges, when two Koreans appeared, and were looking for them. There was another minor incident at the next Rest Stop, as well. The Police Nationale were on hand on the first occasion, and the second was quickly resolved."

"Those two have had quite a time." Head of Operations observed drily. "Carry on."

"Paul Berg arrived at the hotel in Paris this morning, which means that all the parties are together in the hotel; Paul, Nicky and Matt Berg, and Patricia Chen.

"At breakfast, we were joined by Jean-Claude Voisier, Senior Secretary in the French Ministry for Europe and Foreign Affairs, and Lucas Tremblay from the Canadian Embassy.

Monsieur Voisier presented them with the official account of the events involving Nicky Berg, which is, that she was taken severely ill while she was in Beijing with her soccer team. A passing motorist recognizing that she was in distress, stopped, bundled her into their car and took her to the Beijing Children's Clinic, where Doctor Yang Chow attended to her. Because of the language difficulty there were some unfortunate misunderstandings by some of the people who were present. Professor Paul Berg and his friend Doctor Patricia Chen rushed to Beijing. Thankfully, Nicky recovered after a few days, and they all went to rest and recover on the French island of Saint Martin in the Caribbean."

"How did they react to this official version of events?"

"After some initial objections, it was accepted under the coercive threat of legal consequences if they voiced another version."

"Then that is settled. What shape are they all in?"

"A lot better than I would have expected, considering the ordeal of the past few days. Nicky Berg is showing signs of posttraumatic stress, but she is desperately trying to put up a calm front. Tricia Chen contacted me, when they were on their way to Paris, and asked that she and Nicky have connecting rooms. Our security agent has the room next to Nicky Berg, and monitors the activity in her room. She heard screams from Nicky's room around two-thirty this morning, followed almost immediately by Chen calling to Nicky, as she ran through to her. Our agent listened to the murmuring and sobbing until it had settled down. Patricia Chen is a pediatrician, so the agent decided not to intervene."

"What about her father, Paul Berg?"

"Putting together my observations with the information provided by our team in Beijing, it is clear that Paul Berg is very devoted to Nicky, and has found the past few days extremely stressful. I considered the possibility that he could simply collapse, if he is pushed much more. However, his brother, Matt, has assured me that Paul has exceptional mental strength. He is watching out for Paul, and has promised to let me know immediately if he sees any signs of Paul deteriorating. Matt Berg also confirmed my impression that Paul and Tricia Chen have formed a romantic attachment recently. It has not resulted in any discomfort within the group, and there will be strength for both of them."

"How are Matt Berg, and Patricia Chen coping?"

"They have both been absolute rocks, and have been really holding the other two together. In a curious way, they are similar, and yet, quite different. Superficially, Matt appears as an amiable chap, ready to laugh at anything, and Patricia Chen appears to be a quiet, serious pediatrician, happiest when she's helping sick children. And yet, when things started getting rough, Matt and Tricia were the first to jump in, and take the load. It was Matt who located the gite where Nicky was being held, and Tricia who went in and got her out. I have yet to see either of them panic."

"It sounds like they all need to have a calm, normal day. What are the plans for the rest of the day?"

"A shopping trip for Tricia Chen and Nicky, followed by lunch in Montmartre, and a visit to Sacre-Coeur Basilica. This evening, Lucas Tremblay is hosting the group for drinks at Wilde's bar in L'Hotel, followed by a quiet dinner for the Bergs and Patricia Chen."

"Have you encountered any signs of possible hostile activity around the Berg family or Dr. Chen?"

"Nothing has been observed or reported, since the encounters that Patricia Chen and Nicky Berg had at the Rest Stops."

"Nevertheless, I have assigned a full Security Team to the Berg family. They will be close at hand, wherever they go, while they are in Paris. You have the emergency contact information?"

"Yes ma'am, and thank you." She hesitated. "If I might ask, what is the situation with Chief Inspector Lacombe?"

"He arrived in Paris last night. Security was assigned to his family: his son in Paris has a security detail in place, but the whereabouts of his daughter, her partner, and their two young daughters are unclear. There is currently an orange alert associated with Chief Inspector Lacombe and his family. You will be kept informed of the situation."

"Thank you. Has there been any success in identifying who was behind this whole coercion?"

"Not yet, but once we had identified the doctor who was involved in Bergerac, it gave us a strong lead."

"The young female doctor, Sehrish, appeared to be an unwitting participant, ma'am. There was every indication that she believed that she was helping in a difficult medical situation, and tried to give Nicky Berg good care under the circumstances. I was hoping that she could be shown some leniency."

"Yes, I read your report. If we determine that she is telling the truth, it will be taken into account. Is there is anything else?"

"What about the dead woman in the gite, ma'am?"

"It appears to have been a heart attack. In the note she said that she had been told that morning that the Berg girl was a kidnap victim, and to keep quiet, if she wanted to stay out of jail. The shock may have killed her."

"That was what Doctor Chen suspected."

"With respect to the report you sent me, we fully understand that this developed into a difficult situation for you, and your commitment is appreciated. The original time line was for a straightforward escort duty from Vancouver to Beijing, with an immediate return to Lyon. Of course, things became a little more complicated, but at least you are back in France. I can send in a replacement to take over tomorrow, if you want to return to Lyon immediately?"

"I am in contact with Lyon, daily. There is still some time, and the doctor says that it is probably better that I am not there for these last few days. The operation has been scheduled for the fifth of April, next week. I can deliver the group to Saint Martin, and then I would like to return home to Lyon, and start my leave on the third of April. "

"Agreed. I'll make sure all the documentation is completed for you. Anything else?"

"Not at this time, ma'am."

Michelle checked her watch, and hurried down to join the others in the hotel lobby.

CHAPTER 39

The white haired woman paused from pacing around her elegant office, to stand in front of the window, and gaze at the vines flowing down the hillside of southern France. They were her vines, in her vineyard. Everything had passed to her on the death of her husband. She was the custodian of everything that they had achieved together. She clenched her teeth. She would not let his memory down.

She rasped out 'Enter', in response to the expected knock on her door, turning slowly to confront her daughter who had entered.

"What is the latest information, daughter?"

"Michael has returned to France."

"Does he have the material?"

"Unfortunately, not. He informed me that the Chinese authourities took possession of it. The expert he had hired was inspecting it at the National Centre for the Performing Arts in Beijing, when a large contingent of Chinese police suddenly moved in. They arrested the expert, and took all of the material. Michael was fortunate to manage to leave in a crowd of concertgoers." She saw the anger rising in her mother's face, and hastily added. "He assured me that there is no connection to the family."

"Where are Paul and Matt Berg? Can they be persuaded to

recreate their work? Do they have copies?"

"When the Chinese authourities moved in, there was a team from Interpol that took Paul Berg quickly from the Arts Centre to the airport, and put him on a flight to Paris. Our information is that Matt Berg is also travelling to Paris. Michael believes that they could reproduce their work for us, but he is unsure how they can be persuaded to do it."

The old woman gave a long-suffering sigh. "What of the girl that is being held? Is Sehrish still looking after her at the gite?"

Her daughter shuffled her feet anxiously. She could feel perspiration gathering on her top lip, and rivulets trickling down her back. "A woman showed up at the gite in place of Sehrish, and took the girl. We believe they have driven to Paris."

"And Sehrish?"

"She has been detained. Anthony has an avocat working to get her released. The avocat is taking the firm position that Sehrish was simply the physician that had been retained to look after a young a seriously ill young girl, who was being held in a light coma to assist her recovery. There is nothing to indicate that Sehrish knew anything else."

"What a complete disaster." The old woman spat out. "Can my children do nothing without me? Have you all become lazy drones, only capable of living empty lives on the wealth that your father and I created?"

"What would you have us do, now, Mother?"

"Tell Jasar to inform Anthony and Michael that they must go to Paris, and do whatever is required to obtain a copy of the research material from those Berg brothers."

"As you wish, Mother."

"Now leave."

CHAPTER 40

At noon, Paul and Matt were back to the hotel first, and sitting in the lobby when the others returned. They arrived in a taxi, carrying arms full of bags with various store names emblazoned across them. There were bursts of laughter, as they attempted to maneuvre their way, one at a time, through the revolving glass door.

"Looks like you had a successful shopping trip." Paul observed, as he jumped up to help with the bags that appeared first around the revolving glass door, on the end of one of Nicky's arms.

Nicky was first through, and bubbling with excitement.

"Dad, we went to this Rue de Passy that Michelle knew: it was totally amazing. It's only a ten-minute walk from here. We went through these market things in the streets, and they were really cool; they sold everything, meat, and everything, right there, in the open air. Then we got to this Rue de Passy, and the whole street was totally awesome. Michelle said it was because it was sort of an expensive neighbourhood. We went in all these stores, and the clothes were so amazing. Some of the stores had stuff in the window that cost a fortune, so we didn't go in those. We all bought loads of stuff. You know, we had to, after that man said we're going to that Caribbean island place."

By the time she had paused for breath, the other two had negotiated their way through the door, with Matt's assistance.

"It sounds like you have had a great time, and looks like you have a lot of bags there, Nicky. What did you buy?" Matt laughed.

"Lots of stuff, Uncle Matt. I've got a stunning dress for this Wilde place tonight, and shoes to match. It will be perfect for the fancy restaurants on Saint whatsit, too. Then I had to get a swimsuit: it's a really cute two-piece. There was this store that had totally amazing stuff, way different from home. I got a pair of cotton pants, and some shorts: I couldn't walk around a Caribbean island in my soccer shorts. Then there are a couple of tops, and a really wild hat for the sun, plus some personal stuff that I needed."

"Sounds like you have made quite a haul, young lady." Paul chuckled, giving her an arms length hug through her purchases. "Who do I pay for all this?" He asked, looking at Tricia

Tricia waved her hand. "Forget it, Paul. We had so much fun. It was worth every Euro."

"Did anyone else manage to buy anything?" Matt enquired with a smile.

"Oh, yes." Michelle assured him. "Tricia and I managed quite well. I'm not going to tell you what we got, you will just have to wait and see. Right now, I suggest that we head up to or rooms, to unload our hauls, catch our breath, and then we can meet down here again in fifteen minutes."

Matt was the first one back in the lobby, where Michelle joined him after a few minutes.

"This has certainly been the most bizarre several days that I have ever experienced. I suppose that being an Interpol agent, all this has been quite routine for you?" He asked.

"Hardly. Most of my work involves collecting and analyzing data, and interviewing people so that we have even more data." Michelle explained. "This has been an extremely unusual operation for me, first in Beijing, then in France. The whole idea of kidnapping an innocent young girl to coerce information from her father is repugnant. That was probably a major reason for Tremblay and Voisier to create this complicated cover story of you all going to Saint Martin. No government wants what happened to Nicky and her father to become a blueprint for future criminal extortions."

"I can certainly understand that. At least it's all over. It *is* all over, isn't?"

"We hope so."

"You were with Nicky all morning. How do you think she's holding up?"

"She was relaxed, alive, and really enjoying herself." Michelle hesitated, and sucked in through her teeth. "But, after what she has been through, we have to realize that she might crumble at any time. You are her uncle, you know her better than me. We should both keep an eye on her."

"I will. I most certainly will." Matt paused. "One thing has been niggling at me. How did those two thugs know that Nicky and Tricia were at that Rest Stop, on the way to Paris?"

Michelle shrugged. "Tricia may have said something to Nicky about going to Paris, and it was overheard when they were at the gite. It's possible that they had been checking for their car at every Rest Stop on the autoroute to Paris."

"Or there could have been an electronic bug on their car. They're easy enough to buy, or even to make."

"No, there was no bug on their car." Michelle assured him.

“You sound very sure. How do you know?”

“We had a team check it out last night.” She explained. “There was no way that anyone could have bugged Tricia, either. She was never out of my sight, once she had agreed to go to the gite, and she was wearing the other doctor’s clothes, and we had those checked out routinely, when we picked her up. Same thing for Nicky: she wore the clothes that we provided, all the way down to her underwear.”

“I was impressed with the police officer who found them at the Rest Stop, and got them away from the thugs. Could they have somehow got information on where Nicky and Tricia were through the police communications?”

“We checked that, too. It’s possible, but it would have been difficult for them to get to the Rest Stop that quickly through intercepting police communications. We also checked out that Inspector Lacombe, who helped them at the Rest Stop. He has an outstanding record, and two children: a son at university in Paris, and a married daughter, in Bordeaux, with two grandchildren whom he adores.” Michelle explained.

“Are you suggesting that coercion is possible?”

“It’s always possible, with anybody. He arrived in Paris early this morning.”

“I’ve run out of ideas, and you seem to have got everything covered. You have obviously had a busy night. There was no problem this morning, was there, when you three were shopping?”

Michelle shrugged. “Not that I could tell, but the Rue de Passy was busy, and it is a cosmopolitan area with people of just about every race and nationality. Nicky got a bit nervous, once, when she a woman who seemed sort of familiar. I just caught a side and back view, and the woman could have been just a completely innocent shopper. Nicky was understandably jumpy after her ordeal. Who wouldn't be?"

"Here come the others." He paused uncertainly. "If it's not against the rules, would you like to come to dinner with me, after we go to Wilde's?" He asked quickly, glancing towards Paul, Nicky and Tricia. "That would leave the three of them to have dinner together. I think they would all enjoy that, too."

Michelle's answer was precluded by Nicky's animated arrival.

"Sorry, Uncle Matt, Michelle. It's my fault that we're late. I wanted to try on some of the things I got. They are so cute. The shops here in Paris are different from Vancouver, and have all sorts of amazing stuff." She enthused.

"I have to agree." Tricia added, as she and Paul came over to join them. "I can see that I am going to have to put Paris on my list of potential stopovers."

Michelle smiled. "Paris has always been considered a centre of fashion. I'm really glad you enjoyed the morning." She was clearly pleased that her suggestion had been such a success. "How was your morning, Paul? I forgot to ask Matt."

"Very pleasant, and quite relaxing. My head is still in a bit of a whirl after the past few days, what with the jetlag, and all that stuff in Beijing. It was a welcome opportunity to just wander around. We even sat outside at a café, or bistro, as they are called here, and Matt ordered coffee and pastries that were fantastic. We walked across to the Eiffel Tower, there was a carousel going around, with music and everything, but, tempted as I was, I didn't go for a ride on one of the horses."

"I really had to hold him back." Matt added, laughing.

"This is a fascinating city." Paul continued. "However, my stomach seems to still be on Beijing time, so I vote for getting a taxi to this Montmartre place, and having some lunch."

"Me, too, Dad. I'm starving. How do we get a taxi, Michelle?" Nicky asked.

"I'll get the Desk to call us one. I'll tell them that there are five of us, and see if they can get a large vehicle, or if we will need two." She turned to Matt. "In answer to your earlier suggestion, I think that is an excellent idea for all of us."

The hotel called a taxi that was large enough for them all to squeeze in. It raced them across Paris, accompanied by a cacophony of horn blasts, until they had to slow down to wind their way up through the maze of quaint cobbled streets that climbed up into Montmartre. As they weaved their way around the streets, Michelle was occasionally able to point out the beautiful white Sacre-Coeur Basilica that stood majestically above them, on the highest point.

"This is just like Paris in the movies." Nicky exclaimed. "On the way here, I actually saw lots of people walking along with a baguette under their arm." She looked around. "I remember our French teacher telling us about this Montmartre place. It's just how she described it. All the streets are winding and cobbled, and the buildings look so old and, sort of, *French*. Look at those massive steps going up over there, from this street to the next." She pointed excitedly. "It's so different, and totally awesome. The alleyways, the narrow cobbled streets lined with little shops and restaurants, the amazing really old buildings that, sort of, loom over us. I can't believe that I'm actually here." She shook her head in disbelief. "I went to Beijing for a soccer tournament, and end up in Paris. How on earth did that happen? The cars and that are all different, too, and the way they drive." She added, as they eased their way through impossible gaps between a delivery trucks and cars that were stopped on either side of the narrow road

The taxi came to a stop, with the driver explaining that the Rue des Abbesses was a pedestrian street, and he had to let them off there. He pointed out that the restaurant that they had asked to be taken to was across the road, readily identified by its large maroon awnings. The sign proclaimed it to be the Le Relais Gascon, with two floors of large windows that looked out on the street. The pleasant spring afternoon had encouraged a few people to sit at the colourful outdoor tables that were set out on the pavement in front of the restaurant.

Inside, enthusiastic diners occupied all of the dark oak tables. The room was filled with wonderful mixture of aromas, from the mouth-watering dishes that waiters were whisking past. Tricia gazed around delighted at the dark wood beams set into the white plaster on the ceiling, and along the walls, where impressive life size murals filled the intervening spaces. With no available table in sight, they were relieved when the headwaiter hurried over, and confirmed that the hotel had indeed reserved a table for them, as requested. He took them up to the second floor, to a table by the window that provided a fascinating view of life on the street below.

Once they were seated, a waiter appeared beside them, asking what they would like to drink, and handing out menus. They quickly settled on a bottle of white Bordeaux, when Michelle explained that the restaurant specialized in southwest cuisine. Nicky asked if the water was safe to drink, and Michelle assured her that bottled was, adding that bottled fizzy water was popular in France, so they ordered a couple of bottles of that, as well as the wine.

"I'm not sure what half of these things are." Nicky confessed, as she frowned at the menu. "Although, I do know what snails and herring are, and I think I'll give both of those a miss."

Michelle offered to help, which Nicky gladly accepted, admitting that her stomach was not quite ready to take on anything too challenging. The menu was varied enough to meet all of their preferences, from a large Salad Gascon for Nicky, to a rib steak for Matt.

It was approaching two-thirty when they left the restaurant, relaxed, and full of good food and wine.

Matt suggested that they should head on up to the Sacre-Coeur Basilica, to work off some of their splendid lunch, producing a groan from Paul when he looked up at the beautiful church, so high above them. However, Michelle assured him that there was a shortcut that only required a ten-minute walk, well, a bit of a climb, to a funicular car that would take them up the rest of the way, rather than face the grind of the one hundred and forty steps.

In the picturesque Square Louis Michel, Nicky gasped at the carousels.

"Those are actual, real French carousels." She exclaimed, gazing at the incredibly ornate gold and blue merry-go-rounds, with Venetian paintings, and mechanical horses that circled slowly to the sound of traditional French music.

"I suppose I am too old to go for a ride?" She asked hopefully.

"Not at all." Michelle assured her. "Many French adults still like to have a relaxing ride on a carousel horse."

"Go on. Just go and get on." Matt urged her, with a smile. He glanced at his brother. "They go quite slowly, so it will be quite safe." He looked to Michelle "How do I pay?"

"I'll handle it." She replied.

There were quite a few adults, along with numerous children on the carousel. Nicky chose a horse beside a French girl of about her own age, who gave her a friendly greeting, supplemented by an encouraging smile. They slowly circled around, communicating happily in a mixture of French and English.

"What a joy it is to see people indulging in such wonderfully simple pleasures." Paul mused, as his smiling daughter gave him a little wave, as she passed him on the red and white mechanical horse.

CHAPTER 41

As they walked up the final flight of steps, Tricia paused to fully appreciate the splendor of the beautiful Sacre-Coeur Basilica that soared majestically above them. "It looks even more magnificent up close than it does from a distance." She said. "Do you know the history behind Montmartre, and why it was built here, Michelle?"

"But certainly. All of Montmartre has a long and fascinating history that would take far too long to relate. The Sacre-Coeur was a late addition. Following the Franco-Prussian war, it was decided to build a church on the very top of the hill of Montmartre. The Basilica was completed in 1914, but because of the First World War, it was not consecrated until 1919. The view from the outside is quite striking, but you will find the interior even more beautiful."

"But surely, Montmartre is much older than that, Michelle?" Matt asked.

"That is most true. For example, the Rue des Abbesses, where we had lunch, is very old. There was a chapel there at the end of the eleventh century, until it was replaced in the twelfth century by The Abbey of Montmartre that was built by King Louis Sixth, known as 'The Fat'. The original road ran beside the buildings of the Abbey. It had several names, before it was finally settled as the Rue des Abbesses in the late nineteenth century."

"King Louis The Fat?" Nicky gasped, laughing. "What king would want to be known as 'The Fat'?"

"Well, he must have been quite large, which was a sign of wealth and importance in the twelfth century." Michelle explained. "He was also known as 'The Battler', which sounds more acceptable theses days. Shall we go inside?"

The interior of the Sacre-Coeur Basilica was breathtaking, from the north dome to the exquisite mosaic ceiling that Michelle explained was one of the largest mosaics in the world. Guided by Michelle, they absorbed the peaceful ambience, created by the striking colours of the artwork, and the beauty of the stone architecture.

Tricia looked at her watch. "We should probably think about heading back to the hotel." She sighed. "I know I would like to have a brief rest, and freshen up a bit, before we get dressed and head off to meet Monsieur Lucas Tremblay at this Wilde's bar place."

They left the Basilica, reluctantly, and started towards the funicular station.

"There's one of those pay-as-you-go telescopes on the terrace over there. Is it okay of I go and have a quick look out?" Nicky asked.

"This is the highest point in the City, and the view over Paris from here is quite famous." Michelle told them. "What can you see, Nicky?"

"Green grass." She laughed. "All I can see is green grass. Ah, wait a minute. Now I can see people. That's strange." Nicky said, frowning as she stared down below them. "There's a man by the carousel, standing, looking around."

"Who is it? Do you recognize him?" Tricia asked.

"Well, I'm sure that's that man from that café, at the second Rest Stop." She moved back, to let Tricia look through the telescope. "Can you see him, down there? He's coming up the steps with that woman."

"I think you're right, Nicky. That certainly looks like him."

"I don't think this is a coincidence." Matt muttered grimly to Michelle, moving her away from the others.

"Neither do I. We've got to get everyone out of here."

"How the Hell did he find us? That's the question." Matt puzzled.

"What are you two muttering about?" Paul asked.

"I don't like it Paul." Tricia said. "It looks like the man who was in the café with Nicky and me at the second Rest Stop is down below, and coming this way. We must get Nicky away from here."

"They know we're here. They're looking for us. There must be a locating bug on us somewhere." Matt said grimly. "We have to find it."

"How can we?" Tricia voiced her exasperation. "None of us have an electronic bug locating detector with us."

"Wait a minute." Paul muttered. He rubbed his head with his knuckle, to try and erase the lingering effects of jetlag. "Yes. Actually, I think I do. There's an app on my mobile phone."

"Seriously? You have an app on your phone for detecting electronic bugs?" Michelle asked in disbelief.

"The app is actually an rf detector a Japanese colleague gave me at a research lab I visited." He frowned with concentration. "It detects radio frequency. There's a commercial version that they sell in Japan, to check if your microwave oven is leaking radiation. I found it useful at work whenever I thought there might be a leak of rf emissions. It should detect the electromagnetic emissions from the bug."

"That could work. Can you set the search frequency?" Matt asked intently.

"I think so." He pulled out his mobile phone. "Let me see." He started working furiously on it, with Matt pouring over his shoulder, offering the occasional suggestion.

"I'll go and get Nicky." Tricia stated abruptly. She brought a puzzled Nicky over to join the others.

"What's going on? You all look totally serious. What's wrong? You're scaring me. Tricia? Dad? What's happening?"

"It's okay, Nicky. We think that one of us may have an electronic bug on them somewhere, and that is how those men found us at the Rest Stop. Your Dad may be able to set up an app on his phone that will help us detect the bug."

Paul looked up. "Okay, I think Matt and I have got it."

Matt stared at the screen. "There's a signal coming from one of us here, all right."

"I'll scan us one at a time. I'll go first." Paul said crisply, as he slowly moved his mobile phone up and down his body, from head to toe. He handed it to Matt. "Check my back for me, Matt."

They were all holding their breath.

Matt shook his head. "Nothing. I'll go next. Check me out, Paul."

"Nothing. Tricia?"

"Nothing. Michelle?"

"Nothing. Nicky?"

Paul stopped moving, and stared at the screen. "Here it is." He carefully took Nicky's bag. "Yup. It's in the bag. Take everything out one at a time, Matt, and I'll check each one."

"Got it." He held up a small disk that looked like a thick coin.

"It's all been my fault. I want to smash it." Nicky was furious. Tears streamed down her face.

"It's not your fault at all, Nicky." Michelle assured her calmly. "Now we have it, perhaps we can use it against them."

"I'll go and check again." Tricia said grimly.

"Yeah. That's him." She confirmed angrily. "I don't recognize the woman with him. They're on their way up here, walking slowly, and stopping every so often to look around. They're obviously looking for us."

"They would have lost the signal when we went inside the church with its massive stone walls." Matt noted.

Nicky grabbed her Dad's arm. "Come on, let's run. Please. I don't want them to catch me again."

"They won't. I'll make sure of that, Nicky." Paul stated determinedly. "That bastard." He muttered, as he took a quick look through the telescope. "The woman with him, looks a bit like the woman I last saw in the art centre in Beijing, sitting in the café watching me like a hungry hawk."

Tricia turned to Michelle. "You're the professional in this sort of thing, Michelle. What do you suggest?"

"It seems clear that they don't know that we have found the bug, so we can use it as a decoy."

"Right." Matt grunted. "Give me the bug. I'll be the decoy. You know this place, Michelle, can I make my way down, if I go around towards that other side of the church? You three go around this side, and get Nicky out of here. "

"Yes, that will work. From that side you can get back to that area where we had lunch." She grabbed his arm. "Come over here. Look. when you get around that side of the Basilica, over there, you'll see two sets of steps down. Take the second one; it becomes the Rue Chappe. Follow that all the way down to the big five-way intersection. The road on the right is the Rue Yvonne le Tac that we came along on the way up here. Follow that, and you will come to the Place des Abbesses. There's a metro station there, but you will probably manage to snag a taxi before that. Go to the hotel. I'm calling for backup for us, and I'll alert the protection at the hotel."

"That sounds pretty straightforward. I get around that side, and take the second set of steps all the way down to the big intersection and the Rue Yvonne something. Then I turn right along there until I come to the Abbesses Place, and get the Metro, or taxi, back to the hotel. If I get lost, I'll just ask someone. What are you four going to do?"

"We'll head down on the opposite side, over there, and make our way to the Chateau Rouge district. I'm quite familiar with that area. It's a maze of narrow streets that are always busy. There'll be backup there by then. We will be quite safe." Michelle stated brusquely. Her voice warmed, as she looked into his eyes. "You're a special man, Matt Berg. Be careful." She said softly. "Make sure you stay out of sight."

"Don't worry, I will." He gave the others an easy grin. "Time to go. You four must go, too. Take care of them, Michelle. See you all back at the hotel." With a brief wave of his hand Matt was gone.

CHAPTER 42

"This way." Michelle glanced back behind them, frowned and stared for a moment, before she quickly led them around to the opposite side of the massive Sacre-Coeur Basilica, away from where Matt had headed. They raced along, keeping close to the towering white stone wall, until they reached a cobbled pathway that took them under two sets of imposing stone archways with mullioned windows, to where another cobbled street went sharply downhill to the right between a gated park, and a couple of square looking stone buildings that appeared to be residences of some sort.

"This is Rue du Chevalier de la Barre." Michelle explained as she paused to guide them on to the street. "It's a quick way down the hill, but be careful, it's quite steep in places. There is a famous stone stairway ahead that is always crowded, so, Paul, you and Nicky go first; Tricia and I will be right behind you. We need to go quickly, but with caution. The cobbles are uneven and can be slippery, so make sure that you don't slip. It would unfortunate, if one of us twisted an ankle."

Paul and Nicky needed no encouragement; they headed off down the cobbled street at a rapid pace. Behind them, Tricia heard Michelle talking softly.

She hung back, to let Michelle catch up. "Who are you talking to?" She asked curtly.

Michelle touched her hair over her ear. “I’ve got a phone earpiece in. I’m asking for backup to meet us, when we get further down.”

“Is there a problem? You looked back behind us, when we started. Were they following us? Didn’t they follow Matt as we hoped?” She asked softly.

“I thought that they caught sight of us, as we started around the Basilica.” She said quietly. “They looked up, and started pushing their way through the crowds below us.”

“Who the blazes are they?” Tricia gasped, as they hurried to catch up with Paul and Nicky.

“I’ve no idea.” She replied. “Of course, I could have been mistaken. Once we reach the Chateau Rouge district, we’ll be fine. The backup team will be there, ready to take care of things. If that couple is still following us, they will find out who they are. Here’s the stairway.” She said, pointing ahead to where Paul and Nicky had started down, dodging in and out, around the milling groups of tourists who were taking selfies on the picturesque tree lined stairway.

At the bottom of the steps, Paul and Nicky were confronted with a road lined with residential and office buildings.

“Which way, Michelle?” Paul asked, anxiously.

“This crossroad is Rue Lamarck. Go straight across, and keep going on Rue du Chevalier de la Barre, over there.”

She glanced along the road, looking for a break in the traffic so that they could cross. “Merde.” She hissed quietly.

“Problem?” Tricia asked under her breath.

“That grey van, coming along the road at our right. They’re looking for someone. It could be us. I don’t like it.”

““Should we tell Paul and Nicky to run for it?”

“No. That will attract their attention. If we cross the road in the middle of this group, and then make sure they are behind us when we go down the street on the other side, the van will cross behind us, and, with luck, they will not notice us.”

Tricia called out, “There’s a break coming in the traffic. We’ll cross the road with this group, Paul.”

Paul picked up on the urgency in her voice and looked back: Michelle gave a slight nod of her head towards the van that was coming slowly towards them. He saw the van, understood the warning, and maneuvered Nicky into the middle of the group of pedestrians waiting to cross the road.

“Paul, we need to pick up the pace a bit.” Tricia said, moving up beside Paul as they started down the continuation of the Rue du Chevalier de la Barre. “Michelle has been on the phone, and arranged for a ride to meet us when we get a bit further down. The road will be quite busy when we get there, so we don’t want to keep them waiting.”

“What? Oh, yes. I see. Right. Got it.” He muttered, as he grasped the message. “Come on, Nicky, we need to hurry a bit. Michelle has asked for someone to pick us up when we get down to the road, and doesn’t want to have them hanging around waiting. There’s probably no parking, or something.”

“It looks like it ends just ahead.” Nicky pointed out, staring ahead.

“No, it’s okay, Nicky.” Michelle called from behind them. “This street actually makes a sharp right turn, but there’s a passageway down between the buildings, with some more steps. You’ll see it. Just follow it down.”

Sure enough, where the road had appeared to end, it took a sharp right, but there was a short, narrow passageway that went straight ahead between the, once white, plaster walls of two buildings. This led them to a long flight of stone steps, which took them down to a wider, paved alley between buildings that had definitely seen better days. The alley was wide enough for small cars to park on either side, without totally blocking passage.

"Keep going." Michelle called to Paul, who had hesitated at entering the questionable looking alley. "It's quite safe. This will take us to a major shopping street. Rue Ramey. It's just down at the end, there, where you can see all the traffic going passed. It's a one way street."

Tricia touched Michelle's arm, as they panted their way forward. "You hesitated at the top of the steps, back there, and looked behind us. Are we being followed?"

"Yes, it looks like it. The couple I saw originally appears to have split up. I saw a woman at the bottom of the first stairway, but the trees were blocking me from having a clear sight, so I can't be absolutely certain whether it was the same woman, or not. She looked familiar, somehow."

"Why would they have split up?" Tricia asked.

"The man might have followed Matt and the signal from the bug, leaving the woman to follow us. They were probably not sure which way Nicky had gone. Once they realized that Nicky was with us, they would have called the van, and told it to circle around, and try to cut us off."

"How much further before we reach your backup team? Can we make it?"

"I'll see where they are, and tell them our situation." Michelle spoke rapidly into her phone. "They're here." She called to Paul. "Turn right at the road ahead. There is transportation waiting for us at the odd shaped four-way intersection that you will see, to your right. Not far now."

"Thank Heavens." Tricia breathed. "You seem to be much better equipped for this than me. I can handle the stress of surgery, but this is totally different."

When Paul and Nicky reached the road, they slowed down, and gazed around.

"We're safe now, right Dad? We're, like, on a busy street, in the middle of Paris."

Paul put his arm around her. "I would think so, Nicky. In fact, I'm sure we are. Right now, we have to keep moving. Michelle has arranged for someone to meet us here, and give us a ride back to the hotel. There they are, just down the road. Come on."

As Michelle turned onto the road, she glanced back. "Merde. She's standing at the bottom of the steps. How did she get there so fast?"

Tricia was staring down the road at the oncoming traffic. "Michelle! There's that grey van. It's coming this way. They've seen us. Oh shit. What do we do?"

"This looks like it might be the time for us to make a run for it." Michelle said, glancing ahead to where Paul and Nicky were making their way quickly along the road, oblivious to their escalating situation.

"No, wait, this is the support team arriving." Michelle breathed a sigh of relief, at the sound of the wailing siren of a police car. A policewoman standing across from them stepped into the road, and brought all the traffic on the road to a halt.

The police cruiser pulled up on the sidewalk to get around the stationary traffic ahead of it, passing the grey van, before stopping beside a sporty looking blue convertible being driven by an attractive young woman. In the narrow one-way street, the vehicles behind them were completely blocked, in with no chance of moving ahead. The two police officers casually climbed out, clearly not in any hurry to get the traffic moving again.

Michelle gave Tricia a tight grin. "They've got everything under control. Come on. We must catch up with Paul and Nicky. "

"I can't believe it." Tricia said, in a quavering voice. "My legs are shaking. What incredible luck, that police car arriving just then. They have totally blocked the van from getting through."

Michelle gave her a quizzical look. "That wasn't luck, Tricia. The team made sure there was backup at each end of the street, in case we needed some last minute assistance."

They caught up with Paul and Nicky, who had stopped to watch the all the activity in the road beside them. The police officers had told the young woman to get out of the blue convertible, and were taking photographs of her and her vehicle. She was getting quite emotional, as they were pointing at marks on the front of the car.

"Michelle, what's all the fuss with the girl in the blue sports car?" Nicky asked. "What was she doing wrong? It looked like she was just driving along the road. She's not, like, dangerous or anything, is she?"

"No, it's nothing to worry about, Nicky. The officers have everything under control."

"There's something going on that you're not telling me, isn't there?" Nicky said, accusingly.

"Tricia will explain everything, once you are on your way back to the hotel. There's your transportation, just ahead, on this side of the intersection. I recognize the vehicle. Come on, Paul. I'll check you all in with the team.

Ahead of them, the black passenger car that Michelle had

pointed to was parked, half in a driveway entrance, with two wheels on the sidewalk, in the usual Paris fashion. Its lights flashed, to indicate that they had seen Michelle.

As Paul and Nicky climbed in, Michelle pulled Tricia back: she indicated a couple that was sitting at a table outside a nearby restaurant.

"That's two more of our team. I am going to stay here with them. We will find out who the people are that have been following you."

"That was terrifying. Can't the police just arrest them?" Tricia demanded angrily.

"I'm sure that they will think of something that they can be charged with. The officers will take them back to the police station, and hold them for questioning until after we leave tomorrow. The woman who followed us has disappeared. That is not important. No doubt, if the police had questioned her, she would have claimed that she simply took the same route as us down the hill."

"How are you going to find out who the men in the van are?" Tricia challenged.

"The police were actually taking photographs of the van, when they were pretending to photograph the blue car and its driver." Michelle explained. "At the police station, the officers will get each of them to touch something, so that they have their fingerprints."

"Who the Hell are they working for?" Tricia demanded in a furious whisper.

Paul leaned out of the car door. "Come on, Tricia. These chaps want to get going."

"Okay, I'm in." She turned back to Michelle. "Thanks for all you and your team have done, Michelle. I'm very impressed."

She gave a wry smile. ""I do feel a bit sorry for the poor young woman in the blue car: she was just a pawn in all of this."

"Actually, she is also one of ours."

Tricia rolled her eyes. "I should have known. I hope you will join us, this evening at Wilde's bar in L'Hotel."

"I'll be there." She smiled, as Tricia climbed into the car."

Once they were on their way, Nicky turned to Tricia. "Okay, what's been going on, Tricia? Michelle seemed to be filling you in, back there. Someone has been following us, haven't they?" She sounded worried.

"Yes, they have, Nicky. Michelle and her team have been absolutely terrific. They had people ready for every eventuality. The young woman in the blue sports car, the police, they were all part of Michelle's team."

"So who were the people that were following us?" Paul asked.

"Another part of the group that wanted your material in Beijing, Paul."

"Oh, Good Grief. And I suppose they are upset because Renshu took it, and they never got it."

Nicky looked frightened. "Does that mean they haven't given up, and will keep coming after us?" She whispered softly.

Paul put his arm around her. "Don't worry, Nicky, Michelle and her team will make sure that we are safe."

"That's right. Michelle told me that they would take the people in the van back to the police station, and hold them for twenty-four hours. That means that whoever is behind this will have run out of hired help, so that we can relax this evening, and will be free and clear to go to the airport, and leave tomorrow."

CHAPTER 43

As soon as she returned to their hotel, Michelle went to her hotel room to give the Head of Operations an account of the afternoon's events.

"So that's the summary of our afternoon, ma'am. A bit stressful for the Bergs and Chen at times, and as you can appreciate, everyone is quite emotionally charged, after what they have been through. Thankfully, the support team handled the situation effectively, and that really helped. Do we have a fix on exactly who we have been up against?"

"Yes, after the young doctor was so helpful in Bergerac, we have a good idea who is behind all of this, and why."

"Where are the men in the van, who we picked up this afternoon?"

"They are all cooling off at the police station. There were outstanding warrants for three of them, for theft and minor assaults, but that was enough to detain all of them overnight. They have claimed that they had no intention of harming anyone, and were simply contracted to follow your group, and report where you went. They say that their instructions came as text messages, and they have never met, or seen their employer. Apart from the outstanding charges, they are a dead end. How are Nicky, Dr. Chen, Matt and Paul Berg doing?"

"They are certainly pleased to be back together again, and relieved that it's finally over, ma'am."

"Good. Of course, I won't consider it quite over until we have collected up the ringleaders, and I intend to complete that in the next twenty-four hours."

"I suppose we have no idea what has happened to the people who were involved in the Beijing kidnapping?"

"No. There may be some information that filters down about that, eventually.

"Any update on the situation with Chief Inspector Lacombe?"

"Nothing substantive, as yet. There was a rumour that he was back in Paris. I am expecting a report in the next half hour. I will text you with any firm intel. You've had a few long days: you're still comfortable with being involved this evening?"

"Absolutely, ma'am. Will the protection team be around, just to make sure?"

"Certainly. I don't intend to relax until the entire Berg group has left Paris, tomorrow. Are they still intending to go to Wilde's?"

"Yes. I think the best way to describe their attitude is 'defiant'. They are angry at the whole kidnapping episode, and tired of being manipulated, frightened, and made to run around to the kidnappers' agenda. Matt Berg told me that Paul, Tricia and Nicky had all agreed that they couldn't see that meeting Monsieur Tremblay at Wilde's, followed by a dinner at the Eiffel Tower, with Security around them, presented any risk. They are determined to enjoy what they see as a 'normal' evening together.

"I certainly understand their position. They have been pushed around enough, and have decided that it's time to push back. Six o'clock at Wilde's?"

"Yes, ma'am.

"Is the group staying together after Wilde's?"

"No, Matt suggested that he and I leave Paul, Tricia and Nicky to have a quiet meal together. It's been a rough week for them. The three of them are very close, and this evening will be the first time they have all been together since Nicky left for China."

"What about Matt Berg?"

"He suggested that he and I stay out of their way, and eat at some local restaurant."

"I see. Yes. I understand. Be careful."

CHAPTER 44

Paul was sitting on the couch in the lobby of their hotel at quarter to six, the first to arrive for their evening at Wilde's, when Matt and Michelle walked around the corner from the lift. They looked very elegant, with Matt in a striking light grey suit and pale lilac shirt, providing a perfect pairing for Michelle in her soft blue, three-quarter sleeved linen jacket over a delicate peach, low cut silk dress, accented by a single pearl string.

Everyone had been greatly relieved to hear from Michelle that the police had detained all the men who had been following them in the van.

When Nicky and Tricia arrived, Matt was regaling the other two with an amusing account of how he had deposited the bug in a police car, as he was asking for directions back to the hotel from Montmartre. He stopped in mid-sentence at the appearance of Nicky in an emerald green satin dress with an oval boat neckline, three-quarter length sleeves, and a delicately pleated short skirt that ended well above her knees, showing off her shapely young legs. A pair of ankle-length fashion boots, and a tubular gold necklace holding a single maroon stone completed the outfit. Her gleaming shoulder-length, blond hair was loose, with an interesting single, slim braid indicating some assistance from Tricia or Michelle, or both. She was carrying a cream coloured pleather coat over her arm.

"What do you think Dad?" She asked grinning, and spinning slowly around. "Tricia helped me pick it out. The necklace is only 10 carat gold fill, with a fake ruby, we got it at a market stand, so it was really cheap, but it looks great, doesn't it? Tricia is great at picking outfits." She waved the coat. "This coat is soo cool, too. It's got blue trim on the collar, cuffs, and pockets, as well as the little belt at the back. It will even look great with jeans and a sweater. Here, look." She slipped into the coat, and gave a runway pose. "What do you think? Very Parisienne? There is a matching blue tam. I've put it in the pocket, for now."

"You look absolutely beautiful, Nicky." Her Dad gasped. "But what happened to my soccer crazy thirteen-year-old daughter, I knew in Vancouver?"

Nicky laughed happily. "She's still here, Dad, don't worry. This is just me, fourteen, and ready for a night out in Paris!"

"What do you mean, fourteen? Wait a minute. What's the date today?"

"It's the twenty-eighth, of March. I turned fourteen yesterday, Dad."

"Oh, Nicky. I am so sorry I missed the date. Happy belated fourteenth birthday."

"I can't believe that I completely missed it, too, Nicky." Matt added. "My apologies, and happy belated birthday."

Nicky shrugged and grinned. "No worries, I had no idea of the date, and didn't know myself, until Tricia mentioned it this morning. We had a bit of a wild day, yesterday, didn't we Tricia? I don't think I will ever forget my fourteenth birthday." She laughed, and grinned over at Tricia. "Have you seen Tricia, Dad? Doesn't she look amazing?"

Paul looked at Tricia with warmth that was apparent to

everyone. He finally managed. "Yes, indeed. You look absolutely incredible."

Tricia did indeed look stunning in a sleeveless maroon dress, with a halter-keyhole neckline. The full-length mirror on the lobby wall behind her showed a broad satin sash hanging down the back that was open nearly to the waist. She had a silk shawl around her shoulders, and had a grey cashmere jacket over her arm.

"Thank you. I'm glad you like it." She said with a smile and slight bow of her head.

"I don't know that I have ever thanked you properly for getting Nicky out of that gite, and bringing her safely to Paris." Paul added. "Your rescuing Nicky, and getting her away from those people was an heroic achievement."

Tricia dismissed it with a smile. "Nicky and I were sort of thrown into a crazy situation, once the original plan collapsed. Nicky was the real hero, Paul. She was amazing, after what she had just been through. It was a long drive, and I'm just relieved that we made it here safely."

"You were right, Dad. Tricia really did rescue me. I'll never forget waking up and seeing her standing there." Nicky blinked back tears. "It was definitely the best possible fourteenth birthday present I could ever have."

"Thankfully, Michelle has confirmed that is all behind us, and we can look forward to a wonderful evening out in Paris." Tricia looked over at Michelle, self-consciously. "I hope this is appropriate for Wilde's, Michelle? I also purchased a more conservative blue number this morning, and I couldn't decide which one to wear."

"You both look absolutely perfect for Wilde's." Michelle enthused. "It will enhance Lucas Tremblay's reputation in the Diplomatic circles, to be seen there this evening with you two.

I can see that I will have to up my game, to keep up with you."

"You look fantastic, yourself, Michelle. That style and colour really suits you." Tricia quickly assured her. "Matt is a very lucky guy to be your escort for the evening."

"That is so true." Matt concurred, with an appreciative smile. He checked his watch. "There should be transportation, courtesy of the Paris police, arriving for us any minute, and actually, I think it's here." He said as their police driver appeared through the revolving glass door.

They were entranced with the perfection of the L'Hotel, as they walked through the quietly understated ornate white entrance, to the reception area, with its massive star in the beautiful marble floor. As soon as they identified themselves as guests of Monsieur Lucas Tremblay, they were escorted to the Wilde's lounge. Entering between resplendent caramel columns, they found themselves in an opulent lounge with plush seating around fine wood tables. The ambiance was distinctly Victorian, from the discretely located soft lighting, to the furniture, the wall coverings, and the art. The perfect, relaxing milieu was enhanced, of course, by the discrete addition of all the essential modern conveniences.

"I feel like I've stepped back one hundred years." Tricia breathed as they were guided around occupied tables to a semi-private alcove, where Lucas Tremblay rose to greet them. He graciously settled Tricia and Michelle at either end of a long, antique plush green couch, with Nicky between them. There was a long, narrow table in front of them, and Paul was guided to the armchair at the end, beside Tricia, with Matt at the other end, beside Michelle. Lucas gave a polite bow to the women, as he took his seat opposite them.

"Thank you for agreeing to join me, after what I have been given to understand was a rather hectic afternoon." He gave a frankly admiring look at Tricia, Nicky and Michelle seated across from him. "You ladies look absolutely enchanting, and I couldn't help but notice that you caused quite a stir amongst the patrons, as you entered. Wilde's is a popular place to come to people watch, since notable celebrities are frequent patrons, when they are in Paris. You look so elegant, I suspect there are several tables humming with guesses as to your identities."

"You are very kind." Tricia smiled. "Thank you for inviting us to join you here." She glanced around. "It is absolutely exquisite. I doubt we would have ever found anywhere remotely like this on our own."

"Thank you. I am glad that you like the nostalgic atmosphere here." He replied, obviously pleased that they appreciated his choice of venue. "You are quite right: despite being on the popular Rive Gauche, the Left Bank, this little bar is not a favoured destination for tourists." He gave a self-deprecating smile. "I confess, I have been a little self-indulgent: it is one of my favourite Paris retreats, at the end of the day."

"It is really magnificent, Monsieur Tremblay." Matt started.

"'Lucas', please."

"Lucas." Matt continued with a polite acknowledgement. "It is obviously very popular with those who know about it. It will definitely be on my list, next time I am in Paris." He looked around. "I'm surprised that you were able to secure this perfect alcove for us at short notice."

"Ah, now you have forced me to reveal the truth." Lucas laughed. "Alas, I do not have sufficient influence to make this arrangement, but my French colleague, Jean-Claude Voisier, whom you met this morning, certainly does. He was most pleased to assist in making the arrangements." He stopped, as the waiter arrived. "Now what would you like to drink? Also, you must be hungry, so, if you will permit, I will order a selection of small dishes for you to sample."

When the waiter had secured their order and left, Lucas added. "The restaurant here has a Michelin star, and is absolutely outstanding. Unfortunately, even the influence of Jean-Claude Voisier is not sufficient to secure a reservation for this evening."

The drinks arrived with a sumptuous display of appetizers, artistically arranged on their delicate, patterned china plates. Nicky looked at the colourful setting with concern, and whispered in Michelle's ear. She smiled and explained. "Nicky has heard that snails and frogs legs are delicacies in France, Lucas, and she doesn't think she will be able to handle them, after her diet of the past few days."

"Of course. I completely understand, Mademoiselle Nicky." He acknowledged with a slight incline of his head. "I admire how well you have recovered from your unpleasant experience. I am pleased to assure you that there are no snails or frogs legs included in the selection that I have ordered." He pointed to one brightly coloured dish. "You may wish to try that: it is a mild vegetable tapenade, and goes very nicely spread on the bread chips over there."

The evening was a great success. Lucas Tremblay was charming, and kept them enthralled, and laughing, with his stories of his time in Paris. However, at eight o'clock, he offered his sincere apologies, explaining that he had to leave for another appointment, assuring them that he would have far rather spent the rest of the evening with them.

He shook the men's hands, and gave each of the women a Gallic kiss on the cheek, to Nicky's embarrassment.

"You indicated that you were all going on to dinner." He turned to Paul. "Do you have a reservation? It can be difficult to find space at some of the restaurants in Paris. I might be able to assist?"

"Thank you, that is most kind. However, Nicky said that she would like to go to the Eiffel Tower, so we have a reservation at the restaurant, which I believe is on the second level." Paul explained.

"An excellent choice. If you have time, you should take the elevator up to the top. The view over Paris at night is magnificent. I am sure that you will all have a wonderful evening. Au revoir."

After he had left, Matt said. "Actually, Michelle and I thought that it would be an opportunity for you to enjoy a dinner in Paris with just the three of you. It is your first evening together since before Nicky left for China, and you certainly have a lot to talk about."

"Oh, Uncle Matt, Michelle, no, you must come with us." Nicky insisted. "Where will you find a good place to eat, now? Like Monsieur Tremblay said, all the best places will be full."

"That's very considerate of you, Nicky. Fortunately, I did manage to get a reservation at a traditional French restaurant that Monsieur Tremblay suggested. Apparently it has quite an interesting history, and the food is supposed to be very good. It's just around the corner, and I think it will be perfect for Michelle and I."

"No, really. I know I haven't had much chance to talk to Dad, but it doesn't feel right for us to be having a fabulous dinner in the Eiffel Tower, while you go to some dingy bistro around the corner." Tricia nudged her, and raised her eyebrows, with a faint nod towards Michelle.

"What?" It took Nicky a millisecond to catch on. "Oh. No. Restart. Yes. Totally, Uncle Matt. Of course, if you have something already arranged. That's, like, really thoughtful of you." She fumbled. "Tricia and I really want to tell Dad all about what happened to us here, in France, and hear what he's been doing in Beijing. The past few days have been so totally ridiculous. Totally. I can't wait to hear all about Beijing. I just hope Dad doesn't start banging on about physics, I don't think I'm up for that."

Paul's attempt at a hurt look prompted open laughter from the others.

CHAPTER 45

Michelle sighed as she sat back in the taxi. "So what is this 'dingy bistro' around the corner that we're going to, Matt?" She asked with a long-suffering look. "After what we have been through over the past few days, I was hoping for a real Paris meal. At least comparable to that restaurant you took me to, across from the Cloister of Cadouin. Mon Dieu, that seems like a lifetime ago."

"Here we are." Matt said, as the taxi pulled up at the corner of Rue des Grand-Augustins, in front of an old stone building with black, wrought iron gratings.

"Already?" Michelle enquired in surprise. "It really was just around the corner." She peered up at the name, as she climbed out of the taxi. "Mon Dieu, it's Le Relais Louis Thirteenth." She gasped. "Have you really made a reservation here?"

"I hope so." He grinned. "Lucas and Jean-Claude Voisier worked some magic, and by good fortune there was a cancelation. Let's go in, shall we?"

"Matt, this place is legendary. I don't know what to say. It's got at least one Michelin star. I've always wanted to dine here, but I could never afford it when I was a student in Paris, and somehow, since then I have never found the right occasion."

Inside, they were greeted graciously, Matt's reservation was confirmed, and they were guided to their table.

"This is amazing." Michelle breathed as she settled into the soft-backed chair, and gazed around at the ancient house. "Do you know this building dates back to when Louis Thirteenth was King?" She thought for a minute, "If memory serves, it was a convent at that time. Just look at those beautiful exposed ceiling beams, and the stonework walls, with their incredible stained-glass windows. I feel like we've been transported back in time."

"I'm so pleased that you like it." Matt said happily, looking around. "It is beautiful. The ambience is almost tangible. I hope you like the meal I've ordered."

"You've already selected the meal for both of us?" She gave an irritated frown. "Okay, on this one occasion, in this very special restaurant, I'll accept your selection, despite your not even being French. What have you ordered?"

"Actually, I'm not quite sure. Jean-Claude Voisier suggested that his request for a reservation might proceed more smoothly, if I selected one of the complete dinners that the chef produces. Apparently it varies every day." He explained.

"So what did you select?" Michelle asked, as she picked up the menu card that the waiter had placed before each of them. "You ordered Le Menu Degustation?" She gasped. "That's the chef's most extensive menu. There are nine courses."

"We don't have to eat all of them." Matt suggested lamely.

"The Michelin starred chef will be personally affronted if we send one of his dishes back, untouched. Dare I ask if you have ordered the wine?"

"Well, sort of. I asked for the Suggestions du Sommelier." Matt brightened. "Ah, here he comes now, bringing us a glass of Champagne." Noticing a waiter approaching, he added. "This is our appetizer coming as well, if I'm not mistaken."

While they sipped their champagne, Michelle pressed Matt to tell her what had happened after he left them, and took off on his own, from the Sacre Coeur.

"It was all a bit of an anticlimax." He shrugged. "I found the stairway down that you had told me to take. It was exactly as you described, and down I went to the big five-way intersection, where I followed your directions, and turned right on the Rue Yvonne le something." He looked up as the waiter approached, and checked his menu. "I believe this is the foie gras pate, with home made bread wafers."

"How did you end up putting the bug in a police car?"

"Well, I wandered along that Rue Yvonne le whatever road towards the Abbesses place, until I happened to see a police car pulled over. I pretended to be a lost tourist, and asked them in my worst fractured French where the nearest Metro was. While they were patiently explaining and pointing straight ahead, I dropped the bug behind the front passenger seat. The Metro was just ahead at that Place des Abbesses, and I took the subway for a couple of stops, before getting off, and going back up to the street, and grabbing a taxi back to the hotel. That's all there was to it. Pretty boring, really."

Michelle waited while the waiter delivered lobster ravioli, and the sommelier had described and poured his matching selection of a Bordeaux white wine.

"This lobster ravioli is exquisite." She groaned. "When we have finished this, you must tell me if you noticed anyone following you."

Matt finished, and sat back. "That was unbelievable." He took a sip of wine. "The wine is very good, too. You asked if I had noticed anyone who appeared to be following me? Well there was one chap who seemed to notice me heading down the stairway, and started hurrying after me. When I stopped at the police car, he stopped, and sort of turned away. He was quite a way behind me, so I could have been mistaken. He looked quite average, you know, average height and build. Quite smartly dressed. He might have been a Paris businessman."

"What made you think he was a local businessman?" Michelle pressed.

Matt frowned thoughtfully. "Well, he looked too smartly dressed for a tourist, and he was on his own."

"Lacombe." Michelle breathed.

"Who's that?"

"It sounds like Chief Inspector Lacombe." Michelle explained. "The man who assisted Tricia and Nicky at the Limoges Rest Stop. They described him as nattily dressed, with average stature. Who else would it be?"

"Isn't he in the Police Nationale? Surely, he would have come up and spoken to me?"

"I expect that he was just keeping an eye on you, to make sure that you were safe. After he helped Tricia and Nicky at that Rest Stop, he came to Paris, and connected with our Interpol team. However, we have heard that there have been threats against his family. His daughter and her family, who live near Bordeaux, have apparently gone into hiding. I'm sure that we'll sort it out shortly."

As they progressed through the wines the sommelier brought, to match the sequence of courses of tomato tuna salad, fish quenelles, duck breast, a selection of cheeses, and chocolate soufflé with light cream, Matt decided to try and turn the topic of conversation toward Michelle. She explained that she had grown up in the South of France, before attending university in Paris. She had got married after university: her husband had been an avid motorcyclist, and had been killed in a traffic accident.

"Oh, I'm so sorry. That must have hit you awfully hard?" Matt gasped.

"Yes, it did, but I was young, and life does go on." She paused. "It taught me that some things you can control: the rest you have to simply endure. It was over a year later that I saw an advertisement for analysts in Interpol, applied, and here I am."

"An analyst?" Matt sat back, with his coffee. "So you are not always running around, chasing bad guys?"

"No. No. Not at all. It was simply chance that I had just arrived in Vancouver, when the news broke about Nicky being kidnapped. My boss wanted someone to be an invisible escort for Paul to Beijing, and it fitted in with my own plans, so I volunteered. A simple watching brief, with no expected contacts, hostile or friendly, completed with a hand-off to a team in Beijing. In the extremely unlikely event of anything happening, I was to call for assistance immediately, and disappear."

"How did you end up in Bergerac?"

"I wasn't really accomplishing anything in Beijing, and my boss thought that it would be useful for me to be with Nicky, when she was released." She made a vague wave with her hand. "You know, I could tell her that I had seen her Dad, and he was okay, that sort of thing. I was supposed to be just a support member of a team, but unfortunately, as you well know, everything suddenly started to go pear-shaped."

Paul reached across the table, and put his hand over hers. "Thankfully, everything has finally worked out, and here we are finishing a romantic meal together."

Michelle twisted her fingers around his. "Yes, indeed. Here we are, feeling very pleasantly mellow, after an absolutely fantastic meal." She sighed. "I must admit, under normal circumstances, this could qualify as a dream of a first date."

"Second date, surely." He suggested. "What about the dinner opposite the Cloister of Cadouin?"

"You can't count that as a date." She protested. "As I recall, you were rather preoccupied throughout the entire evening. At one point, I thought you were going to jump up, run outside, and chase that car. It was the doctor's car, wasn't it? The one who was looking after Nicky?"

"Yes. I thought I knew where Nicky was being held, but I needed confirmation. What better cover could there be than wandering around, like a tourist, with a beautiful woman for company? Seeing that car had clinched it for me."

"I wasn't sure what you were up to, at first, but I knew it had to be something to do with finding Nicky." She smiled at him. "Since it appears that we were both there under false pretences, that afternoon and evening could hardly qualify as a date, could it?

Matt gave a shrug, and chuckled. "Michelle, you are the most interesting person I have ever met. You have always been one step ahead of me, and everyone else. First, you watched out for Paul and Tricia in Beijing, until another Interpol team could take over, then you came to Bergerac, and used me as a bird dog to find where Nicky was being held. Finally, you persuaded Tricia to go in and rescue her, knowing that she could be relied on to get Nicky to safety, if anything went wrong, didn't you?" He lifted her hand, and kissed her fingers. "You are quite something, Michelle Denis. I am totally captured."

Michelle pulled her hand back with a tight little laugh. "I really like you, too, Matt, and the meal was absolutely wonderful, but we mustn't get too carried away." She paused, before continuing softly. "You don't really know me. These past few days have been very stressful and emotional, and have emphasized our feelings for one another. We are all elated that Nicky is safe. The sober reality is that before we were thrown together in this kidnapping extortion plot, I was an Interpol analyst and occasional agent, and you were a brilliant scientist and entrepreneur. A month from now that is what we will be again, and this will be just a memory."

Matt stared at her, as he slowly shook his head. "I felt a special connection with you from the first minute I met you, Michelle, and that feeling has only increased with every moment that we have been together. From everything you have said and done, I can't believe that you don't feel the same way. What is it that I don't know about you that could possibly affect the way I feel?"

"My job, for one thing, Matt. It's what I do, and I can't imagine not doing it."

"My work is flexible. I wouldn't interfere with your work for Interpol. I could work around your schedule."

She stumbled on, as she tried to explain. "There's things; I am just not in the right space for a serious relationship at the moment, and it is quite possible that I may never be. It's complicated. There are some things that are personal, and must be left alone. At least for now. I really like you Matt, and I would have enjoyed getting to know you better. But the future can contain no commitments or promises." She looked at her watch. "It's late. You've settled up with the waiter, so we should ask the restaurant to call us a taxi."

CHAPTER 46

Tricia and Paul stood beside one of the massive corner bases of the Eiffel Tower, enjoying the pleasant Spring evening, and the casual Paris scene that flowed around them. The coloured lights of a carousel provided a perfect backdrop, its horses galloping slowly up and down, around and around, in time to accordion music that tinkled and wheezed into the night. It was such a peaceful setting that the security team that had been near them all evening had moved back, and were relaxing on a bench.

Nicky had wandered a short distance away, to take photos, and called out that she was going to go across the narrow access road to the park area, to get a picture of the Tower with the carousel in the background. Paul looked across at their police driver, and exchanged nodded confirmation.

They watched her, as she weaved her way through the vehicles that were pulling in to pick up and drop off passengers.

"My little girl is growing up." Paul sighed, as they watched her negotiate her way through groups of tourists, who were making the most of a pleasantly warm evening.

"Girls do that." Tricia observed, with a smile. "She's fourteen, now, and moving into a new, and slightly different, phase of her life."

They vaguely noticed a grey van pull up, just beyond Nicky. Two men climbed out, followed by a familiar figure who pointed at Nicky and commanded, "That's her!"

Nicky looked up: she was confused, and then a look of pure terror took over her face. She screamed, spun around, and ran, her new coat flying out like wings behind her.

Tricia yelled, "Run, Nicky, Run! This way! This way!"

Paul yelled, "Leave her alone", as they raced across the road. Several people saw what was happening, and joined in yelling at the men from the van.

Nicky left the path, and cut past a surprised young couple, as she headed for the shadows under the trees. The crowd around the base of the Tower was yelling for the police, as the grey van starting to careen across the grass after her.

Tricia and Paul's lungs were bursting as they raced past the couple, towards the trees. They were totally focused on finding Nicky, and oblivious to the van that was right behind them, slipping and sliding, but gaining on them, second by second. It slowed to their speed, as the side door was flung open.

"She's gone around the tree." Paul gasped to Tricia.

He turned sharply across the grass, grabbing at the trunk of a massive tree to swing himself around. Nicky's boots had provided better traction, and she was leaving her Dad and Tricia behind, as their feet slipped under them. The van tried to follow, but slewed sideways on the grass, and clipped the tree, spinning to a stop. The driver quickly got it going again, and pulled back on to the path, and raced ahead.

Paul ran as best he could, slipping and sliding across the grass, he followed Nicky who had moved back to run along between the row of trees and the path. The van came to a sudden stop in front of Nicky, and a man jumped out of the side door. He stood between the van and a tree, with his feet apart and his arms spread out wide, sneering at Nicky, as she ran towards him at full speed.

"Leave her alone." Paul yelled, as he tried to lunge forward, but only managed to slip to his knees. He jumped back up quickly, and started forward, watching in horror as Nicky continued to run straight at the man.

"C'est ca. Viens a moi, ma petite." The man hissed.

As he reached for her, Nicky feinted to go to the right, and then suddenly sprang lightly away to her left, landing for an instant on her left foot, spinning around clockwise, and racing ahead. Before the man knew what had happened, Nicky was three metres past him, and he was left, facing the tree, and grabbing at air. Paul was back on his feet, and rammed into the man's back, as hard as he could, driving him face first into the substantial tree trunk, with a resounding crunch.

Another massive man, two metres tall, leapt out of the van, and drove his shoulder into Paul, sending him flying across the ground, before picking up his stunned colleague, and throwing him back into the van. It took off, spraying Tricia with mud and grass, as she stumbled and slid over to where Paul was pulling himself to his feet.

"Are you okay?"

"Yes, yes. Just a bit winded. I had worse hits in hockey." He croaked.

He stood up, took a couple of deep breaths, and started jogging forward. They followed the direction that Nicky had been running, and were confronted by a long, open area, bordered by overhead lights that cast yellow pools along the path. Ahead of them, they could make out small cross paths disappearing into seemingly impenetrable, dark foliage on either side.

Paul stopped, and stood with his hands on his hips, catching his breath. "Why did she run into the park? She should have run to us. The Security team was right there."

"After what Nicky has been through, Paul, she was terrified. She didn't think; basic fight or flight reflex; she opted for flight away from the danger, as fast as she could." Tricia snapped. "Dammit. I'm not dressed for running through this park in the dark. We need help. I'll call Michelle. She'll bring additional Security."

"Yeah. Of course. I'll call Matt."

CHAPTER 47

Matt and Michelle were making their way to the door of the restaurant, when Michelle's phone started to quietly vibrate. It had to be important: she had logged off for the evening. Before she had started to speak, Matt's phone was vibrating as well. Their expressions froze, as they alternated between listening, and firing staccato questions at the callers. Matt was the first to hang up, with Michelle right behind him.

"That was Paul. They are in trouble. Some men in a grey van tried to grab Nicky, when they were standing below the Eiffel Tower. She managed to get away, and fled into the park beside the Tower. It's really bad. I have to go, Michelle."

Michelle was furiously punching the numbers on her phone. "That was Tricia. Same message. She and Paul have gone into the park after Nicky. I've called the backup. Here's a taxi. Let's go."

An elderly couple, who were waiting in the restaurant lobby, stood up, and started to make their way towards the taxi that had arrived outside. Paul and Michelle raced past them, shouting 'Urgence! Urgence!', and leapt into the taxi. Michelle barked 'Urgence. Eiffel Tower, en vitesse!', as she waved her Interpol identification at the startled driver, while Matt waved a fifty Euros banknote at him.

They sat on the edge of the taxi's seat, hanging on to the

handles, as it careened through the Paris streets towards the twinkling lights that pointed into the sky ahead of them.

"Why on earth did Nicky go running off?" Matt groaned. "There would still have been people around the base of the Tower, surely?"

"Nicky ran because she was terrified, after what she had already been through." Michelle said tersely.

"Right. Yes. Of course. What is this park she ran in to, do you know it Michelle?"

"The park is called the Champs de Mars. It's very popular, particularly in the Spring. There are paths winding around trees and beds of flowers. Nicky would have been seen it from the Eiffel Tower."

"Is there lighting? Can Nicky see where she's going?"

"There are lights all along the paths, but it's huge. About twenty-five hectares. If she has run very far, it won't be easy to find her, for us, or for the people who tried to grab her."

"Sounds like a good place to hide. Smart girl."

"Here we are." Michelle said, her hand on the door handle. "Looks like the backup is already here." She added, nodding toward the flashing lights of the police cars underneath the Tower.

Matt shoved the fifty Euros at the driver as they jumped out of the car, and started running towards police at the base of the Eiffel Tower.

"What happened? Have you found them?" He yelled as soon as they were within hearing of the police.

"Who are you, sir?" One of the officers demanded.

Michelle quickly stepped forward, and flashed her Interpol

identification.

"Interpol? That's interesting." The officer said thoughtfully. "Well, according to witnesses, there was an attempt to grab a young girl, after she was crossed the road, over there, to take a photograph. Apparently there was a lot of screaming and yelling: the girl took off, running at speed into the park, and the van with the would-be abductors followed her briefly, and then left. Her parents went into the park after her."

"Have you got a search party looking for them?" Matt asked. "We have to find her before the abductors do."

The officer looked at Michelle. "Since Interpol is involved, I suspect there is a lot more going on here than we know about. In answer to your question, no, we have not instituted a search yet. I'm waiting for more backup. This is a huge park, with many paths bordered by dense bushes and things. If the girl doesn't want to be found, two of us could spend the rest of the night wandering around this park looking for her. We have to wait for help to arrive."

CHAPTER 48

"Where do you think she would have gone, Tricia?" Paul gasped, his eyes frantically trying to penetrate the dark shadows that leaped around them, in time with the flashing sequence of the thousands of lights on the Eiffel Tower .

"She was really scared, and heading anywhere, as long as it was away from the people in the van." Tricia gasped. "This couple coming towards us may have seen which way she went."

The couple had, indeed, seen Nicky race by.

"We called to her; we tried to ask who she was running away from." The man explained.

"She looked terrified. I asked if we could help." The woman added. "She just kept running at full speed."

"Did you see where she went?" Tricia asked, her voice trembling.

"Not really." The woman said.

"From the speed and direction she was going, it didn't look like she was going to stop until she reached the Grand Palais at the far end of the park. Is she in some kind of trouble? I wish we could have helped." The man said apologetically.

Tricia thanked them, and she and Paul quickly moved on.

"So what do you think? We just keep going to the far end of the park?" Paul asked, as they jogged on. "From what they said, it sounds like she just kept running as far and fast as she could."

"We should head that way, but we have to check out this part of the park, as we go." Tricia's voice was shaking. "You take this side; I'll go over there. We'll make ourselves obvious, and call her name, just in case she circled around, and is actually hiding somewhere in the foliage."

"Okay. We'll meet up at the road that I can see cutting across the park ahead of us."

Passing in and out of the pools of light from the overhead lights, Tricia and Paul searched desperately through the dark outlines and shadows of the Park's mature bushes and trees, calling Nicky's name loudly, franticly, as they went. Wherever she was, they had to find her. They must find her.

Where the road crossed the park, the lights of the traffic cast strange shadows, as vehicles moved around a long water-filled pond structure that was circled by quadrants of a solid, dark hedge.

"Was that her?" Paul froze: Tricia raced to join him. They stared into the moving shadows.

"No, it's just the moving shadows from the passing vehicles' lights." Tricia sighed.

"Did you see any sign of her?" Paul asked desperately.

"Nothing so far." Her voice quavered with emotion. "That couple thought she looked like she was going to run straight across that road, and on through the stretch of park that continues on the other side."

"They couldn't be sure, though. That tall hedge thing would have hidden her." Paul said, his heart pounding.

"There's no sign of her so far. We have to keep going. We have no choice." Tricia pointed out. She took a breath and added. "I thought I saw that van that tried to grab her pass me on the side road that runs along beside the park, over there. I can't be sure. I just caught a glimpse of it between the bushes."

"We have to find her, before." Paul swallowed; coughed. "We have to find her quickly." He managed to choke out.

"Paul. Look!" Tricia shrieked. "That grey van. It's on the road, right ahead of us. It's stopped."

"Those men are getting out of it. They're looking to see if Nicky is hiding in the bushes. Come on."

They raced forward, yelling at the men, who looked up, and ignored them, until flashing blue lights in the trees, announced the imminent arrival of a police car. The men jumped back into the van, and it accelerated away.

"They didn't find her." Tricia gasped.

"The police have stopped, and are searching. Let's go talk to them."

"No." Tricia growled. "That will only waste time. Let them look; we must carry on. Come on, Paul. We'll cross the road over there, away from the police. We must keep going. If she's there, the police will find her."

Once they were across the two lanes of the road, and were on the main path through the second part of the park, they glanced back towards the bright lights of the Eiffel Tower.

"The police are at the road here, and they have arrived at the base of the Eiffel Tower. Nicky will see the flashing blue lights on their vehicles, and she might just run to them."

"I'm not sure, Paul. She's really, really scared, after what she's just been through. I think she's in full panic flight mode, and she's a great runner. All she's thinking about is getting far away from those people in the van."

"The police need to get that van. Did you see where it went, after it took off?"

Tricia made a quick frown back at the road. "No. I suspect that once they have checked each side of the Park, they will go up to the end, where we're headed. Come on, we have to keep moving. The same as before; you go that side, I'll go over here. There's that massive glass fronted pavilion place ahead of us: we'll meet up there." She said firmly.

They split up, again, each going to a path on one side of the wide, central open area. They moved along as swiftly as the reasonably could, calling Nicky's name as they went.

Tricia stopped, and peered into the bushes. She shouted across to Paul. "I can see lights along a path winding through the bushes. I'm going to check it out."

She disappeared down the path. Paul paused for a moment, then he, too, headed off down a path towards the road to his right. He found himself beside a children's playground, and basketball court. When he re emerged, Tricia was back on the path.

"Anything?" He shouted.

"Nothing. A couple said they hadn't seen her. You?"

"A basketball court, and a children's playground. "

A few minutes later they were standing together in front of the impressive façade of the building that a sign identified as the Grand Palais Ephemere.

"I can't believe it." Paul panted. "We can't have missed her." He stared around in frustration. "She could have gone out on to one of the side streets."

"I don't think so. Nicky would have wanted somewhere with

people around. From the sound of the steady traffic and lights ahead, there's a major road on the other side of this place. She may have gone there."

They ran around to the street. It was busy with traffic, and a few pedestrians, but no sign of Nicky.

Tricia looked up and down the street. "I don't see her. We're going to have to." She stopped in mid sentence. "Wait a minute. Look at the entrance to that building that's all lit up across the street."

"You mean doorway with those big columns." He gasped. "That movement. Was that a shadow?" He struggled to speak. "Or...?"

Tricia grabbed his hand. "Come on, Paul."

They raced across the road, ignoring the irate hoots from a taxi, calling to Nicky, as they went.

"It's us, Nicky. It's us." Paul and Tricia shouted in unison, over and over.

The top of her head appeared, peering cautiously around the column. As they reached her side of the road, more of Nicky slowly emerged from where she had been hiding, squashed between one of the columns, and the front of the building.

When they reached her side of the street, Nicky raced to them and hurled herself into her father's arms, tears pouring down her face.

"Oh Dad, Tricia. I'm sorry. I was just so scared, I just ran. When I got here, I didn't know what to do, so I hid."

"We found you. That's all that matters. You're safe, now." Tears streamed down Paul's face.

Nicky turned and hugged Tricia. "This is the second time you've saved me, Tricia."

"We mustn't make it a habit. Twice is quite enough." Tricia said weakly, as she wiped away tears.

Paul pulled out his phone. "I'll call Matt, and give him the good news. I expect he and Michelle are with the police. They were on their way when we called before."

After a brief conversation, he put his phone away with a sigh. "As I thought, Matt and Michelle are with the police. Michelle called for top priority assistance, and there are twelve police officers there, plus an ambulance. They will be here shortly. Matt said he had been told to tell us to sit tight."

"You're sure they know where we are?" Nicky asked anxiously.

"Yes." He waved at the building beside them. "Apparently, this is the military officer training college. They knew right away, when I said that you had been hiding behind a column at the entrance of the building at the end of the Park."

"Come here, you two. I need a group hug." Tricia said, holding her arms open wide.

Nicky had her back to the building, as they went into a tight huddle. She suddenly pulled away, and stared past her Dad.

"No! Oh no! Keep them away from me." She sobbed, her face ashen in the artificial light.

Paul spun around. The gray van had stopped to drop two men to their left, and was pulling forward to drop two more to their right.

A fifth man, who Paul recognized as a man he recalled seeing in Beijing, climbed out of the stationary van, looked straight at Nicky. "You will not run away this time." He said with icy calm.

"Don't be foolish. The police will be here at any moment." Paul did his best to sound authoritative, but his voice quavered.

Nicky gave a blood-chilling scream. She was shaking uncontrollably, as she edged back behind the column, where she had been hiding.

A young woman driving past slowed right down, saw what was happening, and put her hand on the horn and left it there.

Tricia started hammering on the massive wooden door behind them, and yelling for help, as loud as she could.

Her knocking was answered when a rugged officer in military uniform opened the door behind them. The four men looked apprehensive, and stopped.

"Que se passé t-il ici?" He demanded. "Pourquoi tout ce bruit?" His eyes narrowed, as he made a swift survey of the scene. Tricia was crouching against the column, with her arm around a whimpering Nicky. Paul was standing in front of them, looking very vulnerable. Their clothes, although crumpled, were clearly intended for an evening out.

"Please help us." Tricia sobbed frantically. These men are dangerous. They are trying to kidnap our daughter. The police are on their way. We need help. Please."

The man slowly turned his head, and barked an order back into the building. There was a clattering, and five muscular young men appeared, in casual military attire. They stopped, motionless, as the leader growled out his commands, then moved smartly to form a line in front of Paul. Their glacial stares made the thugs freeze, unsure of their next move. Time seemed to stop for an instant, as silence engulfed the little tableau.

Two police motorcyclists blasted the scene back to life, as they roared around the corner, with lights flashing and sirens on full wail. That was enough for the two thugs to Paul's left; they turned and fled across the road towards the Park. In seconds the motorcyclists had them cornered against a wall, as they sat astride their bikes with their guns drawn.

The man in charge, and the other two men ran for the van, but, before it had started to move away, two police cars had raced around the corner, and positioned themselves across the road on either side of the van. There was no escape.

Paul and Tricia hugged Nicky, who was shaking and hiccupping, as she valiantly tried to calm down.

“I'm sorry.” She mumbled. “I'm being such a wimp.”

“No, no. We were all scared out of our wits.” Her dad murmured.

Tricia gave a relieved smile at the young men, who were standing watching the proceedings with interest. “Thank you for coming to help us. You slowed them down enough for the police to arrive.”

The uniformed man gave a shrug. “We are pleased to have been of service, Madame, but really we did nothing.” He glanced across at the young men. “I believe these young men were actually hoping for some action.” He gave another shrug. “It is probably best that the police arrived to take over.”

Paul slumped down on the base of the column beside Nicky, and put his arm around her. Tricia was already hugging from the other side. She gave Paul's arm a reassuring squeeze, as Nicky wiped at the tears that were still running down her wet face.

Two police officers walked over, accompanied by a familiar figure.

“Nicky, Paul, Tricia. Are you okay? What happened?”

“Hi Matt. Are we ever glad to see you.” Paul sighed, weakly. He waved at the military team standing in the doorway. “These young men were terrific. They came out and kept the thugs at bay, until the police arrived. We were in a bit of a bind: we had just found Nicky hiding behind this column, when that grey van arrived, and five men jumped out to block us in on either side. It was not good, Matt. I'm about done, and your French is better than mine, could you thank these fine young men for me, and these police officers as well? Correction: I am totally done."

The older military officer waved aside his thanks. "It really was nothing, sir. We are pleased to have been able to assist." He said in perfect, albeit, slightly accented English.

The police officer standing beside Matt added. "You are most welcome, sir, and there is no need for a translator. My colleague and I speak reasonable English. We are just relieved that we reached you in time. We received a message that a group of men were attacking of a couple and their daughter outside the Ecole Militaire. We came as quickly as we could. Would you please tell me what has happened? "

"Good question, officer. A very good question." Paul gasped. "Give me a minute, and I will try and tell you everything that has been happening."

"If you can manage to get into the back of the car, perhaps you can explain while we take you back to the ambulance that is waiting in the open area under the Eiffel Tower. They will check you out."

"Yeah, we can manage that, can't we Nicky? Tricia?"

"Sure. No prob. I think." Nicky mumbled, her knees wobbling, as she tried to stand up.

"Absolutely." Tricia agreed, grabbing Nicky's arm, to stop her from falling.

"Good evening, Professor. We meet up once again. You do

seem to get yourself involved in some interesting situations. Thankfully, this time, all the miscreants already appear to have been apprehended."

Paul spun around in surprise, and stared at the two familiar figures that had arrived. "Good gracious. You two!" His brow knitted in concentration. "One minute. Stefanie and Julia, isn't it? I'm sorry, I can't remember who is which?"

"I'm Stefanie. You remembered our names. I'm impressed." The blond girl laughed.

The dark girl gave Paul a smile. "So am I. You have a good memory, professor. It's 'Julie' actually, but 'Julia' was very close."

"Tricia, Matt, these are the two Interpol agents who whisked me out of Beijing." Paul explained.

"And you must be Nicky. I can't tell you how pleased we are to see you." Stefanie said giving her a warm smile. "We heard how you and Doctor Chen escaped from the gite, and drove all the way here, to Paris. That was amazing."

"It was Tricia." Nicky explained, softly. "She was absolutely awesome."

"Yes, she certainly was." Stefanie agreed, pumping Tricia's hand. "Going in alone like that, rescuing Nicky, and then driving across France, a country that you hardly knew. All that, and I heard that neither of you speak much French."

"Well it didn't seem like we had a lot of choice." Tricia laughed shakily. "Nicky was terrific, considering what she had been through. I don't believe I could have done it on my own. She was an ace with the GPS, and even had some French, which was really useful."

"I didn't actually do much." Nicky said blushing, as Tricia put her arm around her. "It wasn't, like, I could drive, or anything."

Julie turned to Matt and Michelle. "You must Matt Berg. We're pleased to meet you at last. And you must be our colleague who handed over to us in Beijing, Michelle Denis." She added as she shook her hand. "From the reports we have received, you have done a great job."

"Thank you." She gave a Gallic shrug. "I just did what any of us would have done."

Paul had looked puzzled, as the introductions went around, "I don't understand." He finally said. "What are you two doing here?"

"Paul." Tricia admonished. "Let's just be thankful that they are here."

"Don't worry, Tricia, we understand. It's all been quite confusing. When you left Beijing, Paul, there was a general exodus right behind you. The couple who had pretended to be Interpol agents managed to slip through Renshu's net, and left the country immediately, through Seoul, we believe."

"Renshu was furious." Stefanie interjected. "Even though he did end up with all of your scientific material."

"Anyway," Julie continued, "With everyone gone from Beijing, and all of the action apparently moving to France, it was decided that we should come here, since we were familiar with several of the players." She looked around at where the police were holding the five men. "It looks like you've had another eventful evening. However, this should bring this whole unfortunate episode to a conclusion."

"What happened to Inspector Lacombe?" Nicky suddenly asked. "Is he working with you? He really helped Tricia and me at the Rest Stop in that Limoges place?"

"Ah, yes. I'm sorry Inspector Lacombe can't be here. He took the TGV, that's the high-speed train, to Nice earlier this evening. Some threats had been made against his son here in Paris, and his daughter and her family, in Bordeaux. He was furious, and is determined to end this nonsense once and for all."

"Is his daughter and her family okay?" Tricia asked, anxiously.

"Yes, they were quickly moved, and given protection." Julie explained. "Apart from their very unpleasant abducting of Nicky, it seems that this group is more inclined to use threats than action to obtain their desired result. As I said, now that we have grabbed this bunch, I think all that will be left will be the final clean-up."

"That's awful." Nicky gasped. "Inspector Lacombe was really nice to us."

"Inspector Lacombe has been a tremendous help here in Paris as well, Nicky. He made sure that the Police Nationale kept a watch on all of you, and that they coordinated their activities with Interpol. When Agent Denis called for backup, on the way down from the Sacre-Coeur Basilica, Lacombe immediately arranged for the police to put on that intervention on the streets."

Matt frowned. "Why were there no police protecting Nicky, at the Eiffel Tower, this evening?"

Julie shook her head. "That was a mistake of timing. The security team that had been watching Paul, Nicky and Tricia all evening, had started back to the hotel to make sure it was safe, expecting them to arrive right behind them. They weren't expecting a brazen attempt to grab Nicky out of a crowd of late night revelers."

The police officer, who had been standing by patiently while all this had been going on, gave a polite cough. "Perhaps this would be a good time for everyone to move back to the Eiffel Tower, where there is an ambulance crew waiting for the young girl? If she would like to come with us, along with her mum and dad, perhaps everyone else could go with you?" He said looking at Stefanie.

"I'm not actually...." Tricia began.

Nicky cut her off. "Close enough." She whispered, as she gave Tricia a hug.

"But certainly. That would be you two." Stefanie said, looking at Matt and Michelle. "Come on. It's been a long evening, I'm sure you would all like to get back to your hotel rooms."

CHAPTER 49

The Spring sun was starting to warm the balcony of the luxury villa, as the white haired old woman made her way to her customary chair. She settled herself, wrapped the waiting warm blanket around her legs, and gazed across the awakening vines that flowed down the hillside of the Massif de la Clape, in Southern France. Her hillside, she reassured herself once again, with a satisfied smile. Her husband would have been proud of her, and everything that she had achieved since he had died. Now, there was just the one final shining legacy to be established for them both. Her brow clouded. She had carefully planned every step. Surely her children could follow her straightforward instructions, and conclude this last undertaking? It would be a crowning memorial to the achievements of her husband and herself that would last for generations. She stamped her foot angrily. Why was she still waiting for the confirmation from Paris that the girl was back in their possession, and the final steps had been achieved?

Her thoughts were violated by the arrival of her daughter, who burst through the door.

"Good Heavens, daughter. Control yourself. You know I particularly dislike having my noon contemplations interrupted. I only hope that your clamorous arrival can be excused by the news that you are bringing me? I have been waiting far too long to hear that the project has been successfully completed."

"Mother, there are two people here to see you. Well, actually, us. They have told me that I must also attend."

The old woman's features were infused with anger as she turned to her daughter. "How dare you come crashing in as though the place were on fire, and tell me that there are people here to see me during my rest period? Without an appointment no less?" She turned away in disgust. "Find out what they want, and order them to make an appointment to see you, if there is anything significant that they have to offer. Now get them out of my house immediately."

"They insist on seeing you now, Mother. It is the police, and they have a legal warrant."

"The police? Can't you do anything on your own, Daughter? Give them the contact information for our avocats, and tell them that they must not come to this house again."

"I'm afraid that is not an option, Madame."

The old woman spun around with surprising agility to face the speaker, a very confident professional woman, who had just entered the room, accompanied by a smartly dressed man.

"Do you have any idea who you are addressing?" She spat out in fury. "Get out of my house immediately, and I may not take this further with your superiors."

The man ignored her veiled threat. "We have a warrant here." He said, waving a document in his hand. "This requires the detention of both of you for conspiring to kidnap a teenage girl, to physical abuse a minor, extortion, and causing the death of an elderly woman in the cottage near Cadouin, where you held the kidnapped girl under forced sedation."

"Poof. What utter nonsense." The old woman sneered. "Do you realize that I am the head of a huge industrial organization, here in France, and elsewhere? My companies provide significant support for many hospitals and clinics around the country, and I am a personal friend of many of the local leaders, including the Chief of Police for this entire Massif de la Clape region. Give your contact details to my daughter, here, and she will ask our avocats to arrange a meeting with you. They will quickly disabuse you of all of your ridiculous ideas. This meeting is over. My daughter will escort you out."

The visitors gave no indication that they intended to leave.

"We have been remiss, perhaps, in not introducing ourselves." The woman visitor stated coldly. "I am Head of Operations for Interpol, here in France, and my companion is Chief Inspector Lacombe, of the Police Nationale. Several days ago, we arrested your granddaughter, Sehrish, in Bergerac. She was the physician responsible for keeping the kidnapped girl sedated with drugs. The evidence is overwhelming, and she is cooperating fully. She is facing the loss of her licence to practice medicine, although that is hardly significant, since she is also facing the possibility of spending the next decade in prison.

"Last night, your son, Michael, and your grandson Jasar were arrested, together with four other men, when they attempted to abduct a teenage girl in Paris: the same girl that you had arranged to be kidnapped in Beijing, and whom you kept unlawfully confined near Cadouin, here in France. They have both been charged with conspiracy, unlawful confinement of a minor, and flight from the police to avoid arrest. Jasar has also been charged with conspiracy to kidnap, and Michael has been charged with impersonating an Interpol officer, and extortion. Again, the evidence is overwhelming, and indisputable."

"What utter nonsense." The old woman blustered. "Michael has only recently arrived back in France, and has certainly not impersonated an Interpol officer, or anyone else. Where are your witnesses? As for the young girl, I received a request from a doctor in England for my granddaughter,

Sehrish, to go to Bergerac to look after a young girl who required serious medical attention. The doctor said in his note that he had met Sehrish in Africa, where she was with Medecins sans Frontieres. My son, Anthony, was in Bergerac with her, because, the doctor explained, the girl's family held some religious belief that precluded her from having the surgery. The girl's confinement was confidential because it was believed that her uncle was looking for her, with the intention of taking her back to the religious sect. Without the surgery, she would have died. We have the note from the doctor, of course. I suggest that you leave now, before you get into serious trouble." She could not hide the slight quaver in her voice. She turned to her daughter. "Call our avocats. Tell them to come here immediately." She snapped.

"I have already called them, Mother. They are on their way."

"Ah yes, you have just reminded me that your son Anthony was also arrested, and charged with kidnapping and unlawful confinement of the young girl, in the cottage near Cadouin. His fingerprints were found in the cottage, and we have confirmed that the documents and payments relating to the renting of the cottage were all signed, and sent, by him. We have also identified him as one of the people entering the cottage, on several occasions, before the girl was being held there."

"Aren't you listening? I have just explained why Anthony and Sehrish were looking after the girl. If you stop making such ridiculous fools of yourselves, and listen, I have the name of the doctors in Bordeaux who will confirm everything that I have said." The old woman barked angrily.

"The girl is not English; she is perfectly healthy; her parents are not trying to prevent her having surgery, and she is not in Bordeaux. She is now with her father, and she has told us exactly what happened. Furthermore, the two Asian men who were arrested at the Limoges Rest Stop have also identified your son, Anthony, as the person who hired them to find the young girl, after she had escaped from the cottage near Cadouin."

"That's absurd. A thirteen year-old girl who has been heavily sedated could not possibly provide a credible account of what had been happening, while she was unconscious. And, of course, Anthony may have hired two men to find the girl, after he discovered that she had been abducted from his care. He and Michael were very concerned for her safety, and doing everything they could to find her." The woman said, with a discernable sense of desperation in her voice.

"Since you have such an interesting story, we would like you to come with us, write it all down, and sign it under oath. That is not a request, Madame."

"One more thing." Inspector Lacombe added, in a voice that trembled with suppressed fury. "Your grandson, Jasar, was stupid enough to send notes to my family, threatening them, if I did not drop my investigation. It was fortunate for him that I was not with the police team in Paris last night when they arrested him. You can rest assured that the Police Nationale and the courts take threats against their members very seriously. He will be spending a long time in jail."

"In summary, Madame, despite your cleverly concocted story, we have overwhelming evidence that, over the past few weeks, you and your family have planned and have carried out a major criminal scheme, that involved the kidnapping a young girl in Beijing, China, transporting her against her will to France, where she was held under sedation while you attempted to extort valuable material from her father, Professor Paul Berg. Unfortunately for you, your family is comprised of a bunch of very stupid criminals, and they and you will now all have to pay the price."

“”Where are the avocats, Daughter?” The old woman screamed. “Find them! Find them, and get them here, immediately!”

CHAPTER 50

It was mid-morning when Paul, Tricia, Nicky, Matt and Michelle wearily loaded their baggage into two taxis, and left the hotel for the Charles de Gaulle airport. They had agreed that they would rather get to the airport early, than find themselves dragging through the sluggish midday Paris traffic. They were met at the airport by a representative of the Ministry for Europe and Foreign Affairs, who Jean-Claude Voisier had thoughtfully sent to smooth their way through the Departure routine, and settle them into the VIP lounge. Their escort had explained that the events of the previous evening in the Champs de Mars Park, and outside the Ecole Militaire, had generated quite a lot of publicity, and the Ministry thought that it would be preferable for everyone that they leave Paris quietly, before the media were able to locate and harass them.

None of them, not even Nicky, had managed much of an appetite for breakfast, and so they were pleasantly surprised to find that the lounge offered a sumptuous buffet that stretched along one wall. Nicky was concerned that the buffet might be finished, until Michelle pointed out that waiters were still busy, quietly and unobtrusively replenishing any dish that looked depleted.

"I can't believe Nicky is going back for yet another tray of food." Tricia laughed, as she watched Nicky head for the food counter, once again. "I thought the fruit bowl was her finale."

"I think she still wants to sample some of those amazing

desserts." Paul suggested. "It's a mystery to me how she can eat like that, and still remain so slim and fit. She raced up the entire length of that park last night." He glanced across at where Matt and Michelle were standing by the window, looking out at the planes moving around on the apron in front of the loading gates. "Matt and Michelle seem to be getting along well."

Tricia smiled. "I think he's quite smitten. I don't think she has told him yet, that she won't be staying with us in Saint Martin."

"Really? I thought she was going to be with us."

"Apparently, she has a pressing engagement in Lyon. She told me that she is going to hand us over to the consulate staff, who will be waiting at the airport in Saint Martin, and then catch the flight straight back to France."

"Does Michelle or Interpol know who was behind this whole thing, and why?"

"Yes. I had asked her that earlier today, and I was just going through her lengthy reply. She explained that it was planned and organized by the aging matriarch of an extremely wealthy family, and carried out by her sons, granddaughter and grandson, all of whom live in the South of France. There was no one else involved. It was all carried out by this one family, with sole objective of obtaining your medical research. The plan started to unravel after the shooting at the pagoda. When that happened, Renshu stepped in to control the situation, and recruited the man and woman who posed as Interpol agents in Beijing, you know, the one in the lift."

"Ah, yes, that was when you took your clothes off. I remember it well."

"Thank you. I would appreciate your forgetting that episode. Well, anyway, the two sons of the old lady were assigned to run the Beijing and Dordogne ends of the plan: the doctor who was arrested in Bergerac, is the granddaughter, and she was persuaded to look after Nicky, in the belief that Nicky was waiting for a major operation: the chap who was driving the van last night is a grandson. You might have recognized the man who got out of the van, and spoke to us last night; he was the son who was in charge of the Beijing side of the scheme. Apparently, they have all been quite talkative."

"So, why on earth did this extremely wealthy, influential family resort to kidnapping Nicky, just to obtain the research that Matt and I were working on? It makes absolutely no sense."

"Not to us it doesn't, but it made a strange sort of sense to the old woman. She and her husband fled from the war in Beirut, many years ago. They arrived in France in their boat with their young children, and virtually nothing. She was a physician and he was a professor of medical science at the university. They created a massive industrial empire, although, she insists it was mainly her husband's doing, and the French police have suspicions about the legality of how they made their money. Her husband died some years ago, and she is getting old. According to her children, she is building a major new research hospital in Beirut, to commemorate her husband. It will bear their names, and be the crown jewel of their empire."

"I think I am beginning to see the light." Paul said slowly.

"Yes, I expect you are. The hospital will have all of the latest medical and research equipment, and is expected to attract top calibre staff. What she wants is some leading medical research, to establish the new hospital on the international research map. She has lined up several top research teams, but it was the reports of the possible research breakthrough that you and Matt had achieved that really caught her eye."

"Why did we have to go through all this madness? Why on earth didn't she just approach us with an offer?"

"Apparently, she tried that. Do you remember the woman that Matt said he met in Turku? She said that her name was Claire LeBlanc, and she was with Medical Holdings, in Geneva? That is not her real name, of course, and she is actually well known by Interpol for being involved in several questionable technology acquisitions. Once Ms. LeBlanc informed the woman that you and Matt were not going to grant an exclusive licence, she moved to Plan B, which was to kidnap Nicky, and coerce you to give them all of your research."

"Good God. This is unbelievable." Paul gasped. "What terrible misfortune that Nicky's soccer team was invited to the tournament in Beijing. If they hadn't gone there, none of this would have happened."

Tricia gave him a quizzical look. "I suspect that there was not any misfortune involved."

Paul stared at her. "You mean that was all orchestrated, as well?" He shook his head. "I simply don't live in their world." He sighed, adding. "And I definitely don't want to."

"According to Michelle, that is the current thinking at Interpol."

"But why arrange for all of this to happen in Beijing, China, for heaven's sake?"

"That was to isolate you, far away from your familiar Western lifestyle, where you did not understand the language at all, and were completely unfamiliar with the massive city of Beijing. It was designed to disorient you and make you more amenable to their demands."

"Well, they were right about that. I was totally lost, after you left." He hesitated, nodding his head slowly, as realization dawned. "That explains that whole strange business in the lift. They weren't expecting you to come to Beijing with me, so they arranged that scene to send you to France, ostensibly to be there for Nicky, when they released her. You certainly outmaneuvered them there. Where did Renshu fit in all of this?"

"Interpol suspects that Mr. Renshu and the Chinese government were on to them quite quickly, and played along, with the intention of grabbing your research work for themselves at the last minute. As they did."

"What a pathetically tragic debacle. This family had a wonderful plan to establish a major research hospital in Beirut, and they ended up destroying the entire project, and possibly their family, when they got obsessed with obtaining our medical research. If they had approached Matt and me openly with their plan for the hospital, we could most likely come to some arrangement. They wouldn't have got an exclusive licence, but they could have been leading players in the development of the research."

"From what I understand, the old lady wanted her husband's hospital to be remembered as a place that produced a medical advance that saved millions of lives worldwide. When they couldn't buy your work, she tried to force the situation."

"The utter stupidity is that they kidnapped Nicky under the assumption that our research work will actually result in a major medical advance. There is a long, long process ahead, before we will know if our results have any medical significance."

"Unfortunately, as their plan started to stumble, the family became increasingly desperate. Their efforts became detached from reality. That ridiculous stunt here in Paris last night was pure insanity. I can't understand what they hoped to achieve. It was destined for failure from the start."

"And Nicky went through an horrific time because of it." He

growled. Seeing Tricia's expression change, he looked up, and quickly adopted a casual attitude. "Here comes Nicky now, laden with an impressive looking plate of desserts. I'll be right back. I'm going to get something to drink. Can I get you anything?"

"Thanks. A pot of green tea would go down well. Hi Nicky, that's an impressive looking assortment of goodies that you have assembled there."

"The selection of food here is absolutely wicked, Tricia. You've got to try some of these. I just couldn't make up my mind, so I brought a selection, for you and Dad to try as well. Where's Dad going?"

"He's just going to get us something to drink. He'll be right back. How are you feeling? You've had a pretty tough week."

"Um, I'm okay. Sleeping is still kinda difficult, you know, sort of bad dreams and stuff."

"Saint Martin should be really relaxing for all of us, and they have arranged for you to meet with a top psychiatrist, to help you wash all that junk through. I hear Saint Martin has some great beaches, and terrific shopping, and that Jean-Claude Voisier, through the French government has arranged for us to all stay in a luxury villa, quite close to the beach."

"Yeah. It should be great." Nicky said listlessly.

"What's up? Something bothering you?"

"Um, well sort of." Nicky struggled to explain her concerns. "I feel like such a wuss."

"After what you've been through?" Tricia murmured, patting her arm. "You have been absolutely amazing. No one could have managed better than you did. I honestly don't think I could have made the drive to Paris, if you had not been beside me. Of course you will have occasional nightmares: anyone would. Dad and I will be here to help you through, whenever you need it." She put her head on one side, and asked softly. "Is there something in particular that is bothering you, that I can help with?"

"Well, it's just that, at the hotel, it was great with you in the adjoining room, and the door open all night. When we get to Saint Martin, I've been sort of wondering what the sleeping arrangements will be? You know, I don't want to be, sort of, totally, like, on my own. Sorry, that's sounds so childish."

"Of course not. That's a good point." She nodded thoughtfully. "I'll make sure that there are a couple of adjoining rooms that you and I can use. I promise."

"Thanks, Tricia. That would be great." She looked away. "Um. Will Dad be with you? I understand all that stuff, it's just that it would be sort of different. I'm being juvenile again."

"Not at all. I understand. No, your Dad and I will not be sharing a room. There is already a lot of love between the three of us, and that is very precious. If the relationship between your Dad and I moves to another level, we want to be sure that we are all comfortable with any changes."

"Okay. Thanks. I'm really okay with it. It's just that right at the moment, I'm finding the nights a bit difficult." Nicky visibly relaxed, and changed topic, with a wave at the plate. "How about we try some of these desserts?"

"Okay, but I will have to be careful. You've seen that bikini that you encouraged me to buy in Paris. I don't want to be bulging out in all the wrong places."

"I've seen it." Nicky laughed. "Dad is in for a shock."

"What's going to be a shock?" Paul asked, as he arrived back, accompanied by a waiter carrying a tray with cups, pots of coffee and tea, plus a steaming jug of milk, and a container of sugar.

“Nicky and I were just laughing at the effect a long-term diet of these desserts could have.“ She flashed a smile at the waiter. “Thanks for the green tea.”

“Uncle Matt certainly seems to be twitter pated by Michelle, over there.” Nicky commented between consuming mouthfuls of an exotic looking pastry.

“Yes. I was going to go over and ask Michelle about the flight, but Matt seemed so focused that I decided I shouldn’t butt in. I’ve never seen him quite like this.” Paul mused.

Matt Berg and Michelle Denis stood together, chatting, by the floor-to-ceiling window, occasionally watching the arriving and departing planes move around on the tarmac apron below them.

“So this is the end of all the nonsense, at last. It is finally over. Now we can all relax on a Caribbean island, and Nicky will receive some help to get past the awful ordeal that she has been through.” The relief was evident in Matt’s voice. “Was it really all because a very wealthy old woman in the South of France wanted to create a world class medical research hospital in her birth country, as a monument to her husband?”

Michelle shrugged. “Everything points that way. So terribly sad that she would harm the family name by involving them in something like this. What an incredibly stupid thing to have done: kidnapping an innocent young girl, to force you and Paul to give her your research material.” She shook her head. “Perhaps she thought that it would all be over in a few days, and quickly forgotten. Unfortunately, her sons were very poor criminals, and when things started to go wrong, the whole plan quite quickly went from bad to worse. Did I get the saying right, this time?”

"You did indeed. I can't help wondering if I oversold our results in Turku." Matt reflected. "If I had been less positive in my description, perhaps all this could have been avoided. The reality is that, as with all early research, we have no idea if our initial indications will actually hold up. More than nine times out of ten, what, at first, appears to be a medical breakthrough fails to prove out, for one reason or another, when it is put through the required rigorous medical testing procedures."

"Don't blame yourself, Matt. The old woman was convinced that she had found a breakthrough that would cement their names in medical history. She was relentlessly pursuing something that she was convinced would be the final piece to fulfill her dream."

"I'm still confused about a couple of things." Matt puzzled.

"I thought you might be." Michelle said, resignedly.

"Who was the woman in Beijing, who said she was going to impersonate Tricia? Paul says she was watching him like a hawk at the Arts Centre, when the exchange was going through. Was she the same woman who followed you down from Montmartre?"

"We don't know. The team never found her. Somehow, she managed to vanish."

"Were the North Koreans ever involved?"

"No. That was actually just a distraction, what I believe in English you refer to as a 'red kipper' "

"I think the term is 'red herring', but, actually, I like red kipper better."

"So it was a red herring. The two men at the Limoges Rest Stop are actually French citizens, originally from North Korea, they escaped to the South, and then emigrated to France from Seoul,

South Korea. They are Security guards at the hospital in Sarlat. The wealthy family has made some significant donations to the hospital, and the son, Anthony, is a familiar figure around the hospital. They told the Police Nationale that he hired them initially to transport Nicky in an ambulance from the medevac at Bordeaux airport to the gite. He hired them again later, to locate and rescue Nicky, telling them that Tricia had taken her without her family's permission. They have been very cooperative. Apparently their status in South Korea was never formally established, and they were understandably terrified at the possibility that France might send them back to North Korea."

"Who was pulling the strings in Bergerac and Cadouin?"

"That was the old woman's son, Anthony. He has admitted it, but he is trying to claim he believed he was helping a very sick girl, whose family would not allow her to have an essential medical operation, for religious reasons."

"Do you think they will all be convicted?"

"I can't say. That's out of our hands. There is no question that the perpetrators are all members of a wealthy, influential family, and they have created a clever story to explain their actions."

Matt shrugged. "Well, at least they've been caught, and it's all over for us. Now we can relax on the beach for a while." He smiled at Michelle. "I am really looking forward to spending some time with you. I was quite serious with what I said at that restaurant, last night."

Michelle looked away. "I know."

Matt frowned thoughtfully. "I still don't understand how Anthony, or whoever it was, knew where Tricia and Nicky were all the time. There must have been a leak from the police security team. The bug we found in Nicky's bag at Montmartre would only have had a limited range."

Michelle took a deep breath. "I told him. I told him where Nicky and Tricia were, along the road, on their way to Paris, and when they were at the Rest Stop."

Matt stared at her in disbelief. "You? But why?"

"Matt, there is a lot you don't know. I want to explain. We also worked closely with Chief Inspector Lacombe, and the Police Nationale. Once Tricia had told me where they were, I passed the information on to him, and he had a covert team escort them all the way to Paris, switching and swapping the vehicles, so that they were not distinguishable from the surrounding traffic. It wasn't by chance that he showed up at the Rest Stop in Limoges, and helped them to get safely on their way again."

"And I suppose that the woman that spilt the tray of food over the man watching them, in the café at the second Rest Stop, was also part of your coverage?"

Michelle frowned. "No, she wasn't one of ours. We don't know who she was. That must have been just a convenient accident. We thank her, whoever she was. She certainly helped Nicky and Tricia slip away. I didn't know exactly where they were at that point, so we didn't have anyone at that Rest Stop." She stared out of the window. "You are probably wondering how I could pass information on to that Anthony person, and put Tricia and Nicky at risk?"

Matt waved his hand in dismissal. "That's really not important, now. You had a job to do. Everything worked out. It's over. "

"It is important to me. At the restaurant, I told you that I was married, and that my husband died in a motorcycle crash. What I didn't say was that I was pregnant when he died. I have a seven year-old son, Jean-Luc."

"I'm confused..."

"Let me finish. Jean-Luc is in hospital in Lyon. He has a bronchogenic cyst: that's a cyst in his chest. Thankfully, there are excellent doctors and medical facilities in Lyon, including a leading cancer centre. They determined that the cyst is not cancerous, but it must be removed. I took a few last assignments to build up overtime, sick leave and vacation so that I can be with him after he has his operation that is scheduled for next week. The people who wanted your research contacted me, and told that if I did not help them, they would make sure that Jean-Luc did not get his operation. I told my boss, she immediately provided Jean-Luc and the surgeon with covert security, and asked me to play along with them so that we could catch the people behind this whole thing. And, thankfully, we did."

Matt stared at her, shaking his head. "You must have been under unbearable pressure. How is Jean-Luc doing?"

"He has been resting after all of tests, to regain his strength for the operation. Unfortunately, a virus was identified in a young girl in the hospital, nothing serious for a normal healthy child, but the surgeon decided that Jean-Luc had better stay in isolation until his surgery. He's doing well, and will be ready for the operation next week." Michelle explained woodenly.

He reached down and slipped his hand around hers. "Is there anything that I can do? If money is an issue at all, I can certainly help?"

"Thank you, but that is not an issue. France has a good universal health care program, and Interpol provides very good coverage for any additional expenses." She squeezed his hand, and gave him a warm smile. "I really appreciate your concern. You are a good person, Matt Berg. Because of the risk of infection, I was told that it would be better if we did not have direct contact, so Jean-Luc and I have had audiovisual chats every day, online. My Mum and Dad are in Lyon, and are in contact with the hospital, although it has just been a matter of waiting. I check in with them everyday. The surgeon has told us that there is an excellent prognosis for a full recovery."

He stared at her in admiration. "You stayed unbelievably calm, and maintained control of the whole operation throughout, despite your personal situation." He paused, thoughtfully. "Now that it is over, the most important thing is for you to be with Jean-Luc."

"That brings up a final point. I am not staying in Saint Martin. I am going with you as an escort, and handing you all over to a team from the French consulate at the airport. I will fly back to Paris tonight, and on to Lyon."

"Of course. You must be with Jean-Luc. I must say that I am surprised that you came to Bergerac, when you could have left us, and gone straight from Beijing to Lyon. It would have been completely understandable."

Michelle nodded. "That was because Tricia travelled to China with Paul. We were not expecting her, and didn't know who she was. As soon as I reached Beijing, I sent her photo and details to Interpol, and they did an in depth check on her. When I read the reports on her work with children, I was willing to stay with the assignment." She gave a self-conscious shrug. "I talked to Jean-Luc about it, and he insisted that he wanted me to stay and help find Nicky, so I did." She smiled. "He loved the story of how Tricia and Nicky drove right across France, with people after them."

"Jean-Luc sounds like a really great kid. I will be thinking of you both next week. If there is anything I can do, just let me know." He took hold of both of her hands. "I mean it. Promise?"

"Okay. Thanks."

"Now I know that you're not staying in Saint Martin, there is no reason for me to be there, either. There's still time. I will cancel my flight, and grab the Eurostar back to London." He glanced across at where Paul, Tricia and Nicky were engrossed in their own world, and smiled. "The three of them look perfect together. I think they will manage quite well, without me tagging along."

Michelle looked over, and put her head on one side. "I think you're right. Things actually seem to have turned out quite well." She frowned. "The only regret is that the Chinese have ended up with all of your research material."

"Ah, well. Yes. Right. Actually, I have, sort of, a confession. Paul and I have been slightly disingenuous about that. If you remember back when we met in Bergerac, just before Tricia left to get Nicky out of the gite, I said that I had been to Lyon overnight to meet with an old academic friend? You commented that Lyon is known for its medical research."
"Yes, I remember you telling us that. Lyon is my home, so it struck a chord with me, naturally." She nodded, slowly. "You looked like you hadn't slept in days."

"Yes, well, I hadn't. Neither had Paul. He had spent the previous night and day reworking our research material, while I had got to work, completing an academic paper that we had started, for publication. The time difference between Beijing and Bergerac really worked in our favour, on that occasion. To summarize, what the Chinese have is a complete set of research material, but with critical errors that Paul has buried in it. It would probably take me several months to reproduce the key protein string from my notes and my memory, despite having made all of the calculations before. I am sure that it would take their scientists at least a year to realize that the notes they have do not produce a protein string with in any of the claimed properties."

"I'm not sure I follow." Michelle said, frowning. "Are you saying that what Paul gave to the Chinese is worthless?"

"Pretty much."

"So, what is this publication that you wrote? Did you take it to Lyon?" Michelle asked.

"Right. Yes. It was an accurate account of our work: I gave it to our colleague there. While Paul was preparing for the exchange at the Arts Centre in Beijing, she took it on the TGV to Paris for publication in a major medical journal. Once I explained what was going on, she was furious, and vowed to pull in every debt she is owed to make sure that our paper is published in the coming edition. When that paper is published, it will contain all of the correct information on the protein string, for any medical research team to pick up and take further." He paused. "Ironically, that could even include a team from the new hospital in Lebanon, if the family is still interested."

"Could you have stopped the publication, if Nicky had not been released?" Michelle gasped.

"Yes. That was an awful possibility that we had to consider. I arranged with our colleague that if I hadn't contacted her to confirm, she would have stopped the publication. She was thrilled to hear that all had gone well, and Nicky was safe, so the publication will proceed as planned." He took a deep breath. "Paul, Tricia and I were all aware of the frightening reality that, whether or not we handed over all of the information they asked for, if Nicky wasn't freed, the outlook would have been very bleak. We really had no leverage at all." He shrugged. "Anyway, thanks to Interpol and Tricia, it all worked out as planned, and our publication is coming out next month."

"Wait, though. If all of your results are put out into the public domain, doesn't that mean that you have just given away all of your research?"

"Yes, well, sort of, I suppose we have. We are not pursuing our patent applications, and so it will become public property, as soon as our paper is published. If anything comes of it, we will still get credit for our original research, and the publication, but our research results will be available to anyone, at no cost. Paul and I agree: that is the way it should be."

It was Michelle's turn to stare. "You out maneuvered the kidnappers, and the Chinese." She gasped. "That was absolutely brilliant."

Matt shook his head. "It could still all have been a disaster, if Interpol, that being you, had not been in control, and rescued Nicky at the crucial moment that Paul was handing over the material. That was the amazing part."

"Mon Dieu, Paul was under incredible stress. He was sitting in that Arts Centre, waiting for confirmation that they had accepted the reworked, basically useless, research material, desperately hoping that you would call confirming Nicky's release. No wonder he was so upset when Stefanie and Julie suddenly appeared, and started to pull him out." Matt looked puzzled. "They told me all about it." She explained.

"I told you he was mentally tough." He paused. "Um, to go back, I understand how difficult the next little while will be for you, but, whenever you have the time, I would like to know how you and Jean-Luc are doing." He plunged on. "I remember what you said in the restaurant, last night, but I really would like to see you again. When you feel comfortable, perhaps I could come and visit you in Lyon, and meet Jean-Luc. No commitments: I will stay in a hotel, and you can explain to Jean-Luc that I am strictly just a friend." He grinned hopefully.

"If you agree, just tell me when is an acceptable time, and I'll jump on the Eurostar. London to Paris, one quick change, and the TGV to Lyon. It couldn't be easier."

Michelle's smile was answer enough. "I would like that, Matt, and I know Jean-Luc would enjoy meeting you."

"I have your mobile number. Do you have my contact details?"

"Let me think." She pursed her lips, and raised one eyebrow, thoughtfully. "Well, I am an Interpol agent, so I might be able to find you." She said with a mischievous grin.